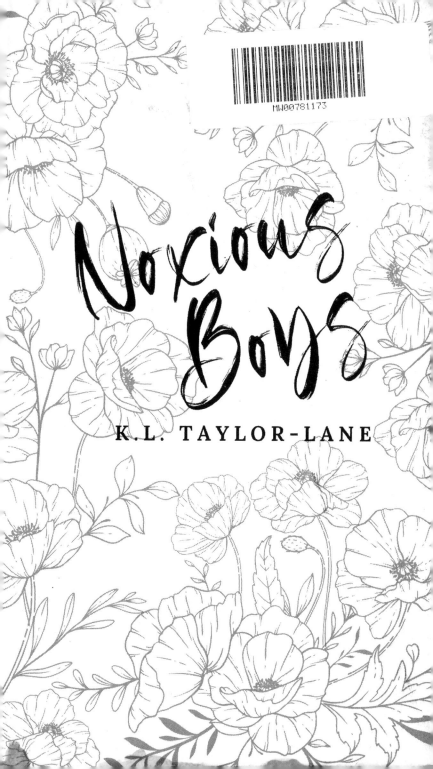

Noxious Boys

K.L. TAYLOR-LANE

ISBN - 978-1-7392089-9-8
Written by - K. L. Taylor-Lane
Edited by - Inga Oake

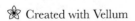 Created with Vellum

Starting at a new college halfway through the school year is miserable. Especially when you have to move halfway across the globe to do so.

My false sense of freedom from the man pulling the strings is crushed, his control crossing oceans with evil eyes watching my every move.

There are a million things that I shouldn't be doing with my new found liberation, however slight it may be.

I definitely should not be falling for my accidental roommate.
Or his brutal best friends.
Or his broody older brother.
Or my slightly unhinged student counsellor.

Falling for them is one thing, but what happens when they decide they don't want me anymore?

For Inga.
The strongest, most kind hearted woman I know.

And because you said you couldn't choose...
Guess that means all of these boys are just for you.

Playlist

Did It Hurt? – Ellise

Somebody else. – Bad Omens

Holding on to Smoke – Motionless In White

Someone Else – Rezz

Don't You Dare Forget The Sun – Get Scared

Alive - P.O.D

bad decisions – Bad Omens

BAD GIRL – AVIVA

Swim – Chase Atlantic

Just Pretend – Bad Omens

Life's A Mess – Juice WRLD

Six Feet Under – Bohnes

Hate You – Boston Manor

THE DEATH OF PEACE OF MIND – Bad Omens

Dirty Mind – Boy Epic

Slow Down – Chase Atlantic

Under My Skin – Dead Poet Society

Blurry – Puddle Of Mudd

Fallen Leaves – Billy Talent

Born Alone Die Alone – Madalen Duke

PLAYLIST

The Grey – Bad Omens
1000 Blunts - $uicideboy$
Fake Love – Capsize
Whore – In this Moment
Brittle – Icon For Hire
Miracle – Bad Omens
I hope you hate me. – Dead Poet Society
Sick, Sick, Sick – Queens Of The Stone Age

Note From The Author

This book is a standalone.
You do not need to read anything else by this author
to understand the events that take place in this book.
Though, it *is* set in the same world as everything else
published by this author.
Please be aware this book contains **many** dark
themes and subjects that may be
uncomfortable/unsuitable for some readers. This
book contains **very** heavy themes throughout so
please heed the warning and go into this with your
eyes wide open.
For more detailed information, please see content
listing in back of book.

The characters in this story all deal with trauma and
problems differently, the resolutions and methods they
use are not always traditional and therefore may not
be for everyone.

This book is written in first person, in multiple points of view, using both British AND American English. The MMCs' point of views are written in American English.

The FMC's point of view is written in British English. Therefore, some spellings, words, grammar and punctuation may be used differently throughout. If you find anything you think is a genuine error, please do not report, instead, please contact the author or one of her team to correct it. Thank you!

This book and its contents are entirely a work of fiction. Any resemblance or similarities to names, characters, organisations, places, events, incidents, or real people is entirely coincidental or used fictitiously.

*Noxious Boys is a dark, college, bully, why chose romance. Please read with caution, the characters in this book do not and will not conform to society's standards or normalities.

This book does have a *happy ever after.**

See full content listing in the back of this book.

X

Poppy

CHAPTER ONE

S now.

In Texas.

I almost laugh.

It's the first week back from the winter holidays. My very first week in an American college, in the middle of the school year, thousands of miles away from home in England, and it's snowing.

When my dad uttered the words 'Groveton College' over a silent Christmas dinner for two. Me at one end of the mile long table, he at the other, and told me I'd be heading to Texas on New Year's Day. Snow was not really what I was expecting. And it wasn't here for the last week that I have been, although, it has been cold.

Blobs of cold, white fluff hit my face. Flakes clinging heavily in my shuttered lashes. Howling wind nips frostily at my exposed ears, long brown hair whipping my cheeks. I'm wet, cold, miserable, but I think I kinda like it, it feels a little like home.

More like home than my actual one does, anyway.

Snow is settling on the brick paved walkway leading back to my dorm. My heavy boots trudge through the slippery mess. Arms curling around my middle, my fingers tugging my too-thin coat closed. A fabric tote bag swings in the crook of my elbow, its contents thudding rhythmically against my hip. I keep my head down and keep walking, jogging up the slippery steps to the entrance.

I stamp my feet on the dark mat, banging off the snow. Sweep my hands back over my hair, getting the wet strands away from my face, fingers of one hand fluffing my heavy fringe out of my eyes. I flick my finger across my brows, one and then the other, clearing the beads of melting snow, wipe my hand down my jean-clad thigh and scan my student ID card. The device bleeps, little coloured light on the scanner changing from red to green allowing me access and I shoulder my way in through the glass door.

Warmth hits me as my boots hit the shiny white flooring, my icy cheeks burning from the rapid change in temperature. Blowing out a breath, I heft my bag of supplies up higher onto my shoulder, tucking it behind my arm, and head in the direction of the stairs. I live on the seventh floor, and that's a lot of steps, but I don't really like getting into lifts.

Enclosed spaces make me think of coffins. Dark, cold, earth. I can smell grave soil in my nostrils as I hit the fifth floor, my breath a little fast, heart starting to thud harder in my chest.

The railing is cold beneath my clammy palm as I latch myself onto it. Slumping my full weight onto the railings that are to stop me plunging over the side to my death. Fingers curling tightly around the metal, knuckles blanching. I stare at the back of my pale tattooed hand, study the finely inked ivy, breathing hard through my nose. Nostrils flaring, I suck in a sharp breath. Squeeze my eyes closed tight. Think of first thing this morning, when I woke to an empty room, the bed beside me still unoccupied. Blinds not closed all the way, the low sun casting its orange rays across the rough navy carpet. And I let myself think of her. For the first time in months, I let myself think of her and it has royally fucked me up.

I flop to my bum on the steel edged stairs, knees spread, I drop my head between them, let my hair dangle down around my face. Try to breathe deep. But this is what happens every time I let thoughts of her in, it destroys me.

Angling myself, I shift my backside up from the step, leaning on one elbow, thrusting my hips up into the air, fingers of my other hand reaching and wriggling inside my tight jeans' pocket. Fingertips catching on plastic, I snag the little bag between my scissoring fingers and drop back down heavily onto the step as I tug it free. Cloth tote bag slipping off of my shoulder, I unthread the handles from my arm, place it on the step beside me, and finger the little clear bag of round white pills.

Sterile white walls, bright strip bulbs, thick straps, locking cuffs, scratchy paper gowns, clipboards, tapping pens, clicking tongues, screaming, screaming, screaming.

BANG.

I jump to my feet. Shoving my second pill of the hour onto the back of my tongue, swallow it dry as I stuff the others back inside my pocket, just as a door below me in the stairwell slams closed. Feet start pounding their way up and I take that as my cue to leave. So in the same rhythmic rush of steps as the person below me, I jog the rest of the way up to my room.

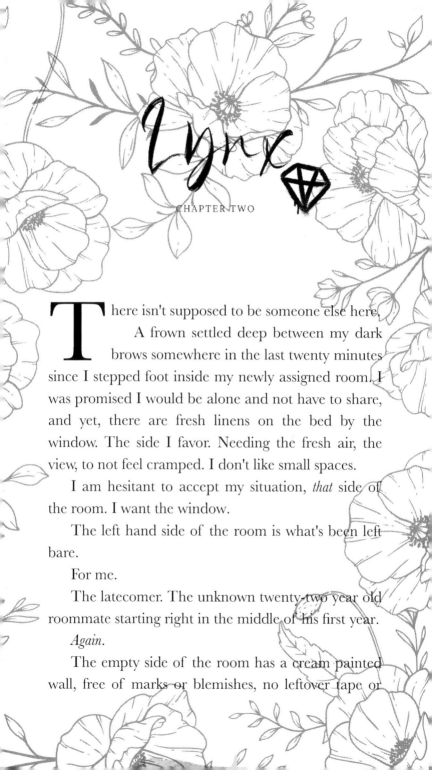

Lynx

CHAPTER TWO

There isn't supposed to be someone else here.

A frown settled deep between my dark brows somewhere in the last twenty minutes since I stepped foot inside my newly assigned room. I was promised I would be alone and not have to share, and yet, there are fresh linens on the bed by the window. The side I favor. Needing the fresh air, the view, to not feel cramped. I don't like small spaces.

I am hesitant to accept my situation, *that* side of the room. I want the window.

The left hand side of the room is what's been left bare.

For me.

The latecomer. The unknown twenty-two year old roommate starting right in the middle of his first year.

Again.

The empty side of the room has a cream painted wall, free of marks or blemishes, no leftover tape or pins from whoever lived here last year. It's kind of admirable actually that the other occupant living in this shared room didn't take over this space too. Unless they were warned someone would be moving in and they had to move their shit.

I frown again.

I wanted to live in the house off campus with my brothers, well, one blood brother, three of them brothers in everything but that, but after what happened before, well, they want the counselor to be able to keep a closer eye on me. A smirk tugs at my lips even as I think of it.

Rattling of the handle at my back snags my attention just in time for me to sidestep and twist out of the way of the inward swinging door.

I freeze, my back to the empty side of the room, the cardboard edge of one of my very few boxes, cutting into the back of my calf as I lean away. A flurry of erratic movement as a girl half-falls into the room, slams the door shut, spinning towards it, and then just sort of slumps against it. Forehead pressing to the wood of the door, her slim, heaving back to me, a black cloth bag thuds heavily to the floor, dropping from the crook of her elbow, slipping down her arm, over her wrist, her balled hand.

Watching her, I make no sound. Unmoving in my position, I study her tall frame. She must be six-foot or close to it as she's almost the same height as me at six-two. Tremors zip through her where she rests against the wood, hands pressing flat against it, fingers splayed.

Deep purple polish on her short, rounded nails, a slim gold band on her right, middle finger. Thick brown hair, streaked with natural gold, brushes the base of her spine. Swishing gently with the motion of her quivering legs dressed in black jeans, wet boots on her feet.

I lick my dry lips, swallowing, nervousness feels like a weight in the very pit of my stomach and I don't know what to do. How to announce my presence now when she very clearly is having some sort of episode.

This is why I needed my own room.

I'm not good with other people.

Not after what happened before.

They know all this, it's why I couldn't be here, had to go away. Why I had to leave.

Fuck.

My fingers knot in my bleached blond hair, the coarse texture of the over processed strands rough in my hands. I tug on my roots, take a deep breath, which almost feels selfish as I watch the figure in front of me struggle to do the same.

That's when I hear her.

Mumbling.

Soft, breathless words murmuring beneath her ragged breaths. Too quiet for me to hear, but I tilt my head to one side as though to listen harder, strain my ears to hear her words, all the same.

And I can smell her. Wet snow, something like sweet buttery pumpkin underlying the stronger scent of damp clothes.

Her back rises and falls slower, and I shift on my feet. The sole of my sneaker making an almost silent scraping sound on the rough textured carpet, but not that silent.

Her head snaps up, her entire body tightening, muscles coiling, she turns to face me, slowly. Her hands drop from the door, fingertips squeaking uncomfortably down the glossy wood as she turns.

Her eyes are large. Pupils blown so wide, I almost miss the unusual lilac-blue coloring of her irises beneath her heavy curtain of bangs. A thin nose, slightly crooked at the bridge, maybe from a break or a fracture, a rounded point for the tip. Leading to pale pink lips, all soft and plush and pouty. Parted, the bottom one looks almost too heavy for her slim face where it hangs, trembling, her chin quivering, cheek-bones high arches on her round cheeks, flushed with an icy sort of pink.

"I'm having a bad trip," she says quietly, a strong British accent soft and light as a feather on her tongue, the sound of it as though a ribbon is floating airily through my eardrums.

I watch her fingertips curling into the door at her back, nails cutting into the wood. I find my fingers relaxing, grip loosening, now that I have something else to focus on. My arms drop to my sides and I think about lighting a joint. But I'm not entirely sure that's what this girl needs to be inhaling right now.

"It's okay, Treasure," her big eyes blink at the rough sound of my voice, maybe at the endearment, clinging onto my thickly accented Texan timbre, trying to reconnect herself with reality.

I know what that's like.

"I'm Lynx." My hand presses to my chest, fingers splaying over the fabric of my white cotton shirt. "What's your name?"

Gasping, she blinks again, staring at me, but not really seeing. And then she inhales a short, sharp breath. The punch of it lifting her chest, breasts jiggling beneath her too-thin coat, loose black shirt underneath.

"Ppp-Ppop-Poppy," she stutters, sucking in her cheeks as she gets the word free from her clattering teeth.

"Okay, Poppy, can you sit there for me?" I gesture with my hand towards what I assume is her bed, dressed with white cotton sheets, little pink flowers embroidered on them.

Glancing at where my own bed still sits bare, I scrunch my nose, thinking about it. This is a co-ed dorm, but there's not usually co-ed rooms. This must be a mistake.

Poppy nods as I shift my gaze back onto her. Throat working, she swallows dryly, and without hesitating, she crosses the space, following my instruction, which does a weird thing to my insides. Her shoulder gently brushing my own, she drops heavily onto the end of the bed, mattress springing up slightly before the metal coils settle beneath her weight. Shoulders slumping forwards, she curls in on herself. Breath rushing in and out, rasping down her throat, eyes wide, unblinking as she stares ahead. I'm not really great at this. This is more Rex's territory, coaching someone through a bad trip, something he has done for me many times before.

But he knows me.

And I, I don't know this girl, she doesn't know me. Are there lines here that I don't know about, trauma, fears, unwanted touch?

The sounds scratching their way up her windpipe sound borderline painful and without thinking any further, I step between her legs, drop down into a crouch and take her trembling chin between my thumb and finger.

I almost flinch. Her soft skin is like ice, her teeth stop chattering as my pinch on her face hardens just a little. Firm but not rough, enough to keep her grounded.

"What did you take, Poppy?" I ask her gently, smoothing my thumb over the round curve of her chin.

"Pp-pills."

I smile at her. Something that feels a little foreign on my face, especially around strangers but I haven't really had much to feel too smiley about lately.

"You know what kinda pills?" I ask, thinking of all the shit pushed out everywhere across campus.

She nods mutely. An eyebrow lifting on my forehead, I wait for her to speak.

"Ecstasy," it's mumbled and slow, a drawl.

Okay, I can deal with that, unless, "Just one?" I ask quietly.

Canting my head, lifting my gaze onto her pretty features crowded beneath her curtain of hair, thick bangs in her eyes.

She shakes her head unevenly like it's too heavy for her shoulders even though I'm still gripping her chin.

"Two."

Fuck.

I blow out a breath, wiping my hands over my jean-clad kneecaps.

Water is the first thing on my mind, but you can overhydrate on stimulants, so I'll need to monitor it. Scanning the space, I quickly locate the mini fridge meant for both of us to share and slowly release her face from my hold.

Opening the refrigerator, there's a couple waters, a bag of grapes and not much else. I kick the door closed with the heel of my foot and just in time to dart back across the short space, catching Poppy before she falls forwards, off of the end of the bed. Dropping the water to the floor, one hand supporting her shoulder, the other on the base of her throat. She mumbles incoherently, head still hanging forward and I think I'm just in over my head here, what if she's got more? What if this is the start of my failure again?

Fuck. Fuck. Fuck.

She breathes hard, saying something I don't catch, my hands supporting her entire body weight now. I lean in, tipping her head back a little, still supporting her so she doesn't hurt herself.

"Hold me," it's a murmured request, but also not really a question, more like an offering of information so I know how to help.

It feels strange, knowing I'm the same way. Always needing one of the boys to keep me in their arms when I'm out of it like this. Some people hate the skin to skin contact when they feel like they've stepped off of the edge of the world, everything too sensitive and tingly it makes touch feel painful, but I need it to ground me. And apparently, Poppy does too.

Vibration in my pocket draws my attention, and I know it'll be one of them. I drag my gaze back up to her eyes, the lilac-blue bright like amethyst as she blinks up at me.

"Okay, Poppy," I shift my feet a little wider, smooth my hand around to the back of her neck, supporting her droopy head by cupping her nape. "I'm going to shift you back on the bed, and then I'll lie with you, if that's what you want?" I make sure she's looking right at me when I ask, those pretty eyes captivating me, glassy and wide, pupils blown.

She nods.

Then I'm smoothing her wet jacket off of her narrow shoulders. Revealing her loose, long sleeved, black shirt, the neckline just grazing her collarbones. Tossing the light outerwear over onto the other bed, still supporting her with one arm. I'm careful not to touch her anywhere that could be deemed inappropriate. The last fucking thing I need is some girl saying I touched her without permission. That'd really set my mother off.

Once I've got her propped up against the pillows that I haphazardly stack one handedly, I gently release my hold on her bicep, her skin hot and damp beneath the thin cotton of her shirt. Her teeth chatter, rattling in her gums, dry lips pale.

Unlacing and sliding her boots off of her stripey socked feet, I let them thud to the floor as I dip down to retrieve the water bottle I dropped. Condensation wets my palm, the inside of my fingers as I curl my hand around it.

It's a welcome feeling, the wet cold in my hand, I feel hot, clammy, as I pause. Watching her. Sweat beads along my temples, at the edges of my untidy bleached blond hair, and my heart thuds harder in my chest. She looks like a messy fucking wet dream. Her eyes are on me, something that should be creepy, the way her eyes are unblinking, but it doesn't really feel like that at all.

Cautiously, I step towards her, swallowing as my fingers tighten around the water bottle, cracking the plastic top free and offering it up to her.

Stepping into her until I'm crouching down to her level, my free hand reaching out, the back of it caressing her cheek.

"Have a small sip," I say quietly, bringing the drink to her lips, she licks them, the tip of her pink tongue just catching on the rim of the bottle. "That's it, Treasure, you're safe." I smile, a small thing, but it feels safe, gifting it to her, reassurance.

And then her lips are parting, the water gently streaming into her mouth as I feed it to her slowly.

All the while, her eyes remain on mine, and words I've never uttered before unconsciously whisper between my lips, "Good Girl."

She trembles, making a little drop of water race down her chin. I think I might want to lick it, but instead, my thumb catches it before it can leave her face. Drawing the bottle away from her mouth, I pop the digit between my lips and suck.

Breath shudders out of her, lilac-blue-gray eyes dropping to my mouth as I hollow my cheeks, slowly dragging out my thumb, teeth grazing over the pad of it. I cup her face, smooth the wet digit beneath her left eye, marking her with me, saliva glistening on her pale skin.

"You want me to slide in behind you?" I ask softly, grateful for the sun beyond the glass to be hidden behind snow clouds, the room in a dull winter gloom.

She keeps staring at my mouth, like she can hear my words by following my lips, "Treasure?"

She lifts her gaze, wide eyes flicking between my own. Clumsily reaching a hand out to me, fingers hooking into the waistband of my sweats as she slaps against my hip. The back of her cool fingers brush over a sliver of my skin exposed between shirt and sweats making my abs tense and roll. She nods, tugging at the elastic of my pants.

Gently, circling my fingers around her hand, clammy palm, long, thin fingers. I smooth my thumb over the inside of her wrist, bringing her hand down from my waist. Trying to keep her from touching me, despite the fact her soft skin sends a chill racing up my spine.

There's a loud pounding inside my head, thumping in my skull, and my pulse ticks like a bomb about to go off as I kick off my sneakers.

She's relaxed, boneless and floppy, but heavy, as I maneuver her forwards, slide in behind her, rest one leg on either side of her thighs, my feet beside her lower calves.

I wonder what she would think of this if she knew the real me. I'm just a frowning, moody, hockey player with a quiet, somber demeanor.

Her thin frame relaxes back against my chest,

heavy with her short breaths, my arms fold across her chest, hands wrapping around either side of her ribs. Her heart thuds through her back, ricocheting into my chest, like fingers rhythmically plucking at my heart strings. My body is stiff, arms tense across her chest.

Anxiety kicking in, ratcheting up and up and up.

I'm nervous. I don't want her waking up in a couple of hours and freaking the fuck out on me. Wondering why there's a strange man fucking cuddling her in bed.

"Lynx?" she breathes out, drowsy and slow, and if it weren't for her heart thudding so steadily against mine, I'd wonder if she was about to die.

I open my mouth to answer, her name on the tip of my tongue, but she beats me to it.

My lips slamming shut as she murmurs, "Be here when I wake up."

A statement, rather than a question. Something of a quiet demand. Something that would usually have my skin prickling, an automatic refusal on the tip of my tongue, at being told what to do.

Instead, I melt into the wall at my back, feel the muscles in my arms across her chest relaxing. And as her breaths slow, deep and even, I let my eyes slide closed with something like contentment.

Raiden

Hands splayed against the white tiles, water scalds down my spine as the shower spray hammers against my back. Drilling into my tense muscles, burning my goosebump pricked skin, in an attempt at washing the day off.

Hudson Cooper, our hockey team Captain, is loud. His laughter booms, echoing throughout the locker room and showers. I get it, he's happy, we had a good practice, and I like the guy. But fuck me, I'd like to be able to decompress in here, even if it's only for a moment.

Anger flows thick and fast then, reinfecting my core as it flows through my veins. My pulse pounds in my temples, my neck muscles straining and despite the whooshing in my eardrums, I can still fucking hear him.

"Yo! Hud!" the words tear out of my throat, gruffness biting its way up my vocal cords.

"King?" he bellows back, and I can hear the smile on his lips, imagine that cocksure, sly grin.

"Think you could shut the fuck up?" I shout back, pressing my forehead to the wet tiles, my black braids sticking to my face as the hot water continues lashing my light brown skin.

Without responding, I hear his voice drop an octave, ushering the rest of the team out. Leaving me alone. We did bag skates today, partly due to half the team turning up hungover, partly because the rest were still drunk. Coach wasn't too impressed, especially considering we're currently undefeated and it's the first time that's happened in years.

College hockey is a blood sport. That's the only reason I even play. It's the only thing that keeps me out of jail most days, since I'm banned from wrestling now. It hasn't been the same though, not since Lynx left.

He's back today. But he didn't want a fuss. Said he'll *stop by*, whatever the fuck that means. I worry he doesn't want to see us, that he blames us.

Me.

I should have seen what was happening, I *did*, I should have done something. More.

Jaw cracking, I grit my teeth harder, hear them squeak as my ears rush with blood. My legs are burning, thigh to calf, and because I had to go home to Mom over Christmas, I did no on-ice training. I feel ill prepared and it only floods the heat of anger through me faster. I'm not weak. Especially not when it comes to my fucking sport, but I've still got to train hard. I need to be the best, so even when I fuck up, they won't kick me off the team. It's why I work so fucking hard to pass my classes.

Taking a deep breath, I straighten, pushing up off of the wall. I scrub my hands down my face, wincing as I catch my eyebrow piercing, irritated from being taken in and out for practice. I finish washing my body, switch off the scalding water and grab a towel, roughly drying off on my way to the gray painted benches around the edges of the empty locker room.

The space opens up, heaps of wet green towels half hanging off of benches, tossed haphazardly across the speckled white lino floor. Pale gray walls house fern-green shelves, all of them labeled with our numbers, and bright white strip bulbs light the space.

Throwing on my clothes, tight black sweats, black sneakers, a white cotton shirt, all of it sticking to my damp skin. Taking my phone from the shelf space, I grab my duffle, slinging it over my shoulder as I check my messages. I shove out of the room, into the wide hall, pausing as the door swings shut behind me, I open the group chat.

REX

Party at ours.

I thumb my reply.

KING

Sweet.

LYNX

Gonna be late.

REX

I can cancel.

LYNX

That's not why I'm gonna be late.

My brow creases as I stare at the messages, Lynx's first day back and we're partying like an old habit. A bad one. For him. And despite our other vocation, dabbling in everything he needs to stay away from, we're determined to treat him like the same old Lynx. And I think that's what concerns me. Is this what we should be doing? He's my brother in everything but blood, in the same way that Rex is, but I feel more... protective of him now.

KING

If you're not ready, we'll cancel.

LYNX

Stop treating me like a kid. I'll be there.

Anger, on his behalf this time, heats through me, and I feel my neck muscles knotting almost immediately. Tension. It thrums through me like simmering wildfire just waiting to be doused in fuel and blown up all over again. I shove my phone into my pocket, slam my way out of the glass doors and make my way to my truck.

I'm back at our off-campus house before I can even process the journey. Blinking hard, I put the truck into park, shove my braids back from my face, grip the wheel and stare up at the house.

It's large, six bedrooms with six baths, a pool out back, converted basement, open plan first floor. It used to house a bunch of Frat rejects back in my mom's day, but then my older brother -*half* brother-, and Lynx's older brother bought it, and they, and now us, have lived here ever since. All except for Lynx. The terms of his return to school without a scandal means he officially has to reside on campus. Unofficially, he'll be living here six days of the week regardless.

Snow is falling again, and that only serves to piss me off further. I stomp up the three wooden steps onto the wrap around porch, shove my way inside and slam the front door behind me, running straight up the first set of stairs to my room.

My sneakers squeak lightly over the dark hardwoods, the walls painted a warm cream. Rex's room is opposite mine, with Lynx's at the very end of the hall, the latter's door is closed, but Hendrix is hovering in his open door frame, one muscular arm lifted over his head, grip loose on the frame. His other is shoved down his pale gray sweats, tattooed chest bare. He watches me make my way down the hall with a sullen lift to his plump lips that's almost teasing.

"Bad day?" he rumbles, my feet stopping me just outside my closed door.

I blink at him, dropping my duffle to the floor, the pale green carpet runner dampens with melting snow as it sluices off of my black sneakers. Inhaling deep, my chest lifting, lifting, lifting, I say nothing.

Rex tilts his head, nose ring glinting in the low light. A strand of ashy, mocha colored brown hair falling across his light green eye, he tucks it behind a pierced ear. His neck stretches, exposing the flakey, drying skin of his newest ink. Coiling, colorful serpents in knotted rings wrap around his throat. It's an interesting placement, but considering the rest of his pale skin is already filled, all of it in color, I get why he chose to have his mark there, serpents are something we're all tattooed with, a symbol of our brotherhood. The rest of him is like a painted ceiling in a ridiculously extravagant religious building some-where, a renaissance masterpiece or some shit. The man likes art.

I grunt in response, shoving my hands over my head, gathering my dark braids into one hand. I lift my other hand to my mouth, using my teeth to pull the thin hair elastic off of my wrist, threading it up onto my fingers to tie my hair back.

"You need to relax, King." Rex is nonchalant

about it, the words he just spoke, instead of his usual teasing tone.

"I know," I grunt again, dropping my arms heavily to my sides. "I know," I shake my head, expelling a breath, and it feels like it's the first time today.

My neck cracks as I flex it side to side, the intricately woven bones beneath my light brown skin pop, helping to release the tension in my shoulders. I shake my hands, flexing my fingers.

"You need to get laid," he shrugs, like he couldn't feel any singular way about it one way or the other.

I eye him. All hulking six-foot-four of him, rocking lightly in the open doorway, his hold on the frame, his light eyes a little dazed and I roll my eyes.

"You just sat in there all day smoking, huh?" I smelled the weed as soon as I got inside the house, but that's nothing new, it's practically ingrained in the walls.

We party daily, nightly, whatever, and we have an endless supply of whatever we want, whenever we want. It's just, we've been cutting back, despite Lynx still saying he's smoking weed, we're trying not to fuck about and tempt him into more now that he's back. Not after what happened last year.

"Not all day." Rex shrugs, spreading his feet wider to help keep his balance, he's two-hundred-fifty pounds of pure muscle, I don't wanna have to pick him up if he falls on his ass.

Not that I couldn't, just that, I'd rather not have to struggle alone.

A thud sounds above us from the third floor, my eyes automatically rolling up as though I can see what it was if I focus hard enough.

With his gaze trained in the same direction as mine, dragging his hand out of his sweats, Hendrix finally takes his hand off of his cock. Rubbing his knuckles over his peeling, inked throat.

"They in?" I ask lowly, still staring at the white painted plaster overhead, delicately carved coving connecting ceiling to walls.

"Not anymore," Rex drawls.

Then he's releasing his hold on the door, dropping his hand down heavily on my shoulder, squeezing the muscle. I drop my gaze to his, a smirk pulling at my lips.

"Let's get ready to party," Rex's own lips twitch as he says it because Lynx is coming home and that means the boys are finally back together.

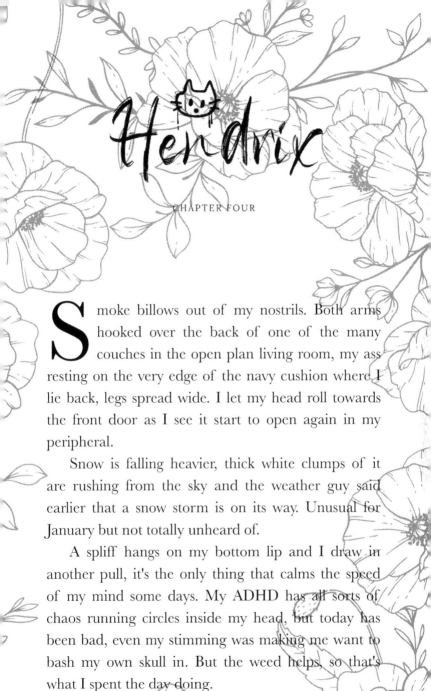

Hendrix

CHAPTER FOUR

Smoke billows out of my nostrils. Both arms hooked over the back of one of the many couches in the open plan living room, my ass resting on the very edge of the navy cushion where I lie back, legs spread wide. I let my head roll towards the front door as I see it start to open again in my peripheral.

Snow is falling heavier, thick white clumps of it are rushing from the sky and the weather guy said earlier that a snow storm is on its way. Unusual for January but not totally unheard of.

A spliff hangs on my bottom lip and I draw in another pull, it's the only thing that calms the speed of my mind some days. My ADHD has all sorts of chaos running circles inside my head, but today has been bad, even my stimming was making me want to bash my own skull in. But the weed helps, so that's what I spent the day doing.

The front door opens fully, and I can't see who's behind it from where I'm sitting. The way this couch is angled. A low coffee table before it, scattered with empty beer cans and bottles, ashtrays half filled with butts. Another couch, matching this one, sits on the other side of it, the back of that one to the door.

Raiden is in the chair to my right, between the couches, in the center of it all. Lounging back, shirtless, like me, exposing all of his black and gray ink, all of it the complete opposite to mine. Tight sweats low on his hips, a half-drunk bottle of beer in his right hand. He lazes back as everyone parties around us, like his nickname would suggest, he watches over everyone like a King.

A couple of his hockey team boys lounge on the couch opposite me. One of them, Barlowe, sandy blond hair with a cruel smirk on his face, has a girl between his legs, her mouth on his dick. I watch for a moment, head cocked, as his hand fisted in blond hair works her up and down his length. And my own twitches, but just barely, even with a girl perched on my own thigh, her hand on my crotch. She's talking to me, potent perfume killing my sense of smell. Lips brushing the shell of my ear with whatever words she's spewing, but I'm not listening, it's always the same shit.

King's eyes follow mine to the opening of the door, waiting somewhat anxiously for our brother Lynx's arrival.

And this time, three hours later than anticipated, he strolls in like he never fucking left. It almost brings a smile to my face. It does bring one to Raiden's.

Lynx slinks in, the door slamming closed at his back, his red-brown eyes immediately finding us. I sit up, shoving the bitch off my lap. I blink as she screeches, Hannah or Harriet, or-

"My name's Heidi," she screeches again, a high pitched whine that I can't stand.

I wince at the sound, even though most of it is drowned out with the heavy bass from the speakers, the echoing noise from the hundred or so people crammed in the first floor. It still hurts my ears.

I stare down at her as she maneuvers herself up from the hardwood, tucking a tit back inside her shirt and scowling up at me. She says something again, but I'm already pushing to stand, giving her my back, dropping the butt of my joint into the ashtray and stepping around the table.

King embraces Lynx first, a cocky smirk on his face as he slaps Lynx on the back. Dropping an arm around his shoulders, turning him to face me. Lynx grins, and he looks less tired, eyes bright, bleached blond hair clean and messy, styled. He looks good. Better.

I step into them both, my arms going around both of their necks. I press my lips to the top of Lynx's head in a fierce kiss and our foreheads all drop together, eyes flicking between each other, I beam, happy, light-

"You're high," Lynx's soft but gruff voice scolds lightly, but he's still smiling.

"And you're sober, don't be a fucking dick," I smirk.

Lynx smiles and King barks a laugh, slapping us both on the back as we break apart, returning to the couches.

Lynx drops down onto the cushion beside me, King in his chair, and fresh beers are placed in each of our hands without needing to ask. Most guys are here because we throw the best parties, but a lot of them also want in with our brother's business. And they think us three are their way in if they voluntarily enslave themselves to us. It makes me want to laugh.

"So," Lynx murmurs lowly, sipping his beer, his warm chestnut-red eyes flicking around the room. "Catch me up."

I bark a laugh at that.

"You've been gone months, what the fuck you think we can catch you up on." I drop my head back, lifting my arms back onto the top of the couch, fingers of my left hand absently twirling the blond hair at the nape of his neck.

"I don't know," he shrugs, "anything," dropping his head onto the back of my hand, stopping my fingers, rolling his attention onto us, but he's still touching me, so I don't object.

"How about you tell us where the fuck you've been tonight," Raiden drawls leisurely, but there's a bite to his tone that let's me know he's not particularly happy.

It's fear.

And it comes from a place of love, but we agreed to let Lynx take the lead on how we go forward now, we're not supposed to be grilling him already.

"Not shooting up, if that's what you mean," Lynx speaks quietly, but his eyes are hard, and my cock finally twitches, drawing my eye, I glance down at my lap briefly.

Thank fuck, little guy, I thought you were dead.

My attention refocuses on King, despite my rapidly growing cock, a dark brow lifting, arching high on his forehead, as the other one pinches atop his gray eye. He says nothing and even I feel uncomfortable. My fingers twitch and my skin prickles, anticipation of what's to come tastes like ash on my tongue, and my fingers flex, wanting to knot, to tap against my lips, but then Lynx relaxes, rolling his eyes.

"I was moving shit into my dorm," he shrugs again, and I frown a little, but I trust him enough to tell us the truth. "And I took a nap."

I flick my gaze between him and King, the latter of whom now has a divot between his brows, but he relaxes it out. The little shit likes to pretend he's just anger and testosterone, fists and brutish words, but I know really he worries about us the most. Probably a bit more than is healthy, but we're his brothers, in everything but blood, and we protect each other fiercely.

I feel the need to lighten the mood, especially as we're currently in the company of others, and although neither one of them sitting opposite me look like they're paying attention, they've both got ears.

I'd hate to have to slice them off.

Curling my arm over Lynx's shoulder, I drag him into a headlock, scrub my knuckles over the top of his skull to noogie him with my free fist.

"We've got our fucking boy back!" I start to chant, grinning wide and bouncing in my seat as Lynx's elbow connects with my gut.

I release him, dropping back onto the couch, my arm still draped over his shoulders, a smile on my lips. I feel light, happy.

We talk shit, drink beer, laugh, and it feels fucking *right*, now that the three of us are back together. As the night wears on, Lynx's tension drains out of him little by little, my arm over his shoulders feeling it in every tiny shift.

And then the front door opens again, a group of girls dressed in colorful booty shorts and crop tops, despite the freezing wind and falling snow, file into the house. Finger-combing their hair and shaking their heads as they laugh, brushing snow off of each other.

Hot girls usually grab my attention, especially in a group, but it's the stiffening of Lynx again. The tightening of his muscles, that has me glancing at him from the corner of my eye, his own on the last girl to enter, pushing the door closed behind her.

She's different from the others she came in with.

Baggy straight leg jeans with giant tears in the knees hang low on her hips. The fraying black denim gaping down her shins, tucked into laced black boots, reveals finely inked floral tattoos. Her arms are bare, though, her pale skin inked with more fine line flowers. Long chocolate hair threaded with spun gold hangs in loose curls down the length of her back, brushing the base of her spine. She's tall, like, really tall, legs that don't seem to have a start or an end, but just go on and on and on. My eyes trace up the length of her, a weird criss-crossed strap crop top on her upper half that barely covers her tits, and her nipples poke through the tight, ribbed, red fabric like they're aching to be touched.

It makes my mouth water.

Her eyes scan over the space, her long fingers, tattoos on those too, and the backs of her hands, she reaches up, brushing her heavy bangs out of her eyes. The girls that came in before her are giggling, turning back for her, grabbing at her hands, but it's like they barely register as her eyes home in on my boy Lynx.

I glance at King, his jaw tense like he's pissed the fuck off, but there's that familiar destruction glinting in his steely gray eyes as he watches her too.

Lynx blows out a breath, rolling his shoulders

beneath the thickness of my arm, and it feels like he wants to shrug me off, but he doesn't and I'm thankful.

I missed you.

I want to scream it at him, tell him not to fucking leave me again, but instead, I stay quiet, watching.

And then the unknown girl is walking off with her friends, heading towards the kitchen, Lynx's eyes following her. My eyes following his, and Raiden King? His eyes watch us fucking all.

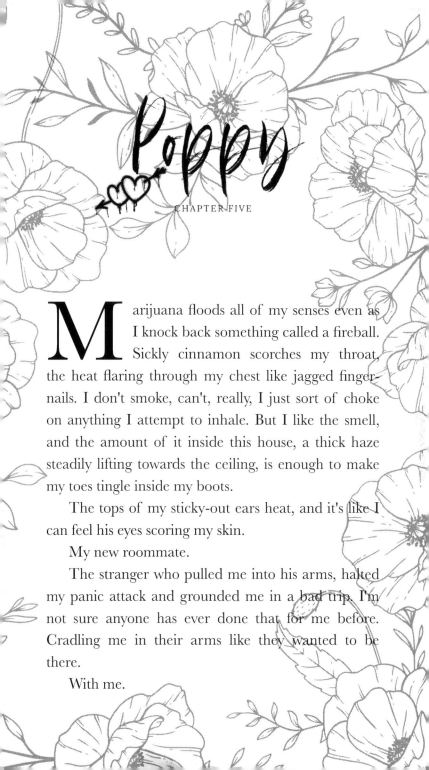

Poppy

CHAPTER FIVE

Marijuana floods all of my senses even as I knock back something called a fireball. Sickly cinnamon scorches my throat, the heat flaring through my chest like jagged fingernails. I don't smoke, can't, really, I just sort of choke on anything I attempt to inhale. But I like the smell, and the amount of it inside this house, a thick haze steadily lifting towards the ceiling, is enough to make my toes tingle inside my boots.

The tops of my sticky-out ears heat, and it's like I can feel his eyes scoring my skin.

My new roommate.

The stranger who pulled me into his arms, halted my panic attack and grounded me in a bad trip. I'm not sure anyone has ever done that for me before. Cradling me in their arms like they wanted to be there.

With me.

But when I woke up, his heavy, deep breaths puffing against the side of my neck, his arms crossed like lead restraints across my chest, his heart drumming easily against my back. I felt safe, so I snuck away.

I tend to get… attached.

Or, rather, I did, once, and look where that got me.

Leaving him sleeping in my bed. I grabbed some clothes and my washbag, stuffed them under my arm and dashed across the hall to Bonnie and Emma's room. Hiding, yes, from this gentle, giant, brute looking stranger with bleached blonde hair and warm red-brown eyes. Large hands, thick fingers, soft skin and-

I stiffen, a shiver tearing its way up my spine, anxiety, again, starting to cloud around my head, making my ears feel like they're stuffed full with cotton wool.

Blindly, I extend my arm, empty red cup cracking in my tightening fingers. Bonnie grins wide with perfectly straight white teeth, she flicks her blonde hair over her shoulder and refills my cup with something else. I don't care what it is as I lift it to my lips, throw my head back and let the alcohol burn its way down my oesophagus. The sounds of the room slowly reconnecting with my brain as I plant the empty cup down on the dark wooden topped island.

Fingers curling over the edges of the surface, I glance down at my purple painted nails, blanching knuckles. I squeeze harder and harder, pale skin whitening, whitening and-

There's scalding heat over my exposed back, nothing but thin straps of my crop top crossing over my spine. My head is down, eyes glazing over as I continue staring at my hands, unseeing. And then lips are brushing my ear, stubble ruffling my hair. The scent of beer is thick in my nose as their humid breath assaults my neck.

"You're new," the male voice hums, and I don't move, don't look up, as a thick arm brushes mine, his front connecting with my bare skin, damp cotton of his shirt the only thing separating us. "I'm Chris," he half purrs in my ear and I grit my teeth, heat flushing up my throat.

"Can you step back, please?" I ask quietly, uncomfortably, shifting my weight from one foot to the other, pressing myself further into the counter.

Chris huffs a laugh against my skin, closing the sliver of space between us and my insides knot, a heaviness building in my chest. He lifts his hands, planting them on the wooden counter either side of my own. Head dipping closer to my cheek, I tremble, penned in. Being trapped has my tongue sticking to the roof of my mouth. I flex my hips forward, pressing myself painfully into the edge of the counter to try and get away, and it's a mistake because he instantly follows.

"Please," I try again, "Please, get off of me," my

voice is barely audible, but it's loud enough for him to hear me clearly.

"Shh," he hushes, suppressing another huffing laugh.

His hips continue pinning mine in place with something like mockery as he curls himself further over my back, his hard cock flush with my arse.

My breath is shallow, and I hear the girls I came with, who I don't really know, giggling between themselves around us like this is all totally okay.

He is suffocating me, stealing my air, and I don't know how to get him to leave me the fuck alone.

"Let me show you upstairs," he slurs, grabbing my wrist overly hard.

I freeze, fear seizing me as he pulls harshly on my arm. But then his crushing weight is suddenly torn off of me. A violent thud sounding at my back, easily heard even over the heavy drumming music.

I spin around, a gasp caught in my constricting throat. Wrist pulsing with pain, my fingers curl into fists, nails carving into my clammy palms as I stare at the back of a huge man, his forearm barred across Chris' throat.

Rippling muscles flex beneath light brown skin, a huge darkly inked back piece covers every inch of it with jagged thorns, cracked skulls, broken pieces of bone, all pulled together with shadowed serpents. It's a macabrely detailed design trailing up over his shoulders, down the tops of his arms. It makes my fingers clench for an entirely different reason.

Black sweats sit low on his hips, sculpted to his firm arse, the stretchy fabric clinging to his thick thighs like they're painted rather than pulled on.

He looks like he exudes no energy, easily pinning a dark haired Chris in place by his pale neck against the wall, Chris' face so red it almost has a purple hue to it.

My head cocks of its own accord. Fascination replacing my fear, as I stare at the back of my saviour.

His dark hair is shaved almost to the scalp on the sides, the top of it long and plaited in intricate braids, all of them tied back, secured with a thin band at the crown of his head. He's a masterpiece. The way he's decorated, the bulge to his biceps, the straining of tendons and vining green-blue veins ridged beneath his skin.

All of this huge guy is tense. Rigid enough to be cut from marble.

His arm flexes, pressing harder, and I think he's cutting off Chris' air supply completely now. Pale fingers clawing desperately into the tattooed forearm keeping him hostage. But the guy doesn't even seem to break a sweat, doesn't flinch, doesn't appear to be doing anything, very much like a statue, except for the heavy rise and fall of his back. Sharp, uneven breaths ripping through his chest.

And just when I think the man who touched me is about to pass out, his dark eyes rolling back, another guy approaches from the main room, and it's the first time I realise, other than the speakers, everything is silent. Everyone is watching, and it's as though the room is holding its collective breath.

The newcomer, tall, broad, of a similar stature, light skin, light eyes, black hair. He doesn't touch the beautiful tattooed statue, instead, he leaves space between them, not crowding him.

"King, man," the newcomer says, something like charm slipping through his teeth. And very quietly he murmurs, "You need to put him down."

And just like that, my saviour, *King*, releases his hold, taking a single step back, and Chris drops to the floor with a pained grunt and loud thud. Hacking coughs tearing from his red fingerprinted throat. But he doesn't say anything, doesn't glare, and the black haired, blue eyed placater drops down into a crouch, grabbing Chris' nape and whispering something I can't hear. I imagine it's something sinister though, because with a quick squeeze of Chris' neck, the new guy hops back up to his feet, leaving Chris discarded on the floor.

Cupping his hands around his mouth, head dropping back, the newcomer howls like a wolf, yelling out, "Let's get fucking wasted, bitches!"

The room erupts into cheering chaos, but I hear nothing over my own thudding heart, banging away in my buzzing eardrums, staring at the back of my silent hero.

I never thought I'd need rescuing. I don't think I ever did before, but then, after everything that's happened over the last year, I don't really know who the fuck I am anymore.

Not since them.

That.

Him.

And then the inked guy turns to face me.

Piercing grey eyes pin me in place, his right eyebrow is pierced, a silver hoop through the arch glinting as his thick, perfectly shaped brows draw together slightly.

King takes a step forward, closer, heat rolling off of his half naked body, he stalks closer all whilst holding my eye. It makes me itch, wanting to drop my gaze, stare at my feet and then silently slip out of the back door, run back to my dorm and hide beneath my sheets.

But I can't bring myself to do it.

I am ensnared, caught, trapped, hooked, and strangely, I don't feel even remotely suffocated as he moves into the vacant space before me. I arch my neck, just a little, I'm six-foot and he's taller by a few inches, and I could just as easily roll my eyes up onto him, but I feel submissive. Instantly. Like I should be rolling over and showing him my belly or something that is the human, and less embarrassing, equivalent.

My mouth is dry, the heat of his body makes it feel as though he's touching me, and I don't hate it.

Even though I'm not high right now and that's usually the only time I can stand touch and not flinch like I've been electrocuted.

His eyes narrow as he keeps his chin tipped up, stares down the slope of his nose at me, the straight line of it rolling effortlessly into an angular square tip, his nostrils flare at my assessment of him. And still, he says nothing.

A nervous tremor runs through me, and it only intensifies the longer he stares. It feels like there's no one else around, the way he holds my gaze. I want to look away, a flare of heat making my belly jump and swoop.

I swallow then, nerves choking me from the inside, but I manage to lick my lips, an action he studies like a predator would his prey.

"Thank you," I half whisper, and the words are sucked in through his nose as he breathes me in deep.

His neck finally allowing his head to drop forward, eating up the sliver of space that was separating our faces. His lips almost brush mine, and it occurs to me suddenly that I really wouldn't mind him touching me, even now, without the drugs I use to get me through social situations like this.

The thought makes me shuffle my feet back, my spine colliding with the counter making me wince. And he closes the scant inches separating us immediately, but we still don't touch. I hold my breath, trying to stop myself breathing him in further, a wicked scent of oranges and smokey black pepper thick in my nose. I lick my lips again, my mouth drier than the desert, my hands gripping the counter like it's my lifeline.

"Who are you?" he grunts, low, gravelly, deep, and I barely hear him, my eyes dropping to his mouth, reading his question rather than using my ears to listen.

"Poppy."

"Where'd you come from, Poppy?" he asks, my name rumbling in his thick Texan accent making me shudder with the way it billows off of his tongue, wrapping around me like coiling smoke.

My breasts brush his bare chest with my sharp inhale, the tattoos on his back wrapping around to his front, licks of black ink up his neck, across his chest, down his abs.

His brows pinch together, his gaze dropping to my mouth now as though waiting for my response. Summoning it forth with nothing more than a look.

"England," I whisper, his thick curl of black lashes shutter closed, and he breathes in deeper, almost like he just can't stop himself.

And for a moment we fall into silence. My breath is held tight in my lungs, and I study his face further whilst his eyes are closed. Watching as his nostrils flare, plump, shapely lips pursing slightly. His eyes flick open, locking back onto mine and I choke down my gasp, a feeling of being caught doing something I shouldn't be assaults me, a wash of heat licking my skin.

Unable to look away, I stare, forgetting where I am as I peer into his eyes, the steely grey bleeding into black as his pupils dilate.

"Come sit with me," he orders gruffly, taking a single step back, flicking his gaze over the top of my head, and that's when the noise of the party filters back in like an explosion.

And without further thought, I turn to follow after him as he prowls back into the living room. The crowd parts for him like he ordered it, despite his silence, his mere presence clearly enough. He stops, halfway back to the cluster of sofas, peering over his shoulder, eyes only on mine, and my feet move as though demanded.

That's when I realise, falling into step beside him, people moving out of my way as well as his, that despite his name, King is not royalty here.

He is a god.

Lynx

CHAPTER SIX

There is a ringing in my ears, a pounding in my temples. My mouth is dry and my fists are clenched. Everything feels too hot and too cold and I wonder how long I've been holding my breath for, because my lungs scream and my pulse soars and all of it sort of dies as I watch King, with her.

Poppy.

The girl that ditched me in her own fucking bed after I helped her through her trip and told me, didn't ask me, to stay.

I glare.

I know I'm doing it, but I also didn't want to have to acknowledge her existence tonight. If any of my boys find out what happened, they would have me moved out of that fucking dorm quicker than I could blink. I laid in her bed, my arms around her hammering heart, and the entire time before I obviously fell asleep, I thought about sliding out from under her. The perfect warm weight cradled between my thighs. Get my shit and leave.

It was unlikely she'd even remember me if she woke up and I was gone. All my boxes, that she likely wouldn't have paid any fucking attention to anyway. The way she threw herself inside the room, oblivious to her surroundings. I used to be like that. Worse.

I should definitely be staying away.

After how hard I've worked on myself.

And then I woke up.

Without her.

And rage, the first real feeling I've had since I got myself together, travels through my veins like a shot of the real good stuff.

I feel high, without the drugs, and it scares me. The hard hit of emotion. Soaring adrenaline pulsing through my veins.

My cock twitches beneath my jeans, the tight black denim practically cutting off my circulation as they tighten across my lap.

"Why's King always the one getting the fresh pussy, man," It's a rhetorical, whiney question from Barlowe, whose dick is still shoved down some random blond's throat.

Barlowe accentuates the non-question with a hard jerk of his hips, the girl's gag loud as he does, but she moans, and my dick dies down at the fake sound of it. Not that it seems to affect the hockey team's goalie.

No, Barlowe's psychotic grin widens, blue eyes flaring as he brings his free hand down on the girl's nape.

"Because you're you," Hendrix deadpans and I force myself not to laugh as Barlowe shrugs nonchalantly.

I flick my attention back towards the kitchen, where, after assaulting his grabby classmate. My fingers curling into fists at the thought of that dick-head Chris touching what isn't fucking his. King is in Poppy's face, untouching, but he's intense and she's bowing back, trying to get away from him and I hope she does.

I don't want to share her.

Which is a redundant thought.

Because Poppy isn't mine.

I blink, my heart thudding even harder, as Rex's fingers tighten in the hair at my nape, knotting, and drawing my attention.

Lazily, he smirks at me as my gaze connects with his. Smelling of weed, beer, smoke and something thick, dark, but sweet like brown sugar. I breathe him in and my cock gets hard all over again. I feel my muscles uncoiling in an instant. A mischievous smile glints in his light green eyes, because he knows how he affects me. And it's been months since I've been with him.

We talked while I was away. Video called and texted. But nothing is the same as when you're physically with the person you think you might have feelings for. Even if they're not reciprocated. I don't really know what's between us. We're probably just fucking. Even if maybe I feel like I want more. I'm not sure Rex really does *relationships*. I'm not sure I do. But he's a bit of an addiction for me too.

Another thing I should be staying away from.

Hendrix Connors' fucking dick.

Rex's tongue peeks out between his smirking pink lips, his straight, white teeth biting down on the pierced tip before he rolls it over his bottom lip.

That's when heat burns through my lower belly, my cock kicks in my tight jeans, hard, and sweat gathers on the back of my neck, goosebumps tearing across my flesh. I tamp it down. The rush of feeling spearing my chest cavity.

And then I glance up, away from Rex, and my eyes instantly fall onto those haunted lilac-gray ones, peering at me from beneath her thick, dark bangs.

King drops down into his chair, leaving the new girl standing at his side. Awkwardly. Five sets of male eyes on her is intimidating in any circumstances, but the way King is looking anywhere but directly at her, is what has me concerned.

He never steps in like some sort of hero, especially not when his team captain is here. Hudson will always sort that sort of shit out. Not because he's a hero either, he's the fucking spawn of Satan, but he does keep his players in check 'round the clock. They're on a winning streak and he won't let the sloppiness of his boys fuck it up.

Poppy's fingers knot together before her, her thumb nail absently picking at her purple polish. Her chin is dipped, and I see those enchanting eyes flick between me, King and Rex. Never once looking at the two sitting opposite us. As though she can already tell, we're the ones here holding the power.

"You can come sit here, Kitten," Rex smirks, patting his thigh furthest from mine, widening his knees, causing everything in me to lock up.

Jealousy, or something else, worse, stomps on my lungs. Then I think of what she might look like pressed between us and I breathe again.

Rex's head cants, pierced tongue licking over his lips as he drags his gaze down her. I can feel it, the moment he's going to say something wildly fucking crazy. I want to stop him, before he does, but I don't need to.

With a surprised yelp, Poppy's flopping onto King's thigh, her legs between his, she sits side on to him, his fingers a shackle around her dainty wrist, her other hand planted on his bare chest to catch herself. She's looking up at him, lips parted, eyes wide, but she says nothing, even as a tremor runs through her, she doesn't object, doesn't try to stand, move away.

"I said, sit with me," Raiden rumbles lowly in that deviant, smoky timbre, releasing her wrist and slouching back in his chair, thighs wide.

Poppy sits stiffly. Still staring at him, the delicate column of her throat working as she swallows. Glancing down at where her hand is planted against his chest, her fingertips flex the tiniest amount against his hard muscles, and then she's tearing her hand away like he burned her. Likely did, my best friend is made of fucking hellfire.

"No fucking fair," Rex grumbles beside me, fingers still playing with my hair, but he's staring at them with a frown and a pout. "But they do look edible together," he murmurs, licking his insatiable lips and just like that, tongue bar clicking against his bottom teeth, he's smiling again.

I want to disagree. Lead Rex upstairs. Let King have her. Keep her as far a-fucking-way from me as possible. With those innocent looking big eyes. Tempting, fat, pink lips, tall frame with miles of leg and delicately tattooed pale skin.

She'll fucking destroy me.

King'll fucking destroy her.

And I'll let him.

Won't I?

"So, new girl," Rex starts and I force myself to relax, to not let anxiety pierce my chest with the stress of whatever shit's gonna inevitably come out of his unpredictable mouth. "You got a name, Kitten?" It's husky, alluring, coaxing, the way he asks, sex drips off of him without any effort on his part at all.

"Poppy," she answers with caution, squeezing her hands in her lap.

"Poppy what?"

"Foster." It feels frail, hollow, the way she delivers it, disconnected.

"Foster, Poppy Foster," Rex sing-songs, cocking his head, my eyes only on him. "What brings you here?" he dips his chin, eyes glazing as he flicks them up. "You're British, correct?"

She nods, following it up with a quiet, politely spoken, "Yes."

Rex hums. Raiden looks anywhere but at her, even though she's seated like an upright corpse in his lap, and I stare at the side of Rex's face. Watching him watch her. Trying to ignore her subtle reactions in my peripheral.

"Why'd you come here?" he asks again, his smirk starting to dissolve on his lips, his interest already waning, he's not really a fan of the quiet ones.

"Why not?" she fires back suddenly, unexpectedly, her bottom lip pushing out, irritation straightening her spine further, instantly renewing Rex's interest.

He lifts a brow, and even King is staring at her now, intense, smoldering, hungry.

"Easy, Kitten, it was just a question," he chuckles darkly, dropping a hand onto my thigh, his fingers squeezing.

"To go to school, what else would I be doing

here?" she arches a brow then too, mimicking his expression, daring him to ask more.

She very clearly isn't interested in this little 'get to know Poppy session'.

Raiden sips his beer, hiding a smirk and I glance at her then, waiting for Rex's comeback.

"They don't have schools in England, your Royal Highness?" he drawls mockingly, dragging the words out like he doesn't give a fuck about her answer, he just wants someone to irritate.

"They do," she blinks, like he's stupid, and King swallows another mouthful of beer, using the glass bottle to hide his amusement.

Poppy leans forward, Rex moving at the same time, meeting her in the middle, their noses almost touching, my gaze and King's following the pair like we couldn't possibly look away.

"And next time you address me," she whispers just loud enough for us to hear her over the music. "It's Your Majesty," she says with a half snarl, top lip curling up and over her teeth.

For long seconds neither one of them moves. I can't see Rex's face with the angle he's leaning at, but I can imagine the hedonistic glint in his green eyes because she just set some sort of challenge in his mind.

Poppy, on the other hand, glares at him like she's imagining his death in an endless amount of violent ways, perhaps even considering the most effective to commit right now. Then she blinks.

Her eyes going dead, like she just shut herself down. She stands from King's lap in one fluid movement. And all three of us watch her, not trying to stop her as she stalks away, rejoining the group of girls she arrived, not ten minutes ago, with. All of them instantly huddling around her, handing her another drink, whispering and giggling as they glance between her and us.

She turns her chin back over her shoulder, flicking her unusual lilac-blue gaze between the three of us and shakes her head. Dismissing us with nothing more than a cold, blank look.

"Oh, fuck me," Rex hushes, rubbing the heel of his hand over his cock before grabbing it harshly and squeezing it through the fabric of his sweats. "I want her," he breathes, biting his lip as it curls up into a smirk.

King says nothing. His steely gray eyes zeroed in on her, but still, his expression gives him away. The aggressor in him unable to hide his own reaction to the girl. Soured, cold rage. Putrid and dark, but it's the little glint in his narrowed eyes that makes my own heart thud.

And then he says sinisterly, "Me too."

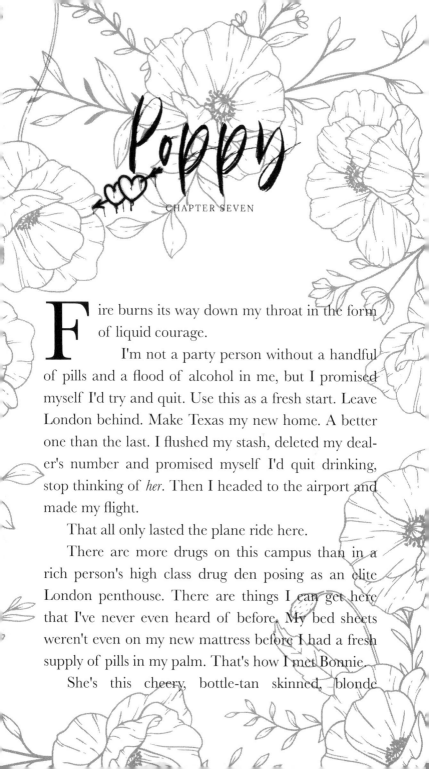

Poppy

CHAPTER SEVEN

Fire burns its way down my throat in the form of liquid courage.

I'm not a party person without a handful of pills and a flood of alcohol in me, but I promised myself I'd try and quit. Use this as a fresh start. Leave London behind. Make Texas my new home. A better one than the last. I flushed my stash, deleted my dealer's number and promised myself I'd quit drinking, stop thinking of *her*. Then I headed to the airport and made my flight.

That all only lasted the plane ride here.

There are more drugs on this campus than in a rich person's high class drug den posing as an elite London penthouse. There are things I can get here that I've never even heard of before. My bed sheets weren't even on my new mattress before I had a fresh supply of pills in my palm. That's how I met Bonnie.

She's this cheery, bottle-tan skinned, blonde

haired, blue eyed beauty with petite facial features, naturally pink lips and boobs the size of footballs. She lives in the dorm room opposite mine with a girl called Emma. Who has delicate warm brown skin, bright brown eyes and beautiful thick, long, black curly hair. Equally as cheery, equally as friendly.

In the short week that I've known them both, they are constantly popping uppers, it's like they're in a constant state of hyperactivity. Which is not really my thing, I like to pass out and forget. Let my mind black out and relax for just a while. It's the only thing that seems to help.

Watching the girls throw back shots, passing me one each time they drink, and cheering like high pitched wolves when they toss them down the hatch. I feel included, for one of the first times in my life. And it's warm, inside my chest, the feeling of friendship, regardless of how deep it is, surface only. Although, I honestly don't know how we'll function when classes start tomorrow.

Regret clouds inside my head. I need to do well or Dad'll send me away again, to the place that's so much worse than here.

Still, I swallow down my drink, something fruity and spicy, and my limbs start to loosen, brain starts to melt. So when Bonnie and Emma each take one of my hands, I don't object as they pull me onto the makeshift dance floor in the centre of the room.

They sandwich me between them, rolling their

hips against mine in some semblance of clothed sex that supposedly passes as dancing, but I don't care.

Heat thrums through my muscles, two sets of delicate hands resting lightly on my hips, their fingers locking together, holding me in place. I let the alcohol rush through me. Fall into my new friends' movements, and the three of us sway and move and grind together in the centre of all the other sweaty bodies doing the same.

Letting go.

It's all every therapist I've ever seen has ever told me. Every single one of them. It's like a chant that rings inside my head. Mockingly. Because I can't. I cannot let any of it fucking go.

Let it go. Let it go. Let it go.

My eyes snap open as the light feminine scents surrounding me are suddenly replaced with heavy imposing male ones. A swirling concoction of fresh orange and dense black pepper at my front. Weed, beer and a subtle sweetness like soft brown sugar at my back. And I realise immediately it's not my new roommate.

Lynx.

The one I knew I'd be getting this week, but had no idea it'd be a guy. I think there must be a mistake, they said co-ed dorms, not rooms. There's nothing I can do about it until tomorrow when the administration office reopens, and that's exactly where I'll be going when it does.

But then my eyes connect with King's grey ones. His hands close over my hips, his forefingers clamping onto the bare skin exposed between my jeans and crop top, and it's as though he's the accelerant to the raging inferno sparking beneath my skin.

That's when I feel the second pair of hands.

Rougher skin with thicker fingers lace through King's from behind, a tall silhouette falling over me, shadowing King's face as I twist my neck to look back.

Playful light green eyes stare at me from beneath wisps of ashy mocha coloured hair. A black nose ring stark against his white skin, hooked through his left nostril. Which flares as he dips down to the bare skin of my shoulder and sucks in a breath of me. His jaw is wide and square, his lips thin and pink, with flakey, tattooed snakes curling around his throat. I swallow hard, looking into the eyes of the man I verbally sparred with earlier.

Warm fingers flex on my waist, softer than the green eyed man's, drawing my attention back to King.

"You didn't let me introduce myself," the guy at my back says when I'm no longer looking at him, sounding like he's pouting.

Dropping his chin onto my shoulder as both men close in on me, eradicating any sliver of space between us by plastering themselves to my front and back, all of their hot, hard edges cutting into my soft.

"I'm Rex," he says huskily, teeth nipping at my earlobe.

Together, the heat of their naked upper halves burns my body. Sweat builds under my arms, beneath my hair at the nape of my neck, but their hold on me moves my hips, which had stilled when I felt their presence. Rotating and rolling me between them, moving me to the beat of the music, they dance with me, and neither one of them speaks. We just move in sync to the music, but even as we dance, Rex's chin on my shoulder, his breath sliding down my neck, I glance back to their friend.

Lynx watches us with what would be perceived as a blank look. Unfeeling. Cold. But it's his eyes, these pretty red chestnuts that flare with fire and darkness the longer he stares. The subtle clenching of his fingers against the top of the sofa cushions where he sits with his arms slung casually over the back of it.

I study him too, only little wisps of him are bright in my cloudy memory from earlier. His coaxing voice, his warm calmness despite my panic. The feel of his skin on mine, everything was hypersensitive, my goosebump rippled flesh, his rough fingers, the weight of his arms folding over my chest.

I wonder if he told his friends about me and that's why they're giving me their attention. It feels wrong. To be dancing with them both, in front of him, not even offering him my thanks, leaving him alone in my bed. All after he helped me and didn't have to. He could have left me. Pretended he saw nothing. But he was kind and calm and warm. He smiled and it might just have been the most genuine thing I've ever seen.

Soft fingers firm on my chin draw my attention back to King, his hand quickly dropping back to my waist. My eyes fix on his steely dark grey ones peering into mine like he can bore his way into my soul if he just stares hard enough.

I lick my lips, my mouth dry, head fuzzy, and finally bring my hands up to his tattooed chest, splaying my fingers over his hard, tattooed pecs. His nostrils flare at my touch, thick, black lashes fluttering over his pretty, dangerous eyes and it feels as though he moves in even closer, despite us already touching. Everywhere.

Chin tilted up, angled a little to the left, giving Rex more space to nuzzle his face into the crook of my neck. I feel his lips pull up, pressing a hidden smirk into the side of my throat.

"Eyes on me when my hands are on you, Princess," King husks and a tremor rips its way up my spine like his words are tearing the bone straight from my flesh. "Lynx is just jealous," he murmurs lowly, a sinister smirk pulling at his lips as he flicks his teasing gaze in his friend's direction.

"He wishes he were us, Kitten," Rex says directly into my ear, his teeth latching onto my lobe and making me shudder. "He might even wish he was you," he chuckles darkly, his mocking laughter vibrating through tendon and bone as he sinks his teeth into the side of my throat.

Licking a stripe up the length of my neck with the flat of his tongue, his teeth relatching onto my pierced lobe. He flicks his tongue, just dipping inside the shell of my ear, his tongue bar sending a chill down my spine. He huffs a laugh against my flesh making me tremble in response before his teeth find more places on my neck to mark.

King stares at me with the harshest gaze, like he's trying to drill his way into my brain cavity and pick through all of my innermost thoughts. Then he drops his face so it's level with mine.

The three of us still moving and grinding against one another.

Rex continues biting, sucking on my throat, my exposed shoulder, dragging my skin between his teeth. I know I should get him to stop. Tell him no, but it's like my tongue has been swallowed down my throat and is currently being dissolved in acid. Because King is in my face, his mouth ghosting over mine in something that is not quite a kiss and I pant against his plump, parted lips.

Heat travels up my neck, the assaulting attention almost hard enough to be called violent, but I like it, and I don't stop, and I want to close my eyes. Escape the intensity that is clearly Groveton College's own idol. The way his grey eyes turn to flint the longer he stares at me should feel intimidating. But it feels strangely safe. The way he defended me earlier. *Saved* me. This man is clearly no hero, but he feels kinda like mine.

A hero just for me.

Rex and King's hands sweep over my body, up and down the exposed skin of my sides, over my jean covered arse, the tops of my thighs. Rex's bare chest is plastered to my back, his body almost draping over mine like some sort of human skin cloak and it feels good. I can't remember the last time I wasn't high and actually enjoyed being touched. I feel all of my wound up insides uncoiling, but then the lights go out, the music stops and everything inside me becomes granite.

My nails carve into King's chest, clinging to him as Rex's mouth unlatches from my shoulder and he says something to King. A rumbling in my ear. Deep, melodic, but it's as though it's drifting away from me. Sound. Their warmth and this room. Blackness infecting me like it's being injected into my every orifice. Wisps of bleakness curling around my organs and constricting like a boa of emptiness.

"Poppy."

My lungs heave, my nails bite down harder into the solid surface beneath them and my eyes see nothing, my head too heavy for my shoulders.

There's panic.

It shows itself like red spiderwebs in the whites of her pretty blue eyes.

She speaks to me, but I hear nothing as my nails claw into the back of her hand splayed over my little chest. She pushes me back, with a finger to her red lips, the top one shaped like a little heart. She forces me to the back of the kitchen cupboard, pressure on my shoulder making me sit. My bottom hits the wood beneath me, knees drawn up to my chest, but I don't release her hand and she yanks it away, leaving me with bloody fingers on my chubby hands.

The door is closed on me, and I breathe harder. My eyes wide, trying to see in the dark. I don't have my little bear with the light up tummy in here, Mummy said I can press him to light up whenever I feel afraid in the dark.

I stay quiet as I hear Mummy speak, but she's too far away from me to hear what she's saying. I frown at the tone, she sounds like me when I fell and cut my knee. She wiped my tears with soft thumbs, gave me that warm, comforting smile, and kissed it better, getting blood on her lips which made me gasp and her giggle.

There's thudding, and I don't move. It's a constant sound, and my mummy cries.

Thud, thud, thud.

Over and over and over, and then there's screaming.

"Poppy!"

My eyes fly open, the room is still in darkness, a mass of voices muffle in my buzzing ears, but I can see him. King. His hands on my upper arms, someone else's hand fisting in my thick hair, forcing my head back so I'm staring into dark grey eyes.

I draw in a deep breath, his fingers flexing on my bare skin. Rex at my back is wrapped around me, craning his head over my shoulder to get a good look at my face.

"Treasure?" a third voice calls and my attention diverts on autopilot to it.

Him.

Lynx.

His big hand is coming towards me, then it's on my face, cupping my clammy cheek. Concern creases between his dark brows, his peach coloured lips thinned into a line.

My chest rises and falls heavily, my lungs feeling like lead balloons.

"You okay?" he asks lowly, his voice a soothing rumble.

I nod, slowly, cautiously, swallowing dryly, I breathe him in. Red berries and rich cedar, warm and bright.

"I'm okay," I almost whisper, dropping my gaze in shame.

Embarrassment is hot in my cheeks, clawing its way up my neck from my chest. Red blooming in my pale skin which thankfully they cannot see.

The room is in darkness, but laughs and hoots and giggling whispers start to reach my ears. Penetrating my panic. I swallow again, King's finger and thumb on my chin, he directs my face back to his, Lynx's big hand sliding to the side of my throat.

"Look at me, Princess," King says smoothly, my eyes rolling upward, flicking between his from beneath my shuttered lashes. "It's just a power outage 'cause of the storm. That's all," his face is bright even beneath the thickening shadows. "'Kay?"

I lick my lips, his gaze dropping to follow the movement of my tongue. I nod, trying to find my words, praying they don't laugh at me. Don't ask me what's wrong with me. A bolt of fear races up my spine, dangerous spears of fresh panic light up through my skull.

Rex digs his chin into my shoulder a little harder, his lips pressing lightly to my throat, breath like a cool breeze ghosting across my overheated skin.

"You need a light on, Princess?" King asks me without mocking, and the usual shame accompanying my fear of such is absent.

King's fingers hook beneath my chin, forcing me to lift my gaze once more, Lynx's thumb strokes softly over my rapidly hammering pulse.

"Yes, please," I reply quietly, swallowing again.

Before I can think about it further, King releases my chin, reaches into his pocket, drawing out his phone, it lights up as he touches his thumb to it. Illuminating his features with the cast of blue light from the screen. His bone structure shadows his features, the slight hollowness to his cheeks, his strong chin, razorcut jaw. Then the torchlight flares bright, the screen dying back to black and his free hand covers one of mine, still planted on his chest, nails cutting in. I gasp as I realise, but he just smothers his smile, plucking my fingers one by one from his flesh.

"Here," he murmurs, placing the phone in my hand, torch aimed at the floor. "We need to check the breakers," he says over my shoulder, looking at Rex who's nodding against me where he's resting in the crook of my neck. "You stay with Poppy," he says next, flicking his gaze onto the man on my left. "We'll be right back," he tells me, tapping his curled finger beneath the point of my chin.

His phone in my hand, I squeeze it tighter, watching as he and Rex make their way through the crowd. Screams and laughter grow in volume, and I drop my gaze back to my feet as Lynx takes King's place at my front. His black trainers, the cuffs of his jeans, the only thing I can see.

"I'm sorry," I say quietly, wincing at the weakness in my voice. "I should have stayed, to thank you," I wince again. "Because I am. Grateful, thankful, that is. For what you did." Wondering if I sound as pathetic out loud as I do inside my head, I open my mouth to apologise for my shitty apology.

"It's fine," Lynx says, interrupting my runaway train of thoughts. "I, urr," he clears his throat, drawing my attention, he reaches up, squeezing the back of his neck, his gaze flicking up, my eyes connecting with his pretty red-brown ones. "I actually understand better than you might think."

My gaze flickers over his face, his strong jaw dusted with light stubble. A little dimple in his chin, freckle beneath his right eye, another, lower down on the same cheekbone. He drops his hand from his nape, licks over his peach-coloured lips, making them glisten with the shadows from my torchlight, angled now so I can see with it, but making sure it's not blinding him nor I.

"I'm not," I swallow again, feeling like it might be my tongue cutting me off rather than the dry, anxiousness of my words. "I'm not like that everyday," I shamefully whisper, feeling like I need to defend myself, make sure he doesn't think badly of me like everyone else I know.

He shrugs, but he doesn't look away. Like he knows I'm not really telling the full truth, but isn't going to call me out on it.

My face heats further, as I realise his hand is still on the side of my throat, over my racing pulse. I didn't need to tell him I'm a liar, he can feel it all for himself. I drop my chin, gritting my teeth.

"Poppy, it's okay," he tells me, and it's comforting, but he's lying too.

I shake my head, still staring down at my boots, but I don't say anything to call him out on it, in the same way he didn't call out mine. He steps in closer, his trainers on either side of my feet, his chest against mine, his hand squeezes lightly on my neck, the other snaking around my lower back.

"I haven't told them about the room situation," Lynx reveals in a hush, his face so, so close to mine, it's heady, his scent, decadent red berries and cedar.

"Why?" I find myself asking.

Regardless of the fact that I am absolutely going to the administration building in the morning and asking for a room change. I'm still curious as to why.

His attention, fixed on me, dark eyes more red than brown, boring into my own. I feel hot, like I want to strip layers I'm not currently wearing, and I like feeling his skin on mine. Forearm scorching the bare skin of my lower back where it's firmly wrapped around me. All corded muscle and tight, warm, tanned skin.

Lynx steps into me, his hips finding mine like they were made to meld together.

"I don't want them to know about the nights," he smiles, dropping his gaze.

"The nights?" I ask, my brow creasing.

"The nights I'll get you all to myself, Treasure," he rasps deeply, tilting his chin, moving his mouth so it slants directly over mine, untouching, teasing, staring into my eyes. "You see," he licks his lips, catching me with the tip of his tongue, making me sway into him. "We always share. Always have. Since we were little kids." Glancing down, he eyes my mouth, my lip wet from the flick of his tongue before dragging his attention back to my eyes. "We made a pact, actually, all of us. Promising to never let a girl come between us."

I shake my head on autopilot, about to interject that I would never, but I don't get a chance.

"So, after tonight," his lips curling into some semblance of a wicked smile, "when we share you." He lifts a brow, watching for my reaction, "Press you between us," he says lowly, running his thick fingers across my back. "Feast on you," he breathes over my mouth, lips parted with short, fast breaths. "*Fuck* you." He presses a light kiss to the corner of my mouth and I want to moan at how good he feels, soft and warm. "Then I'll get to have you again," it's an assumption, the whole thing is an assumption I'll fall at their feet and let them take me however they want, but I don't object as he continues talking. "Every night. All week. In our tiny little room that no one else knows about." His eyes flicker over mine, and he smiles wider at what he sees, wicked in its intent. "Just you and I. My captured little treasure."

His lips brush mine, swallowing my muted gasp, and I bow forward. Arching my spine, pressing my front to his, leaning into every hard, carved inch of his body.

"You want me to kiss you, Treasure?" he whispers over my mouth, "To thank me?"

My entire body is vibrating with need for it, for him. The darkness surrounding us long forgotten, even as I squeeze King's phone, the torch still bright on our feet, in my hand. Lynx leans in, his teeth sinking into my thick bottom lip in quick, carnal violence. I moan into his mouth, against his teeth as the tip of his tongue brushes just the very tip of mine, swallowing the thick sound from my throat.

That's when the lights come back on.

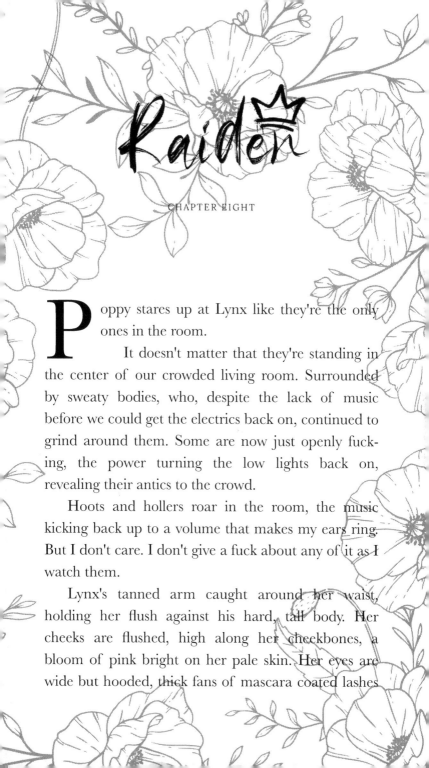

Raiden

CHAPTER EIGHT

Poppy stares up at Lynx like they're the only ones in the room.

It doesn't matter that they're standing in the center of our crowded living room. Surrounded by sweaty bodies, who, despite the lack of music before we could get the electrics back on, continued to grind around them. Some are now just openly fucking, the power turning the low lights back on, revealing their antics to the crowd.

Hoots and hollers roar in the room, the music kicking back up to a volume that makes my ears ring. But I don't care. I don't give a fuck about any of it as I watch them.

Lynx's tanned arm caught around her waist, holding her flush against his hard, tall body. Her cheeks are flushed, high along her cheekbones, a bloom of pink bright on her pale skin. Her eyes are wide but hooded, thick fans of mascara coated lashes fluttering over her unusual colored lilac-gray eyes. My cell is still in her hand, the flashlight still bright, beam of it pointed at their feet.

I can't take my eyes off of them. Everyone else is moving around them, dancing, drinking, grinding. Leaving them in the center as though they're in an invisible bubble.

Impenetrable.

I want to burst through it.

This insatiable need to get between them, my brother, this… girl.

I want to fucking devour her.

I feel Hendrix when he slinks up beside me, moving silently, the both of us protected in shadows in the entrance to the basement. No one is paying us any attention, not with the position we shield ourselves in. Surveying the room. The people. Specifically *them*.

Lynx speaks soft words over Poppy's parted lips, her chest rising and falling in dramatically fast move-ments. Her breasts lifting, lifting, lifting, and then she exhales and her spine bows and her free hand moves unconsciously, clinging onto the soft cotton collar of Lynx's black shirt, fisting it in her purple painted fingers.

"I want to fuck him whilst he fucks her," Rex says almost dreamily beside me, his bare arm brushing mine as his chest inflates with his deep inhale, an unlit spliff clenched delicately between his thin pink lips.

It's a familiarity, that. The way we can touch, look

at each other, be there for one another. We've been together since we were so young.

Rex and I have lived next door to each other our whole lives. We were born only three weeks apart and have been inseparable ever since. So when Lynx moved in with me at the age of nine, along with his mom and his older brother. It felt only too natural for the two of us, Rex and I, to welcome Lynx into our circle.

We went through a few rough years. Lynx's dad was gone, his mom distraught. All of them trying to rebuild a life.

These guys aren't only my best friends. They're my brothers in every sense of the word. We don't need to share DNA to love each other.

I grunt in response, my dick growing hard, all of my blood rushing south so quickly it gives me headrush.

"She's a pretty thing," I murmur, watching her body bow into Lynx, all of her soft, pale flesh melding into his hard, tanned body.

Rex adjusts himself, hand over his erect cock, his arm flexes against mine as he squeezes it through his sweatpants.

"Real pretty," Rex agrees, licking his lips, my gaze on our friend with Poppy, but I hear him wet his lips. "I don't want no one else looking at her," he says then, something thick and feral in his tone.

I'm already nodding, unable to tear my eyes from

the pair as Poppy drops her gaze, Lynx presses his mouth to the underside of her jaw.

Fuck me.

Unsure why I'm even staring, there are plenty of beautiful girls in this room. Lots of them. Some of them I've even sampled. I'm on the hockey team, I'm good looking, have money.

Power.

Maybe I'm just excited to see someone new. But unbeknown to the general population of Groveton, I'm no fuckboy. I could fuck myself into a coma if I really wanted to, women would lineup at my feet like they're there for a holy fucking communion, but it's not me. I'm not interested in that. I want to build a connection with something, *someone,* that isn't going to force a wedge between me and my boys.

And for some reason, this quickly, less than hours of meeting, I have something weaving its way through my chest at the thought of her.

I have a strange draw to this girl with unusual eyes. Thick hair that hangs too close to their rare color, hiding them from me, like her bangs are a personal affront. Still, I stare at her, color sitting high in her cheeks, parted lips a natural red, climbing ink of fine lined flowers and leaves and vines crawling all over her exposed skin. I swallow down the strange feeling in my throat. The foreign ache in my chest.

It's not her eyes, not their perfect shape, eye catching color, it's what's in them. Really in them.

Something that I've seen reflected in each of us, our older brothers', at one time or another.

Emptiness.

It is a disease.

Festering.

Eroding.

Soul sucking.

It's why I stepped in with that tool, Chris. Her body trembled as he draped himself all over her. I could see some of my teammates watching. Waiting. We're close, the boys on the team, and I'm not their leader, don't wanna fucking be. But this is my house. They were waiting to see what I'd do.

If someone says no. Even if they say nothing. Silence isn't a yes.

It's why I had to intervene. I've said no before and been ignored. I won't let it happen again, and certainly not to someone else under my fucking roof.

Blood pulses through me, most of it shooting to my cock. I feel feral, animalistic, unhinged, a part of me untamed and reckless.

I think back to Rex's previous statement, not allowing anyone else to look at her, and it shakes me free of my thoughts.

"Agreed," I rumble thickly, my voice half choked in my throat, drying up as my eyes flare back to life, instantly colliding with hers.

Poppy stares at me over Lynx's shoulder, his lips to her ear, nose nestled in her hair. Her hand fisted in the back of his shirt now, like she's holding him to her with everything she's got.

Fuck.

My insides feel tight, and I'm striding towards them before I can talk myself out of it, people parting out of my way like they know I'm on a mission. To get to her. Them.

Rex is at my back, a gleeful *"Fuck yes,"* hissing under his breath, his hands grip my shoulders and he jumps up and down at my back, I can practically feel his grin.

I don't stop until I'm plastered to my best friend's back, Poppy's scrunched fist between us, her knuckles digging into my sternum, my nose touching hers as I crane myself over Lynx's shoulder.

Her breath halts, eyes widening, pupils dilating like she's trying to suck me into her fucking orbit. But I'm already there. I've had three beers, no smokes, and it's crazy to believe I'm thinking clearly. Because as I grip her chin, Lynx's lips suctioned to the same side of her throat that Rex was feasting on not ten minutes ago, I brush my lips over hers. Soft, silky, warm, wet. All of her is supple and soft and right.

"I'm going to kiss you, Princess," I whisper over her lips, the words seeping into Lynx's ear, making him draw back, his deep red eyes flicking between us, his mouth just as close to mine as it is to hers.

Rex slinks around us, gluing himself to her back, hands sliding up her sides, smoothing the bare skin beneath her tits. His nose to her hair, he sucks in a deep breath, inhaling her scent, sweet and buttery, his eyes closing, he tilts his head back, sighing loudly.

"You smell like fucking heaven, Kitten," he growls into her ear, the vibration of his chest against her spine making her shudder.

"Any objections, Poppy?" I ask her, my finger and thumb a sharp pinch of the point of her chin.

Lynx's lips feathering down her cheekbone, he meets Rex's over the gentle slope of her bare shoulder in a dark, biting kiss. Poppy's eyes flick to her right, widening briefly before shuttering, a tremor rocking through her as she watches the savage way they devour one another, all the while holding onto her. Lynx's arm around her back, Rex's fingers ghosting over her tits. She looks up at me, blinking heavily like she's already three orgasms deep.

Not long, Princess.

Her chin lifts, lips puckering, still parted slightly, her tongue darts out, wetting her lips, glistening with saliva in the low orange light. She shakes her head.

And that's all it takes.

My mouth crushes against hers, my free hand fisting in the hair at the crown of her head, my other still on her chin, guiding her head this way and that, so I can lick into her mouth. My tongue glides over her teeth, wrapping around her own before I'm sucking it into my mouth, groaning at her tiny, breathy whimpers. Soft, little moans climb their way down my tonsils as I swallow them from her tongue. I bite into her lip, plucking it away from her bottom row of teeth. Teasing the plump flesh between my clenched jaw.

She blinks up at me as I release her lip, suckle on the corner of her mouth. Dominate her with something that can't even really be called a kiss. No. This is more. Something I feel all the way down to my toes.

This feels like something real.

And just like that, I'm tearing myself back from her. Forehead dropping against hers. We share breath. Needy pants gruffly escape my tightly corded throat as I grit my teeth. Soft, gentle groans fall from her swollen lips and I want to fuck her right here. Right now. Make this real. Show every fucking person in this room that she is fucking mine.

Ours.

It sort of hits me like a freight train.

There's no fucking logic behind it.

Chemistry thickens the air around us. Something bone deep and primal. I want to bite, claw and maim. But I want to keep. Protect.

I close my eyes, unable to see her face anyway, my own too close, vision blurred, but I know she's looking at me, because I'm touching her. Because I told her to. My grip is tight on the back of her skull, crushing, I can feel it, the pressure in the front of my head where our skulls connect like we're two stones of the same wall collapsed against one another in some semblance of balance.

That's what it feels like.

Support.

It's illogical. The draw I feel. The way the breathy little *'oh,'* that drops from her throat has my cock pulsing with my entire fucking blood supply. Anger, my number one chosen emotion at all times is nowhere to be found, even as i claw for it, search through my fucking bone marrow, it's as though my body's forgotten how to turn rigid, muscles locking up then loosening before a fight. But that word, the *'oh',* has me pulling back. Slow. Gentle. Something I'm not sure I'll be able to show for much longer. I peer into her eyes, these hollow pits of sparkling blue-gray-lilac starbursts. So full, so dead.

Didn't think I'd ever see anyone else with the same gravelike look in their eyes as I did when we were younger. Then, when we were older. A year ago. When Lynx had to go away.

To save him.

A reminder I chant to myself daily. It rattles around my hollowed out insides until there's some sliver of content over the fact we had to send him away. And it's my fault. I didn't have him under control. Not like I should have. I should have noticed. Paid better attention. I still don't know how I didn't see any of it.

Until it was too late.

This thing inside me, trapped and barred behind the bones inside my chest cavity, hammers against its jail bars. A demand, bone deep, to replace that coldness with something more.

I'm protective of my boys. They of me. But I have never wanted to bring anyone else close.

Until now.

Knowing nothing more about her than she has a pretty name for a dying soul, I already feel like that's enough.

But this shit, right here, this is messy. It's more than a risk, it could be fucking suicide. But I already feel like it's worth it, enough. As I draw back further, taking in air that's not full of her humid, rapid breaths, her eyes flicking between mine. I realize what the soft, breathy *'oh'* really was for.

Lynx and Rex.

Their hands are all over her wedged between them, their mouths on each other, lazy pulls on each other's tongues. Teeth clashing as they devour each other's lips. Much the same way that I devoured hers.

I let her look, watch them as I watch her, her scalp feeling like fire beneath my knotted fingers in her hair, I tighten my hold. Her dark hair thick, threaded with strands of natural gold, it's like looking at the sun through the shadows.

Unable to resist, I dip my face back down to hers, resting the point of my chin onto Lynx's shoulder, I lick my lips, look up at her through my inky lashes.

"You like that, Princess?" I rumble, knowing smirk flitting to and from my lips before she has a chance to see it.

Her attention returns to me, all small features, fat, swollen lips, dark brows over light eyes. And she nods, breathless, licking her lips, pulling her bottom lip into her mouth, she glances back at them, Rex's kiss mouthing at her cheekbone as Lynx curls his tongue inside Rex's ear.

"You like watching them?" I ask her huskily, throat thick. She goes to nod her head again and I shake mine, her lips parting, "Words, Princess," the demand rattles through me, making my fingers tremble against her.

"Yes," she says immediately, hungry for it, them, me. "Yes, I like watching them."

"Who? Who d'you like watching?"

"Rex and Lynx," she spits fast, breathy, heady, the sound going straight to my cock.

Fucking hell, this girl's like a shot of heroin.

I groan at the same time she does, Lynx's tongue in Rex's ear, Rex's tongue in Poppy's, but her eyes are on me.

Only me.

Propelling me forward in a rush, I drop my mouth back to hers. Nipping her lower lip, she hisses, and I flick my tongue over the sting, sucking on her mouth, her tongue, my savagery finally showing, my kiss clinks our teeth together.

91

Someone hollers my name, and she flinches, knocking her head back into Rex's face making him grunt, tearing her lip from between my clenched teeth, a ruby of blood beading on the torn skin. That's when I feel it.

The anger.

Rage.

It's bitter and twisted. Thick on the back of my tongue. So when I answer the incessant, drunken fucking bellowing of my name.

King.

It's a roar that spears out of me like jagged, inverted claws, the type that tear and shred and kill, "EVERYONE OUT!" my voice booms around the room, over the music, the dying laughter, giggling. "NOW!" I bellow.

No one questions it, me. The music cuts, the front door opens, and I feel people leaving more than see or hear it.

Ears buzzing, back rising and falling rapidly with my quickened breaths, my heart races until it feels like it's going to burst free of my throat.

Poppy's fingers connect with my spine, her hand cautious as she wraps it around me, fingertips feathering over my heated skin and then they're braver, her hand splaying over the center of my back, my phone still pressed beneath her thumb, into her palm, between us now. A firm reassuring pressure to my spine that has the steam billowing out of my ears, deflating my chest.

Slowly, inhaling a deep breath, I turn to look at her, a crease between her brows. She says nothing and I think, maybe, I want her to, but then Rex is walking around us both, jerking his chin in an *'I got this'* motion.

"Everyone out," he calls, cheerier than me, he continues his chipper bullshit with, "thanks for coming… Great to see you… Sure thing, see ya… Bye now."

The door slams, Poppy's hand drifts away, and I'm spinning around at the loss of contact, catching her dainty wrist in the lock of my encircled fingers, taking my phone back and shoving it into my pocket.

I can't speak, baring my teeth, as I stare at her, only a few inches shorter than my six-foot-five frame. Poppy looks up at me, chin tilted like my finger and thumb still hold it towards me. She lifts her other hand, eyes on mine, and places it to my chest, over the hammering of my heart, her gaze dropping to it for just a second, before lifting her sight back to me.

Lynx is at her back now, but he doesn't touch her, encroach on my space, waiting for my temper to implode or explode. Sometimes it's both, always one or the other, but it's never been neither.

Lynx's red-brown eyes are a shock of warmth against his bleach-blond hair, light skin. I've missed his face, this past year, nothing has been the same. We're going to have to re-find a routine, something organic. Not forced. Healthy. Better.

"You good, brother?" his deep, sullen voice asks, no smile on his lips, but I imagine one there, playing pretend for just a moment, I nod and he exhales.

"I can go," that's what she says.

"Do you want to?" I ask her, "Go?" a frown on my brow I can't help forming. "Lynx can walk you back to your room," I offer, because he has a room on campus now too, by order of the dean, a condition of his return.

Poppy's eyes flicker over her shoulder, catching Lynx's gaze as he steps up beside her, checking her briefly, like he's making sure she's in one piece. It's the same look we all give each other, whenever one of us has a moment. It's like she's one of us already, and she doesn't even know it. Has no idea what we're like. Who we are. What we do. How we work.

"I can leave if that's what you want," she lifts a slim shoulder in an unbothered gesture, but I feel the stiffness of the action like it were my own limb aching.

I reach up, tucking a strand of thick hair behind her ear, a row of piercings lining the length of it, lobe to cartilage, the spiked backs catching the pad of my finger.

"I want you to stay," I tell her, watching the most miniscule of pinches of her face, seeking out her true reaction. "Only if you're comfortable here. If not, we'll take you back."

She swallows, looking down, and I feel deflated, expecting her to want to leave.

"I'd like to stay," it's barely a whisper, but it's enough, the spoken words immediately being locked up tight in the vault inside my head.

Acceptance.

I curl a finger beneath her dipped chin, dragging her attention back onto me, her eyes lifting as her neck cranes back.

"Then you'll stay."

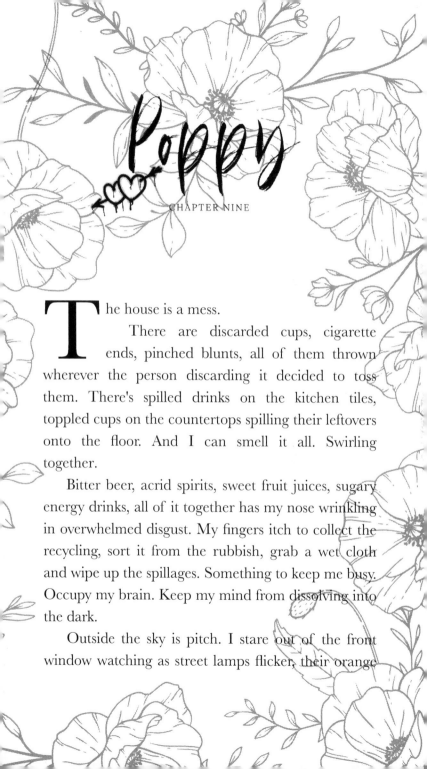

Poppy

CHAPTER NINE

The house is a mess.

There are discarded cups, cigarette ends, pinched blunts, all of them thrown wherever the person discarding it decided to toss them. There's spilled drinks on the kitchen tiles, toppled cups on the countertops spilling their leftovers onto the floor. And I can smell it all. Swirling together.

Bitter beer, acrid spirits, sweet fruit juices, sugary energy drinks, all of it together has my nose wrinkling in overwhelmed disgust. My fingers itch to collect the recycling, sort it from the rubbish, grab a wet cloth and wipe up the spillages. Something to keep me busy. Occupy my brain. Keep my mind from dissolving into the dark.

Outside the sky is pitch. I stare out of the front window watching as street lamps flicker, their orange glow fading in and out as stormy wind violently whips around large white chunks of snow.

I don't know why I'm still here. Why I'm not already half way back to my dorm, with or without Lynx. Like a compulsion, I feel the need to stay, *want* to stay. It might just be the stupidest thing I've ever done. I don't know these boys, *men*. I've only been on this continent a week and I'm already agreeing to things that are wholly unlike me.

Maybe that's why I'm staying.

Maybe it's the storm.

Changing winds.

Maybe it's the fact I freaked out in a room full of strangers and the two boys I was with didn't laugh at me, mock me, point and joke and ridicule. One of them held me tighter, the other handed me a torch.

On instinct, like they just *knew*.

I shiver as Rex presses himself into my back, the metal through his nipples icy against my overheated skin. He curves his arms over my bare shoulders, holding his own hands where they hang over my belly. His chin comes to rest on my shoulder, and I watch him in the reflection of the window as he smiles at me, watching me, too, in the darkened glass. My hands climb to his forearms automatically, fingers curling over his colourfully inked skin.

"We're going to bed," he rumbles, deep, thick, low, the sound travels through me, ricocheting through my skeleton.

We're.

My head tells me he means him and his friends.

Instinct tells me he means *us.*

The four of us together.

His lips skate over the blooming purple patches on the side of my neck, courtesy of him and Lynx, a sharp sting making me tremble as his teeth grate over it. His light green eyes honed in on our reflection, he rocks me in his embrace, swaying us side to side, continuing to mouth at my throat.

"You want to sleep between all of us, Kitten?" he rasps, nipping my bruised skin, rocking his hips into mine, pressing the hard swell of his cock against the top of my arse.

Breath sails through my parted lips. Heat spearing throughout my lower belly, my thighs clench, nails digging into his arms. His low chuckle rumbles down my spine, exhales hot in the crook of my neck.

Heart hammering, I squirm in his arms, clutching his muscular forearms tighter, closer.

"Words, Poppy," he demands, nipping and sucking on my throat. Drawing back, his eyes on my neck, he groans, flexing his hips into me, "I want to mark you like this all over. Make sure everyone fucking knows this was me."

"And Lynx," I half whisper, half choke out.

His smirk reforms, chin coming back to my shoulder, "Mmm, and Lynx," he hums in agreement.

"That where you wanna be? Between us, watching us fuck, but feeling our hands on you."

I'm trembling in his hold now, full body rattling with need. His words raking their way up my spine like a winter's chill.

"I'll show you jus-"

"Rex," King says gruffly at our backs, his huge, god-like body stepping into the frame of our reflection. "Poppy," he rasps, eyes on mine in the glass. "Ready?"

I glance down, all of Rex's pale skin decorated like a renaissance painting, all colourful and delicate, like he's a ceiling mural. Grand, spectacular.

"You don't have to do anything you don't wanna do, Kitten," Rex whispers in my ear, but loud enough for King to hear. "We can just sleep."

"Okay," I reply, nerves firing through me because there's no way I'm going upstairs with these three men and only sleeping.

I won't be sleeping at all. Not with the lights out. It's that reason I should have taken up their offer of walking me back to the dorms. Where I have my lights, the open blinds, a street lamp right outside of it.

Rex's arms fall off of me, his big, rough hands skating down my arms, goosebumps pricking beneath his touch. Using his loose grip on my upper arms, he turns me towards King.

King's hands are in his pockets, his posture

relaxed. His braids are loose now, out of their tie, and hanging in his eyes. His chin dipped, the straight lines of his jaw are sharp, shadowed. He flicks his eyes up, onto mine, holding me captive. I am so still, Rex at my back, King at my front, two lions and a mouse. Nothing worth them hunting, but they could play with me if they wanted, swat me about with their big claws, and then toss me aside when they get bored.

It should be enough to put a stop to this. Whatever this is.

Rex applies gentle pressure to the base of my spine, and my feet move me toward King, our eyes fused together, a snapping tension in the air. King removes a hand from his pocket, reaching it out to me, and my own hand lifts towards him without any thought on my part.

His large fingers close through mine, his skin so, so soft, it almost makes my own feel rough. His other hand lifts to my jaw, cradling my face in his hold, he licks his lips, tilts my chin.

"You're in control," he rumbles, rough and deep, my eyes flicking between his, I nod, and then he's turning me in the direction of the stairs.

Every step I take feels like air is harder and harder to draw in. The higher I climb, the more my ears buzz. Echoing everything around me. Rex's steps at my back, King's in sync with my own as he climbs the stairs at my pace. Letting me lead, have control.

My boots feel heavy as I follow the pale green runner carpet down the hall, dark wood underneath thumping and creaking with every step. King's hand solid and warm in my own cool, clammy one. Rex's fingertips teasing my spine, his body a slightly less intimidating presence than King's.

We stop between two doors, both closed, but we turn to the one on the right, Rex stepping in front of us to push it open. The room is in darkness as he makes his way inside, but LED tubing runs around the edge of the ceiling, casting the room in bright blue light. Eradicating the darkness of the night without being too bright. My hand flexes in King's, tightening around his thick fingers.

Maybe the room is always like this.

Maybe they put these on just for me.

I swallow sharply, watching as Rex saunters further into the large room, more like an open plan suite than just a bedroom.

Two closed doors are on the far left of the space. Dark grey leather couches set around a TV and game consoles set further forwards, a small table between them. A large window with drawn blinds stretches across the wall directly in front of the doorway we stand in. The large bed sits off to the far right, dressed with various shades of dark and pale grey sheets, a mass of black and green pillows atop it.

One of the doors to our left opens revealing a now topless Lynx. His tanned skin is inked with realism looping serpents, thorny looking vines, all of it in various shades of grey and black. Little dribbles of water smatter his chest, rolling down the hard structure of his abs, soaking into the waistband of his low hanging jogging bottoms. Feet bare, arms raised high above his head, fingers hooked into the doorframe, he rocks in the doorway, his muscles twitching and jumping.

I'm staring at him, his temple resting on the edge of the doorframe, a darkened bathroom at his back as the door behind me clicks closed. The sound ominous in the silent room. Loud, final.

Rex stalks forward then, slow, deliberate. Dragging his gaze up my body, licking his lips, his head cocked, he looks up at me from beneath his lashes, stopping before me. He bites into his bottom lip, canine snagging the pink skin.

Slowly, he lifts a hand between us, extended fingertip tracing along my collarbone to the hollow in the base of my throat. He drags the digit down the bare skin of my chest, over the criss-cross of thin straps holding my crop top to my breasts. Rex's fingertip drags over the thin cotton of my top, nail pricking over the stiff peak of my nipple. He circles it, eyes on mine from beneath hooded lids, he watches me, sucking on his bottom lip.

My breath pants, feeling three pairs of eyes watching me.

King's hand still tight in mine, he lifts it to his lips,

mouthing wet kisses across my knuckles, stealing my attention, as a third body closes in on me.

Lynx's scent floods the space, rich cedar, sweet berries, his mouth instantly finds the cap of my shoulder, his teeth scraping deliciously down my flesh.

I tremble between them, my eyes locked on King's even as Rex palms my breast, flicking his thumb over my nipple. Eliciting a shudder, I gasp as King's tongue flicks over my fingertips, sucking them, one by one, into his hot, wet mouth. My eyelashes flutter as large, hot hands smooth up my back, down my arse, over my sides.

Lynx's hand sweeps up my spine, beneath my curls, his thick fingers threading into my hair, fisting it at the root. He jerks my head towards him, unlatching his teeth from my shoulder, crashing them into mine.

His lips and teeth and tongue war with mine. Straddling the line between too rough and too gentle. I want to fold myself into him, let him take his fill of me. His tongue wraps itself around mine, before he sucks it eagerly into his mouth, pressure of his sucking pulling at the very back of my tongue.

A moan catches in my throat, swallowed by Lynx as Rex suctions his lips to the corner of my jaw, his hot breath sweeping down my bruised neck. King's mouth licks and sucks its way up my arm, pulling and nipping with his teeth as he suckles on the inside of my elbow.

My free hand fumbles as I grab onto Rex's shoulder, my short nails carving into his colourfully inked, pale skin as I take hold of him. He nips my jaw, along the length of it to the tip of my chin, and then his tongue is lapping upwards, disconnecting my kiss with Lynx to push his tongue into my mouth alongside his friend's. Our mouths are clumsy, three tongues licking and tasting one another's, teeth nip at my bottom lip, another set biting into my top and it feels like I'm the toy in a tug of war. Both of them kissing me, and each other as we pant, and moan, drawing in each other's humid breaths.

A gentle tug on the ends of my hair has me pulling back, neck craning. Watching down the length of my nose as Lynx and Rex's mouths crash together in my absence.

Their kiss is violence. A collision of tongues, a clash of teeth. Just as catastrophic and beautiful as a thunder and lightning storm.

King's fingers join Lynx's in my hair, tugging the ends sharply, earning a breathless gasp in response, my eyes roll onto him and I'm caught in the storm I find in his cloudy grey eyes.

"Open up, Princess," he rasps thickly and my lips part of their own accord for King to spit into my mouth before his tongue is thrusting inside.

He groans deeply, sending the primal vibration rattling through my teeth, the fizzing current shooting all the way down to my core. King kisses me with his whole body. Every part of him moves into me, against me, his heat scorching my tingling skin. His fingers are looped in the ends of my curls, brushing my lower spine, but they work effortlessly against the knotted lacing across my back. His thick fingers deftly unthread the strings of fabric over my back, feeling my top drop to my hips, exposing me.

I shiver, the room cool, but their bodies so, so hot.

King draws back, breathing me in with a salacious smile on his thick lips, their dusky rose glistening with a sheen of saliva. His and mine. I arch into him, biting into his bottom lip, suckling it softly into my mouth. His grip tightens in my hair, on my arm, and I bow my back, pushing in closer to him.

Lynx's hand still fisting the roots of my hair, Rex's long, wandering fingers curling into the low waistband of my loose jeans.

I fall into King. Let his mouth consume me, erase my reservations.

"Fuck me," Rex whistles lowly, heavy breath panting free with his rough words. "I knew you looked edible together."

Lynx chuckles darkly, his strong fingers massaging my scalp hard enough to hurt. But it sends the whine climbing up the back of my throat free. Another whimpery sound that King dissolves with his tongue, licking up the needy sounds and swallowing them down like they were created just for him. *By* him.

Hands cover my breasts, two very different hands, but neither one of them King's.

"Fuck, she's pretty," Rex rasps, plucking at my nipple with his rough fingertips, calloused almost, the skin hard, I wonder what he does to make his skin feel like that.

"Real fuckin' pretty," Lynx whispers into my ear, his thick accent rumbling through my flesh, sparking every nerve ending I have into a frenzy.

His teeth latching onto the lobe as he drags a thumbnail over my erect nipple forcing a cry to lift from my mouth.

Lips leaving King's to arch my neck, stretch my back, bow into the cradle of the three of them. Ripped, hard bodies, sculpted like they're carved from blocks of marble. Their greedy hands tugging sharply at my breasts, cupping the flesh and tweaking my overly sensitive nipples. King's lips devour me, his tongue laving over my pulse point, his fingers still tight in the ends of my hair, the sharp tugs softened by Lynx's grip at my roots.

Rex drops into a crouch before me, the cool air of the room rushing to meet my heated skin in the space he leaves. He tugs my loosely laced boots off, my socks following, and it's Lynx's hand that snakes down my belly, making me shudder as King reaches up. His velvety soft skin cupping over my breast to replace Lynx.

Lynx unfastens my jeans with sure, deft movements, the knuckle of his thumb grazing over my pubic bone as he sends my jeans dropping heavily down to my ankles. Rex immediately takes over, still in a crouch, he lifts my feet, one then the other, free of the rough fabric, tossing them aside with a soft thud.

Dense, soft carpet beneath my spread feet makes my toes wriggle, Rex's rough hands sweeping over the tops of them, up the front of my shins. His long fingers hooking around my upper calves, fingers dragging deliciously over the backs of my knees. I drop my chin to glance down at him. My spread knees, his weight on his own, he straddles over my feet, his chin lifted, my hand drops to his mocha coloured hair, fingers running through the messy strands on his head.

"Any limits, Princess?" King asks, drawing my attention back onto him with intent, even as my body buzzes with their combined touch making it hard to concentrate.

"Any hard nos," Lynx says at my side, his fingers stilling against my scalp, encouraging me to speak up.

Looking back at him, his face dipped beside my shoulder to catch my eye, I glance down at Rex still at my feet, having pushed in closer, my knees widening automatically to make space for him, his fingers working the tight muscles of my calves.

"Umm," I worry my lip, picking at the flesh with my front teeth.

"Anything at all, Kitten," Rex purrs up at me.

My gaze flicks up, sight running across the tubes of light framing the ceiling.

"Please can you keep the lights on?" I whisper almost inaudibly, vision blurring where I stare into the fluorescent blue.

"Absolutely," King growls, diving back down to capture my lips.

And then hands are moving everywhere.

My skin prickles as Rex hooks his fingers into the waistband of my knickers, pulling them down my thighs. King's mouth smothers my own, his tongue fucking between my teeth with long, hungry strokes. Lynx eats his way down my shoulder, bicep, biting into the pad of my thumb.

Long fingers part my knees, nails digging into the flesh of my thighs, and then Rex's breath rushes over my pussy and my legs almost buckle as his lips suction over my clit.

Quiet laughter comes from Lynx as his mouth finds my breast, teeth grating over my nipple, he sucks hard, swirling his tongue. Drawing back, he blows on the wet flesh, sending a smattering of goosebumps skipping across my skin, before he takes the other into his mouth offering it the same treatment.

King kisses my mouth like he's in competition with Rex on my pussy. The two of them sucking my tongue and clit in a tempo that should be illegal. My knees shake, but Rex only grips harder, driving his fingers deeper into my flesh as he laps the flat of his tongue over the lips of my sex.

Holding me up, Lynx and King keep me supported between them, their hands gripping me so tight I almost forget to breathe.

Breaking my kiss with King, Lynx fists my hair harder, ripping me from his friend's mouth, who doesn't seem to mind as he drops his greedy lips to my sensitive nipples. Lynx sweeps his tongue into my mouth at the same time Rex drives his own into my pussy. Forcing an animalistic groan to tear its way up from my vocal cords, the sound rattling in my throat, echoing in Lynx's kiss.

So when King's teeth drive hard into my flesh, the suction of his mouth sealed over my nipple, Rex bites down on my clit, Lynx sucks on my tongue and an explosive whine rips its way free of my tonsils as I come.

My hips jerk, my body feeling too heavy, too hot, then lighter, warmer, a simmering bubble of something like happiness lapping at the surface of my skin. It's almost too much when the boys don't stop. Rex's tongue lazy now, leisurely lapping between my thighs. King's mouth suckling over my chest, slowly, carefully. And Lynx's kiss turns softer, no less hungry, but his pace is more controlled. All of them coming down slowly with me.

My eyes flutter open, heavy draping lashes shuttering me from the blue glow of the room. Lynx pulls back, pecking my swollen lips. It feels like they're done, over, and I feel a sudden wash of embarrassment start to flow over me. I'm completely naked, they're all still semi-dressed, and my mind begins conjuring those nasty, intrusive thoughts.

But then long, rough fingers grab hold of my arse cheeks, and Lynx and King are lifting my legs over Rex's shoulders, supporting my weight as he rises from his knees, threading his arms up my back.

Rex's face nuzzles into my pussy as he lifts me up, up, *up*. Biting at my folds, my hands flying to his head as he lifts me, my legs over his broad shoulders. Four extra hands supporting my back keep my upright, and I fist Rex's ashy light brown hair between my fingers, holding me to him as he walks us towards the bed, still feasting on me.

With a thud, my back hits silky soft sheets, Rex dropping me like a wrestling move to the mattress. He chuckles darkly as the air oomphs from my lungs, my body bouncing on the firm bed. I'm open to all of them. Sprawled wide and bared in the centre of the oversized sheets.

At the end of the bed, the three of them stand like worshipping gods, their attention so intent, my skin burns under their watchful gazes. They stare down at me like I'm their altar. Perhaps, a sacrifice laid bare before it. I swallow hard, head tilted up, neck straining, my gaze flickers between them. All hard packed muscles, beautifully painted ink, white, brown and tanned skin. All of it has saliva building on my tongue, beading at the corner of my mouth.

Breathily, uncertain, I lift my hand in their direction, limb shaking as a whimper claws its way off of my tongue. But they take it for what it is.

An invitation.

Poppy

CHAPTER TEN

King moves first.

Kicking his joggers down his legs, peeling them from his thick thighs, toeing them off when they gather at his ankles. His knees hit the bed and I barely feel it move as he crawls towards me, boxers still tight on his hips.

Muscles taut, flexing and bunching beneath his beautifully warm, light brown skin, tight body cast in shadows beneath the fluorescent lime coloured lights around the ceiling. His knuckles sink into the sheets on either side of my waist, making the bed dip under his solid weight. Black braids with curled ends drop into his eyes, fists holding himself above me. King stares down at my exposed body like I'm something too precious to be devoured. But in this moment, those grey eyes coming to mine, dark and hungry. He looks like the type of man who isn't going to mind consuming all of my broken, jagged pieces.

"You gonna spread those creamy thighs for me, Princess?" King rasps thickly, the darkness and blue light swirling around like a cloud of safety.

My feet shift to sit flat against the sheets, knees bending up on either side of his hips, toes curling into the silky linen. King dips down to lick across my pout, my eyes closing, lips parting, I arch into him, pushing up onto my elbows to seal my mouth to his.

Heat envelops me, rushing high to settle in my cheekbones, trickling like tropical rainwater down the length of my spine. King's hips press into mine, the hard grind of his erection startling against my soft, wet heat. He grunts, biting at my tongue as I lick into his mouth, my bare breasts rubbing with delicious friction against his sculpted pecs. His hips roll, the pulsing length of his hard cock grinding harder against my sex, a slow, steady pace that shoots stars beneath my closed lids, cold sweat rolling between my breasts.

"Wrap up, bro," Rex calls, tossing a foil packet to the bed beside King's hand.

My eyes flare open, a frown scrunching my brow as King leans back, lips parting to let them know I'm covered and have a clear bill of health. But then I think about the last time I actually remembered to take my contraceptive pill amongst the other, more fun, ones, and I keep my mouth closed.

"Gotta keep our kitten safe," Rex winks at me as

Lynx sucks along the strong, square bone of his jaw, his hands pushing at the open waist of Rex's jeans.

"What'd I say about eyes on me when I'm touching you, Princess?" King grunts into the side of my throat, nipping at my skin.

He lifts up onto one fist, raising himself over me, his grey eyes flare black, stud through his right brow glinting under the blue glow of the room. He licks his lips, biting down on his bottom one, dragging it between his teeth.

My breath pants noisily through my teeth in anticipation, and I stretch up, circling my hands around the back of his neck, nails dragging over his hot skin.

"Take what you want, Princess," he breathes the words, hot and humid breath slanted over my mouth, and my lips chase his, connecting with a clash.

"I want these off," I speak through kisses, maddening and desperate, shoving at his boxers with my feet.

One fist holding him up, the other trails down the valley of my breasts, knuckles grazing over my sternum. He runs his hand down lower, thumb hooking into his waistband, the back of his hand resting over my pubic bone.

I shudder beneath him as he pushes them down, hardly shifting on the huge bed as he rolls them down his thighs, kicks them off. King's long, thick cock thuds heavily against me, wetting the skin of my hip with a smear of sticky precum. I glance down, wanting to see, but his dark chuckle snaps my eyes onto his just as he whips my elbows out from beneath me, sending me sprawling flat to the mattress with an oomph.

"You'll see what I want you to see," King says, taking my lips with his in a sucking kiss. "When I want you to see it," he breathes out teasingly, biting on my lower lip with sharp teeth, and a slick tongue.

"You said take what you want," I whine, breathy and high pitched and foreign sounding to my own ears.

"Hmm," King hums with a low rasping laugh, "You're right, I did."

And then he pushes up onto his knees, his weight a presence I instantly miss, despite him never having rested on me fully. His cock stands proud, jutting out, dark thick inches with a gentle upwards curve in its long length. A dark blushed head, reddening the longer I stare at it, licking my lips as I watch a bead of clear fluid form on the slit of his crown.

Breathing in deep, I stare up at King, expecting to find cockiness in his gaze, but its absence stills my tongue. I was expecting some sort of comment, a look, knowing, but there's none of that there. Nothing I can see to make me feel anything but sure about this.

Groans sound at King's back, shuffling feet, grabby hands, Lynx and Rex out of my line of vision, but not out of my head. There's a gentle pressure against the sheets, a tugging against the softness beneath me when they fall to the foot of the bed.

King is patient, careful, as he drops back down over me, holding himself up with one balled fist, knuckles driving into the mattress. His other hand sweeps hair behind my ear, the pierced shell of it hot and itchy with his attention. Cock nudging over the crease of my thigh, he lets his hips lower further, a welcome pressure against my own.

Without any further hesitation, I let my thighs widen, arching my neck to reach his lips, his chin dipping to meet my kiss halfway. His large palm smooths softly up my side, cupping over my breast as his tongue rolls over my own, needy but slow and sure, patient. Agonisingly slow. It's me that draws a grunt out of him, my teeth sinking into the point of his tongue, his finger and thumb pinching my nipple sharply in response.

Fingers clawing at his shoulders, I arch up into him, crushing myself to his chest. Hooking my feet around his hips, I climb my way around his body, forcing all of our bare skin to fold together, arms and legs circling around him. Teeth scrape my lip, my chin, the hot trail of his tongue making me squirm against him, rubbing myself over him with subtle grinds of my hips. His hand tugs out from between us, his thick fingers immediately digging into the flesh of my arse. Gripping me tightly to him with fervour.

And I want him. This. Them.

I don't understand it, this overwhelming feeling of comfort. I'm not sure I've ever felt anything like it. It's just pure instinctual need. Like these men could look after me. They already have. I've never had a one night stand, and although that's exactly what I'm doing, I want it anyway. Despite this being a really bad idea, I don't let it stop me.

My head drops back at the slip and slide of King's bare cock over my sex, nothing between us but want and need. And as though he reads my mind, he draws back, removing his lips from the column of my throat, his hands working on the condom.

"You ready for me, Princess?" he breathes, nipping savagely at the point of my chin as I nod. "Wanna feel you," he rumbles against the column of my throat.

King lays me back down, smoothing my fringe back from my sweat-dampened forehead. My fingers slipping over the silky skin of his hips, thumbs smoothing over all of his dips and muscular ridges.

The intensity of his stare only increases, every time my eyes connect with his, it feels like I'm staring at someone I know. *Really* know. Have known. For a lifetime.

A hand cuffs my ankle, making me freeze, my leg jolting at the contact of thick, firm fingers.

"You didn't think we weren't here for you too, did you, Treasure?" Lynx chuckles from over King's shoulder.

Breath catching in my throat at King's curl of a smile, I roll my head to the side, peering beneath King's arm, to see Lynx wrapped around Rex in a contortionist type cuddle. All clingy arms, bare skin and glistening sweat, cheeky, almost cruel smiles on both of their faces as they stare at me under King.

"Me first." King says, swallowing my whimper with the finality of his words as his mouth comes back to mine, his fingers finding my folds, slippery and aching, eliciting a strangled howl from my throat. "That's right, Princess," he growls, suddenly plunging a thick finger deep inside of me.

I keen, arching my back, twisting my neck, my thigh muscles tightening and uncoiling, trembling as my pussy sucks hard on his finger.

My mouth releases his, breath panting as he sits up on his knees, my nails scratching deeper into his back, trying to keep him close.

"So fucking tight," King rasps, rapture on his face, in his words, as he watches the place his finger is curling out of before pressing back inside me with a second.

Pressure has me clamping down on his thrusting digits, heat soaring through my core, lower belly coiling and tightening and I think I'm going to come, just like this with barely more than three pumps. But he pulls his fingers free, sucking them into his mouth at the same time his cock thrusts inside of me.

My back bows, a high pitched wail tearing free

from my throat, scratching and clawing its way through my tonsils. His cock hits the entrance to my cervix with one hard punch and my spine curls like a coiling serpent.

King fucks me with long, hard strokes of his cock, too long and too thick, but deliciously so. My walls quiver around him, trying to suck him deeper, the noisy wet slap of his pelvis smacking against my wet cunt with every thrust makes my keening cry only seem louder.

His hands grip my hips with bruising pressure, fingertips flexing over the curved bones, thumbs pressing into my skin like weighted darts. King breathes hard through his teeth, throat rolling with a thick swallow.

I want him nearer as he slams his way inside of me. My hands dragging desperately over his back, scratching and pinching the skin of his shoulders in a desperate attempt to claw him closer.

"Kiss me," I whisper, a furrow between my brows when he only smirks in response, not slowing his speed, not dropping his body to mine.

"Don't mind if I do, Kitten." I gasp as Rex flops into the space to my right, Lynx on the left.

My head knocks in both directions, lips parting, a shy heat starting to creep its way up my neck. But King growls, fucking me harder, deeper, longer, with violent pounding strokes.

It's Rex's fingers that find my face first, twisting my

head towards him with a crack of my neck, and crushing his lips to mine. I groan into his mouth, his own moan of desperate pleasure echoing in our kiss. And Lynx curls over my left, the heat of him prickling my skin, and his mouth scorching my breast as he sucks it into his mouth.

The noises that tear out of me are unrecognisable. Lynx's thick fingers sliding down the dip of my belly, my chest heaving in the clenched bite of his teeth. All of my groans and moans and breathy cries of pleasure are eaten straight from my tongue as Rex licks into my mouth with long, languid strokes, his piercing clicking over my teeth with every sweep of his tongue.

The contrast of Rex's hungry mouth, King's cock, eager, solid claps of his hips, and Lynx's teeth secured in my breast, pad of his finger pressing easy, hard circles into my clit, is what has me clawing relentlessly at King. My left hand drops to his hip, nails delving into the skin, as though to force him into me harder and harder.

"Gonna make you see fucking stars, Princess," King grunts, breath punching out of him with every slam of his cock in my cunt. "Seeing you like this, between the three of us…" he sucks in air through his teeth, cutting himself off and I find myself desperately hoping he'll finish whatever it is he was going to say.

Instead, Lynx's teeth plucking at my nipple, my mouth still fused with Rex's, Lynx lifts his lips to my ear, whispering, "You look like a fucking angel. So perfect for us, Treasure."

Stars shoot across my closed eyelids with that. Lashes fluttering over my cheekbones as I scrunch my eyes, squeezing them tighter. My release fizzes through me, the tingling build up slow and steady, and then it takes hold. Firing through my limbs like an explosion of fireworks on New Year's Eve. It aches and it burns and my breath screams in my lungs as Rex continues to feast on my mouth. Lynx's canine snagging on my earlobe. The orgasm slows, teasingly lapping at me in heady waves threatening to drown, my body melts into the mattress, tension leaving my face, but King's voice lulls me back with his praise like a lighthouse across a stormy sea.

"That's it, Princess," King rumbles in approval. Praise grunting from his lips with every smash and pound of his hips. "Fuck." *Thrust.* "Such a." *Thrust.* "Good." *Thrust.* "Fucking." *Thrust.* "Girl."

I keen, my body rolling, Rex's lips pulling from mine, moving to suckle at my jaw instead. Allowing me the freedom to arch up, Lynx's finger on my clit almost painful as he continues to roll his digit over it, hand pressed between King and I. But it's the dip of King's head I'm desperate to meet, his teeth finding my mouth, tongue lapping at my parted lips and delving inside. He kisses me like he's trying to devour me, and I kiss him back with just as much vehemence.

Then, releasing my mouth, my upper body thudding back flat to the bed, he really lets go.

We fuck like we already know every inch of each other's bodies. Every dip and curve and nerve ending. Nothing to be left unexplored.

Six hands wander across my body, mapping my skin, my own spread out on either side of me, searching for the two cocks waiting patiently for my attention, whilst the third slams home like a punishment with each thrust.

My right hand finds Rex first. Straight, thick length pulsing in time with his heavy breaths as my fingers close around him. Warmed metal curls through his tip, both surprising and not. I've never felt a pierced dick before, but I shouldn't feel any shock that it's Rex that's pierced. He has a lot of piercings I've already noticed, including pierced nipples that I can feel now, brushing the side of my breast where he rolls into my side. Thrusting his cock into the palm of my hand with a low, dark chuckle.

Heat flushes my cheeks when my other hand finds Lynx. All smooth skin and thick veins lining the underside of his velvety, steel length. My fingers just manage to close all the way and he throbs as my fingers and thumb make tight, squeezing contact around him.

"Fuck, Kitten," Rex chokes out, his humid breath rushing over my damp skin before he sinks his teeth into my collarbone, his hands curling over my skin like smoke.

I moan, arching with a squirm as Lynx bites into my opposite shoulder. Daggering his teeth in like sharp little pinpricks, pressure builds again, my eyes flicking wildly between the three men. King's eyes are so wide, so dark, swirling vortexes of thunderclouds in the blown pupils engulfing the grey.

Lynx grazes his teeth up my shoulder, biting my earlobe between his teeth, his hand still wedged between me and King, torturing my swollen clit.

"Come for us again, Treasure," he breathes, hard, hot breaths against my throat as I work my hand up and down his length in a tight corkscrew.

Rex pulses in my hand, his own fingers closing over my fist and stilling the squeezing pulls of his length, "I'm gonna bust, Kitten, and I'd really like to be inside you when I do."

A shout echoes through me as I come, teeth biting down into my bottom lip in an attempt to smother my heavy groan. But it's no use. King's fingers tighten over the curve of my hips and with one final, bruising smack of his hips into mine, a grunted groan falls from his lips, something similar echoing from my own as he comes. His hold on my hips sweeps gently down my outer thighs, my lower half lifted up from the mattress in his hold, legs curled limply around his back where he holds me tightly to him.

King dips down, keeping my legs wrapped

around him with his hold on my thighs. His mouth finds mine in a sweaty, leisurely kiss. His tongue strokes across my lips, the top then the bottom, before he plunges inside, licking across my teeth, the roof of my mouth. We pant hard together, Lynx's hand crushed still between us, my aching clit pounding in time with the rapid crashing of my heart.

King kisses me like it means something. Like *I* mean something. The soft grazing of his fingers smoothing over my goosebump peppered skin, he sucks on my tongue, my lips, pecking at my mouth one final time before he lifts up onto his knees. Lowers my legs, and stares down at me like some sort of demonic looking god.

"Fuck, you're beautiful," he praises, rolling his eyes down my sweat slicked body to where he's still buried deep inside me, before flicking those dark, steely eyes back onto mine. "You ready for more worshipping, Princess?" he asks me with a curling twist of his lips.

I swallow, my hands still on Lynx and Rex's cocks, each of them twitching with interest at the question. I glance at Rex, then at Lynx, the pair of them pushed up onto an elbow, cheeks propped on curled fists.

"Think you can take more, Treasure?"

I glance at Lynx, feeling King twitch inside of me, hardening again already. I twist my head, looking at Rex, a smirk on his thin, pink lips, right eyebrow lifted in soft challenge. I nod, slowly, his smirk curling into a decadent grin I want to lick right off of his face.

Turning my head, I look back at Lynx, a loose smile on his mouth.

"I can take more," I whisper.

And just like that, I'm lifted in King's arms, my hands flying to his shoulders, clawing myself into his chest, as the two boys shift beneath me. King shuffles back, standing from the foot of the bed, clutching me tightly in his arms. Hands on my thighs, he lifts me off of him, his cock slipping free. He adjusts me higher, my core wetting his rippling abs as he tugs the condom free, flicking it into a waste paper bin off to the side.

"You ever been fucked in the ass before, Poppy?" King rasps into my ear, my body shuddering in his arms as he curls them tighter around my back.

I bury my face in his throat, shaking my head with hot cheeks and a shivery spine which he soothes with the soft sweep of his hand.

"They'll be gentle with you," he whispers, kissing my temple, and just like that the tension of nerves dissolves with a single press of his lips.

Hendrix

King carefully places Poppy down on wobbly legs, her grip on his arms steadying her as he twists her in his hold, turning her back to face the bed with his arms crossed over her chest.

Over my shoulder, Lynx lies flat on his back, naked, glistening sweat-slicked skin, a muscular arm propped behind his head, other hand lazily stroking his cock. A dimple daggers his right cheek, eager smirk on his face as he watches Poppy, red-brown gaze dragging appreciatively down her bare body.

Twisting back around, I lick my lips from my place at the end of the bed. Legs spread wide, feet flat to the floor, elbows perching on my parted knees. Teeth dragging my lip into my mouth, I bite down on the flesh, pinching it hard between my teeth. Trying hard not to lift my fingers to my mouth, tap my lips like my brain constantly forces me to.

I stare at them together. King and Poppy. Standing like they're a newly wed couple on the first night of their honeymoon. Her cheeks flush. A glint in King's eye, protective hold on all that gloriously naked skin.

I reach out a hand, waiting. Being patient for the first, and possibly the only, time in my life. I've never fucked a girl slow before either. Not sure I know how, but I already know I'm gonna. Watching King, the way he held himself back, taut with tension, making sure he didn't hurt her. Not sure I've ever seen him with so much control before. He did it right. Didn't spook her.

She's afraid of the dark.

I blink as her hand slips into mine, stilling the unconscious movement of my fingers against the inside of my thigh. King at her back, plastered to her like they're stitched together. His dark gray eyes a warning as I gift our girl a smile. *Don't hurt her,* he tells me with nothing more than a look.

My fingers close around Poppy's clammy ones, pushing to stand as she steps between my thighs, bringing us face to face, her height only a couple inches less than mine, she lifts her chin, her lips parting, ready and wanting for my tongue.

Tongue bar clicking over her teeth, I push between her plump pout, licking over her mouth and groaning as her lips suck on mine. My hands smooth up her sides, skin smattered with goosebumps, my thumbs caress her nipples as I cup her breasts, running my hands higher, resting them on either side of her pretty little neck.

"I told you earlier how pretty you'd look crushed between us, didn't I, Kitten?" I breathe over her mouth, her soft, quiet pants making my cock scream. "Get on that bed and straddle our boy, yeah?" I draw back from plucking at her lips, her eyes blissed out and heavy lidded on mine.

She nods in my hold, gaze flicking over my shoulder. She swallows, eyeing Lynx, and then she glances back to me. Her hands coming to my belly, her gentle touch sending a tremor through me, she looks up at me, seeking reassurance.

"We're gonna be real fucking gentle, Kitten," I tell her seriously, promising her, something I find strangely easy to do, like instinctually, I know I mean it. "Okay?"

She nods, just once, firm, and then she moves past me, King's eyes on her, my own following as her knees hit the bed, her splayed hands next, and then she fucking crawls.

"Jesus Christ," I hiss, biting on my tongue as I watch the round globes of her ass flex, her hips swaying side to side as she crawls her way to Lynx on the oversized bed.

I don't think she even realizes she's doing it. Seducing us. Melting our brains out of our fucking ears.

It propels me forward, watching the rapture on Lynx's blissed out face as she climbs over his legs, long, thick curls dropping forward over her shoulder, curtaining them for that first kiss. Lynx rears up, biting into her mouth, grabbing the sides of her face with his big hands. She whimpers into the kiss, folding herself into his hold, and I'm moving.

Shifting at her back, settling myself between Lynx's calves, pushing up onto my shins, leaning forward on my knees, I curl my arms around Lynx's back, sandwiching her between us, pressing my lips to her cheek. Breathing the two of them in, sweet, sugary butter mixing with that familiar earthy cedar and sharp berry scent, as they consume each other's mouths.

Lynx's back ripples beneath my touch, Poppy's back heaving against my chest where I close her in between us.

"So fucking pretty," I breathe in her ear, flicking my gaze onto Lynx, his eyes opening, focusing on me as his tongue twists with hers.

"Mhm," Lynx hums, breaking off their kiss, her mouth chasing his before he grips her chin. "Be a good girl for us, Poppy. Rex is usually such a good boy for me," he breathes over her mouth. "When he wants to be," he says, glancing at me briefly over her shoulder, and a shiver rips its way up my spine, my pounding pulse hammering at the back of my skull. "Bet you can show him up, huh? 'Cause you, you're a real good girl, aren't you, Treasure?" he smirks wide, white teeth glinting blue under the lights when she nods her agreement, my fingers carving divots in his back.

Tipping her head back against my shoulder, unusual lilac-blue eyes lifted onto mine.

"Let's get him inside you first," I say, making her shudder. "You want that?" I flick my tongue over the tip of her nose, staring into her eyes. "Both of us inside you at the same time, Lynx in your pussy. Me in your pretty little ass, Kitten?" I move a hand from Lynx's back, scratching my nails down his skin, bringing my fingers up between where they're pressed together and clutching her tit. "I can be so careful with you," I rumble against the sensitive skin below her ear, my gaze on Lynx. "Just ask our boy here," I smile, hiding it in the crook of her neck as she trembles between us.

"King?" she whispers, an almost whine in her throat that makes me frown.

"He's here," Lynx soothes, smoothing his hands over her sides, flicking his gaze over her shoulder as King moves up beside us, boxers on now, but failing to hide his erection.

"You look so fucking beautiful," he purrs, pressing his lips to her sweaty temple. "Show me how crazy you can make 'em, Princess." Then he drops to his ass, propping himself at our side with a mountain of pillows at his back.

Poppy turns her face towards me, still resting back against my shoulder, and I capture her mouth with mine. Lynx leans back, my other hand sliding from the hard planes of his back to the soft, smooth skin of her front, joining my other. Fingers running up her thighs, over the flare of her hips, dip of her belly, until I'm cupping her breasts, small, weighty handfuls, nipples tight between my fingers.

Lynx rolls a condom over his shaft, licking his lips as he eyes us both. Poppy's eyes shut tight, my own, half lidded slits to watch him with. I groan as Lynx reaches for Poppy, taking one of her hands and tugging her gently toward him, the both of us shuffling on our knees to get closer.

Nudging her forwards, I tear my lips from her's, I reach around her, taking hold of Lynx's hard cock and giving it one nice long tug. He groans, his hips lifting from the mattress, chasing the touch as I guide Poppy higher up onto her knees, directing his cock to her entrance.

"You ready, Kitten?"

And without answer she slides her way down, taking Lynx inside of her with one slow glide. The look of euphoria on Lynx's face, the tightness in his features, tells me just how good she feels. His hands grab her hips, dragging her closer, before gripping the back of her neck, pulling her in for a heat filled kiss.

King tosses me a bottle of lube without even looking in my direction, his entire focus on Poppy's face. He looks like a man possessed, the way he watches her, like she's his missing piece. Maybe she is. Maybe she's all of ours.

Shaking my thoughts, of a girl we don't know anything about, free. I try to make this just about sex as I roll on a condom, slick myself with lube and press myself forward, closing the gap between me and them. My cock thuds against the parted crease of her ass where Lynx now holds her cheeks open, her chest plastered to his, their mouths fused together. He fucks up into her in slow, gentle thrusts, nothing sharp or violent like we usually are, but the movements are just as desperate.

It feels strange, as I pepper Poppy's back with kisses, her warm, slick skin sticking lightly to my lips. I whisper soothing words as I circle her puckered hole, slipping past the tight ring of muscle with one slick finger, her entire body shuddering as I pump it slowly inside of her, building her up to a second, scissoring them inside of her when she pushes back into me.

"Such a good girl," I breathe against the shell of her ear, her head thrown back, light gaze arrowed on me from the corner of her eye. "You and Lynx are fucking beautiful together, Kitten." I twist my fingers in her ass, the muscles clenching tight, sucking me deep, a low whine slipping free of her lips, "That's it, you're so ready for me. Can't wait to feel Lynx inside of you too."

Poppy pants hard, Lynx's gaze coming to mine,

pupils blown, dimpled cheek shadowed under the fluorescent blue glow of the lights. Leaning back, I pump more lube onto my cock, drip it down the exposed crease of her ass where Lynx's tanned fingers spear into her flesh, spreading her wide. With one final pump, I slip my fingers free, the head of my cock immediately taking their place and pushing inside of her without any hesitation from her or I.

Her entire body quivers around me, my cock pulsing and hardening even more as I feel Lynx moving shallowly through the thin wall inside of her. Goosebumps raze across my flesh, my dick suctioned so deep inside of her, I wonder how I'll ever be able to pull out. I'm frozen, unmoving, Lynx stilling as he senses my control. I'm not used to slow fucks. Never careful of the other person. This is all… new. Feels different, not wanting to hurt her.

Feels kinda scary.

"You okay, Princess?" King rasps, his own control fucking award worthy because he hasn't even cupped his own dick, despite it pressing against the thin cotton of his underwear, the whole time.

"I'm-" she licks her lips, my gaze so intent on her face, I feel like I can see into her fucking soul. "I feel really full," she breathes out, adjusting herself on our cocks making both Lynx and I groan loud and low.

"You like it?" King asks her, her hips rolling just once and the way her ass clenches around my cock, I wonder if I might die.

Lilac-blue eyes widening, pupils like saucers, she nods her head, the long, dark, golden streaked tangle of her hair falling over Lynx's side.

"I like it," she breathes and I can't help my long, hard thrust.

She gasps hard, but pushes back, Lynx flexing beneath her, his cock throbbing against mine inside of her. And with an approving nod from King, the pair of us move.

I fuck her like I've never fucked anyone before. I pull out, Lynx pushes in. The give and take making a vein pulse in my temple, sweat dripping down my spine, even as my fingers can't help but drum over her ribs in a staccato rhythm.

The little breathy noises she makes, the way her ass clasps my cock like it was made just for me, all of it has me seeing stars. I hammer my way inside of her like I'm trying to burrow my way into her gut, my hips slamming into her ass, the back of Lynx's hands still between us. I knock his hands away, not that he seems to mind as he fists her hair, rolls her tit and bites into the bone of her jaw.

The palm of my hand claps her ass cheek, red instantly rushing to the surface of her pale skin as I draw out of her. Slamming my way back inside with the finesse of a feral caveman. I slap her flesh, one cheek and then the other, alternating between hard, sharp thrusts. Her pale skin heats my own as my pelvis smacks into her. The abused skin bright red and burning hot.

Lynx's hands come to mine where they fold over her shoulders, crushing her further into his chest as I rise up on my knees and fuck her like an animal. My head thrown back, her ass gripping my cock like a vise, my cock swells and swells and swells and then *boom*. I'm coming so hard I see stars. Breath held, chest puffed up, my movements slow, the hard slamming turning to nothing more than uneven stutterings of my hips, my fingers still tapping over her ribcage. I collapse over top of her just as she comes. Lynx coming too. Our collective heavy pants echoing around the room like we're in an amphitheater.

Lynx arches up, finding my face over her shoulder, I dip my own down to meet his lips in a searing hot kiss. All of the warm familiarity of *us* coming swarming back in.

We stay like that, the three of us piled atop one another, our breaths too shallow to be comfortable with crushed lungs. And I know I should move, lift my huge weight off of the girl who just let me take her ass for the first time. Unknowingly, helping me reconnect with the boy I think, just maybe, I might love. But it's King's hands that come beneath mine, rolling my weight off of them and rolling me onto my side, cock slipping free, wet against my thigh.

I watch through heavy-lidded eyes as King cradles Poppy in his thick arms, lifting her from the bed and disappearing with her into the bathroom, leaving the door ajar so the blue light filters in.

I roll towards Lynx, pulling off the condom and dropping it lazily to the floor.

"I missed you," I whisper, my eyes closing as Lynx drops his head onto the same pillow.

His heavy breath on my lips, his hand coming to my face, the touch of his palm solid as it smooths over my cheek, curling over the side of my throat. A heavy, comforting weight.

"I missed you too," he rasps, and it's the last thing I hear before everything goes black.

Bennett

CHAPTER TWELVE

My nose wrinkles at the scent. It smells like fall in here, pumpkin without the spice, vanilla, salted butter, warm and homey, but somehow cold in this room. There's none of my younger brother in this dorm. The one he was not supposed to be sharing. Especially with a female.

Dancing my fingers across the small desk, on what is clearly *her* side. A few textbooks piled atop it, a black uncapped pen, a half finished kid's juicebox, the cardboard crushed in the center, the concertinaed bend of the straw pinched closed. There are floral patterned sheets on the bed beneath the window, an undressed mattress on the opposite side of the room, pushed up against the wall. But I know this is Lynx's room. His small cluster of belongings that he uses daily sits in cardboard boxes beside the unmade bed. Cologne, hairbrush, hockey jersey balled up on top.

Pinching the material of my designer pants at

mid-thigh, I tug and pull them up to sit down on the made bed, the fabric stretching tight across my thick thighs, surrounded by that soft feminine scent as I rustle the linen. That's when I get a hint of him, Lynx's berry-cedar scent flooding up from the cold fold of the sheets.

A brow lifting on my forehead, lips pulling into somewhat of an impressed smirk. *Good job, little bro.*

Taking my time surveying the room. Eyeing all of the little touches that reveal things about the woman my brother is likely fucking. There're little lights strung up over the window, small round bulbs linked on a black string. A plum coloured throw blanket screwed up in the desk chair, a hairbrush full of dark and light stands balanced on the very edge of a shelf over the refrigerator.

Then there's a thud against the door, a hissed curse, light and breathy and oh so feminine. My smirk morphs into a grin almost instantly as the door flies inwards, bouncing off of the wall, and a tall, long legged creature that smells like buttery pumpkin and sex, all but falls into the room.

"Fucking door," she grunts in a British accent, toeing it closed behind her with a loosely laced combat boot.

She flicks her hair back over her shoulder, lifting her head as she sweeps her forearm across her heavy bangs, little melting flakes of snow flicking to the floor, that's when she spots me.

"Hello," I greet, cocking my head as she backs up with a jolt into the *fucking door.* "You must be Lynx's roommate," I say politely, laying on my thick southern charm, pushing to stand, movements effortless and predatory in the easy glide of my suited body.

She blinks, chin lifting with every step of my approach until I'm drawing to a standstill a little less than a foot away from her. Lifting my hand in offering, she eyes it warily, hands splayed over the door at her back, blue rings sunken beneath her pretty lilac eyes.

"I'm Bennett," I say, watching the panic ooze from her pores, it has every instinct inside of me wanting to drag her out into a dark field and force her to run. "Lynx's brother."

My hand is still held out between us, but she makes zero effort to take it. A flustered blush highlights her sharp cheekbones, and I watch her throat roll in a swallow with apt attention. My extended fingers are almost itching to feel it, clasp her throat in my palm, squeeze the tips of my fingers into the sides of her pretty little neck.

Letting my hand drop between us, I take a step back, sliding my hands into my pockets with an easy smile.

"And your name is…?"

She swallows again, my eyes automatically following the movement, and then she pries her hands off of the door, straightening her spine, standing on her own, unaided by the wood at her back.

"I'm Poppy," she lifts her hand this time, not in offering to me, but to sweep her hair back over her shoulder.

Dark hair streaked with fine golden strands shifts, revealing the plume of plum-purple hickeys decorating her neck. She must not even notice the way in which her fingers trace teasingly across her collarbone, dipping a little to the skin displayed at the base of her throat, but I do.

Milky pale flesh peeks out from the poorly zipped hoodie, something that I notice quickly because of the hockey team emblem, the jersey number, is Raiden's.

My eyebrows twitch, desperate to lift in surprise, the boy never cares about anyone, let alone lends them clothes. King's a fucking asshole, it's one of the things I like the most about him. But this, her wearing his hoodie, his *number*, knowingly or unknowingly by her, he's claiming her.

"Poppy what?" I pop every *'P'* in her name with preppy pronunciation which only heightens the bright colored blush in her cheeks.

"Foster," she says quietly, eyes wide, their unusual color both light and dark, as though beneath the clear lilac-gray-blue surface, something almost black lurks.

My smile grows, fingers clenching in my pockets at her nerves. It sends signals to all of my own, each signal from my nervous system yelling *chase, fuck, kill.*

The wiring in my brain is wrong, mangled as a young boy. It's why I've managed to get to where I am today. From slinging shitty drugs in back alleys to supplying high quality product to the highest class of clientele all under the guise of a respectable business.

"If you don't mind-" Poppy starts, this quiet, thoroughly accented, overly polite request.

"I do mind, actually, where's my brother?" I ask with a raised eyebrow, cutting her off.

Her mouth gapes, brow digging in an arrow shape formation, a flustered breath skittering through her teeth. So stereotypically British, I almost roll my eyes.

"Not here."

That's what she says. And it's like a little fire lights behind her eyes. Something I instantly want to coax out. Head cocking, gaze dragging up her body, booted feet, shredded jeans, oversized hoodie. All of this *mess* leading to such a pretty, innocent looking face.

I want to fucking eat her.

"Clearly, but you were with him, obviously," I drawl, wanting to see what other sort of reaction I can tempt from her.

"Not this morning." It's a sharp snap that's still soft and quiet but something conflictingly confusing.

"Really?" I ask then, smirk growing wider.

I step into her, closing all of the politely spaced distance between us. And to her credit, she holds her ground. Only a few inches shorter than me, I let my face dip, head canting to the side to catch her gaze, her eyes dropped. I plant my hand beside her head on the wood of the door, watch as she flinches at the movement, heart thumping in my chest like I've just won a prize.

"You smell like him," I breathe into her ear, emphasizing my point by dragging in a deep breath of her, catching more than just the scent of my brother. "I know you've fucked him in the last twenty-four hours, Lolli*pop*. So why don't you just tell me where my brother is?" I could text him, call him, likely would find him at home if I had just gone there first, but antagonizing this soft little creature feels much more fun.

She jolts with my words, blinking, and just as I expect her to slink back into the wood of the door, her hands come up in the sliver of space between us, and she pushes at my chest with the heel of her hands, *hard.*

Letting her move me, I step back at the firm nudging of her fists, watching her step to the side. Arm stretching across the door, her fingers latch onto the handle and she's wrenching it open so wide, she's almost hidden behind it.

"Leave," she orders, a tremble in her body, quiver in her voice, all of it screaming prey, but she doesn't shrink away.

I wonder how long it'd take for her to crack. Maybe she would cry. Shout. Crumble to the floor. I wonder how long I could stand here, just like this, to get any of those reactions out of her.

Tongue licking over my lips, I feel myself start to move back in towards her, her entire body snapping straight as though she can sense it, but the sudden ringing of my phone stops me.

"See you soon, Lollipop," I grin at her, stepping out into the empty hall, hearing the door slam at my back, feeling it vibrate through the soles of my shoes.

Retrieving my cell from my pocket.

Flynn.

I swipe the screen, lift it to my ear, listen to him speak for a short minute. Tapping my foot as I reach the elevator and press the call button. Flynn rumbles in my ear, feeding me the information I've been waiting on, and then I'm stepping inside the elevator, letting the doors close me in before I cut him off.

"Poppy Foster," Flynn stops speaking, silence between us for a beat.

And then, "What you want on her?"

I grin, wide, sinister, chaotic, "Everything."

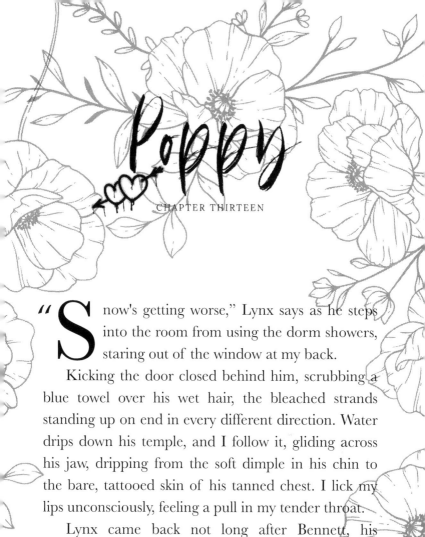

Poppy

CHAPTER THIRTEEN

"S now's getting worse," Lynx says as he steps into the room from using the dorm showers, staring out of the window at my back.

Kicking the door closed behind him, scrubbing a blue towel over his wet hair, the bleached strands standing up on end in every different direction. Water drips down his temple, and I follow it, gliding across his jaw, dripping from the soft dimple in his chin to the bare, tattooed skin of his tanned chest. I lick my lips unconsciously, feeling a pull in my tender throat.

Lynx came back not long after Bennett, his brother, left, leaving me with a sense of unease and a feeling of eyes on the back of my neck, but I didn't say anything to him about it. Not when he walked in smelling of sex, *with me,* looking like sin, and wrapped me up in an embrace that felt much too comfortable and familiar for a stranger.

A stranger that you were fucking last night.

"Didn't know it snowed in Texas," I half-shrug, pushing away thoughts of our previous night's activities.

Having done zero research on the new country I'd be living in in the short amount of time I'd had between being informed of my impending departure and my actual departure. I know next to nothing about my new home.

"Thought it was always hot and humid, huh?" Lynx's mouth lifts up on one side, dimple carving deep into his slightly hollowed cheek, "It is. Usually. Maybe you brought the cold weather with you frommm…?"

"England," I say quietly, dropping my gaze back to the book in my lap, hiding my smile beneath my hair.

"Har *har*," he says, but his smirk transforms into a smile that I catch with lifted eyes beneath my lashes.

"Surrey," I offer up then, lifting my chin to look at him fully, one leg tucked beneath the other where I perch on the end of my bed.

Lynx flicks the damp towel over his shoulder, cocking his head to one side as he grabs his hairbrush from the end of his freshly made bed, "What's it like?"

Lonely, I think to myself. A big empty house with a man who doesn't want to know me.

I swallow around the lump in my throat, try not to think about that.

"It's fine, there's a nice little tea shop around the corner from my house that I liked to spend my Saturday mornings in," I smile a little, thinking of the park I cross through to get there.

"Tea." Lynx wrinkles his nose. "Dunno if I've ever had it. I'm not really a hot beverage person."

"I brought some with me, you can try it if you like. I like mine with lots of sugar."

"Ah, a sweet tooth," he grins, and my cheeks flush instantly as though I've been called out for something. "So, I don't know of any tea shops," Lynx starts, smirking at my obvious flush but not addressing it further. "But there is a great bakery not too far from here that serves these little cream puffs. They have all kinds of sweet fillings with different coloured toppings. They might serve tea, I usually just grab a protein shake."

"They sound good," I nod in agreement.

"I'll take you," Lynx steps closer, forcing me to lift my chin to keep my eyes on him. "Tomorrow, maybe?" he reaches out, thick fingers curling a lock of hair behind my ear I don't want him to draw attention to, they stick out too far, a weird shape to the cartilage. "Just us."

I feel a little breathy, light headed, I thought after last night he'd gotten what he wanted from me. I was easy in giving it up, they didn't really have to try, and I just… I thought I felt something with them, each of them, but shook it off as still being a little high. Clear headed enough to consent, but just, maybe I was reading into things that weren't there.

"Why?"

"Why?" Lynx repeats back, a frown creasing his features. "What d'you mean, *why*?"

"I just…" I wrinkle my nose, unsure of what I even want to say. "You don't have to be nice to me or anything just because we live together. I can get a room change, and, after last night…" I frown harder, worrying my lip. "I won't tell anyone."

"Wait. Hold up, we'll circle back to the roommate thing, but why would you say that?"

"Say what?" I pout, confused.

"That you won't tell anyone, why wouldn't we want you to tell anyone?" Lynx's heavy accent curling with his deep voice growls with the words.

"Just, I'm not, ya know, and you're all, well, you," I stutter stupidly, lifting a hand up and down to gesture to him, all six-foot-two of broad shoulders, tanned skin and beautiful ink.

"Okay, and in that case, that means that you're all, well, what?"

I squirm as he repeats my stuttered words, pinching my chin, tilting my head back further, my neck arching almost painfully as I swallow. Lips parting as I look up at him. Those deep red-brown eyes intense on mine.

"Um, just me," I shrug one shoulder, feeling exposed and like I would quite like to die in a hole.

Lynx's eyes flicker between mine, deep chestnut red-brown, assessing, *seeing*, all of it making me want to squirm but I don't move an inch, don't breathe. After long suspended silence, he hums, releases my chin and lifts the towel from his shoulder, swiping it back over his head again.

"You've got class," he says, turning away from me to lift a deodorant from the end of his bed, rolling it under both arms. He lifts a fresh white t-shirt over his head, threading his arms through, dragging it down his slightly damp body, little droplets of water instantly soaking into the fabric. "I'll walk you."

I frown down at the book in my lap, staring hard at the pages, all the words blurring together. I feel like I'm torn open. The way he saw me. My nails claw over my thumbs, digging deep and marking the skin with dimpled crescents. I feel exposed. Itchy, hot, suffocated.

Seen.

It's only when Lynx walks me down the corridor towards my first class, one of his big pullover hoodies beneath my acid-wash denim jacket, drowning me in cedar-red berry scented fabric, something he leant me to keep me warm, that my chest starts to thaw. His big hand dwarfs my smaller one, his thick, warm fingers threaded through mine, our upper arms brushing, I feel like I can breathe, just a little.

But when he stops us outside what I assume is my first class, I hardly remember how we got here.

He releases my fingers, turning me to face him. Tilting my chin, his warm eyes flicking between mine, he says nothing, and I tremble, so many things rushing to the forefront of my mind, but I can't pick through any of it. I have nothing and everything to say. It feels like he's burning a hole through my soul, big enough to climb his way inside of.

My breathing is a hard rush, my eyes flicking over Lynx's shoulder, watching other students rushing past us, throwing varying looks of curiosity our way as they enter through the open door at Lynx's back.

"I'll be here at eleven."

"You don't have to-"

"I know I don't have to, but I will be." His warm palm comes to my cheek, thumb smoothing beneath my eye. "You look beautiful," Lynx murmurs, and before my cheeks have time to heat, his lips press to mine, no teeth, no tongues, just this delicate plucking of his lips on mine.

Regardless, I'm still gasping when he breaks the kiss, a small smirk on his face as he turns me with his hands on my shoulders and walks me into the classroom. Takes me up the stairs, sits me in a seat. Everyone staring with open mouths as he passes me my bag and books he carried all the way from the dorm.

"Treasure," he whispers, bracing his hands on the sides of my small desk, making me shrink down in my seat.

He engulfs me, the immediate area, the entire fucking room, all I can see, smell and feel is Lynx.

He licks his lips, leaning in close so we're face to face, I glance side to side, trying to see how many people are staring at us because I can practically feel eyes burning my skin, but he's everywhere, blocking my view. He drops his lips to my ear, his cool cheek pressing to mine.

"Be a good girl," he speaks huskily, his tongue curling over the shell of my ear, I shiver, fingernails biting into my tight, curling fists. "See you at eleven."

Then he straightens, looking down at me, looming over me like a god with a smirk on his handsome face, a devilish twinkle in his eyes. He turns away, taking the few steps down in the auditorium and saluting the teacher as he passes her in the entrance.

Heart fluttering with enough winged creatures to take flight, I sink down deep in my seat and make sure my dark hair covers my burning ears.

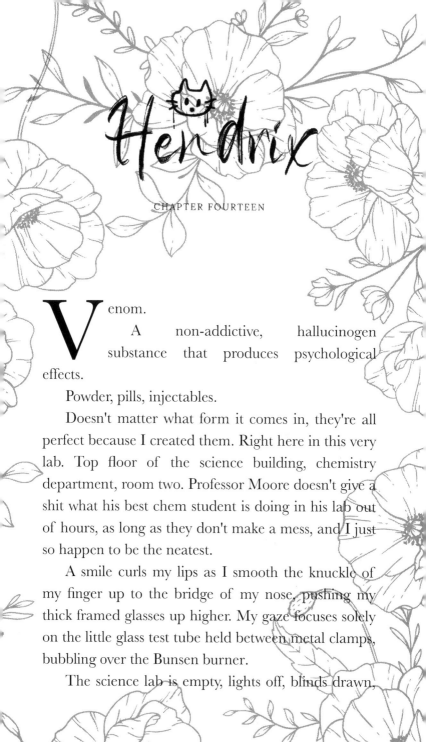

Hendrix

CHAPTER FOURTEEN

Venom.

A non-addictive, hallucinogen substance that produces psychological effects.

Powder, pills, injectables.

Doesn't matter what form it comes in, they're all perfect because I created them. Right here in this very lab. Top floor of the science building, chemistry department, room two. Professor Moore doesn't give a shit what his best chem student is doing in his lab out of hours, as long as they don't make a mess, and I just so happen to be the neatest.

A smile curls my lips as I smooth the knuckle of my finger up to the bridge of my nose, pushing my thick framed glasses up higher. My gaze focuses solely on the little glass test tube held between metal clamps, bubbling over the Bunsen burner.

The science lab is empty, lights off, blinds drawn,

nothing but the hiss of gas and my own thudding heartbeat filling my ears. I'm trying a new chemical compound that I know is going to work, but I want to test it out just once more before I let Bennett put it into production. I don't trust anyone to make it as perfectly as me, but it's something I'm working on.

Letting go.

The wood of the desk vibrates under my elbows, and then it buzzes again, again, *a-fuckin-gain*. I don't even glance at my cell, knowing I'll have to start over if I fuck this up. So I ignore it, even as my teeth grind, a bead of sweat rolling down my temple.

And then my timer's going off. I kill the heat, plunge my test tube into the waiting slush-filled ice bath, and wait another minute. Counting the sixty seconds in my head along with the timer. Precision. I lift the tongs, tap out the crystallized contents onto the glass slide and place another over the top, sandwiching the two together. I slip onto the wooden stool beside me, pull forward the microscope and place the slide under the lens.

I get lost in what I'm doing, forgetting all about the incessant messages my cell was trying to alert me to, so I shouldn't be surprised when the wide, wooden door bangs open, ricocheting off of the drywall and sending the vibration of Smiley's entrance through my bones.

"Yo, Rex, my man," Smiley hollers, lifting a big hand to wave.

Without lifting my head, I flick my gaze onto him, watching as he swaggers across the room, muscular body loose and comfortably slumped, arms swinging casually by his sides. His brown eyes skate across the room, calculating the space and its contents in the same way he does as a left winger on the ice. The only time I think he has half a brain cell is when he's strapped in hockey gear, holding a stick and smashing someone into the glass.

The bones in my neck crack as I twitch, having spent the last few hours in this exact position, Smiley's over-happy, idiotic demeanor is an irritation I'd rather not have. This is the only place I'm serious. Ever. Well, and when I'm beating the shit out of someone, but that's more about enjoyment, the seriousness comes in the first act; intimidation.

This shit, the drugs, is just something I'm good at. And I'm probably a bit of a perfectionist with it.

"What?" I ask lowly, rolling out my shoulders to straighten on my stool.

Smiley's face falls, anxiously shoving a big hand through his short brunet hair, he shifts on his feet.

"I texted you," he shrugs a little awkwardly, "Hudson said to pick up the product for the team party."

Fucking Hudson.

The hockey team Captain, Hudson Cooper, blue eyes, black hair, cocky, sinister smile. He's one of the only people that King will listen to outside of our family, for reasons unbeknown to me. It's not personal, I just don't really like anyone outside of my family. So I tolerate him, along with the rest of King and Lynx's teammates, for the sake of my brothers.

I'll never understand their obsession with hockey, I mean, we all played it back in high school, but I thought they'd drop it like I did when we got to college. They didn't. If anything they only played harder. Lynx plays because he's passionate about the sport, probably dreaming of making it to the NHL, maybe in another life. And King plays because it's one of the only legal ways he can beat the shit out of people with a stick and be cheered on for it.

"Right."

He relaxes as I slide off of the wooden seat, shove my glasses up into my hair and cross the room to where I dumped the rest of my stuff. Fingers flicking open the duffle bag, I grab two baggies of pills, tossing them at Smiley as I turn back to face him.

"Thanks, man," he sing-songs, beaming at me, bright and happy again, over-eager with too much sunshine for any normal fucker, probably taken one too many pucks to the head.

"You're good," I flick my chin towards the door in suggestion, and thankfully he takes it for what it really is, *an order.*

Knocking my glasses back down onto my face, I get back to work, relaxing back into what I was doing with every one of Smiley's disappearing footsteps down the hall.

"Kitten," I husk directly into Poppy's ear, my hands smoothing around her sides, fingers drumming over her ribs as I wrap my arms around her, draping myself over her back, chin resting on her shoulder.

I lift my head in greeting to Lynx, red plastic tray in one hand, his other linked with our girl's, that coy, playboy smirk lifting one corner of his filthy mouth.

Satisfaction.

Yeah, feels real fucking good having her between us.

Shuddering, Poppy peeks at me over her shoulder, gaze lifting from beneath her lashes, those lilac-blue pools just tempting me to dive right in.

I want to ravish her.

"Hi," she replies, quiet and shy, and it makes my fucking balls draw up, dick hard, desperate to get back inside her.

She's damp from the still steadily falling snow, little flakes melting on her acid-washed denim jacket, the fabric stiff beneath my clingy hold, but she smells fucking edible. Breathing her in, I bury my face into her hair, sweet, buttery pumpkin filling my nostrils. Drawing away with a nip to her purple marred neck, courtesy of me and Lynx, maybe a little bit of King, and a kiss to her cold cheek before I prop my chin back on her shoulder.

Peering around the cafeteria, dark wooden flooring, matching paneled walls, green leather chairs pushed beneath rectangular stained oak tables. I smirk at all of the eyes on us, some discrete, most outright staring, it all just makes me grin. This isn't high school, there's no hierarchy so to speak, but if there were, we'd be up there, sitting at the top. As it stands, I don't really give a fuck about status, these people are nothing to my life. But they know the three of us guys are inseparable, and they've never seen us like this with a girl before. Ever.

However, when my little kitten leans further back into me. Lynx in front of her, piling food for the three of us onto a single tray. His thick fingers popping with ridged green veins more and more as he adds a mountain of dishes, dragging us along at his back as he works his way around all of the foods. I feel her anxiety, the lifting, lifting, lifting of her chest as she draws in breath, doesn't let it go. Presses back further into me like I'm her shield.

I'll be whatever the fuck you want me to be.

Lynx glances up, then down, flicking those warm red eyes between the tightening of her fingers in his, and the uncomfortable expression on her face.

"Kitten?" I nip her earlobe, shuffling us closer to Lynx as he turns to close in on her front, placing the tray down on the counter at our side, cupping her cheek.

I stare at her side profile, her eyes on Lynx, wide and shining. Lynx smooths hair back from her face, brushing her cheek with his knuckles and a tremor wracks its way down her spine, her body vibrating in my hold.

"You good?" Lynx rasps, deep voice low, a crease digging its way between his dark brows.

"Everybody is staring," she whispers in that sexy British accent I want to eat right from her tongue, forcing Lynx to lift his gaze from hers, flick his attention, just briefly, across the rest of the room.

"Let 'em fucking look," I growl, mashing my lips into the side of her throat, squeezing her tighter in my arms. "You're ours."

It's a snarling statement I have no right to make, but I feel it in my fucking bones. This weird, wiery, rapidly tightening attachment. It feels like she was made for us, *born* for us. Barbed wire wrapping around my thudding heart, coiling tighter and tighter every time I think of her. And the look Lynx gives me in this moment, this smoldering agreement that has sharp fangs and razor claws, just daring anyone to protest it, only makes me feel steadier in my resolve.

Poppy makes this raspy sort of gasp, shallow and breathy, turning her face so she's barely an inch from mine. Her blue-lilac eyes flash between my own, wide and unsure, she nibbles on her lip, sucking on the inside of her cheek. And when she wrinkles her nose, it takes everything in me not to bite it. Strip her bare right here, spread *her* out on the display counter and tongue fuck her cunt for the whole world to see. I imagine Lynx's bite to my ear as I eat her, his quickened breath on my neck, '*good fucking boy*' he'd rasp and I'd die right here.

"Rex," Poppy breathes, lips brushing mine and it's like an angel singing my name, calling me back to the present, all sunshine and heavenly beams exploding inside my temples.

"Mm, love when you say my name, Kitten," I speak over her mouth, plucking at her top lip before sinking my teeth into her bottom one.

Lynx moves in even closer, a hand clamping down on my shoulder as Poppy's tongue slips into my mouth, "You've made your point," he breathes against our cheeks. "Now let's eat before I make you put on a real fucking show." The ordered growl rips straight from his chest, vibrating along the bones of my face, and then he's yanking Poppy's mouth from mine with a fist in her hair, "Ours," he snarls, sinking his tongue into her mouth like he's trying to lick out her tonsils. "Now," he sucks in a breath, drawing back.

Eyes flicking between us both, haunting and consuming all rolled into one, it makes me want to drop to my knees for him, lick his cock like a melting ice cream cone, let Poppy suck him with me. Both of us side by side, our cheeks pressed together, tongues lapping at our man, one of his hands on each of our heads. Patting and praising and saying, *'good fucking boy. Good fucking girl'*.

And as though he knows exactly what I'm imagining, my cock rapidly swelling in my tight jeans, already weeping for his, and her, equal attention, Lynx smirks and says, "Lunch first," winking at me and smiling at Poppy as he leads us to a table in the back.

And just like that, my heart combusts in my chest.

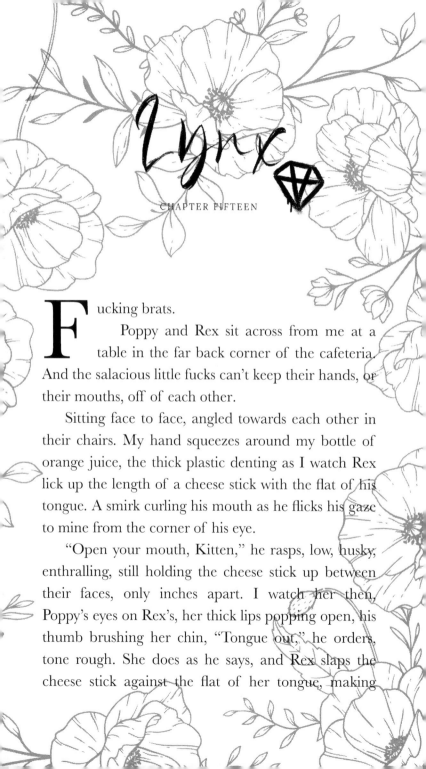

Lynx

CHAPTER FIFTEEN

Fucking brats.

Poppy and Rex sit across from me at a table in the far back corner of the cafeteria. And the salacious little fucks can't keep their hands, or their mouths, off of each other.

Sitting face to face, angled towards each other in their chairs. My hand squeezes around my bottle of orange juice, the thick plastic denting as I watch Rex lick up the length of a cheese stick with the flat of his tongue. A smirk curling his mouth as he flicks his gaze to mine from the corner of his eye.

"Open your mouth, Kitten," he rasps, low, husky, enthralling, still holding the cheese stick up between their faces, only inches apart. I watch her then, Poppy's eyes on Rex's, her thick lips popping open, his thumb brushing her chin, "Tongue out," he orders, tone rough. She does as he says, and Rex slaps the cheese stick against the flat of her tongue, making both her and I blink. "Take a bite," he whispers then, leaning in closer, her lips close around it, teeth biting through and then he drags it away from her mouth, a stretch of mozzarella between his pinched thumb and finger and her lips that he rips through with his own teeth.

"Mmm," she moans, turning her head to face me as she chews and swallows, at the same time Rex's pale green eyes find mine.

My hands slam down on the table making Rex smirk and Poppy flinch. And I can't think of anything except the way my dick kicks in my fucking pants.

"Up, now," I growl it, low and sinister, leaning closer to the pair of them over the table. "You wanna play fucking games with me," I look between the two of them, Rex's smirk lifting even as he bites his cheek, he knows the drill, it's why he started playing this game with Poppy. "That's fine, I'll show you exactly what I do to brats who test me." I walk around the table, lifting Poppy's tote bag, "Come," I order them, waiting for them both to rise from their seats. Their fingers lace, "Walk," I instruct and both of them start to head towards the exit.

Poppy glances at me over her shoulder, Rex whispering in her ear and a slow smile crawls onto her plush mouth as we walk down the hall. She bites her lip, pressing her cheek to Rex's shoulder as they continue to glide down the hall.

Two angels trailing to their punishment. Onc, The

Holy. Thick white wings, a golden aura surrounding her, visiting from a sacred land is quickly corrupted by the other. The Fallen, black winged, smoking feathers. He whispers into the ear of The Holy, coaxing her into the darkness with seductive murmurs and wicked tongues.

That's how I picture them inside my head as I direct them through a first floor lecture hall, into an empty Professor's office. Locking the door at my back as I enter behind them, enveloping the three of us in shadows.

Poppy's sharp inhale prompts me faster towards the desk, flicking on the small table lamp, dropping her canvas bag onto the chair. I lean back against the desk, crossing my ankles, arms folding over my chest. The two of them standing before me, holding hands, matching smirks on each of their faces, our girl's a little shyer than Rex's.

My cock fucking weeps and I want to fuck them both at the same time, devour them, bruise them, make sure they both know they're mine.

"Get on your knees," I breathe, controlling my tone, keeping it even.

Slowly, sinking to their knees, hands still together, it makes me swallow, the sight of it. Their joint submission.

Poppy's lips are slightly parted, her eyes wide, and it's like as soon as her shins become flush with the wooden floor, she hits subspace. Rex's chest rises and falls, his eyes only on mine, waiting, he licks his lips, and I see the corded muscle in his forearm flex as he tightens his grip on Poppy's hand.

I stare between the two of them, silent, waiting, their combined breathing heavy and fast. It takes everything in me to keep control of my own.

Uncrossing my legs, I drop my arms, keep my chin high, looking down the length of my nose at them.

Kneeling.

For me.

My head spins, lust like a cloud of smoke lulling me under, but I straighten from the desk, standing tall, towering over them.

"Treasure, you're such a good girl for me usually," I lick my lips, tongue slowly rolling over my bottom one. "You let this bad boy corrupt you today?" I ask her, lilac eyes glazed, face shadowed, my silhouette falling over her.

She shakes her head, breath escaping her parted lips, "No," she whispers, eyes only on mine and my heart hammers.

This is a girl I could love.

And she's sitting beside the man I *do* love.

Both of them waiting.

For me.

"Come take out my cock, Treasure," I rasp, low and deep, and like the perfect fucking girl she is, she *crawls* towards me.

Her knees probably aching against the hardwood,

but she doesn't wince, her ass swaying. Rex's eyes glued to it as he watches her close the three feet between us, his teeth in his lip. Her eyes on mine the entire time. She stops, right at the toes of my sneakers, tilting her head all the way back, her neck arching, her chin almost brushing the top of my thigh as she presses up on her knees. Long fingers curling beneath the waistband of my pants, her skin grazing mine like a shock of electricity bolting up my spine. She tugs down my boxer briefs and sweats, my cock springing free, her breath fanning over the weeping head of it makes me flinch in surprise. She drops down to her haunches, her eyes on my cock, and licks her lips.

"Rex," I rasp, husky and low, my eyes lifting to his light green ones, "come show our good girl how much of a good boy you can really be for me."

Rex shifts, as though he's going to rise to his feet and I cluck my tongue, stopping him with one foot flat to the floor, a knee raised, "I don't think so," I whisper sinisterly. I lick my lips, raking my eyes down his cut, muscular body, "Crawl to me."

Rex's thick throat bobs with his swallow, his eyes holding mine, smirk gone, he drops his knee back to the floor, hands going out in front of him, he starts to crawl.

I glance back at Poppy, her entire body in submission, and it might just be the most beautiful thing I've ever seen.

My cock jumps, the cool air of the room chilling my skin, but beneath it, I feel so, so hot. Anticipation a fire igniting beneath my flesh.

Rex stops beside Poppy. But where she's resting back on her heels, he's pushing up onto his knees, their thighs brushing as he does. Straight strands of ashy-mocha colored hair fall across his forehead as he looks up at me, shuffling even closer. His long fingers curl around the base of my cock squeezing my length in his rough palm as his lips part and he takes me all the way into his mouth. Twisting his fist at the base as the tip of my dick taps against the back of his throat.

Rex hollows his cheeks, sucking me deep, those pale green eyes locked on mine, and I can't help lifting my hand, placing it palm down on the top of his head. His hair silky beneath my touch, I resist the urge to twine my fingers in it, grip him hard and yank him further down on my cock.

Instead, I rumble, my voice thick, "Such a good fucking boy for me," and I pat his head.

His eyes roll into the back of his head, lashes fluttering as he sucks me even deeper, and I'm kneading my fingers into his scalp, making him moan. Vibrations running down the hard length of my cock, warmth growing in my lower belly. Letting him suck me hard, working his lips up and down my cock, the metal through his tongue trailing the underside. And then I'm fisting his roots, wrenching him back, strings of saliva connecting us. I lean forward, his neck arched so far back, I'm sure it's hard to breathe, but he doesn't protest, a small whimper catching in his throat as he drops his hand.

"Share with our girl," I murmur over his lips, my eyes flicking up from his mouth to his eyes.

He nods in my hold, trying to swallow, his square jaw clenched. I release his hair, but he doesn't drop my gaze, our lips brushing, I draw back, just enough to see him better, and trail my hand down the side of his face. Pinching his black nose ring, I give it a little tug, his nostrils flaring.

"Show Poppy how we play," I tell him, slapping the flat of my hand against his cheek, his pale green eyes glazing at the gentle contact.

My lips curl up as he nods once again, a broad smirk lifting my face. I straighten back up, stare down at my cock, precum oozing from my slit. Lifting my gaze to Poppy, already pushing up on her knees, leaning forward, Rex's fingers still laced with hers.

"Don't waste any, Treasure," I say gently, her lilac eyes coming to mine.

Her chest heaving as I weave my fingers into her hair, curling a strand behind her pierced ear, something I know she hates. But she doesn't have to hide that shit from me. Her insecurities. Plus, I think the way her ears catch fire at their slightly pointed tips when she gets embarrassed is overly fucking adorable.

"He tastes like candy," Rex whispers, loud enough for me to hear as he presses his open mouth to her cheek, nuzzling his nose in her hair. He drops his cheek to rest on her shoulder, both of them looking up at me, each of their mouths so fucking close to where I want them it's almost hard to breathe, when he says, "Let's share."

Two mouths suck along either side of my cock, starting at the base and wrapping their tongues together around me, the tips flicking over one another as they suckle around the head.

Rex draws back, Poppy still on my cock, "Taste him, Kitten," he encourages, his breath making my dick jump.

And then the flat of her tongue is lapping up the length of my slit, her mouth suctioning over the tip, hollowing her cheeks as she swirls her tongue around me, poking the tip into the slit.

I want to close my eyes, drop my head back, but I don't want to stop watching.

Rex licks around my shaft, one hand lifting to cup my balls, his long fingers massaging.

"How's he taste, beautiful?" he rasps then, Poppy sucking harder and harder on my tip before she pops her lips off of my cock.

She blinks those big eyes at Rex, his hand not on my sac lifting to her face, cupping her cheek, thumb resting along her swollen bottom lip.

"Delicious," she breathes, flicking her gaze up to me, eyes wide, face flush, and I feel like I could come from that alone.

"Well, we better not leave him wanting then," Rex chuckles, squeezing my balls before he moves that hand to her face as well.

Gripping her cheeks, he pulls her towards him and they meet open mouthed. Tongues visible between their parted lips, they stroke along each other, Rex's tongue bar clacking over their teeth as he winds his tongue around hers. She whimpers, and he groans, and my fingers are biting into the wood of the desk at my back so hard they feel like they'll snap. And my heart is pounding so fucking hard, I think there's a real possibility I actually might be dying.

But then Rex pulls away, Poppy's eyes snapping back to mine, even as he keeps hold of her face, pecking at her lips.

"Suck my finger, Kitten," he finally glances at me then as she looks to him, both of them still on their fucking knees. "Get it real nice and wet." I'm panting, breathing so hard as Poppy opens her mouth, Rex pushing his middle finger all the way to the back of her tongue, making her gag and then swallow as the digit hits her tonsils. "You wanna be a good girl for Lynx, huh, Kitten?" She's nodding, bobbing her head as she sucks his finger. "What you wanna be for Lynx, Kitten?" he breathes, his eyes on hers, hers coming to mine.

Rex removes his finger from her mouth, glistening wet with her saliva. His hand coming back to my balls, the wet finger sliding back even further, circling my ass.

"I wanna be your good girl," she breathes, licking her lips and as Rex's finger breaches my asshole, the intrusion making me jolt as he grips my balls firmly. "I wanna be your good little treasure."

I groan as she says it, my head finally tipping back, at the same time both of their mouths come back to me, hands resting on my thighs. Rex pumps his finger in and out of me, both of their tongues running down the length of me. Poppy's small hand gripping my base, swirling her tongue around my tip as Rex sucks the underside of my cock, their lips touching and she's twisting her hand, corkscrewing the base.

The picture of them before me, taking it in turns to suck my cock, spit dripping down their chins, lips glossy with each other, with me, as they lap at each other's faces.

It's fucking obscene.

I've never seen anything so fucking erotic, so fucking *mine*, in all my life.

My chest heaves and my lungs burn, cock jumping as they both suckle on the head, taking it in turns to pull my cock deep into their throats. And then a second, much slimmer, finger is sliding into me along-side Rex's. And I can't fucking breathe as they drag me to the edge, heat unfurling inside my belly. And my hands are lifting to the tops of their heads, heat spiking in the bottom of my spine, as in tandem, they curl their fingers together, rubbing on that soft, spongey place inside of me.

I come with a shout, cum erupting from my cock, spurts of it painting their faces, their mouths as they continue to lick and suck.

My hands are patting the tops of their heads, and I'm groaning, "Good fucking boy." Rasping, "Good fucking girl." Panting, "Don't stop, keep fucking sucking me." I'm squeezing my eyes closed, stars shooting behind my closed lids and I'm in heaven.

Because as their fingers slip out of me, their hands smoothing up and down my thighs, kneading my trembling muscles. I blink, looking down, both of them looking up at me, with wet faces and flushed cheeks, soft smiles. I know I must be in fucking heaven.

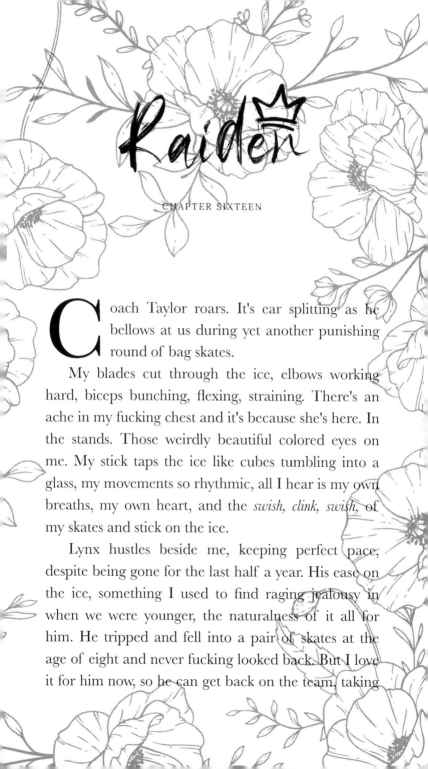

Raiden

Coach Taylor roars. It's ear splitting as he bellows at us during yet another punishing round of bag skates.

My blades cut through the ice, elbows working hard, biceps bunching, flexing, straining. There's an ache in my fucking chest and it's because she's here. In the stands. Those weirdly beautiful colored eyes on me. My stick taps the ice like cubes tumbling into a glass, my movements so rhythmic, all I hear is my own breaths, my own heart, and the *swish, clink, swish,* of my skates and stick on the ice.

Lynx hustles beside me, keeping perfect pace, despite being gone for the last half a year. His ease on the ice, something I used to find raging jealousy in when we were younger, the naturalness of it all for him. He tripped and fell into a pair of skates at the age of eight and never fucking looked back. But I love it for him now, so he can get back on the team, taking his rightful place, be here with me. Keep me just a little bit sane.

Coach blows the whistle, screaming and cursing, veins in his temples looking ready to explode, but I can hardly hear any words over my ragged breaths, my gaze flicking straight to the stands.

Poppy and Rex sit huddled together, his arm lazily draped around her slim shoulders, her knees jumping with jerky little movements because she's cold, maybe a little anxious. Lynx brushes his arm against mine, staring up at them pressed together, I hear his sharp inhale, watching Rex's hand pinch Poppy's jaw, her eyes remaining open, focused wholly on us as he twists her head towards him, takes her lips with his.

"Shit," Lynx hisses, gloves creaking as he tightens his grip on his stick. "How much longer you think we'll be here for?"

I shrug, "Dunno." Rex forces Poppy's head back, his hand engulfing the entirety of her long throat, his thumb on the corner of her jaw, turning her to face us as he bites into her neck.

"I'm gonna bust in my fucking shorts," Lynx grits out, his eyes laser focused on the two people he's obsessed with.

My sexual obsession is only with Poppy, but Rex is my brother and I love my brothers harder than anything else. But there's something about *her* that I can't seem to get my mind off.

I grunt an agreement, my cock angry at being so

restricted in so many layers of bulky clothing. I'm sweating beneath it all, my muscles screaming, bones aching, but my chest pounds harder and harder and I wonder if this is what a heart attack feels like. Poppy's eyes are only on me and the brother at my side, while our third devours her like a fucking snack.

"What we gonna do?" Lynx shifts beside me, the rest of the team starting to leave the ice, heading towards the locker room, I hear Coach shouting still, but the sound is moving further away. "When *they* find out about her?" I swallow just as hard as what I'm sure he does.

I grind my teeth, back molars aching as they creak with the force of my locked jaw, "We don't tell them."

"Dude, they're gonna know, someone will tell them. It's not like we've kept her a secret. We agreed, no girls would come between us."

"Just," I huff out an exasperated breath, "I can't stay away from her." It's why I fucked her, something drew me the fuck in, I thought I'd fuck her out of my system, but all that really did was sear our fucking souls together.

It's been less than a week of knowing her, four fucking days of hanging out, talking, fucking, fucking, *fucking*... I don't think I've ever gotten attached to anyone so quickly before. Or as deep. It's like I can feel her essence in my marrow, corded around my heart, pumping through my veins.

"We're out tonight," a statement, not a question, Lynx sounds a little… deflated about it.

Dragging my gaze to him, his red-brown eyes already on me, I cock my head.

"Yeah, at Graves. You struggling?" it grates me, the way I have to ask, it means I'm not paying him enough attention, like I swore I would, to keep him safe, protect us.

"No," he shifts again, gaze flicking back to the stands, I don't look, watching him instead, keeping my focus where it needs to be. His face creases, something like pain in his eyes, "But I think-"

"Yo! Dipshits! Fucking hustle!" Coach Taylor bellows from the tunnel, cutting Lynx off and making my neck crack with the jerking pull of my attention.

Lynx claps me on the back, skating away without another word, and when I glance back up at the stands, Rex and Poppy are already gone.

Poppy literally takes my breath away when she walks in with Lynx. I feel like a fucking kid on Christmas when she steps into our house in a tight little dress, plum in color, tight and short, strappy like most of her clothes, despite it fucking snowing, but she has knee high cowboy boots on and I smirk.

"Lynx got me them," she laughs, "he wouldn't let

me leave 'til I put them on." She steps into me, my arms wrapping around her freezing body.

"Because it's the middle of fucking winter, Princess. Where's your coat?" I talk into her hair, feel her shrug, her shoulders lifting and falling inside the circle of my arms. "Huh?" I lean back, pinch her chin, tilt her head back. "You wanna freeze to death or something?"

Her lilac eyes tighten with her smile, something sincere, plum painted lips curling at the corners.

"You need to wear a coat."

She shakes her head, her smile growing, "Nu-uh, that's what I got you guys for, always draping your-selves over me," she shrugs again. "Think I'm good."

I lift a brow, trying to smother my smirk, "You're good, yeah? That's what you think?" her smile is wide now, toothy, dimples carving in her flushed cheeks. "You ever do as you're told, baby girl?" I rasp, drop-ping my mouth to slant over hers as she swallows down her sharp intake of breath. "You tryna antago-nize me, Princess?" I smirk now, licking over her parted lips, tasting the waxy texture of her pout. "You wanna stay in tonight and see how it feels to disobey me?"

All I can see in my mind's eye is her pale ass stinging red with the imprint of *my* fucking hands. But I've been gentle with her, so fucking gentle it makes me grind my teeth when she grinds her cunt down on my dick and I have to hold myself back.

There's just something *fragile* about her.

And I sorta wanna protect her. From me, my brothers. Our other brothers…

Maybe from herself.

Poppy shudders, this time, not from the cold, her breaths short and sharp against my mouth, I drag my bottom lip across hers, flicking my tongue over her cupid's bow.

"You still think you don't need a coat?" Her heavy bangs catch in her eyelashes as she blinks, licking over her lips as her eyes dance between my own.

"I'll get a jacket," she whispers over my mouth, her words on my tongue.

We are so, so close and I want to fucking eat her alive, but I step back, flick my gaze over her shoulder, my arms still around her, and watch as Rex saunters closer. A long pale gray coat in his hands, sharp collar and big round buttons, he places it over her shoulders, another shudder curling through her tall body.

Lynx leans against the closed door, one foot kicked up, thick arms crossed over his chest. He lifts a brow, drags his gaze down her body, taking in the miles and miles of her long legs as I turn her to face them.

"Told ya," Lynx winks, licking over his teeth, he pushes to stand as Rex takes Poppy's hand, me at their backs as, collectively, we walk towards the front door.

"Yeah, yeah, mister know-it-all," she sasses Lynx, I can practically *hear* her eye roll, our girl has some fucking bite.

So why are we always so careful with her?

Lynx just smiles at her, a tightness in his eyes that makes me feel like he's struggling. So I promise myself, I'm going to watch over him tonight. I failed him once, I'm not going to let it happen again.

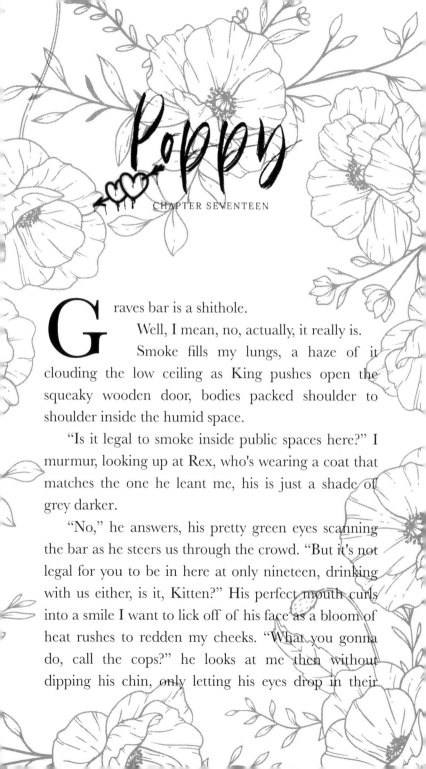

Poppy

CHAPTER SEVENTEEN

G raves bar is a shithole.

Well, I mean, no, actually, it really is.

Smoke fills my lungs, a haze of it clouding the low ceiling as King pushes open the squeaky wooden door, bodies packed shoulder to shoulder inside the humid space.

"Is it legal to smoke inside public spaces here?" I murmur, looking up at Rex, who's wearing a coat that matches the one he leant me, his is just a shade of grey darker.

"No," he answers, his pretty green eyes scanning the bar as he steers us through the crowd. "But it's not legal for you to be in here at only nineteen, drinking with us either, is it, Kitten?" His perfect mouth curls into a smile I want to lick off of his face as a bloom of heat rushes to redden my cheeks. "What you gonna do, call the cops?" he looks at me then without dipping his chin, only letting his eyes drop in their sockets to glance down at me. "If you wanted me in handcuffs, you only had to say." Rex licks his lips, my own parted, and then Lynx is snatching me out of his hold, shouldering between us with a smug look on his face.

The wooden floors creak, every step I take is hard work with the way my shoes stick to the grimy floor, it's like super strength glue trying to tear the soles off of my new boots. There's Groveton College paraphernalia plastered all over the walls, everything in Groveton green and white. Posters and articles, photographs, flags and jerseys, all pinned up, covering the dark wooden walls.

King and Rex walk right up to the bar, leaving Lynx and I wrapped around one another to find a booth. And I don't know how because the place is wall to wall, there's no way we'll find-

"Move," Lynx barks, and the occupiers of the booth he's stopped us next to, full of hulking guys and pretty girls, all stand at the command, grabbing their drinks and the guys actually *thanking* him as they give up their table.

"They'll get bored of her so fast," someone hushes under their breath as they hurry past me, making my neck crack as I twist to look over my shoulder, but all of the girls Lynx just forced out of their seats are whispering together.

It could have been any one of them.

I frown as Lynx ushers me into the corner seat,

leaning forward and wiping the cracked seat cushion with his hand before I sit. Then he climbs in beside me, eyes roving over the rest of the bar, his arm snaking around my shoulders, he leans back, slouching, relaxing, and my tongue goes dry the longer I look at him.

"That was mean," I say, meaning him and his demanding dismissal, but the girl's words ring true inside my head too.

They will get bored of me and not want me hanging around anymore, just like my dad.

I frown, staring at Lynx's handsome face, dark eyebrows, messy bleached blonde hair, full lips, plush mouth and straight nose. Small, dark freckle beneath his right eye, a matching one on the same cheekbone.

His peach lips twist up on one side, but he doesn't look at me, his fingers tightening over my shoulder cap. It makes me feel safe. The way he holds me, all of them, always touching, always watching, like I have twenty-four-seven security guards. It should probably feel invasive but all it does is make me feel seen.

I am so desperate to be seen. Not by the world, just by someone, someone that gives a fuck, about *me*. And these boys, *men*, they do.

It is sickening.

Me.

I'm disgusting.

The way I crave them now, after one stupid night

that never should have happened. A few days where I've revelled in their attention.

I must reek of desperation and I wish I could stop this now. I should have stopped this before anything happened at all. I never should have gone to their party. Admittedly, I didn't know Lynx would be there, I didn't know he had connections to the men who lived in that house.

But I should have stopped it all the same.

I've spent so many years alone, isolating myself, feeling uncomfortable in my own skin, around other people, worrying everyone I meet would think I was weird or strange.

My shoulders curl forwards, gaze dropping, studying the marked, worn wood of the table. I've spent the last four days in some state of weird fantastical bliss. It's not normal, it can't last. It *won't* last. And I'm forming attachments to men who, once my shiny new toy label wears off, won't want anything to do with me. We'll pass each other on campus like strangers, and my heart will bleed and they will move on to the next girl with easily spreading legs. They probably laugh about me when I'm not around because I'm so fucking pathetic.

I shouldn't care. I shouldn't be feeling any sort of attachment to these men. I'm just a warm place for them to shove their cocks into.

I'm *fun*.

My thighs clamp together, muscles tensing.

Shame.

It threads through me like a fizzing hot wire of electricity, but it's not going to start my heart, it's going to fucking flay it.

Lynx's hand is on my shoulder, his fingers smoothing back and forth over the exposed skin of my collarbone beneath Rex's loaned coat, and it feels like razor blades cutting my flesh.

I'm flying to my feet, knee smacking into the table, the coat falling from my shoulders to the seat before I even have time to think.

"Poppy?" Lynx's rumble that normally strokes its way across my flesh feels like gouging shards of ice in my veins.

"I have to pee," I announce, shuffling my way around to the other side of the booth, pressing my fingers to the sticky surface of the table as I make my way around.

"Okay, I'll come with you, it's really-"

"No!" I shout, the force of my word stopping him half risen from his seat. "No, no, it's fine, I'm fine, I'll be right back."

He stares at me with a long blink, and I know he's going to say more, even as I'm shimmying out the other side of the corner booth, but King arrives, stopping at the edge of the table, drinks in hand. He frowns, flicking his gaze between Lynx and I, the former still staring at me, gaze hard, and I, I just bolt.

Shouldering my way through the mass of people, I almost crash into Rex.

"Woahhh, easy, babe. Where you off to in such a hurry, Kitten?"

"Have to pee," I call over my shoulder, eyes bulging, breaths too sharp, it feels like the air is attacking my lungs.

I don't know where I'm going, I don't know where the restrooms are in this bar and I feel like I can't fucking breathe. So when I hurry towards the first hallway I see, elbowing my way between bodies, I break through the sweaty mass, heaving for breath in the slightly clearer hall.

The lights are low, everything wooden and dark and dingy, no one is looking at me, no one is staring, but it feels like there are a thousand eyes glued to me. I straighten my spine, taking my time to walk down the hall, trying not to fall apart.

I should have stayed in the booth, knocked back a few drinks and let the liquid courage drown out my anxieties, if only for just one more night with them. And yet, I'm here, meandering down a crowded hall and finally pushing into a restroom.

Tiles cover the floor and walls in a dirty shade of ageing yellow-grey, but there's no one by the sink and the two stalls' doors are swung open revealing they're empty.

Yet, despite the space being deserted, it still feels like I'm suffocating. My heart racing, lungs screaming, my head pounds like something is knocking on the inside of my skull.

Bracing my hands on either side of the sink, I bow my head, squeeze my eyes shut, listen to the drippy tap plink drops of water into the sink.

My heart hammers so hard in my chest it feels as though it's going to burst straight through my rib bones. My skin itches, fingers tightening on the sides of the basin and I sway, black spots blurring beneath my closed eyelids. I feel light headed and over-whelmed and I just need to *not*.

I think of the little white pills, the ones that make me better, make me happier, more likeable, fun. I've never been called rude, stuck up or boring when I take drugs. And the bloom of warmth they force through my chest cavity makes my head feel light and my worries disappear, even if it's only for a short while.

I reach into the cup of my bra, pull out the little bag. I tear the plastic open, tip one of the little white pills out into the palm of my clammy hand and just as I'm about to toss it back, a warm hand clamps gently over my shoulder and I flinch so hard I bash my hips into the countertop in my panicked thrust forward, my pill dropping into the sink, clattering before it disappears down the plughole. A groan leaves my lips, face scrunching up, eyes squeezing. I whip around with a hand to my heart, quickly tucking the bag of remaining pills back into my bra.

Lynx holds his hands up in surrender, his back to the door as my entire body shakes, a cold, sticky sweat breaking out across my skin, goosebumps erupting over my flesh.

"It's okay," Lynx coos, and it feels sincere, but it can't be, can it?

Not when this doesn't mean anything.

I squeeze my eyes shut tight, the backs of them burning.

Shame.

At being caught, at being *desperate.*

"I'm right here, Treasure."

But no one's ever been *right here*. Not for me. I don't even know what the fuck that really means. And all of these nicknames, *endearments,* they're not really meant for me.

My body sways, head bowing forward, it feels like my skull is full of sloshing water. I feel Lynx approach and my hands fly out in front of me, warning him away. I've already fucked up, I should be the one ending this shit now, I have no idea what it is I'm doing.

"Poppy, I know what it feels like."

"No! *No!* You don't!" I yell back, biting off my groan, fisting my hands in my hair, I straighten, taking a breath, arms dropping by my sides. "I'm not- This isn't-" I want to scream in frustration that I've let myself grow close to people who won't want me past the weekend and I just, "I need to go."

I push off of the sink, marching past Lynx, not looking at him even though I want to throw myself in his arms, beg him to never walk away from me.

Don't leave me.

It's been less than a fucking week, and this is how weak I am.

Desperate.

I wrench the door open, but it slams back closed as Lynx slaps a hand above my head, and shoves himself into my back, slamming me against the wood.

My lungs seize, palms flattened, elbows bent, my entire front is plastered to the surface of the door, Lynx flush with my back. Cheek squished against the wood and I squeeze my eyes shut tight until I see stars shoot across my closed eyelids.

Lynx's breath ghosts down my neck, his berry-cedar scent filling my nostrils, his heat flooding through our clothes, warming my spine, the backs of my bare thighs.

He drops his lips to my ear, "Where'd you think you're going?" his tongue flicks my skin with every pronounced word. "You think you can get away from me, Treasure?" his thick southern accent vibrates down the column of my neck, the heavy drawl like spiders creeping over every boned disk in my spine. "You think because I've been treating you so nice, you can do whatever you want?" I shiver, his hands flat against the door on either side of my head. "You think I'm ever gonna make walking away from me that fucking easy?"

I bite down on my tongue, saying nothing.

Lynx's hand squeaks as he slips it down the door, his fingers coming to my chin, he wrenches my head further back towards him, twisting my neck, my temple smacking the wood. He slants his mouth over mine, and I squeeze my eyes shut tighter and tighter as my spine crunches at the base of my neck.

"You're mine now," his breath hot on my parted lips. "Ours," he emphasises with a nip to my bottom one. "I get to decide when you walk the fuck away from me, and it's not until I'm done with you," he hisses, licking over my mouth. "And guess what, Treasure? I'm not fucking done with you yet."

Yet.

My heart slams in my chest at that, *not until I'm done with you.*

Because they will be. Done with me, and I already know it's going to ruin me, but with his weight against my back and his breath across my mouth, I can play pretend for just a little while longer.

"I don't know what you've done to me, Poppy," he groans it, the words coiling around my heart as I taste them on my tongue. "It's like you've bewitched me," he half-laughs, but there's no humour in it, his huff of warm breath heating my chin. "You taste just like I've traded one addiction for another."

Toxic.

That's what addiction is.

A craving for poison.

That's what I am to them.

I've infected them, they've addicted me, like a sick-ness, they're burrowed inside my bones, and it's going to leave me with nothing more than just a memory of these seductively, noxious boys.

I freeze, my eyes fluttering open, and I know the moment he feels me go stiff beneath him, because his entire body does the same no more than a second later.

"You've been such a good girl for me," he breathes, relaxing his hold on my chin. "But you've got bored of that, huh?" his finger and thumb pinches harder on my face. "You thought tonight you'd be bad?" he grinds his hips into me, the length of his cock hard and thick against my arse.

"No," I gasp out.

Hot breath panting against the door, chest heav-ing, Lynx pins me in place, wrenches my chin further and further, like he can twist my neck at a complete one-eighty. It feels like he's going to break my spine, but as his other hand drops from the door, clamping onto my breast, fingertips digging in hard enough to bruise, I think, perhaps, maybe, I won't mind.

"You thought you could run from me, my atten-tion, now you're all I can fucking see, Treasure, and I think you need a reminder of who's in charge here."

His words sink into me, heavy and dizzying, threading through my limbs like they're on strings.

Releasing my breast, he flips up the skirt of my dress, revealing my lace knickers, the rough denim of his black jeans harsh against my backside. I watch him from the corner of my eye, my neck screaming with his grip on my chin.

His knuckles graze over the exposed skin as he pops his jean's button, yanks down the zipper.

"Bend," he grunts, his eyes between our bodies, his cock smearing me with precum.

I slip down the door jerkily as he tugs on my chin, his other hand on my hip, he yanks me back into him, my temple banging against the door.

"Get your hands on your ass, Poppy and spread those beautiful globes for me," he grits out, his booted foot kicking mine apart, forcing my spine into an arch, my arse up.

"The door," I breathe on a whine, panic broiling in my chest. "What if-"

"You let me worry about the fucking door," he spits, verbally and literally, his saliva hitting the base of my spine at the end of his words, slipping down the crease of my arse, making me jerk forward. "Now, get those hands where I want 'em. This is gonna be hard and fast, Treasure."

And just like that, fingers digging into my own flesh, weight resting entirely on my cheekbone against the door, Lynx shoves my knickers aside and thrusts into me.

My groan is drowned out by his, echoing around the grungy bathroom. My pussy feels like it's on fire, the way he is so, so deep inside of me, his crown tapping at my cervix like it wants to be welcomed deeper.

Lynx fucks me hard, my face smashing into the door with a thud on every brutal thrust. My muscles clamp down around him trying to suck him in at the same time they want to force him out and he chuckles in my ear, draping himself heavily over my back. He licks my ear, bites my jaw, sinks his teeth into the bruised side of my throat.

Lynx pinches my clit, my head feeling like it's going to explode as pleasure shoots through my skull.

"You're a dirty fucking girl," he rasps in my ear. "So. Fucking. *Bad*." A thick finger slides into me beside his hammering cock making me whimper, stretching me far beyond pain and pleasure, a pressure too intense to do anything with but groan deep from within my chest. "That's it, Treasure, you like it when I'm rough with you, fucking come for me."

And I do. With his weight on my back, burning heat along my spine, humid breath down my neck, I fucking detonate as he fucks into me with his cock and finger, going harder and harder. Face bashing into the door with every punishing thrust. Pleasure swells, swells, swells, and then crashes over me like an icy wave. Chills race down my spine, sweat breaking out across my forehead, back of my neck, as goosebumps crawl their way across my skin.

And Lynx is grunting into my ear, his teeth driving into the underside of my jaw, his cum filling me with heat as he slows his pace, little jerky movements as he fills me with his release.

That's when panic sets in, feeling him still, his bare cock throbbing inside me.

I can hardly breathe as he pulls his finger out of me, brings it to my mouth, "Open," Lynx snarls, and my lips part for him, his thick finger sliding to the very back of my tongue. "Suck," he commands, and my cheeks hollow, tongue swirling around him, the taste of us thick in the back of my throat, the idea of what we just did heavy in my heart.

"You really are such a good girl," he chuckles, burying his face in my neck as his finger pops free, his hand cupping my chin in a caress, he smooths his thumb along the length of my jaw, breathing hard against my neck. "So fucking good for me."

"We didn't use protection," I choke out, my eyes wide and unseeing with panic, "I'm not taking anything else, that's why we'v-"

"Stop," Lynx pulls out of me, a rush of him slipping down the inside of my thighs. "Look at me," he turns me in place, pushing me gently back against the wood of the door, his red chestnut eyes flicking between my own, frowning when he sees how pale

I've gone. "I'll sort it, okay? I- *Fuck*, I wasn't thinking," he pushes his hand through his bleached hair, dropping his gaze for a second, he tucks himself back in his pants, the zipper loud in the room, even over the pounding of my heart rattling around the inside of my skull. "Poppy, I won't let anything happen to you," he says fiercely and the lump in my throat triples in size, my chin trembles, and I don't look away in time. "Hey, *hey,*" he dips his chin, cocking his head, trying to catch my eye. "I swear, I won't let anything happen to you."

I shake my head, my eyes squeezed tight, I try to swallow, but when I do, all I taste is *us*. I want to heave, eject the thought of us from my brain, take the last twenty minutes back, hell, the last week.

"Poppy," he whispers, and my heart cracks. "Please, look at me, did I... Did I hurt you?"

I shake my head, ignoring the thud of pain in my cheek, the teeth marks in my neck, because none of those things hurt as much as my own stupidity.

"Do you want me to get one of the others?" he asks lowly as my breath shudders into my lungs with another shake of my head. "Okay, okay," he says more to himself than me, "I'm gonna clean you up, sweetheart, okay?"

Trembling against the door, I nod my head. Lynx goes into a stall, crosses to the basin, then sinks to his knees at my feet, he looks up at me, my eyes burning at the backs with the urge to cry, I look away. Trying to smooth out his expression, a knot between his brows, he swipes wet paper towels between my legs, and humiliation strikes through me. I drop my head back against the door with a thud, draw in a trembling breath and try to ignore the feel of his hands on my thighs.

I'm not good at this, I'm not good with people, let alone men, I'm not even good with myself. I've been alone since I was five, since my mum, boarding schools only helped my isolation, my dad was always too busy for me. I didn't have friends, always moving from one school to another every other year. Then I found a way to let go, to sleep without nightmares, to walk down a dark street without having a panic attack.

Now I don't know how to breathe properly without filling myself full of chemical happiness.

"When's the last time you took something?" Lynx's hand brushes over my cheek, making me flinch with the touch of pain in the bone. "Sorry," he hushes, crowding my front, "it's bruising," he lifts my chin to get a better look at my face, but I keep my eyes lowered, my shame filling the room like smoke, toxic, overwhelming, suffocating. "I hurt you."

"You didn't," I shake my head, blinking hard as I draw in a ragged breath, "I hurt me," I swallow. "I just used you to do it," It's a whispered confession that feels ripped straight from my soul.

Because it's true.

"Popp-"

"Please," I glance up then, looking into his warm chestnut-red eyes, "I just wanna go back to the dorm," I swallow hard, trying not to throw my arms around his waist, let him bury me in his chest, band his arms around me so tight I can't think about anything else.

"Okay, we'll stay in an-"

"No, I... I wanna be alone. You stay, I'm just gunna go to bed," I whisper it at the ground, because what I really want is to fucking disappear. "You stay and have fun, there's tonnes of girls out there who would love to have your attentio-"

"Woah, wait, *what?*" Lynx jerks my chin up, his eyes hard on mine, and I bite down on my back teeth to keep my chin from trembling, my cheeks flushing crimson. "You think we'd even fucking *look* at anyone else if you weren't here?"

"Well, I just though-"

"No, no, no. Stop. Poppy," he takes a deep breath, cupping my tender cheek. "What the fuck is going on in that pretty little head of yours? Have we made you feel like that? Something we've said, done?"

"No, but I-"

"Look, I know this has been really fast. I think," Lynx blows out a breath, shoving a hand through his messy hair again. "I think we should like talk? Or something, I want you to trust us with you, but it's been like a week and it's fast and we're all kinda riding a high and no one's thought to like, *talk* about it, right? So maybe we just need to do that first?" Lynx tilts my chin, slants his lips over mine, stares into my eyes, pleading, "I want you to trust us, tell me what to do, whatever you want. Let's go home together, all of us, let's talk and we can, we can slow this all down."

"This has gotten out of control," my chin trembling, I bite my lip, glance down. "I'm tired," I choke out almost silently, the lump in my throat growing, but this is what I wanted wasn't it? To end it before they did? "I just want to go to bed," I whisper, "I don't know what I'm doing." Lynx looks like I just slapped him across the face, he steps back, dropping his gaze, his hand, gritting his teeth. "It isn't you, I just, I need to press pause for a minute."

I want to cry. To scream. To throw myself at him. But above all, I just want to die.

"I didn't mean to hurt you."

"I know you didn't. You didn't hurt me. It's not that, I just," I choke on my own words, feeling like the world is spinning off of its axis. "I just need…"

To go home, to grab some pills to knock me out, so I can forget all of tonight ever happened, and I can-

"You need a night in, with us reassuring you that we're not going to leave you, not unless it's what you want. I get it, I know we look like fuck boys that have never had a girlfriend before, but Poppy, you're different, this is different. I don't want to push you into something you're uncomfortable with. And I know you think you wanna be alone right now, but I don't think that's really what's in your best interest. Let us take you home, we'll put on sweatpants and watch trash TV and order pizza. Let us try and show you how we feel, and if you decide you don't want this, we'll walk away, we'll leave you alone. But I want to show you just how much we want you and even though this is fast, it doesn't change how we feel about you." He swallows, glancing at the sliver of space between us before dragging his gaze back onto mine, "It doesn't change how *I* feel about you."

I am so fucked.

Our mouths meet in a frenzy, tongues tangling, teeth clashing, his hand is planted over my chest, shoving me back into the door. Heart thudding against his palm, he shoves his knee between my thighs, using his other hand to drag me up to his chest, grinding my cunt over his thigh, his hand trapped between our heaving chests.

He kisses me like he can entangle our souls together for eternity with nothing more than his tongue. And as I melt into him, throwing my inhibitions out of the goddamn window, I promise myself the inevitable pain will be worth it for just a few more precious moments like this.

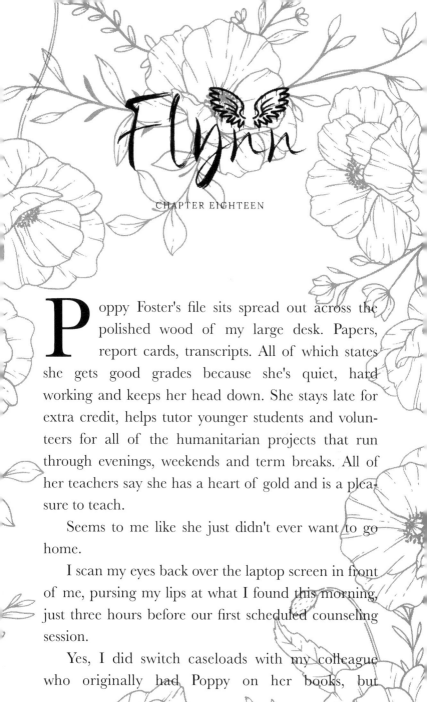

Flynn

CHAPTER EIGHTEEN

Poppy Foster's file sits spread out across the polished wood of my large desk. Papers, report cards, transcripts. All of which states she gets good grades because she's quiet, hard working and keeps her head down. She stays late for extra credit, helps tutor younger students and volunteers for all of the humanitarian projects that run through evenings, weekends and term breaks. All of her teachers say she has a heart of gold and is a pleasure to teach.

Seems to me like she just didn't ever want to go home.

I scan my eyes back over the laptop screen in front of me, pursing my lips at what I found this morning, just three hours before our first scheduled counseling session.

Yes, I did switch caseloads with my colleague who originally had Poppy on her books, but

Bennett asked me to look into her, and what better way to really scrape out the inside of someone's skull than to *counsel* them? Plus, hacking the school system to make the switch was nothing, my colleague, Julia, won't have even looked at the poor kids she's got on her register until they're sitting in the chair opposite her with shitty tales of their rich kid upbringings and how it's just so unfair that their mommy didn't love them more.

I'll be a qualified psychiatrist in less than a year, but I'm not sure that's really what I wanna be doing with my life. Plus, I work for Bennett's security business, and do some of his other, less shiny jobs.

I refocus on the screen, glaringly bright in the dim light of my dark office, all rich woods and deep green carpet, walls lined with shelves of volumes of books I've never read. A free standing lamp emits a warm orange glow at my back in the corner. Blinds shuttered over the large window, heavy, velvet curtains drawn across them too.

Carrington.

The name is seared into my memory as though it were my very own. Something I can't forget, *won't*, not after what Michael Carrington did to my best friends' family, my brothers in everything but blood. It's the entire reason we're all so close. We always wanted to build a better life for their mom, look after her since their dad was locked up.

And Michael fucking Carrington was the offshore accountant behind it all.

And what did he fucking lose?

Nothing.

But now, halfway across the planet, in *our* fucking lap, is the daughter he presumably tried to hide. Different last name, a blank history, addresses of boarding schools and live-in academies instead of a home, a life built with no mention of a parent anywhere. There was just nannies, ones that seemed to change as quickly as the fucking weather.

A grin pulls at my lips, twisting the corners with savagery.

Poppy Foster is Poppy Carrington and there's no greater vengeance than the hurt that comes with ruining a man's precious daughter.

FLYNN

How do you want to work this?

I ask, sending off the text to Bennett. We grew up together, lived in the same house since we were kids. My mom, stepdad and younger half-brother, Bennett's mom and his younger brother. We formed a bond, along with the kid next door, my brother's age, and the five of us became inseparable.

BENNETT

Play with her.

Tongue licking over my teeth, I try not to smile, I

211

try so fucking hard not to grin, but I can't stop it. My lips kick up, teeth on display and a huff of laughter escapes me in the silence of the room. I spin in my chair, leaning back into it, I let my head drop back on my shoulders, stare up at the ceiling. This is what I'm good at. And I'm *never* allowed to play.

Minds are fragile things.

Knocking on the door has me clearing my throat, straightening up in my chair. I shuffle the papers together, turning them face down, and exit out of the folder on my desktop, closing the laptop.

"Come in," I call, hands clasping atop my desk, back straight.

The wide door creaks open, bright light spilling in as a dark haired girl pushes into the room, blinking in the darkness with a divot between her brows.

"Ah, you must be Poppy. Please, come in," I smile.

She straightens, entering the room, slowly pushing the door closed at her back, her light eyes flicking across the space. I let her look, waiting until, eventually, her gaze lands on me, just briefly, like she's unable to hold my eye. She shifts her weight from one leg to the other, knotting her fingers together anxiously.

"Take a seat." I gesture to the armchair opposite me, dark brown leather with wide square arms.

She shuffles forward, thick bangs in her eyes, waist-length hair draped forward over one shoulder. She wears a black hoodie beneath a light-coloured, distressed, denim jacket, holes and fraying at the cuffs and hem. She crosses her long legs as she sits cautiously in the chair, and then finally, *finally*, she looks at me, and it feels a little like my heart stops. Wide lilac eyes, a thin nose, rounded at the tip, thick lips and high cheekbones.

Fuck she's pretty.

Blinking, I clear my throat, just to give me a moment to collect my scattering thoughts.

"I'm Mr. Marshall, but you can call me Flynn," I smile again, and her shoulders start to drop from their hunch. "As you know this is just a mandatory session to check on your wellbeing, to see how school is going and if there's anything you want to talk to me about, or request help with. Anything to help your integration into the school, that's what I'm here for."

She nods, squeezing her tattooed hands in her lap. But she says nothing, and I'm silent too, for a beat too long, waiting for her to speak, to hear her voice.

I take a deep breath, "So, how's your first week of classes been?"

"Fine, thank you," she says quietly, British accent thick, something I thought I wouldn't give a fuck about, but apparently, my dick *really* fucking likes it.

"No issues with finding your way around?" she shakes her head. "Professors are all okay?" she nods, letting her gaze drop to my hands, her focus on my laced fingers. "People are being nice?" she nods again, and I want her to fucking speak. Craving the sound of her already, "And you've checked in with your psychiatrist?"

Her gaze flashes up onto mine then, eyes flicking between my own, I watch her bruised neck roll with her hard swallow.

An admission of guilt.

"You know that's one of the conditions for you to be able to stay? That you check in weekly," I say softly, cocking my head in an attempt to catch her eye.

"I know," she whispers, swallowing again, "I'll call him today."

Him.

Something tightens in my chest, sharp and hot. I don't know why it didn't occur to me before that her therapist could be a guy. I guess I just assumed they'd be a she. I don't know why I care.

Poppy reaches up, fingers absentmindedly grazing over the bruising on her throat, and as if she forgot about the tender flesh, she winces, quickly dragging her hair further forward to hide it.

A bright blush sits high in her cheeks, her eyes darting to mine, and it takes everything in me not to catapult myself over the table, launch myself at her, tip the chair backwards, pin her to the floor and lick up the length of her pretty little throat, add my own marks.

"Good," I nod, swallowing thickly, cock pulsing hard in my slacks. "And you're taking your medication?"

Antidepressants. Anxiety medication.

Her cheeks flush even redder, spreading like groping fingers down her throat. I wonder how far the blush extends. Does it smother her chest, drag its way down her tits, darken her nipples?

She nods, looking back down at her tattooed hands, the tips blanching white where she squeezes them so tight.

A lie.

"I know we've just met," I say gently, "but you can tell me the truth," I coax quietly. "I'm not going to report it," I hedge, cocking my head further, dipping my chin in an attempt to catch her eye.

Look at me, look at me, look at me.

As if she heard my silent summoning, she looks up, our eyes connecting and for long moments she holds my gaze, something so delicately vulnerable in her wide orbs.

I want to break it.

I grit my teeth, my insides knotting, intestines coiling around my liver and kidneys like some sort of noose.

Her dad destroyed my brothers' lives.

So we'll ruin hers.

And I do so like to break pretty little things.

Moving forward with my assumption, "Is there a reason you're not taking them, Poppy? Are you having a reaction, hallucinations, headaches?" She shifts again in her seat, staring down at her lap, "This is a safe space," I reassure her. "Confidential."

"Are you a doctor?" she asks then, a small crease between her dark brows, her long lashes tickling the arch of them.

I wobble my head on my neck side to side, thinking about what to say.

"No. I'm a qualified student counselor with a background in psychiatry," is what I decide on, the truth, more or less.

She hums, fidgeting again, and I'm wondering whether we should just sit here in silence for the hour. The dim light of the room, the silence, uncomfortable on her part, somewhat satisfying for me. I need her to be *just* uncomfortable enough that we can move forward from it in future appointments, so I don't want to push her. Too far. Not yet.

"Aren't you like super young?" she suddenly blurts out, her eyes wide as she realizes what she's just said.

I chuckle, a smile transforming my face as I give in, let her see *me* if only for a second, I clear my throat, "I'm thirty," I tell her. "If that's all right with you," I arch a brow, cock my head, curl my bottom lip in, snagging it between my teeth.

I watch her blush deepen, heat practically boiling in her cheeks, the red bloom traveling down her neck. I think of the knife in my desk, imagine what her pale skin would look like decorated in a different form of crimson.

"Sorry, that was rude, I-" she swallows, flicking those lilac colored eyes up onto mine, wide and blood-shot, which is when I notice her pupils are like pinpricks. "I didn't mean any offense. I get foot-in-mouth syndrome when I'm nervous."

My mouth curls up again, twisting sinisterly at the corners and I don't try to hide it this time. I lick my lips, dip my chin. Think of all the opportunities I could have, locked in this room, alone with an anxious girl. Who's high…

So much fun.

"Am I making you nervous, Angel?" I ask, my deep voice thick like curling smoke hoping to choke.

Her eyes widen even more and I'm transfixed on her tiny pupils.

What have you taken?

She half sways in her chair, fingernails breaking skin where she grips her hands together so tightly.

Slowly, I stand from my seat, her head tipping back to look up at all six-foot-four of me. Rounding the desk, I come to stand before her in the space between her and the desk. Her plush lips parted as she stares up at me, the bottom one looking like it's too heavy for her slim face.

I want to sink my fucking teeth into it.

Leaning back, butt resting on the edge of the desk, I cross my arms, head canting to the side, I suck on my bottom lip, taking her in. Letting my eyes wander down her body, long, lean legs, small, perky tits, so many layers of clothing covering up all of her pale skin. I wonder if it's as flawless as her face.

I want to strip her bare, spread her out over my desk, slice her with my knife, lots of long shallow cuts, maybe I'll fuck her with it after, then I'll lick up all of her blood.

Suppressing a groan, I look at her from beneath my heavy lashes, narrow my dark blue eyes on her, and she is captivated, her entire attention honed in on me, her light eyes flicking rapidly over every single inch of me. Taking in my black curly hair, pale skin, sapphire eyes, thick arms and strong thighs. Her breaths are quickening and it's like she's readying to bolt, or drop to her knees and beg to suck my dick, I wonder if she would. But I need to draw this back, we're not quite there yet.

Even still, it, her attention, feels heady, liberating, fucking dangerous.

Fuck, I'm going to wreck you.

"Hm?" she suddenly asks, eyes snapping back to mine, I sweep my fingers up and down my bicep, muscles bulging where they're crossed over my chest, tension straining beneath my crisp white button up.

I chuckle darkly, "You were about to tell me why I make you so nervous, Angel." I grin wide, her mouth slack, she blinks rapidly, shifting to sit up straighter in her chair and I feel like a wolf readying to chase a rabbit.

"I'm not- You don't, I-"

"It's okay," I soothe, bending forwards until we're barely half a foot apart.

I can feel her warm breath, quick, on my skin, it's addictive, the innocent look on her. Leaning even further forward, our lips almost touching. I reach out to tuck a strand of gold streaked-brown hair behind her heavily pierced ear, smoothing the rough pad of my finger over the cold metal hoops.

I shift my weight on the desk, widening my thick thighs just enough to relieve a little pressure in my pounding dick, her eyes dropping right to my crotch as I do, before flying back to my face in panic, that plume of red growing once more.

"Like I said, this is a safe, *confidential* space," I tell her quietly, so many fucking meanings entangled in those words. "No one will ever know what happens inside this room." It's a warning laced truth because as I think of all the things I want to do to her, I know I'm going to do every single fucking one of them.

And no one's going to be able to stop me.

Not my brothers.

Not even Bennett.

I know the boys have been fucking her, hiding her from us, thinking, stupidly, we wouldnt find out. They forget we see and hear everything. There are no secrets between us.

And I'm gonna be this druggie girl's new safe space.

I hold Poppy's gaze, her teeth sinking into her bottom lip as she stares up at me, fingernails cutting into the leather arm rests of her chair as she tightens her grip.

I make a show of glancing down in the sliver of space between us to check my watch. The tips of our noses brushing, her creamy, buttery pumpkin scent filling my nostrils as I inhale her slow and deep. Savoring her scent so I can fuck my hand to the memory of it as soon as she leaves. I flick my gaze up from the pearlescent face of my gold watch, lick over my lips, tip of my tongue *just* catching on the crease down the center of her fat bottom lip.

"Session's over," I whisper across her mouth, eyes boring into hers. "I'll see you tomorrow, Poppy," I smile then, sly and terrifying, before I sit up straight, look away from her.

Rounding my desk, fingertips trailing over the polished wood, the door slams at my back. I drop my big body back into my seat. Smug satisfaction humming through my veins, I unzip my pants, take my cock into my hand, and come like a two-pump chump to thoughts of bloodshot lilac eyes.

Raiden

Poppy curls into me, her naked body pressing into my side. I've got one arm around her back, holding her close, the other propped up, elbow bent, behind my head. The ceiling lights are on, a cast of blue light falling across the room, the dark sheets pulled up to our waists.

I trail my fingers over her tattooed shoulder, goosebumps lifting on her skin. My lips pull up into a small smile as she shudders.

Looking down my nose at her, her eyes closed, lashes a curled fan against her high cheekbones, she looks peaceful, and I'm not sure she ever really does.

"You cold?" I ask her, for no other reason than wanting her attention back on me.

Those big lilac eyes opening, lashes fluttering as she looks up at me, she shakes her head, a small smile on her lips.

"Hungry?" she shakes her head, her smile lifting. "Thirsty?"

Swatting at my chest with a tut, she giggles, "No!" she laughs, sighing softly, "I'm just per-" she shifts her shoulders in some semblance of a shrug, clearing her throat, "I'm just fine."

Perfect.

Her smile dies.

She was going to say perfect.

You are perfect.

She smiles again when she realizes I'm frowning, but it doesn't reach her eyes. Something I've noticed happens more often than not. I grip her tighter to me, holding her as close as I can get her without crushing her.

"Princess?" I rumble after an extended silence, comfortable, easy.

Her leg shifts over my thigh, knee beside my cock, but I don't think about that. The way the smallest touch from her sets me on fire, gets my dick hard.

"Yes, King?" she answers, and I suddenly think of her telling Rex to address her as *Your Majesty* and I want to laugh.

"Raiden," I rasp, fingers gripping her shoulder tighter. "My name's Raiden."

She smiles again, a soft smile, this one feels more real, her eyes squinting a little, "Raiden," she breathes, and it's like a shot of lust and love all tangling around my heart and dick alike.

"I like how you say my name," I smile down at her, her eyes still on mine.

"Yeah?" she smiles wider and my heart thumps.

"Yeah."

She drops her forehead to my chest, hiding her face from me, but I can feel her smile against my skin, feel it when it falls.

"What are you thinking about?" I whisper, staring down at her, face to my chest, hand over my heart, her pulse against my heartbeat feels so right, I never want her to move. "Look at me, Princess."

Slowly, she lifts her head, replants her chin back on my pec, flexing her fingers, her nails just grazing my skin.

She frowns a little, brow scrunched low, "My mum," she swallows, biting her lip, I want to bite it for her.

"Yeah? What's she like?" I ask, smoothing my hand over the ball of her shoulder. She hesitates, dropping her gaze, "If she's as pretty as you, we better keep her hidden, I reckon Rex has a thing for older women, ya know."

She chuckles at that, lifting her eyes, but they're sad, turned down at the corners, and I feel my own smile fall, my laughter fade.

"She was prettier than me," *was*, "she had these big blue eyes, tiny little freckles across her nose." Poppy's eyes glaze over, mouth turning down, "I can hardly remember what she sounded like now." She swallows, looking up at me, chewing on the inside of her cheek.

"What happened to her?" I ask her softly, holding her tight.

"She was killed," she looks away, choking a little on the words, "by an intruder," her eyes seem to glaze, frown lines marking her head, and she bites her lip, doesn't say anything more.

"I'm so sorry, Poppy," I tell her, feeling the small tremor wracking through her.

"That's why I don't like the dark," she whispers like an unconscious confession, "because of the cupboard."

"The cupboard?" I repeat back, trying to remain smooth in my tone, even though anxiety pricks at my skin.

"She put me inside a kitchen cabinet, and told me not to come out until she came back for me." She swallows, holding my eye, "I listened to her... as she was raped and murdered in the front hall," she drops her gaze. "She never came back for me." Her eyes flick up onto mine, glassy, "I was five." *Five.* "I found her," she whispers, "I found her."

"Jesus, Poppy," I breathe, smoothing my hand over her hair. "I'm sorry, Princess." I shake my head, offering her a small, sad smile, "That must have been really hard, growing up without your mom."

She nods, sniffing, she swallows, "Yeah, I get like, anxiety and stuff now," she frowns hard like she's somewhere else. "It took me a long time to try and move past it," she rasps, her voice low and cracked. "Don't think I ever will." There's that almost guilty look in her eyes as she looks away, something haunting her, but she doesn't elaborate.

"What about your dad?" I ask next, instantly regretting it as she tries to smother her wince.

"He was never very good with children." Poppy wrinkles her nose, "With me."

"How come?" I shouldn't press, but it's like my insides compel me to push, like I need to know.

She seems to think about her answer. Like she's reliving something and it makes me want to pull her back from wherever it is she went. I don't want to ask her any more fucking questions.

My lungs seize, heart slowing to a frightening thud in my chest.

"Poppy?" I say, fingers squeezing her shoulder. "You okay, Princess?"

"Yeah," she shakes her head.

Wiping a lone tear against my chest, sniffing quickly as she looks back up at me, getting herself composed, like she's just flipped a switch. Smiling a little with dead eyes again.

My heart thuds harder, aching for this girl, I'm not sure it's ever hurt for anyone before. I peer over at the wall, thinking about my own mom, happy with my dad. *Lucky,* she says we are.

I should call her soon.

"Tell me a secret," Poppy whispers, her warm breath ghosting over my nipple, hardening it into a point and I want to flip her over, fuck into her all over again, make her forget for just a moment. "Something no one else knows."

Secrets are something I only share with my brothers, because I never feel safe. I don't like to feel vulnerable. But my mouth runs away without me anyway, like she could summon my demons, pet their heads to tame them. And I could… purge them, *with her*.

"When I was fifteen I was… *touched*," my heart skips a beat and Poppy stiffens, my thumb brushing up and down against her warm, soft skin. "I thought boys couldn't get raped by girls. So I didn't tell anyone that I had said no." I shrug, staring across the blue lit room, lights I leave on every night now just for Poppy, even if she's not here. "When it kept happening, I thought it was cool, I *convinced* myself it was good. It felt good. I should like it. What was wrong with me that I didn't? That I didn't want this older woman touching me and making me come." I swallow, whispering, "I thought I was gay. I had to be. To not like it."

I think of crying as I came in her hand, her mouth. I think of the vomit, the bed wetting. The night terrors.

"One day, Lynx came home early from practice," I swallow, thinking of his red sweaty face, his damp hair, those warm brown eyes seeing it all. "He stopped it," I breathe, "he threatened to hurt her." *If you don't get the fuck away from him, I'll slit your goddamn throat.* "She laughed it all off, said we were just *playing,* but I grew up with Lynx in that house, he knew me too well for that shit."

"What happened to…" Poppy swallows, glancing down at her hand on my chest, big eyes coming back to me as I look at down at her, chin dipping. *"Her?"*

Bennett and Flynn took care of her.

"My older brother reported it, but the woman ran. No one's ever heard from her again."

"Oh my god," Poppy gasps, digging her nails into my skin. "So she could be out there somewhere still, what if she-" Poppy's eyes flick between my own. "What if she comes back?"

Earthworms will have finished her off by now.

I smile, and it feels real, "She won't be coming back, Princess."

"Raiden," she whispers brokenly and my heart drums, *for her.*

"I'm fine now," I kiss her head, looking at her, her looking at me. "We're both fine now," she bites her fat bottom lip, chin to my pec. "Safe, Princess." she nods, but it's like she doesn't believe it, doesn't feel it. "I promise you that you'll always be safe with me."

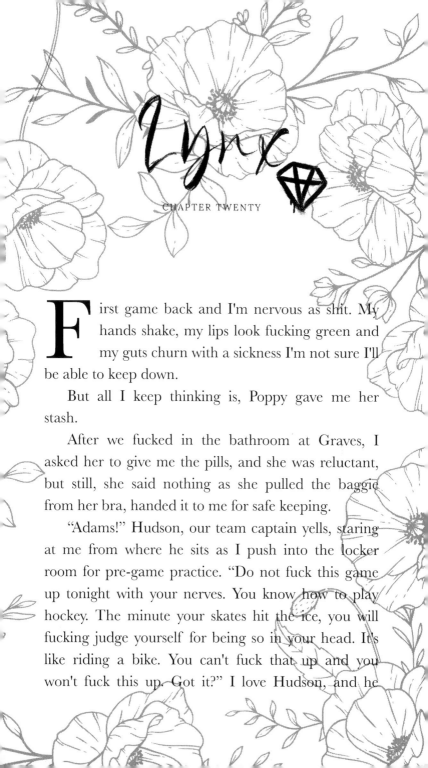

Lynx

First game back and I'm nervous as shit. My hands shake, my lips look fucking green and my guts churn with a sickness I'm not sure I'll be able to keep down.

But all I keep thinking is, Poppy gave me her stash.

After we fucked in the bathroom at Graves, I asked her to give me the pills, and she was reluctant, but still, she said nothing as she pulled the baggie from her bra, handed it to me for safe keeping.

"Adams!" Hudson, our team captain yells, staring at me from where he sits as I push into the locker room for pre-game practice. "Do not fuck this game up tonight with your nerves. You know how to play hockey. The minute your skates hit the ice, you will fucking judge yourself for being so in your head. It's like riding a bike. You can't fuck that up and you won't fuck this up. Got it?" I love Hudson, and he thinks of himself as some sort of motivational speaker, which he isn't, but fuck, I know he's right.

Head nodding, I grimace, trying to hide it, "Yeah, I know. First game back nerves," everything else I say is hardly audible above the violent thrumming inside my head.

Hudson rolls his eyes at my anxiety, "You're my guy, you know my moves before I make them. There's nothing to worry about. Just let the magic fucking happen." He stands, walking over to me, dropping his arm over my shoulder, squeezing me against him, "Tell your nerves they are no longer needed. We are fine. You are fine," he assures me, quiet enough not to be overheard. "Now, let's go play some good old fashioned puck!" I push him away as he yells it, some of the guys cheering and banging their sticks against the floor.

I turn towards my locker space, breathing deep when King comes up on my left, dropping his bag on the bench.

"You've got this, bro. You and me, yeah?"

I nod, swallowing bile as I dress in my gear, pulling on my pads, hockey pants and finally my jersey, number eleven and 'Adams' in big white numbers and letters on the back. It feels good to get it back on officially after so long, the weight of my gear like a blanket of comfort. Familiar.

King claps me on the back, fingers tightening over my shoulder,

232

"All right boys! Let's fucking go!" Hudson bellows, the guys whooping and hollering, as we make it down the tunnel towards the ice.

I feel better after practice, the game now only twenty minutes away, and I'm pumped. Muscles burning, head clear, everything preparing me for the game against Texas State. Confidence fills my chest like an inflating balloon is shoved beneath my ribs, my heart kicking in my chest, adrenaline pulsing through me. King sits on the bench to my right, elbowing me with a slick smirk as Coach Taylor yells at us about our 'goddamn chant'.

Check hard. Play hard. Fuck hard.

Which is apparently a part of our new pre-game ritual. Gotta admit, it's better than the last one. So that's what we echo in the room, sticks clashing, voices booming as he continues to yell at us. My laugh is a bright bursting chuckle as his face reddens, blue veins protruding along his temples.

It's Smiley that stands first, thrusting his stick in the air, and throwing his head back, "All right, boys, let's get 'er done!"

There's ten minutes left in the third, and we still haven't scored. I'm so frustrated I want to scream, because this game should be a fucking breeze. State have spent all their fucking time forcing us back into our own zone to defend Barlowe in goal, but that determination slowly decreased, and now they just look fucking tired.

Good.

The linesman's arm goes up. *Offside.*

"Fuck's sake," I mutter under my breath, shaking my head as Play stops and we're forced into a face off in our zone.

King's shoulder connects with mine where we sit on the bench, legs bouncing in time with one another as we wait to go back out. Reassuring me that we're in this together as we both breathe hard, his light eyes narrowed in on the other team.

Time seems to slow as I hone in on the puck, watching it drop to the ice. State wins it as Raiden roars beside me in frustration, and our guys immediately battle for the puck. It's a struggle. The guys bust their asses to keep it out of the net, Barlowe looking like he might drop stick and tear someone apart instead of defending goal, but he doesn't.

My heart pounds in my chest as it's finally time, and I'm jumping over the boards. Legs pushing hard as our line heads out, pumping my arms, stick sliding effortlessly over the ice, I keep my chin dipped, eyes up as I watch Hudson snag the puck and hit center ice.

The air is frigid, my muscles are on fire, and the rage to win burns through my core, splintering out like razored talons in my soul. The sickness from earlier is long forgotten as I race over the ice, skates carving their way across the rink. And just as I make it to Hudson, the whistle blows, Play stops again and hooking on State is called.

Two minute penalty.

I grin.

Powerplay, baby.

Hudson takes the faceoff, winning. The crowd fucking roars as we effortlessly power across the ice, the puck passing between Smitty and Hudson, our skates in sync as our formation takes shape, fucking flying towards State's goal.

I feel fucking alive, a grin so wide on my face, it must look feral with my blood-red mouth guard in, all because I can feel her eyes on me. Somewhere, up in the stands of five-thousand people, sits my girl and I want her to see us fucking soar.

A lightness washes over me, happiness that feels foreign striking me in the heart, but I know this is real. This feeling that makes me ache all the way down to my toes. I get it every time I think of her.

Poppy.

Something I've never, ever felt before. And my chest swells, my heart aches, and my breath comes fast and uneven. She's the only girl I'll ever wanna take home to my momma, and I'm fucking going to. This weekend, in fact, if we win this fucking game. I don't care it's so soon, I don't give a fuck what my brother'll say, I already know, despite whatever shit she's battling with, she's it for me.

Her and my brothers.

We're fucking *it*.

State scrambles to protect their net, as we pass the puck back and forth, waiting for the right moment. Smitty whistles, State's attention diverts to him, thinking that's where the puck's heading. And then Hudson is passing the puck to me, the opportunity *right fucking there*, I shoot.

The *ting* of the puck makes my eyes widen, breath still, as it hits the metal goal post, and it feels as though the crowd goes silent. Maybe it's just in my head as it buzzes so loud it feels like nests of bees are settling in my ears.

Time seems to slow, I can't watch as the crowd collectively gasps. And as I look up towards the stands, everyone's eyes on the puck, but not hers, no, her eyes are on me. My gaze finds her instantly like she's my lighthouse in a stormy sea.

And she is.

My light in the fucking dark.

Rex beside her, his eyes on the goal, mouth agape. I think I stop breathing as she smiles at me, bright and toothy and wide.

Lifting a hand to my chest, palm splayed, I tap my fingers over my heart, she drops my gaze, looking at her feet, and my heart fucking stops, but then her hand comes to her own chest. Eyes reconnecting with mine, fingers tapping over her own heart, and I notice she's wearing our jersey, *my* fucking jersey. Then the crowd fucking roars. Rex grabs her shoulders, shaking her as she laughs, the two of them cheering, jumping up and down, both of them pointing at me with huge smiles.

The puck goes in.

The team rush me, grabbing me, slapping my helmet, jumping on my back. A lump lodges itself in my throat and I choke back the feeling, blinking the heat from my eyes as Hudson grips my shoulders, lifting my head up to meet his blue gaze.

"Check hard, play hard, fuck hard," I laugh with a shrug and he claps me on the back before skating off to center ice.

"Proud of you," King says, skating into me, gripping the back of my helmet, he brings my head forward, resting against each other. "I fucking missed you, brother."

I sniff, grabbing the back of his helmet in return, gripping him to me so our heads are pressed together.

Yeah, I fucking missed you guys too.

Bennett

CHAPTER TWENTY-ONE

T he boys won their game, and it's one-a.m. before they roll in through the front door. Rex's loud bark of laughter is like light in the darkened room, King's thumping footsteps come next, then he bolts the door at his back. That's when Flynn flicks the lamp on.

"Holy fucking *shit!*" Rex shrieks, dramatically high pitched and too fucking loud.

Flynn barks a loud laugh, "You're a fucking pussy, Hendrix."

"Get fucked, shit for brains. It's not everyday some dickhead's sitting in my living room in the dark," he shoots back.

"We live here," Flynn deadpans, that foggy, psychopathic look twinkling in his dark blue eyes.

"Yeah, well, you don't usually sit in the fucking dark like some sort of wannabe mafiosos," he growls back with lilting humor.

"Sit." I click my tongue, losing my patience for this bullshit. I cross my legs, ankle resting atop my opposite knee where I sit in an armchair beside the front door, "This won't take long."

"I'll call Lynx," King says automatically, business head instantly switched on, thinking I want them to do something for me.

"No. Leave my brother with the girl."

That gets their attention.

Mentioning her.

Someone they think I know nothing about.

Flynn flops down onto the couch to my left, his huge, bulking body making it groan under his weight, denting the cushions. He spreads his tattooed arms out across the back of the leather, a white tank top clinging to his muscular chest, tucked into his royal blue slacks, thighs wide, taking up almost all three seat cushions. And the two boys come to sit on the one opposite me.

"Look, we-"

"Shut the fuck up," Flynn barks at his younger brother, silencing King before he can finish.

"What's this about?" Rex asks cautiously, trying to read the room.

He's not related to any of us by blood but he's been in our lives ever since he moved in next door to Flynn and Raiden, before Lynx and I had even moved in with them.

"Poppy Carrington," Flynn says, my gaze drifting

ever so slowly to him, he's two years older than me, but I'm the one that holds *his* reins.

Rubbing a thumb across the tip of his nose, a blank expression on his face, waiting for the other shoe to drop. And, in a strangely unpredicted turn of events, it's Hendrix that understands first.

Falling back in his seat, eyes wide, Rex drops his head to the back of the couch, staring unseeingly at the ceiling, fingertips coming to his mouth, drumming over his lips, *"Fuck."*

King stares at me, always the leader of the younger three. My own brother, Lynx, too quiet for that role, viscous but silent. Rex has always needed a leash, similar in the ways that Flynn does too. King can keep them under control, unlike his temper, but that's what he plays hockey for.

Control.

This boy has it in spades. Unlike his older brother, a seemingly sensible college student counselor, but who really has a penchant for blood and playing with knives.

"It can't be the same family. It's a coincidence." King stares at me hard, unyielding, something he never normally does, challenges me.

I stare back, unblinking until he drops his gaze, swiping a hand over his braids.

"Poppy Foster is the daughter of Michael Carrington. The same Michael Carrington that fucked over my dad, got him thrown in jail and left my mom, *us,* with nothing." I let the reminder of what happened in our childhood sink in, not that it *needs* to be said.

I don't have to say anything else, we've been working on ways to destroy the guy that ruined my family's lives without ever having to go overseas anyway, this is just… well, you couldn't write this shit could you? The convenience of it all.

What with my booming empire in personal security for the elites, home security systems, alarm panels, surveillance and personal bodyguards. Serpent Security Enterprises is now a multimillion dollar company in its own right. The little bits on the side, like the drugs, *Venom*, that's just pocket change. But it keeps the boys busy while they're in college, hustling, plus, Rex is a fucking good chemist. Creating shit that isn't addictive, doesn't have lasting effects, won't leave you nursing a two-day come down and it doesn't show up in drug tests. He doesn't need me to do that shit at all.

King's gray eyes lift to mine, a divot deep between his dark, crinkling brows, he glances at his brother, knowing it will always be him doing the background checks, "You're sure?" his voice is low, quiet, almost soft and I think of the girl.

Gold streaked, brown hair, pretty lilac-blue-gray eyes, plump lips and pale skin.

Ah, fuck.

A dark brow arches high on my forehead, "You got feelings for her, Raiden?" I ask lowly, teeth crunching as I bite down on my molars.

He says nothing, Rex glances between the two of us. Flynn dragging his arms from the back of the sofa, leaning forward, forearms on his thighs, hands hanging between his knees, his blue eyes lift from beneath his dark lashes, a curly tendril of black hair hanging across one of them. He watches us too, probably hoping for some sort of blow up, but that's never been the way we sort shit out.

King blinks, smoothing out his expression, he swallows, but he doesn't look away, "What do you want us to do?"

And just like that, we form the plan to destroy the daughter of a man who condemned us as kids.

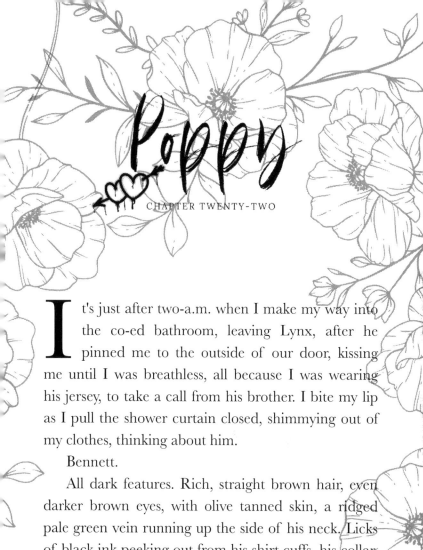

Poppy

It's just after two-a.m. when I make my way into the co-ed bathroom, leaving Lynx, after he pinned me to the outside of our door, kissing me until I was breathless, all because I was wearing his jersey, to take a call from his brother. I bite my lip as I pull the shower curtain closed, shimmying out of my clothes, thinking about him.

Bennett.

All dark features. Rich, straight brown hair, even darker brown eyes, with olive tanned skin, a ridged pale green vein running up the side of his neck. Licks of black ink peeking out from his shirt cuffs, his collar. He was tall and muscular and intimidating, kind of a dick. He called me Lollipop, and I… I liked it. The way he popped the *pop*.

I giggle out loud, smacking my fingertips to my lips, hiding my smile even behind the curtain, because despite it being two-a.m., there are other people in here, showering, washing their faces at the sink. But I can't stop the giggle from escaping again.

I think of the Molly I took back in our room, after Lynx stepped outside for his phone call, promising he'd come join me as soon as he was done.

Lynx was riding a high after his win, I was getting overwhelmed, he wanted me to be excited and I was, until I wasn't.

Too many people were huddling around us as everyone celebrated the team in Graves. And I thought about giving Lynx my stash the last time we were there and it made me itch all over thinking about him flushing them. It's not that I couldn't get more, I already had more, back in our room. I have pills hidden all over in it, but I didn't take any with me to the game or the after party and I was anxious to get home. I wanted to be happy for him.

So it's the first thing I did the moment I was alone, the high settling in me almost instantly as it mixed with all the alcohol I'd consumed throughout the night.

Hot water beats down on my face as I angle my head back, letting the shower spray soak my hair, washing the smell of cigarettes and cheap beer down the drain. The boys wanted us to stay with them, but Lynx wanted me to himself tonight. Wanted to talk to me, he said. King and Rex didn't seem to mind, looking proud that Lynx's first return game was played so well. It was my first hockey game ever, if I don't count watching their training, and every moment of it felt like I was riding a high. I couldn't take my eyes off of Lynx or King as they dominated the ice, and Rex talked me through everything that was happening. It was exhilarating.

And when Lynx scored that goal, his eyes on mine instead of the puck, my belly swooped and my ears popped and church bells fucking chimed in my skull.

But only for the moment. Then the darkness rushed back in, a reminder that the happiness was temporary.

I should end this now.

My heart races in my chest, pulse thrumming in my neck, I can hear my blood rushing in my ears. I feel heavy and light and I'm smiling even though I have an insane urge to cry. But the high of the Molly and the heat of the alcohol keeps me afloat enough not to let my smile fall.

Cold air hits my hot skin as Lynx wrenches open the shower curtain, a shrill sound escapes me, choked off by his hand as he climbs into the stall wearing all of his clothes, his boots.

His red-brown eyes are wild, flicking between my own as he digs his fingers into the sides of my neck, squeezing his palm over my windpipe, his thumb crushing the corner of my jaw.

My face twists into a frown, hands flying to his, my breath stalled in my lungs, no oxygen able to get in or out. Twisting me around in his hold, he lifts me off my feet, and I heave in a great gasp of air as his hand momentarily leaves my throat. But then he's slamming me face first into the tiled wall, knocking all of the air from my lungs. I ignore the bruising pain in my right cheek, my brow, the same one he slammed into a door only days ago as he presses me into the wall.

Lynx drops his weight to my spine, ripping the shower curtain closed at his back, some of the metal rings pinging against the wet floor as they tear free.

"Lynx," I groan, my breath a puff of condensation over the slick tiles.

Gasping at the feel of his rough jeans against my bare, wet thighs. The shower spray directed only on him now, my body shivers, goosebumps razing across my flesh. The tiles cold, my skin wet, Lynx's heat heavy and welcome over my back.

Everything hurts, but I'm laughing anyway, giggling even as pain bolts through my teeth, jaw smashed into the tiles. Lynx's breath is a quick rush down the side of my throat, my hands splayed on the wall, he kicks my feet apart. Using one hand to hold my head flush to the tiles, pressing heavily against the side of my face. The back of his other grazing over the flesh of my arse, he reaches between us flicking open his jeans, tearing down the zipper. And then his cock is thrusting up inside me.

A moan trembles through my chattering teeth, pain aching in my face, but it feels good too, the way it spears out from my cheekbone, up through my temple, pulsing in my nose.

Lynx says nothing as he fucks me hard and fast, his hips smacking into me, my head swimming, it fucking hurts, but I'm laughing again. Teeth clacking, I grind my jaw, let my high flood through me. I am so desperate for Lynx's big hands on me, his rough skin traversing my smooth, but I kinda want them anywhere but where they currently are. Applying his weight to my head, a bruising grip on my hip. My head feels as though it might explode with the pressure from his palm but I moan anyway as he pounds into me from behind, his forehead dropped to my shoulder, all of his clothes on.

An orgasm builds, sweeping through me, tumbling around in my belly as it grows faster and faster. I bite down on my tongue, taste blood and I want him. I want him so badly, and he isn't looking at me, he isn't touching me, not really.

"Lynx," I groan out, no longer giving a fuck about anyone else listening, but the thought of that, of people listening, only makes me wetter. "Lynx, please," I almost sob, his fingers almost tunnelling their way beneath my skin. "Lynx, Lynx, Lynx, please," I chant, trying to lift my head, trying to see him through the slight gap in his splayed fingers smothering the side of my face. "Please, Lynx," it's a wailing now, pain and pleasure rolling through me as my release climbs higher and higher, "Kiss me. Please, *Lynx*, kiss me."

He doesn't. Instead, grunting against my left shoulder, he buries his teeth into my flesh, biting so hard I scream behind gritted, bared teeth with the pain, his own sinking deeper and deeper into my flesh. Tears prick my eyes, the intensity blinding me as I squeeze them closed tight. The edges of my vision blurring black then white and then I'm coming with him as he slurps at my shoulder. Teeth still sunken, tongue rolling over the painful skin, he fills me with his release. His cock pumps into me as he finishes, once, twice, my pussy tightening around him, trying to suck him deeper, and then he's pulling out of me painfully.

He releases me from his crushing hold, from his teeth. Cold air rushing in to greet my goosebump smattered skin. I slump against the wall, breath heavy, misting the wet tiles, his hand cracks against my arse, the clap a loud echo in the silent room, nothing but our shower water making any sound.

I glance over my shoulder, ignoring the dark purple colouring I can see in the very bottom of my vision, my line of sight only wanting to find him. But Lynx isn't looking at me, his hands fisted at his sides, cock already tucked away as if he didn't have it inside of me just a few seconds ago.

Pain, a different kind of pain, the emotional kind, the kind I've been drowning with pills and booze for as long as I can currently remember, starts to wash over me. And suddenly, I want to cover up, the Molly long forgotten even as it still pulses erratically through my bloodstream. I cross my arms over my chest, my feet at the ankles, attempting to hide myself in yet another moment of vulnerability. *Shame.*

My mouth is so dry, my tongue too heavy, the shower still switched on and pounding the tile floor between us. Time seems to slow as Lynx shakes his head, that beautiful red-chestnut-brown gaze still directed at his feet, and even though, in this moment, I want to hide my body from him. I really, really need him to look at me.

I swallow, half-choking on my nerves, "Lynx?" it's a barely audible whisper, but he flinches with the sound as though when my voice hit his ears it caused him physical pain. "I'm sorry," I breathe the word as my heart bangs in my chest, I don't even know what I'm sorry for, I haven't done anything, I just know I want to fix this silence, the way he won't look at me.

That's when the Molly makes a reappearance, not that it ever really left, but my lips curl up into an unwanted smile like I'm the cheshire fucking cat, and I wish I could just bite them off.

In this moment, I almost want to bash my head against the tiles until blood comes out of my ears and I'm not even sure why. I'm not even sure why, but my high is a curse as a giggle bursts free of my lips, my jaw aching and heavy and that's when he finally looks at me.

"You're a fucking mess," he spits at me, fury and vitriol, malice pronounced in every word.

That's when I flinch.

"You're a junkie fucking whore. Can't go one night without fucking pills. I could have been anyone just then, slamming his way inside of you, and you wouldn't have cared would you? Just want a cock shoved so deep inside you that you don't have to think."

"Lynx, *no,* please, I don't- I'm sorry, please, I'm sorry," my bottom lip trembles even as my skin aches with the need for him to touch me, if he would just touch me, everything would be better again. "Please, Lynx, it's not like that, I don't- I thought…"

"Yeah," he huffs with mocking, a strangled sort of dark laugh puffing between his pretty lips. "I don't really think you actually do that."

"Do what?"

"*Think,*" he hisses, shoving a hand through his wet, bleached blonde hair, revealing more of his smooth face, that luscious olive tanned skin. "You don't use that fucking head of yours at all, if you did, you wouldn't be fucking high right now, naked, in a co-ed fucking shower room with a guy you just fucking met."

I blink. It's true, we only just met, but there's

something more. Here. Between us. We're something more. *He* said that. Lynx said that. He told me…

I don't understand.

I don't understand what's happening.

The Molly rips through my veins now, and my trembling lips curl up into yet another smile that I don't want. Can't stop. My entire body riding a high that has my cracking heart pounding in an insane rhythm.

My limbs ache, but my body's numb, and as cum drips down the inside of my squeezed thighs, I think I'm going to pee at the realisation that we just had unprotected sex. *Again.* And I'm not prepared for a responsibility like *that*.

Just some *junkie whore*.

"We're done with you, Poppy. All of us. We're done."

The world starts to tumble down around me, crashing and swirling and breaking apart.

"Oh my god," I whisper it, the words spilling from my tongue like I wish the ground would fucking swallow me up. *"Oh my god."*

I knew this was going to happen. I knew they were going to do this to me. So why the fuck does it hurt so much?

Because I let them in.

Shame floods my cheeks with heat.

I drop my gaze, hate my fucking self, and I'm going to pee, and I'm laughing again, with tears in my eyes, I'm fucking laughing, because of the Molly, the shame, self-hatred.

God, I fucking hate myself.

Lynx walks away. He just walks away, he steps backwards without looking at me, out of the shower, shaking his head, leaving the curtain open as he turns his back on me, and the bathroom is *not* empty. A camera flashes in my fucking face, laughter flooding the echoing space, steam being sucked out of the cubicle into the cold room. But I can't even reach forward to pull the curtain closed. Watching, dumb-founded, as Lynx stalks past the small group of people and out of the door, all without looking back.

Once he's gone, finally, my limbs seem to work again, and I tear the curtain closed. My brain feels like it's on fire. Tears spill down my cheeks and my ears ring, pain bolts through my cheek, my head, my jaw and I clench my teeth, grinding my molars and I still can't wipe the drug induced smile off of my face, even as my tears wash down the drain.

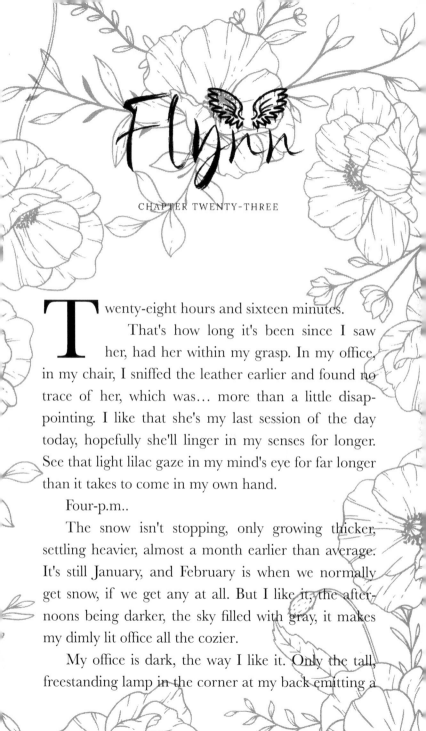

Flynn

CHAPTER TWENTY-THREE

Twenty-eight hours and sixteen minutes.

That's how long it's been since I saw her, had her within my grasp. In my office, in my chair, I sniffed the leather earlier and found no trace of her, which was… more than a little disappointing. I like that she's my last session of the day today, hopefully she'll linger in my senses for longer. See that light lilac gaze in my mind's eye for far longer than it takes to come in my own hand.

Four-p.m..

The snow isn't stopping, only growing thicker, settling heavier, almost a month earlier than average. It's still January, and February is when we normally get snow, if we get any at all. But I like it, the afternoons being darker, the sky filled with gray, it makes my dimly lit office all the cozier.

My office is dark, the way I like it. Only the tall, freestanding lamp in the corner at my back emitting a dull orange glow. It makes it feel warmer. In my opinion. And people always spill their darkest secrets when they feel at ease. That's how you get blackmail material.

Forty-two minutes to go.

Maybe less.

Poppy Foster -Carrington- is a goody-two-shoes. She'll probably be early.

I hope.

Have to admit, seeing her all wet, naked, and bruised, eyes the size of saucers, evidence trailing down her leg of being freshly fucked, had me taking my dick in hand before six-a.m..

Twice.

That's why I hacked every server and cellphone within a four-hundred mile radius to erase all evidence of her beautifully fucked body from the planet, well, apart from the copy I saved for myself... Shame I can't erase the image from the heads of all those fuckers that witnessed it in person. Although... Perhaps I can beat their heads in until the memory slips its way out of their ears in a satisfying stream of crimson.

My cock pulses again, violence and sex on my mind. I lift my arm, check the time on my gold watch.

Thirty-four minutes.

Christ.

Cock aching, I squeeze it hard through my pants, gritting my teeth as I suck in air through my nose. I've never jerked off so many times in one day before, well, actually, maybe that time when I- *no*, I think this beats that too.

Without conscious thought, my chair is sliding back, length whipped out, pulsing in my palm, and I only just manage to tear my shirt up and out of the way in time. Clenching the white egyptian cotton between my teeth to avoid jets of cum splashing over the fabric.

The sticky, wet heat hits my abs, the rest of my release spilling over the tight curl of my fist, dripping down my fingers as my cock continues to pulse, weeping. I drop my head back, eyes squeezed shut, breath heavy exhales from my open mouth. And I imagine painting Poppy's lips with it. Her chin, neck, tits.

We're supposed to make her life hell now. Which is one of my favorite pastimes. But I usually use manipulation, mind fucks and physical violence. Although, I'm six-foot-four, weighing just over two-eighty and she, well, she isn't, so using physical violence seems a bit redundant, I could just flick her in the forehead and she'd likely tip over.

A laugh bursts out of me at that.

I'd actually find that kinda funny.

But my heart does a funny thing in my chest, it sort of thuds harder, a little faster, even though I'm not jerking my dick, but I picture Poppy falling backwards. Cracking her head on the wood, blood swelling in a pool around her halo of thick, dark, gold streaked hair, and my throat feels a little tight. But then, just as quickly, I imagine painting her with the blood spilled from her head, fucking it into her cunt, licking it off of her face, and my heart starts beating normally again.

A groan rumbles free, although it sounds a little like a purr which is startling to say the least.

I wish she were here right now, for me to punish, to use, to fill with my cum instead of wasting it on my hand.

My eyes blink open, locking on the jug of orange juice atop my desk as my cock starts to harden once more. This load doesn't necessarily have to be wasted…

Poppy

I've been walking around on tenterhooks all. Day. Long. Just waiting to see images of myself, naked, wet, abandoned in the shower, plastered across the walls, my classes, social fucking media. Not that I've logged into mine for months. The longer the day has dragged on without incident, without snide remarks, without seeing myself stuck to every single surface I pass, the worse my anxiety builds.

I feel like I'm suffocating and nothing's even happened yet.

Lynx wasn't in when I finally got my shit together enough to make my way back into our room this morning. I spent the night in a single bed sandwiched between Bonnie and Emma because when I knocked, I told them I just wanted someone to hold me. And they were high too, so they didn't question my blooming black eye, bite mark on my shoulder, or the tears down my cheeks, they just cuddled me and the three of us giggled together until we fell asleep.

But I don't think any of us were really laughing.

They have demons too.

I haven't seen any of the boys today, which isn't totally unheard of, I only share one class with each of them and we don't have any of those on a Friday.

That's one good thing I suppose, that it's Friday and I can try to talk to Lynx tonight when he gets in from practice, apologise for the pills. For ruining his night. I mean, that's what it must be, he was fine with me before the shower, great even. Happy.

He doesn't mean what he said.

My cheeks flush, heart pounding as I think about watching him dominate the ice, stare at me in a crowd of thousands and tap his fingers over his chest. My stomach swoops at just the memory, but then I think of what he said to me in the shower.

'Fucking mess.'

'Junkie whore.'

'We're done with you, Poppy. All of us. We're done.'

My heart bangs harder, threatening to crack through my ribcage and that heavy lead feeling of dread resettles in my belly. I can stop taking pills anytime I want. I will. For him. *Them.* I can be better.

I hurry my steps as I cross the quad, large flakes of white fluff assaulting my cheeks, and I suddenly wish I could stay out here a little longer because the icy air feels amazing against my swollen face.

I reach up, hover my fingers over the tender, heated skin, hidden beneath my curtain of hair because it was just too painful to press concealer into, even more painful to think of the way Lynx held me down. I shiver, from the cold, from the thought, drop my hand. Suck in a sharp lungful of frosty air and continue hurrying towards the far building for my counselling session.

I hate that I have to do this. Meet with a stranger who knows nothing about me. Mr Marshall, *Flynn*, is intimidating to say the least, so I dunno how he's supposed to be my what? Some sort of college life coach? Someone who's a safe space, can help me with school issues, job applications, he can't really help *me*. He spoke to me more like a creepy, invasive therapist. But that wasn't even the worst part. The worst part of it all was how beautiful I thought he was.

Easily six and a half feet, broad shoulders, thick, curly black hair, long on top, short on the sides. A light covering of dark stubble, that is definitely intentional, along the hollows of his cheeks, the wide square bone of his jaw. Full pink lips, pale skin, and muscles in his thighs that definitely belong to a rugby player. He is criminally gorgeous and too old for me.

'Thirty. If that's all right with you?'

That's eleven years older than me.

I've never felt attraction to older guys, not that he's old, definitely not that, just... I've never really felt attraction to anyone before I came here. The way I lost my virginity. How I ended up with that guy. I shudder just thinking about it, him, *her*. The laughing. What came after it…

Why the fuck am I thinking about this?

Shaking my head, knees protesting as I rush up the wooden stairs towards Flynn's office, I disregard all thoughts of him and those devilish blue eyes. God, they're like molten hellfire smouldering against pit black pupils.

I lick my chapped lips, tasting vanilla-pumpkin chapstick and rush to reapply it. I didn't drink enough water last night and now I'm suffering the consequences of dehydration. Which reminds me, yet again, that, fuck, I'm thirsty. But I'm late, I'm never late.

Shit.

I run the rest of the way down the long empty corridor, only the third floor entrance to the library and the closed doors of Professors' offices lie ahead.

Coming to an abrupt stop outside of Mr Marshall's door, I breathe in deep, feel my insides start to squirm and then I lift my hand, rapping my knuckles on the brightly polished wood of the door beside the shiny gold plaque of his name.

"Come in," he calls immediately, a deep, deceptive rumble, luring you to safety only to then look like he's going to eat you alive.

Reluctantly, I ease open the door, darkness

greeting me, my eyes instantly searching out the lamp in the back corner of the room. I hold onto that as I enter, trying to ignore the dark shadowy spaces filling the rest of the room, close the door at my back, and take a seat before he invites me to sit.

I can't bring myself to look at him across the wide expanse of the desk as I knot my tattooed fingers in my lap, studying the intricate lines of ivy, not ready to see him yet. My breathing is rough, quick from my running and I stare down at my bony knuckles until the pain in my lungs from the freezing air starts to ease.

I've never liked counselling, therapy, psychiatrists. Everything about them is too invasive and prying and it feels like a drill bit is whistling its way into my brain cavity. I don't deal well under pressure, and questions cause me stress.

Sweat is breaking out beneath my arms, and I shove my thick jacket off, swallow hard, my mouth dry, like sandpaper, I need a drink, water or-

"Hello, *Poppy*," Mr Marshall says, cutting off my erratically spiralling thoughts, but he doesn't just *say it*.

It's a curling rumble that feels ferocious as it slithers from his mouth, like a seductive spitting from a forked tongue. The sound wrapping around me like a boa constrictor. Because, for the first time since yesterday morning's session, I remember what he called me.

'Angel.'

My eyes snap onto his like they couldn't stop if I plucked them out, and I swallow hard, staring at the smirk on his mouth. I really take him in then, studying his face. Plush pale pink lips, an arrowed, defined cupid's bow. A strong, straight nose, thick, neat, black brows, a light layer of purposeful stubble over hollow cheeks. High cheekbones, square jaw, round ears that stick out, just a little, and I love them. They remind me of my own, too big for my head, too sticky out not to be teased for them, it's why I always cover them with my hair, but I don't mind them, I actually kinda like them, I only hide them so I'm less of a target.

"Poppy?" I realise with a flush of heat soaring high in my cheeks that I'm staring.

But what's worse is that, at the sound of my name on his lips, I like it. A little *too* much. His deep voice caresses like a tongue down my spine.

"Y-Yes?" I stammer, tongue sticking to the roof of my mouth, gaze dropping to my lap, I squeeze my fingers harder, circling them around my thin wrists, letting my nails carve into the inside of them.

"Did you hear anything I just said?" he asks cautiously, hesitantly.

My brows knit together, fingers biting deeper, nails gouging further.

I didn't hear anything he said. I didn't hear anything. Was he even speaking when I was staring at his pretty face, ignoring his soul sucking eyes. Admiring his *ears*. I flinch at myself, the desire to reach up and make sure my own ears are covered is excruciating. It tingles all the way down to my toes, the urge to spring up out of my chair and get the fuck out of here. Hide away in my room.

But then I think of Lynx and pain bursts inside my chest like I'm having a goddamn heart attack.

Panic swoops through me, knocking the air from my lungs because I blacked out again without actually blacking out. I zoned out, didn't hear anything he said and I scare myself when I get like that, everything goes dark.

I can't go back in the dark.

"Poppy?"

Fingers beneath my chin have me catapulting from the leather chair, my feet clumsily trying to get beneath me, and they're not going to and I'm going to fucking fall. I'm going to fall on my arse in front of a faculty member and make a fool out of myself when I've been trying so hard to be normal.

Why the fuck can't I be fucking normal?

A firm grasp on my elbow stops me from falling, but rather than only steadying me, Mr Marshall pulls me towards him, his fingertips singeing my skin, but I let him reel me in like a proverbial dying fish on a hook. That's when I notice he's on the wrong side of the desk.

His huge, broad body towers over me like he's eclipsing the sun, and even though I'm steady on my feet now, he doesn't let me go. In fact his grip only tightens, and he yanks me closer so hard it feels like my arm is going to rip out of its socket.

Drawing in a ragged inhale, I finally find the courage to glance up at him, a frown creasing my brow because his deep sapphire eyes aren't looking at me, instead, they're gazing down, and his other hand is grabbing my own, bringing it up so close to his face, I can feel his warm breath on my skin. His long, thick fingers grasp my hand so delicately, handling me like fine china as he flips my hand, smoothing out my fingers and stroking over my palm.

My face heats, eyes locked on him, studying the look of concentration on his own, the purse of his lips, the scrunch of his brow, lines wrinkling his forehead.

"You usually make yourself bleed when you're upset about something?" he rumbles in some semblance of a whisper, but it's enough to freeze me to the spot, my entire body stiffening.

Slowly, I stare down at my blanched fingers, quickly realising with no small amount of horror that I have, in fact, made myself bleed.

Shame fills my belly like lead, nausea swirling in my gut as bile rushes up the back of my throat.

"Poppy?" Mr Marshall's voice rings like pots and pans crashing inside my head, banging and clanging and- "Angel," he coos, smoothing the rough pad of his thumb over the bloody crescents in my wrist. "Look at me."

I try to snatch my hand back, tugging sharply, but his hold only tightens, bruising grip crushing my elbow. Air knocks out of me with an oomph as I suddenly drop backwards into the chair, a big hand planted on my chest, finger and thumb pinching savagely at my chin.

I can't not look at him then, *see* him.

Because his face is almost flush with mine, nothing between us but my ragged breaths, his slow, measured ones.

"Let me go," my lip trembles, but he doesn't, he doesn't stop staring either, he only grips me harder, my hand, my chin. "Let me go," it's a weak demand, an order without backbone.

And a man like Mr Marshall is clearly not someone to take an order from anyone, let alone some silly little girl like me.

"Poppy," he growls my name like it personally offends him, with bared teeth, gritted and caged. "Do you always do shit like this to yourself?"

I'm hot. So hot. Flushing all over like a volcano is going to erupt inside of me and I've got no way of stopping it. My vision blurs at the edges and I feel it, the swaying of my body, the cold, empty feeling in my legs.

"Angel," I hear it, but I see nothing.

Falling, falling, falling, swallowed by the black abyss, a cold sweat washes over me and I sink into the feeling of being heavy then light.

Sharp pain surges through my bruised cheek, head knocking to the side, but then someone stops it, massaging along my jaw, my eyes blink open.

I'm on the floor, my back against the leather armchair, my jean-clad legs flopped open, arms heavy. I think I might be sick. I swallow, *hard*.

"Mr Marshall, I'm-"

"Flynn," he counters, smoothing his thumb across my jaw, the skin hot beneath his touch.

He hit me.

I swallow again, and without looking away from his hand on my face, he passes me a glass of orange juice.

"You need to drink this, you're dehydrated, you fainted, it's got everything you need inside that glass," he eyes the glass then, those dark sapphires locked on where I take the juice from him, bring it to my lips.

His hand stills, his gaze lifting to my mouth, he licks over the sharp definition of his cupid's bow, and when the glass pauses, my hand trembling, he cups the base of it, tilting it up until I taste sharp, fresh juice on my tongue. He lifts it higher and higher, slowly, carefully, watching my throat work it all down like a man possessed, so focused on his task -making sure I swallow the orange juice- that you'd think he's personally getting something out of it.

"Such a good girl," he hushes under his breath and I almost splutter on the last mouthful.

A drop escaping my lips, dribbling down my chin. His thumb traces it as he releases the empty glass, allowing me to place it on the floor at my side. His gaze still on me. The pad of his thumb catches the drop of juice at the tip of my chin, sweeping it back up towards my lips, he rubs it across my bottom lip, eyes glazed as he studies his own movements. But my eyes remain on his, the entire time I'm watching him as though these things are happening to someone else.

Then his short nail is tapping at my front bottom teeth, and without conscious thought, my mouth is opening, his thumb pushing inside, gliding over my tongue, to the back of my mouth, sweeping across my tastebuds. It's the first time I've ever really smelled him, sandalwood and vanilla, masculine and strong, but creamy vanilla cutting through it all.

My lips close around his thumb as saliva pools in my mouth, and I suck on the digit, tasting his skin, breathing him in, that's when his eyes lift to mine.

Deep, dark, sapphire blue, they flick between my own, and I keep sucking on his thumb, his fingers curling along the length of my jaw. He doesn't even blink, letting me suckle on him like it's the cure to calming me down. Maybe it is.

Heat flames in my cheeks, spreading down my neck, warming my chest because this is my *teacher*, kind of, either way, he's a member of the college faculty which in turn means he is one hundred million percent off limits. And yet, he doesn't snatch his hand back. I don't spit out his thumb. Continuing to suck on it, cheeks hollowing with my slow, gentle pulls. I can't get enough of the taste of his skin, so warm and thick and *right* for my mouth.

Our gazes are locked on one another and I don't want to be the one to look away first. *Flynn* is sat down on the hard floor in front of me. Knees bent up, feet spread so he's sort of cocooned around my awkwardly flopped legs. His breathing is faster, and his other hand comes up between us, but I don't look, unable to divert my attention from him, the feeling of his thumb in my mouth, fingers on my jaw, splaying down over the side of my neck.

His hand lifts to my bruised cheek, thumb pressing against it overly hard. I wince, my teeth coming down on his thumb, and he stills, I still, eyes widening just slightly, and then he laughs. This low, rough sounding chuckle, something dark and violent and not safe. He presses on my bruises again, forcing my mind back to Lynx and I want to cry.

"I think you look beautiful in blue," he rasps, applying more pressure to my bruised face, his other hand still on my jaw, thumb in my mouth. "I love bruises," he tells me whimsically, like he's not even really speaking these words to me. "I think," he swallows, Adam's apple bobbing heavily, up and down, in his throat, "I like these more because they're on you." He swallows again, the movement in his thick, corded neck captivating, "I wonder how pretty you'll look when you really bleed."

That's what has me snapping back into the room. I'm not even sure what I really hear through the cotton wool feeling in my static ears. I wrench my head back, swatting his hands away as I escape out of his grasp and pounce up to my feet. Head spinning, I grip onto the arm of the chair, grabbing my bag and jacket, and fling myself away from him.

Flynn chuckles darkly as I exit the office without looking back, bootsteps pounding down the wide hall. I shove my hand into my tight jean's pocket, pulling out a little bag of pills as I race toward the library instead of the dorm. I can't face Lynx like this, if he's even there tonight. I'm not sure I can face him anyway, now I'll really have to chase the housing administrator for a room change.

My mind spins, head a mess. I can't apologise for upsetting Lynx if I'm not thinking straight, I want him to know I'm serious when I say I'll stop the drugs, that I'm sorry for doing them last night. For ruining everything. Instead of just enjoying the moment with him.

"We're done with you, Poppy. All of us. We're done."

But then Flynn's dark chuckle reverberates around my skull and I think of what I just did, with my *coun-*

sellor. What he said, how I just… wasn't really there, until suddenly I was.

I pluck out a pill, stuff it in my mouth and dry swallow it down.

I'll stop tomorrow.

Tomorrow I'll stop.

Hendrix

CHAPTER TWENTY-FIVE

T hink I understand addiction now.

It's so much harder than I thought to stay away from her.

Poppy moves, breathes, coughs, and I watch her.

Captivated.

Intoxicated.

A drug running through my veins.

I make them, but I don't dabble, other than weed, I have no interest in getting fucked up, my ADHD is a high all on its own some days.

But this is different. I could touch her before, and now, now I *can't*. And I'm already not coping with it. The stimming is worse today, worse than last night, my lips are dry and cracked from tapping my fingers against them constantly. And yet, I still can't stop.

When I was with her, she made everything go quiet.

And now, everything is loud again.

Poppy bursts out of Flynn's office, the fucker, her boots thumping down the hall, she rummages around in her pocket, not seeing me, even as I shamelessly lean against the wall opposite Flynn's office. She draws something from her jeans, hand to her face, she throws her head back, still running until she slams her shoulder into the library door. Smooths her hair down, and then she walks calmly through the second set of doors, swiping her key card to gain entry.

I follow behind her, not trying to hide, hands sliding into my pockets as I make my way inside. It's Friday evening, classes are mostly over. There's a party happening in a frat house just off campus and most students are likely getting ready to head there later, so the library's empty.

It's warm in here, a welcoming hit of heat from the icy temperatures outside. The lighting is low, tall, green, glass shaded floor lamps fitted with soft orange bulbs. Dark green carpets, and rich wooden furniture. The shelves tower over everything, so many aisles laid out like a labyrinth. The study rooms are empty, lights off, and I watch Poppy casually stroll past, glancing at them as she passes, her pace quickening just a little as she does.

She's afraid of the dark.

A smirk curls my lips, watching as she heads to the far back corner, sitting down on the curved bench seat built into one of the four towers. Her tote bag hits the floor with a thud as she draws her knees up, presses herself into the corner. Unless you were *really* looking, you wouldn't see her.

I study her face as I move closer, no one around, my heart thudding in my chest. The reality is, my brothers come first, none of them are my blood, but they're my glue. I would take a bullet for any one of them, any day of the week, but this, the fucking bully bullshit feels wrong.

Is wrong.

And I'm a fucking coward because I didn't fucking say anything. What Bennett says goes, he's our official leader, I respect him, love him, but still, I always look to King.

Raiden's been my best friend since we were kids, and although he has a temper problem, because the guy's a control freak, he's one of the most level headed people I've ever met. He thinks shit through, plans, is rational. You'd never guess he was related to the blood lusting, psychopath Flynn. Sure, they have different dads, but they were both brought up together by Raiden's father. Flynn's only ever met his bio dad once, he wanted nothing to do with him from then on, and he's always treated King's dad as his own.

I stared at King, waiting for him to protest this shit when Bennett explained who Poppy really was. We always swore we'd find the guy, Michael Carrington, we'd make him pay for fucking over Bennett and Lynx's father, for taking their dad away from them. Forcing them to move in with the Kings when they lost everything. Their dad going to jail, all of their assets being seized, their mom's manic depression. They lost both parents that day, even though only one got put away. They lost their home, cars, bank accounts. The clothes on their backs were all they had left when Raiden and Flynn's parents took them in. The families having always been close.

Then they brought me into the fold.

The weird, hyper kid next door. They embraced me as I was. Never wanted to change me like my parents did, they were always trying to feed me pills to suppress my active nature, get me to calm down. Not the families next door. I spent more time there than in my own house.

My loyalty is with my boys, forever and always, but if anyone could sway Bennett, it would be King. And he didn't even try. He just… *nodded*.

I wanted to grab him and shake some sense into him. Tell him, *fuck no*, that's our girl. She didn't fucking do any of that shit, she woulda been like five or somthing. How could she have been the master-mind behind the demise of a successful businessman like Jason Adams. On another continent... She couldn't. It's not her fault her dad is a fucking lowlife.

But I didn't fucking say any of that, did I?

Because Bennett knows this. King knows this. Flynn knows it. Lynx knows it. And none of them care. They don't care because it's not about Poppy. She's just an easy way to get payback.

Ruin her life to ruin her father's.

I'm sure it won't end there.

Once Bennett latches onto something he doesn't stop, but step one is ripping apart Michael Carrington's daughter.

I walk right up to her, sit down beside her feet, her face buried in her drawn up knees, her entire body trembling, arms wrapped around her legs.

Lynx told her we were through with her.

Done.

I'm not sure that'll ever be true. At least, not for me.

Addicted.

"Kitten," I purr, reaching out to cradle the back of her head, snatching my hand back before I make contact with her silky hair.

Her head lifts slowly, lashes blinking over bright lilac eyes, half-lidded, bloodshot, pupils blown. She stares straight through me, her head swaying as though it's too heavy to hold up on her neck.

"Poppy?"

I feel a pull in my chest, an ache, a memory.

Lynx, the needles, the blood.

I move without conscious thought, snapping her neck back with my fist in her hair, my nose pressing against hers.

"What the fuck are you doing?" I shake her, strands of her beautiful hair snapping free, tangling around my fingers.

A whimper slips from her throat, her bitten, dry lips, mirroring my own, parted. Her breath rasping in and out through her mouth, puffing warm, sweet, orange scented air directly onto my tongue. My cock thickens in sync with my anger. How dare she fucking do this. After everything with Lynx.

Everything she doesn't know about.

I take a deep breath, force my eyes shut, let the shudder ripple through my bones, my teeth squeaking where I bite down on them. I give myself a minute to try and get control of my temper, but it's like trying to hold onto smoke.

Blowing out a breath, I open my eyes, one of hers hidden behind her hair, the other, wide and wet and *hurt*. And mine snap closed again in an instant, I don't even see her, not properly, unable to look at her like that. Yet, I can't loosen my grip, I can't clear the cloud of red rage fogging my vision.

"You're a fucking idiot," I snarl, biting down on her bottom lip, driving my teeth into the flesh and tearing into the skin until I taste blood.

I force her knees down, straddling her, trapping her down on the bench, her back to the wall, legs laid out along the seat. I don't even think, letting her lip pop free, I force my tongue into her mouth, hers unmoving as I twirl mine around her mouth, and then she kisses me back. Slow, sad, fucking terrified, she kisses me back and I can't look at her, my eyes squeezed shut so tight they hurt, but I can't see another person I care about doing this to them fucking selves.

Hand tangled in her hair, I keep her head snapped back, throat arched as I work my hand between us, yanking her jeans open and thrusting my hand into her panties.

We groan in unison, the sounds echoing in each of our throats, and I eagerly swallow it down. She's so hot and wet, I crave to be inside of her.

Oh, god, what am I doing?

Even as I think it, my fingers work between her folds, thighs forced tight together between my own, no room for her to widen her legs. My wrist screams with the angle it's twisted at, my fingers working through her wetness, dragging it up and around to circle her clit. She whimpers against my mouth, our noses smashed together, our breaths heavy, mingling between savage kisses.

I thrust a finger inside of her and nearly come in my fucking pants. She's so fucking tight and hot, it's like a fire burning between her thighs. I grunt, forcing my middle finger deeper and deeper, my weight on her knees where I arch over her.

I want so desperately to look at her.

To see her.

To kiss her like I care.

But I can't, I can't fucking do it, but I can't stop either, fucking her with my finger, the heel of my hand grinding against her clit, and she's groaning, deep and throaty from the angle I hold her head at. I feel her tightening around me more, even as I violently shove my ring finger inside her too, both fingers fucking into her harder and harder.

Hurting her, but she's moaning, and writhing and she tightens and tightens, and my thumb is vicious as I circle her clit, my teeth in her tongue, holding it inside my mouth to suck on it. Her breaths are erratic, her hands fisted in the front of my shirt, she clings onto me, pushing me away at the same time she drags me closer and I want to fuck her, I want to fuck her and I fucking hate myself. And she's so close, I can feel it, taste it in the desperate sounds that claw their way up her throat like I'm exorcizing her demons, consuming them for myself.

I wish I fucking could.

And as her back arches, my fingers cramping where her cunt sucks on them so fucking hard, I rip my hand out of her panties, tear my mouth from hers, releasing my hold on her hair, and fall back on my ass, not letting her finish.

My cock weeps, my head pounds and my heart fucking dies, because I'm a fucking asshole. Which means I'm doing it right.

I scrub my hands over my face, smearing her all over me, the tangy, tart scent of her sharp in my nose. My back against the wall at the other end of the bench seat, and finally, like the fucking coward I am, I finally open my eyes. If only to prove to myself I can do this, I can ruin this girl for my brothers.

That's when I see the bruising on her cheek. Inky blues and violets, strawberry spotting on her perfect pale flesh, along her temple, curling around her outer eye, the top of her cheekbone, and it's like everything falls away. I feel myself deflate, the anger gone, something like fear swooping in to take its place like lead in my gut.

I don't know how I didn't see it, I just didn't want to look at her, her hair was covering her face, and I- *I didn't wanna fucking see her cry*.

"Who the fuck did this to you?" I growl it, because I know my brothers, not one of them would physically hurt her, not to *hurt*. "Poppy?" I bark it, teeth bared, I sit up, looming over her as she gapes at me, her chest rising and falling so quickly, I wonder if she's having a heart attack. I swallow, peering into her pretty eyes, studying the plume of bruising, "Poppy-"

"Shut up," that's what she whispers, dragging her hair over her face, throwing her legs over the side of the bench, feet to the ground, she sweeps her bag from the floor, tosses it over her shoulder, and she stands, to get away, escape.

Me.

I realize with horrifying clarity, she wants to escape *me*.

Not until I find out who did this to her.

I leap forward, hooking my fingers through her

inner elbow, snatching her back, she tumbles into me, unsteady on her feet. I grip her chin, angle her head back, she shakes her head, trying to get out of my hold, but my arm's around her waist, my other on her face, holding her still. She has no choice but to look up at me.

"Poppy," I say lowly, trying to keep my anger in check. "Who did this to your face?"

Her scowl is etched into every feature, but her eyes glisten with tears that threaten to break me. Tell the rest of them to fuck themselves and let me keep her, protect her, *from them.*

I'm so fucked up.

I. Am. So. Fucked. Up.

She scoffs loudly, even though the sound cracks in her throat, "This is a joke," she scoffs, her finger stabbing at my chest. "Lynx," she clarifies, "but then, I'm sure you already knew that, seen the videos, the pictures."

I blink, brow pinching, "What the fuck are you talking about?"

She laughs, loud and deep, shaking her head, snatching her chin from my hold, "Don't pretend like you don't know, and then look at me like you *care,*" that last word curls off of her tongue like she's spitting venom. "You're all done with me, Lynx delivered the message when he smashed my head into a wall, and you're here for what? Just to further the mindfuck? Is that what this is?"

I blink again, cracked lips parted, mouth dry. There's no way Lynx would hurt her like that, she looks like she's gone ten rounds in the ring. I shake my head, words of defense for him on my tongue. I swallow, open my mouth to speak, but the words die as she hefts her jacket back up her shoulder, straightening her bag straps.

"Stay away from me," she trembles as she says it, something more than hurt in her words, a scary tremor of fear there too.

I release her, stepping back, looking at her without really seeing anything, because she's telling me the truth. She's telling me the truth and my best friend fucked her up. He *bruised* her.

Poppy's gone when my ears finally stop ringing, my heart a dull thud in my chest, an ache rumbling in the rest of me. I don't know what to think, there's really nothing but shock burrowing inside my marrow as I take empty steps towards Flynn's office. My mind a mess, I don't knock, letting myself inside, drop into the leather chair opposite his desk.

I look up at him, blinking like I'm not really sure I'm even here. His lips twist up into a slow smirk, hands clasping behind his head of black curly hair, blue eyes flashing in the dark as he leans all the way back in his chair.

"Ah, she got to you too, didn't she?"

Bennett

I t's been a long fucking day in the office, and I'm still in my shirt -sans tie- pressed slacks and dress shoes. I toss my suit jacket over an empty bar stool, sliding up to sit on the one to its left. Lifting my hand up at the bartender, I signal for my usual.

Graves is dead, as it usually is on a Friday night when there's a frat party happening. I'm not a college kid anymore, but I was once, and there's something comforting about drinking here after a shit day at work.

Drumming my fingers against the sticky bar top, a glass of bourbon is placed down in front of me, no coaster, no napkin beneath, just the glass straight on the wood.

That's why I like this place, there's nothing fancy about it, there's no pretenses, anyone that walks in can feel comfortable because there's nothing to make you feel inferior. And I've felt that way a lot of my life.

Even now, sitting in the top office of a sixty-floor building I own everyday, I don't always feel good enough. I've worked fucking hard to get to where I am, I've had to do some less than legal shit to get here too, but the point is, I did get here.

It's for my dad, my mom, all of this is for them, my brother. To protect them.

I would, and do, do anything to protect my family, that extends to my three other brothers too, no blood is shared between us, but that means nothing. Our bond is something else. Other level.

The final step has always been to destroy the man who tore apart my family, and now, even that ball's rolling. In the form of the slouched woman at the opposite end of the bar.

Poppy slumps against the far wall, ass barely hanging on to the cracked, leather cushioned stool, face propped up on her curled fist, elbow atop the bar. She swirls a short black straw around in her glass of melted ice, staring at it like it holds all the answers to the world's problems. The bartender places another drink down in front of her, a subtle dip of her chin is her acknowledgement, but she doesn't move to touch it right away.

I watch her slowly make her way through three more drinks after that, as I remain on my first. The place is still dead, no one sits between us on the seven empty seats available, until the door opens at my back as I'm sipping my second bourbon. Still watching her without her seeing me as icy wind whips through the bar, cooling my back, the door banging shut with the arctic wind howling beyond.

The guy that enters passes at my back, like he knows his intended destination before he even stepped foot in the place. I watch with narrowed eyes as he sits down on the stool directly beside Poppy, who doesn't so much as flinch at his sudden appearance. He turns fully towards her, dipping his face close, and my hand tightens around my glass as I watch them.

She doesn't push him away, ask him to move, she doesn't seem to make a sound as the guy speaks to her, something I can't hear over the low humming music. But then the guy gets up, steps back, and Poppy, her eyes on his, head still resting on her fist, she sits up, wobbles to her feet. Using his forearm for balance, they walk towards the hallway that leads to the restrooms.

I squeeze my glass so hard it shatters in my hand. I don't even feel it, the jagged shards piercing my skin, the blood running down the inside of my wrist, soaking into the cuff of my white button up. I think of what she's doing, who he is, why they're together.

My feet are moving before my brain has a chance to conjure anything else, like images of Poppy fucking some random guy, sucking off some random guy. *Kissing* some random guy.

I'm going to murder him.

Her.

Both of them.

I storm down the hallway, slamming my palm against the women's restroom door with an audible crack as it ricochets off the tile.

"Get. *Out.*" The words rip off of my tongue like a bullet out of a gun, "Now," I growl it, my chest rumbling, my eyes narrowed in on the back of the guy where he crowds Poppy by the washbasin.

He turns to face me, multiple baggies of pills and powders in his hand, and like a deer caught in head-lights, he freezes, lips parting, mouth opening and closing, wordlessly, like a gasping fish.

"Get the fuck out," I bark and the kid tucks tail and runs.

I breathe in deep, trying not to see red, trying not to say anything. If Poppy wants to ruin her life with drugs, I should let her get on with it, saves me a fucking job if she destroys herself. But that isn't going to lead to satisfaction at knowing *I'm* the one respon-sible for it. Fucking up the daughter of the man I intend to ruin. I need my revenge.

Poppy hasn't moved, her back to the basin, baggie in one hand, phone in the other, one that's lit up and buzzing in her palm. It's as though she doesn't even notice I'm here as she fumbles with the phone, seem-ingly panicked. Her thumb and fingers swiping over the screen with no direction, and I'm assuming she was attempting to hang up on whoever it is because when she answers the call, on speaker, nonetheless, her eyes are so wide, they look like they might burst in their sockets.

"Poppy?" a man's voice rumbles on the other end, the deep British baritone filling the tiled room. Poppy shakes then, like she's *scared* and then the man continues. "Poppy!" the voice snaps, "I have been calling you for the last two fucking days! Dr. Soren says he has not heard from you since you touched down in fucking Texas! When will you get it through your thick skull, girl, you need to do as you're told or you're going straight back to Briarmoor. Do I make myself clear, young lady?"

A brow arches on my head, Poppy's gaze down, hair hiding her face, those fucking eyes I see inside my head when I lie in bed at night, hidden beneath her bangs. I find myself stepping closer when her body trembles, and she doesn't say anything, I'm not even sure if she can. She crushes the baggie of pills inside her other hand, fingers blanching, nails puncturing her palm with little crescent shape indents.

"POPPY?!" the man bellows, "are you listening to me? And, for the love of god, take your goddamn pills! If I get one more notification about you missing pick up at that pharmacy, I'm going to go into cardiac arrest!"

She flinches, and I'm striding across the room, snatching the phone, my eyes on hers as I say, "I'm sorry, Mr. Carrington, Poppy can't come to the phone right now, but I'll be sure to pass on your message."

Without waiting to hear his response, I end the call, slip her phone into my pants pocket and my palms are on her cheeks, my bloodied hand smearing her in red.

"Poppy, did you take any of what that guy gave you?" I angle her head back, flicking my dark eyes between hers, the ones that haunt my dreams, lilac ringed in blue-gray, "Lollipop?"

She blinks, lashes fluttering over blown pupils, nostrils flaring, like she's breathing me in, filling her lungs with *me* and something strong flits through me. Possessiveness hits deep in my gut as her eyes roll slowly in their sockets, up onto me, and her lips part, brow furrowing.

"Bennett?"

The way my chest heaves with the sound of my name on her tongue plays tug of war with my insides, I don't know what to do about it either. This loss of control. Because one minute I'm cradling her cheeks, the next, I'm lifting her up onto the basin, stepping between her parted thighs, angling her face *just so* to get a better look at the purple bruising on her face.

"What the fuck is this?" I spit, the rage brewing over hearing that phone call now morphing into something worse.

"Oh, stoppp, you just wanna hurt me," she swats at my hand on her jaw, trying to get me to let her go, but she's so fucking sloppy, she misses me completely. "You're all the same."

My jaw ticks, nostrils flaring at the strength of

liquor on her breath, but I know how much she drank, I watched her.

"All the same? I'm the same as who?"

"Your brother," she squeezes the words out like they hurt her to say, and she must see something in my expression that gives away my shock because she attempts to shake her head as an invisible knife plunges into my gut. "I dunno why you all look so surprised."

"Who's *you all*? Poppy, look at me," I shake her in my hold, forcing her lolling head to rest in my hand. "Who knows about this?"

She looks at me then. Lazy blinks of heavy lids over bloodshot lilac eyes, her lips curl up on one side, but it doesn't look anything like a real smile.

"Everyone," she whispers and the knife in my gut twists.

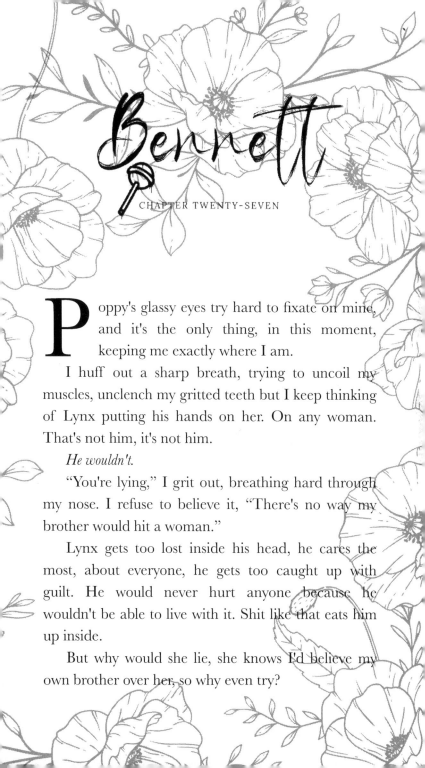

Bennett

CHAPTER TWENTY-SEVEN

Poppy's glassy eyes try hard to fixate on mine, and it's the only thing, in this moment, keeping me exactly where I am.

I huff out a sharp breath, trying to uncoil my muscles, unclench my gritted teeth but I keep thinking of Lynx putting his hands on her. On any woman. That's not him, it's not him.

He wouldn't.

"You're lying," I grit out, breathing hard through my nose. I refuse to believe it, "There's no way my brother would hit a woman."

Lynx gets too lost inside his head, he cares the most, about everyone, he gets too caught up with guilt. He would never hurt anyone because he wouldn't be able to live with it. Shit like that eats him up inside.

But why would she lie, she knows I'd believe my own brother over her, so why even try?

"Whatever," she slurs out, shimmying closer to the edge of the washbasin, intending to escape me, but all that does is put her flush with my hips.

She blinks as she feels it, slow realization of what it is pressing solidly between her legs has me hating my fucking self.

"Oh," it's this soft, whistling little sound she exhales through her teeth.

Her light eyes flick down to where my raging erection throbs in protest against the tight confines of my pants. I grit my teeth to the point of grinding them into dust, watching her face. Her head sways just a little on her neck, her blinks slow, she glances down, looking at the sliver of space between us. I don't move, don't try to hide it, even though I know I should.

She blinks again, finally dragging her eyes back up to mine. This time there's no smile, no confusion in her eyes, it's like she sees me, and I don't fucking like it, but I can't look away.

"Does your dad always shout at you like that?" she flinches so hard, she grinds her cunt along the length of my cock and we both freeze.

She swallows at the same time I do. Our chests heave in unison, her tits brushing my pecs, the heat of her cunt seeping through the layers of fabrics separating us, sinking into my cock in the same way I'd quite like to sink it into her.

I feel out of my depth, out of my mind, my heart

thudding so hard in my chest it feels as though it's going to break free of my bones.

"Why'd you care?" she shrugs one shoulder with the question, a frown line nestling between her dark brows, as though no one's ever done that before.

Cared.

Shrugging it off as nothing, even though it definitely feels like something, I tut, "Just… humor me?"

She glances over my shoulder, clamping her mouth shut, but her jaw has a mind of its own as she struggles to keep control of it. Still, I wait, not pushing, I'll stand here all fucking night if I have to. I've got nowhere else I'd rather be.

That's what hits me like a bullet to the goddamn heart.

This is *exactly* where I want to be right now, of anywhere in the world, I want to be right here. In this dank little restroom with this fucked up girl in this old shitty bar.

I already have everything I thought I wanted, I don't need anything but my boys.

I didn't think.

I don't think.

I look into the eyes of this girl as she finally draws them back to mine, my hands on either side of her thighs on the washbasin, my blood on her cheek. I don't even feel it, the gash in my palm, cuts along the insides of my fingers from the shattered glass. I just look at her, staring into her wide eyes, seeing the tremble in her chin, I hate it, that look. A look my younger brother has worn so many fucking times.

Hopelessness.

I swore I'd never walk away if I saw that look on another face again.

That I'd do something about it if I did.

Possessiveness is like a punch to the face, a kick to the solar plexus, because it hits me all at once, making me see stars. All I see in her big eyes is pain, like my brother's pain, and I don't know what to do about it.

She's derailing my plans as quickly as I make them. Knocking down my walls as quickly as I build them. Bulldozing through the carefully constructed bricks of her own downfall and she doesn't even know it.

But that's the point isn't it? She doesn't know it. She doesn't know anything. She doesn't know why Lynx broke it off with her, she doesn't know what she did, she doesn't understand anything.

She would have been five.

No good can come from this, *absolutely* no good can come from this, and yet, it's the liquor I blame as my mouth crashes into hers.

She surrenders to me with zero hesitation, my bloody hand sinking into the crown of her hair, clutching her to me. She moans into my mouth, lips parting, my tongue plunges between her teeth, quick, full licks over her tongue. Her hands fist in my shirt, clenching the cotton tight between her fingers, she wrenches me into her with the same savagery I drag her in towards me.

We clash like fuel and flame. Explosive. I dominate our kiss, sucking on her tongue, biting her mouth, bruising her skin with my fingers digging into her spine, pulling on her hair. Her soft, breathy whimpers funnel into my mouth and I greedily swallow them down. Inhale her scent, smelling her soft skin, creamy and buttery beneath the sharp tang of liquor.

Smoothing my hand around from her lower spine, sweeping it up her belly beneath her loose shirt, I cup her tit, flicking my thumb over the taut point of her nipple through the rough lace of her bra. She groans louder, arching her neck, her back, pushing herself into me, my hand. I flex my fingers in her soft flesh, then yank the cup down, dipping in to free her breast, holding down the fabric with the heel of my hand.

Breaking the kiss, I lean back away from her, fondling her tit, pinching her nipple. I watch her throat bob as she drops her head back on her shoulders, hair swishing along her lower spine. Wrenching my fist from her hair, I feel wildly out of control, slamming my splayed hand over her chest, her shoulder blades connecting with the cold surface of the mirror. She shivers, feeling it through her thin shirt, crown of her skull knocking at the reflective glass where I force her back.

I loom over her, her chest heaving, my hands coming to her outer thighs, smoothing up and down the rough denim of her black jeans, fingers pausing on the tops of her knees. I bite my lower lip, watching her eyes flutter open, dropping in their sockets to look down at me.

Deftly, I flick open my pants, releasing the tight material imprisoning my cock. Those lilac-gray-blue eyes on my hands the entire time. I'm slow with it, waiting for her to kick me away, to tell me no. Watching her face, watching her watch me, seeing her reaction. But I don't want to take this slow, I can't, desperate to get inside of her.

In a flurry of unconscious movement, I'm tearing at her jeans, ripping them down her legs, yanking them off of one leg along with her underwear and boot, hearing it thud to the floor as I wrap her leg around me. Neither one of us really notices though because I'm surging inside of her in one quick punch of my hips. Stilling us both at the sudden intrusion with deep synchronized groans.

It's animal, the deep grumbling sound that rips free from my throat as I draw my dick out of her, look down at it glistening between us with her arousal, only my crown still secure inside of her opening. And I can feel her clamping down around me, her walls working to suck me back in.

"Look at us," I grit out. "Look at where we're joined," I huff out, clenching my teeth to avoid coming right away.

She's so hot and tight and *right*.

Wrong…

Everything about this is wrong, wrong, wrong.

Poppy's supposed to be our enemy, the object of my obsession to ruin her father, but here, in this moment, my cock in her cunt, she's something else entirely. And I don't know how I'm ever going to claw my way back from this.

"Fuck, you feel so good. Look at us, Poppy."

She whimpers when she looks. My hand still firmly planted on her chest, keeping her back to the mirror. Her hands curling over the edge of the counter, knuckles prodding at the front of my thighs, she glances down her body, seeing where we're joined, before flicking those haunting eyes back up to my face. And as they connect with mine, I thrust back in, eliciting a groan from both her and me.

And I'm possessed.

I don't think of anything else as my hips piston, cock pounding into her over and over, holding her still, a leg curled around my waist, heel of her foot digging into my ass. Her heart thudding beneath the palm of my hand, just as hard as mine is.

I watch my slick cock disappear inside of her as far as it can get, and her pussy squeezes, her hips rolling, grinding herself against my pelvic bone, coating my skin with her arousal.

Her quiet cries, whimpers, her fingers of one hand stretched out to touch my skin, I watch her face, eyes dazed with lust, lips parted. She stares at me, looking at me, *seeing* me, and it makes my stomach flip.

In a frantic rhythm of hard, brutal thrusts, muscles crunching and rolling with every smack of my hips, my thumb rubs vicious circles over her swollen clit. With a short, breathy wail escaping through her clenched teeth, she climaxes.

And not a moment later, her muscles so tight it's hard to push through, I start to come, realizing too late that I'm still inside of her, I quickly pull out of her, fisting my pulsing cock, coating her pussy and inner thighs with the last of my release.

My eyes squeeze shut, head dropping forward, hand leaving her chest, I sweep my fingers up her neck, resting them against her face, my thumb on her chin. Trying to catch my breath, get my bearings.

Opening my eyes, I look up, her chest heaving, cheeks flushed, but then she glances down, a small crease forming between her brows.

"Poppy?" I breathe out raggedly, a look I do not fucking like starting to form on her face.

A shuddery breath whistles out of her, her face paling. She shakes her head, wincing as she looks down at herself. I tuck myself away, drag her closer with my hands on her hips, sitting her up from the mirror.

"Lollipop?"

Throat rolling with a hard swallow, her eyes slam shut, and even when she opens them, she doesn't look at me, "Please don't call me that," it's a barely audible whisper, but it's like a sledgehammer to the sternum. "I want to stand up," the words shudder, her breathing uneven.

Gritting my teeth, I take a step back, "Let me just-" I rake a hand through my dark hair. "Let me just clean you up first, okay?" I'm gentle with my words and I don't know why because it's her, this fucking girl, this isn't supposed to be happening.

She shakes her head, still not looking at me, "It's okay, I got it."

She slips from the counter with a pinched expression, and it's like the petals of a flower closing, the way she shutters herself. Not bothering to wipe my cum off of her, she shoves her leg back through her jeans, foot into her boot. Deft fingers work her jeans, and she runs her hands over the crown of her head, smoothing the wild hair in the back.

When she's done, my jaw cracking with the pressure on my molars from gritting my teeth so hard, she knots her hands in front of her, and all I can think about is my cum soaking into her panties, her jeans, the rest of it inside of her...

I don't know what to say, I don't know what to do, and I always know what to do.

This was a colossal mistake.

I fucked up.

I'm fucked up.

"Lolli-"

"That shouldn't have happened," she says sharply, admonishment in her voice that I don't really feel like is aimed at me. "Oh my god," the words are whispered, hateful, devastation fills the room like a sudden tsunami. "I'm so sorry," she whispers, and honestly, I don't know who she's talking to now. "So, so stupid," she hisses it and before I can even register what happens, her open hand comes to the side of her head, heel of her palm slamming into her temple, once, twice, three times.

"Poppy, Poppy, Poppy, stop," I rush forward, closing the small gap, grabbing her wrist away from her face, the other coming up to pummel my chest, and I let her, watching her face screw up with something like devastation, a choked, raspy cry lunging out of her mouth.

"You're Lynx's brother," she chokes on my brother's name, a sob catching in her throat. "You're his brother." Her fist thumps against my chest once more, but it's lost its strength, her fist slipping down, knuckles curling into my abs. "You're his brother, and I'm just a fucked up druggie who can't keep her legs closed."

I wrench her into my chest, banding my arms around her tightly, protectively, possessively.

Like she's mine.

That's when she sobs, and as much as I hate to admit it to myself, it breaks me.

Raiden

"**K**ING!" my team mate Landon bellows my name, I can hear him perfectly, even over the roaring crowd, five thousand fans screaming as I push forward. Carving through the ice as we pass the puck between us, Lan passes to Lynx, Lynx to Hudson, back to me.

I don't keep track of the score, I don't know if we're winning, losing, I'm just moving, muscles surging, blood pumping, adrenaline pounding. Going with the motions, I can play hockey without thinking, my body does all the work, muscle memory driving me. Anything I can do to keep my mind from wandering back to *her*.

I clamp my teeth down harder, digging them deeper into my mouthguard until my jaw aches. I glance up to where Rex sits in the stands, brain automatically expecting to see her. Wanting. *Wishing* She isn't here. I've not seen her for over a week.

Avoided her for over a week.

The snow storm came, forcing everyone to remain inside, classes were canceled, Lynx stayed with us, stayed away from her. Yesterday was the first day back, and she didn't show. I know Lynx is heading back to their dorm tonight, and I know it's just to fuck with her.

I know he's going to be a fucking asshole.

I know I'm going to be a fucking asshole.

Lynx has taken the news the worst. Slamming every door he walks through, banging every pot, pan and piece of cutlery he's had his hands on, and fucking Rex so hard every night, not only have I had to listen to it, but I've had to watch Hendrix limp his way around the house the following mornings for an entire goddamn week.

I skate across the ice, tuning everything out except for the tap of my stick against the rink, the blades of my skates cutting through the surface.

I pass the puck to Lynx, watching him skate side by side with Hudson, Landon elbows me as he passes, tapping his helmet, telling me to get my head in the game. I can hardly bear it. Functioning like everything's normal when nothing is even fucking remotely normal. Nothing is okay.

After everything I confessed to her.

Too soon.

I miss her.

The way she makes me feel.

And yet, I'm here acting exactly like everything is okay.

Before I can think about what it is I'm doing, I'm skating off the ice, Coach Taylor screaming my name at my back, but I hardly even hear it. Stripping my gear as I make my way back to the locker room. I toss it all into my locker space, roughly pulling on sweats, sneakers, stick clattering to the floor, and then I'm out of the arena.

The snow is melting, but the wind isn't going anywhere. Bitter slaps of it hit my sweat slicked face, hands fisted at my sides, I stride across campus, feet taking me where they need to fucking go. Instinct, the only thing driving me.

My fingers curl over the top of the doorframe when I get to my destination. Only the wood of the door between us, separating me from her. Glancing down, there's a soft glow coming from beneath the door, but not much else, I listen through the wood, waiting to hear shuffling, movement, footsteps. Anything.

"She's sleeping," a woman's voice sounds at my back.

Without moving away from the door, fingers still tight to the frame, I glance over my shoulder, the door of the room opposite is open, a tall, attractive, athletically built girl stands in the frame in workout gear. Dark brown skin sweat slicked, thick pile of braids twisted up high on her head. She runs her dark gaze down my body, her upper lip twisting like she finds me severely lacking, and then she pops her hip, lifting a brow.

"You're not good enough for her," she states, like *A,* I give a flying fuck about what she thinks, and *B,* like she knows my girl better than me.

Fuck that.

"Yeah?" I toss back, hatred in my narrowed gaze, but the girl doesn't even shift.

"Yeah. Y'all are a bunch of fucking assholes. Leave her the hell alone. If you don't fuck off, I'll call campus security." Then she slams her fucking door so hard it makes my brain rattle inside my skull.

I keep staring at the door over my shoulder, and I can hear the girl inside, muffled voices, and I wonder if she's already calling them. That's the last thing I fucking need.

Without hesitation, applying pressure to the round, locked door knob, shoulder straining, my entire body trembles with the force I apply. Vein pulsing in my temple, tendons standing rigid in my neck, I twist the handle in the wrong direction, and with a metallic rattle and crack, the lock gives way.

I move into the room, closing the door at my back, which absolutely does not close properly anymore, I glance around in the darkened room, little stringed bulbs around the window alight. I grab the desk chair, propping it beneath the busted handle. That's when I hear the door opposite open again, holding my breath, I listen, waiting, and then the door closes, no footsteps outside in the hall.

Heart thundering in my chest, breath sails out of me, her scent in the room, my fists flexing by my sides as I stare at her.

Splayed out on her bed, beneath a thick comforter, a dark coloured blanket, her arms on her pillow, curled loosely around her head. Messy tangles of dark, gold-streaked hair fan across the white pillow, her chin tilted up and to the side.

In sleep, she looks peaceful. I've watched her before, like this, that first night we met, her deep, even breaths puffing across my bare chest, her small hand splayed over my heart. I could barely sleep, even with my brothers on her other side, Rex spooning her back, Lynx on his other side, their combined weight pushing her against me closer. I wanted to touch her again, her face, her hair, her delicate features, her soft skin, round breasts, but instead, it was as though I could hardly breathe. Having her in my bed, between me and two of the closest people to me, my brothers.

We'd never shared a woman before, not for more than running a train on some sorority girl at a house party once. And that's where that ended, the girl told everyone she was dating all of us and the whole thing was a fucking mess, that's why we stopped. I didn't wanna fuck around with anyone, not if they were gonna run their mouths after. I don't need everyone hearing about my dick and what I do with it.

That's why I couldn't sleep.

We promised each other a girl would never come between us, and there we were, with one literally between us. And I didn't hate it.

Poppy came into our lives and in an instant of merely seeing her, I didn't want her to ever leave. Then I got her in my bed, where she burrowed beneath my skin, infected my heart and filled my head with nothing but her.

It wasn't love at first sight.

It was something else.

Something more.

And now I'm going to ruin her life.

Silently, I move closer, needing to see her, needing to be close, and it's best she doesn't see me. The vile things I could do to this beautiful girl gnaw at me like rodents feasting on my internal rot.

Looming over her, listening to her steady, even breaths, watching her chest rise and fall, so slow and deep, I know she must have been asleep for some time. I can't help but touch a strand of her hair, even tangled, it's still so silky soft, it makes me think of the rest of her. All of that pretty, pale skin, the bright blushes that hit her cheeks with a beautiful red, then travel lower, down her throat, over her chest, down her breasts.

Carnal desire rushes through me, my cock beating with my pulse as my heartrate flies higher. I can't help myself, tracing a lone finger across her open hand, knuckles against her pillow, limp fingers curling in toward her palm. My fingertip brushes across hers, each one, just a subtle touch. I stare at her chipped nails, the warm cast of light from her string bulbs around the window just enough to see her.

Her luscious lips are parted, the bottom one so heavy and thick, it almost looks like it's being dragged down. My thumb grazes over her forehead, curling around her temple, across the arch of her cheekbone, down the length of her petite nose, stopping at her cupid's bow. The defined shape of it so enticing, I want to glide my mouth over it, trace the edges with my tongue.

She sighs, this soft, breathy deep exhale, a tiny satisfying sound threading through her lips. I still, feeling the rush of breath against my hand, sending goosebumps up the length of my arm. My gaze drifts down from her face, over her chest covered with the comforter, and I can't help it, I can't suppress the urge to see her.

Fingers curling over the top edge of the comforter, I slowly roll it down, revealing her tiny, white tank top. Her nipples puckering beneath it at the exposure to the cold air, my mouth salivating to warm them with my tongue.

I keep pulling down the sheets and blankets, flicking my eyes between her body and her face, ensuring I don't wake her. I need to be close to her right now, but she can't know that. I want to be soft with her. I want to comfort her, to rock her in my arms, to wipe away her tears, to tell her I-

Stopping my thoughts, I shake my head, moving my gaze back down her body, the dip of her belly, shadow of her navel, and then the small cotton panties low on the jut of her hip bones. I suck in a small breath through my teeth, seeing her like this, exposed to me in the darkness, like I'm the monster that just crawled out from beneath her bed, waiting for a moment exactly like this.

I flip the covers off of her, only one foot still hidden by the sheets, and stare at the rest of her. The long, long length of her smooth legs, the delicate lines of her floral tattoos from her feet, up her shins, over her knees and thighs. I want to trace every inch of her with my tongue. Paint her with a glistening trail of my saliva.

Mark her.

Claim her.

Own her.

My fingers dance over her thigh, my eyes on her face, peaceful and calm. My cock thumps in rapid succession of my heartbeat, a cold bead of sweat running down my spine.

I shouldn't be here.

I don't even know why I came.

Right in the middle of a game, abandoning my team, my brothers. All for this.

What would I have done if she were awake?

Short tank top rolled up above her navel, I blow out a breath as my wandering fingers glide across the low waistband of her underwear, and she moves. Making me freeze, study her face, watch for every twitch, every flutter of her lashes, but there's nothing, just a small shift of her hips as though she's inviting me in.

I trail my middle finger down the length of her covered pussy, but the thin cotton between us can't hide the blinding heat between her thighs. Head dropping back, I clench my teeth, squeeze my eyes closed tight, fisting my hands by my sides, trying to get control of myself, but then she shifts again, my eyes going wide, I blink, looking back down at her as she spreads her legs wider. A shiver from the cold room pricks goosebumps across her flesh, and I can't stop myself, I touch her again. Pressing a little harder against her slit, tracing and teasing the line of her folds through the fabric.

I breathe in deep, holding the scent of her in my lungs, and let my fingers travel, smoothing a little firmer at the inside of her thigh, along the seam of her panties, always going back to her pussy.

I rub her through the fabric, soft, gentle strokes of my fingers, pushing in a little deeper, fingertips forcing the cotton between her folds. I stare at her face, watching in case she wakes, but she's serene in heavy sleep, completely unaware, or so I think.

A small patch of wetness starts to form, glistening

on my fingers through the thin, white cotton, only encouraging me more, urging me on. I touch my thumb to her clit and as though I send a bolt of electricity through her with my touch, her hips kick, back arching. I don't stop, even as she starts to turn onto her side, facing the window, clamping my fingers between her legs, my hand between her thighs, her back to me.

She sighs as I loom over her, my other hand pressed to the bed for balance, the length of my forearm grazing her spine. I keep stroking her through her underwear, biting down on my bottom lip as her arousal coats my fingers through the material.

A low groan rumbles in my chest, molars grinding together to lock the sound inside. I pull my fingers away from her, my breathing ragged, I stare at the side of her face, one hand beneath her head, the other planted on the mattress in front of her face.

Hand tracing over her outer thigh, my finger slips beneath the leg of her panties, curling beneath to pull the fabric to one side. I hook my ring finger in them, curling the material away, my knuckles brushing over her soaked flesh, exposing her. My groan rips free, and she moves again, rolling back onto her back, a small crease forming between her brows, eyes tightening.

Teasing her folds, I can't stop touching her, but if I don't do something, she's going to wake up, and I don't think I want her too. I'm not ready to face her.

I'm not ready to face myself with her yet.

Because everything is different now, even if she doesn't understand it.

I lean over her as she twists her head, still asleep but more aware, bringing my lips to her ear, "Shh, go back to sleep, Princess, you're safe."

And just like that, her chest inflates with a slow, deep breath, the crease between her brows smoothing out.

She trusts me.

Even in sleep.

And I hate my fucking self.

But I don't stop.

Circling my slick fingers over her clit, I press my thumb to her entrance, gathering the evidence of her arousal by smoothing it around her tight hole. Then I switch, thumb pressing to her swollen clit, I glide two fingers down the length of her cunt, my eyes captured by her peaceful face, I plunge them inside of her.

Her closed eyes tighten, lashes fluttering, parted lips releasing a soft breath.

Like a man possessed, I fuck my fingers into her, slow and careful, her pussy releasing more and more fluid, lubricating my fingers with her slick. Her heat is like fire, and I want to get burned, so I keep going. Thumb rough on her clit, fingers getting harder as they push through the slowly tightening muscles of her pussy.

"Fuck, I wanna be inside of you," I whisper

beneath my breath, leaning back over her, smoothing my free hand across her pretty face. Bringing my nose tip to tip with hers, "Good girl," I hush over her mouth, unable to help myself.

I swallow, glancing down the length of her body, watching the movement of my hand, breathing her in, the creamy, buttery scent of her mixing with the sharp tang of her arousal. I breathe deep, watching my hand thrusting between her thighs, her warm breath against my cheek. I let my eyes close, enjoying the feel of her wet, sloppy cunt gripping my fingers, sucking me inside.

"King?" my eyes snap open, but my hand keeps moving, fingers thrusting in and out of her harder and harder.

"Go back to sleep," I tell her, deep voice rough and gravelly.

I feel her tighten around me further, a shuddery exhale leaves her, as a stuttered one of my own is drawn in. I don't look at her even though I'm dying to.

"Raiden?" my eyes slam shut, hearing her so unsure, calling me by my name, like we're close, like we're more.

"Go back to sleep," I tell her again, feeling her stillness beneath me, my fingers working like they're a separate entity.

But in this moment, under the cover of darkness,

where no one can see us. Theres no one to witness my sin in the shadows.

My head twists on my neck, bringing us nose to nose. Lips aligning with hers, my eyes on pretty lilac ones, we both suck in a sharp breath. Her heavy lashes flutter, fanning across the top of her cheekbones, her tongue flicking out to wet her lips, catching mine as she does. My hand flies up, fingers digging into her cheeks, the juncture between thumb and forefinger squeezing the curve of her chin.

"Shhh, this is all a dream. You're just dreaming, Princess," I whisper over her mouth, "Let me look after you, go back to sleep," she gasps softly, saying nothing and I keep fucking her with my fingers.

Our breaths hard, she holds my gaze as I curl my fingers inside her, grinding the tips against the spot that quickly drives her wild. Poppy arches her neck as much as I allow her, spreading her legs wider, the sloppy, wet sucking sounds of her cunt as my fingers drive in and out of her have me in a frenzy.

"Raiden," she pants, my name on her tongue, her lips brushing mine.

I can hardly breathe, feeling her tightening around me, her walls clenching tighter and tighter. Her thighs begin to tremble, her breath hard against my mouth, and I can't hold back any longer.

"You want this, Princess? You want me fucking you with my fingers? Is it making you feel good?" she

323

thrashes in my hold, and it's not in rejection. "Your greedy little cunt is sucking on my fingers so hard, you're gonna fucking break them. I won't be able to play hockey for the rest of the season, you want that, huh? Me all to yourself." She groans then, her hands finally, *finally* coming to my shoulders, her nails biting into my skin. "Mmm, you like that, Princess? My fingers making this pretty little pussy gush. So fucking sloppy for me."

I grunt as her nails grip harder, my cock impossibly hard, I'm lightheaded. And I can't take anymore, can't wait, can't resist. My mouth crashes to hers, crushing her lips to her teeth as I add a third finger, two already enough, but three, three is way too much. She whimpers against my lips at the stretch, opening her mouth and I immediately sweep my tongue inside, tangling it with hers.

Fingers curling, thumb menacing as I circle her clit with it, she tightens impossibly hard around me, and I tear my lips away, breathing hard over her mouth.

"Beg me," I breathe, eyes flicking between hers. "Fucking beg me to let you come."

And like a dream, she chants, "King, *Raiden*, please, please, *please*, let me come."

"Good fucking girl," I rasp, biting her lips, licking into her mouth.

Poppy cries out in my mouth, and I greedily swallow every sound she feeds me as she comes. Her cunt gripping, pulsing, tightening, pulling and pushing as I continue to fuck my fingers into her. She pants into my mouth, our chests heaving, I slow my movements, slipping my ring finger free to continue lazily stroking her inner walls. She trembles around me, thighs shaking, breaths quick, heart thudding hard.

Our kiss is slow. Lazy laps of my tongue over hers, stroking, twirling, caressing. I kiss her like I'll never get to again.

Carefully, I pull my fingers free, separating our mouths, I straighten her panties, covering her back up with the comforter. Her eyes are open, heavy lidded, and I can't hold her gaze any longer. I peck her lips, release my hold on her face, smoothing my fingers down over her eyes, and she closes them like I need her too.

I smooth her hair back from her face, press my lips to her forehead.

"You're sleeping, Poppy," I whisper against her warm skin, pressing the words into her flesh.

She sighs, her breaths deeper, I straighten from where I lean over her. Staring down at her pretty face, tension between her brows.

"Sweet dreams, Princess," she doesn't hear me as I leave the room, pulling the door closed as well as I can.

I wander a little way down the hall, making sure I can still see her door, I stop, kick a foot up against the wall, licking and sucking on fingers that taste of her, and keep watch until Lynx comes back.

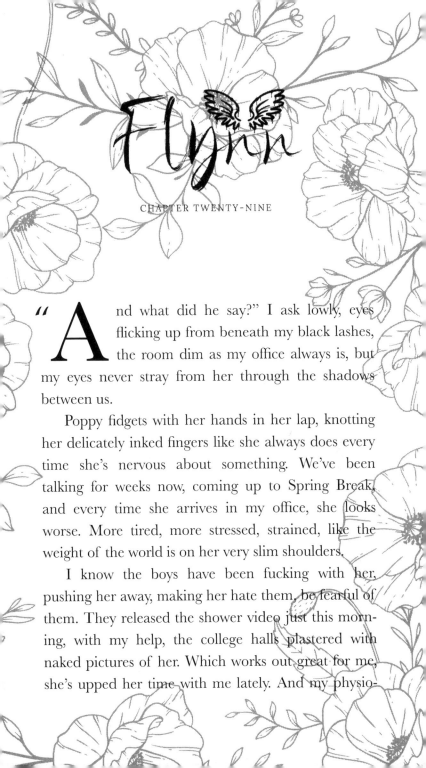

Flynn

CHAPTER TWENTY-NINE

"And what did he say?" I ask lowly, eyes flicking up from beneath my black lashes, the room dim as my office always is, but my eyes never stray from her through the shadows between us.

Poppy fidgets with her hands in her lap, knotting her delicately inked fingers like she always does every time she's nervous about something. We've been talking for weeks now, coming up to Spring Break, and every time she arrives in my office, she looks worse. More tired, more stressed, strained, like the weight of the world is on her very slim shoulders.

I know the boys have been fucking with her, pushing her away, making her hate them, be fearful of them. They released the shower video just this morning, with my help, the college halls plastered with naked pictures of her. Which works out great for me, she's upped her time with me lately. And my physiological mind fuck sessions with her are just the cherry on top of the cake.

I love breaking apart pretty things.

Those boys have violent plans for this girl, they're going to push her so much further, she might not make it back after tonight, at least, not in one piece anyway. She'll give up trying to make Texas work for her, and run home to her daddy. Broken, desecrated, ruined.

I don't know why she hasn't left yet, considering the mean shit they've been doing to her. Most of it's petty, well, all except for Lynx. He's really stepped up his fucking game, even I was surprised by.

Speaking of which, "Tell me about the door," I encourage quietly, switching my question, watching for the flinch I know is coming.

She's been sitting in this room with me for the last six weeks, an hour a day, five days a week, because that's one of her enrollment conditions.

But tonight's different.

It's Saturday.

And *she* asked to see *me*.

She flinches, just as I expected, at my question. A tremble tearing through her core, shoulders twitching, she shakes her head, sucks in an almost silent breath that I'd miss if I weren't paying incredible attention. It's as though I can feel it in my own chest, sharp and uncomfortable.

I am fixated on her, on playing with her. Her

328

every breath, every sound, every word, every fucking second of her existence, I watch her. Through camera feeds when I can't follow her around campus. In person the rest of the time. She is my newest obsession and I've been holding back, staying unseen, but tonight, tonight, it's as though she knew I was there, specifically *for her.*

She flicked that addicting lilac gaze over her shoulder, wind whipping strands of her long hair across her pale face, her eyes locked on mine, her head tilted, and she mouthed my name like a question. My feet moved me towards her across the quad like she tugged on an invisible tether, as though she opened her demonic book of tricks and summoned me with not much more than a blink.

I think of her voice, the way she rasped her question, *'May I see you later today? If you have time for me, Mr. Marshall.'*

I bite down on my teeth, jaw cracking as my molars squeak, my dick rising to fucking attention, once again.

"Poppy?" I clear my throat, cocking my head.

"Right," she whispers, drawing my eye to the length of her pale throat as it rolls with her dry swallow.

"The door?"

"It was nothing," she says quickly, my lips pulling into a slow smirk, I drop my gaze, dipping my chin to hide my reaction.

"Somebody removed your dorm room door, and you didn't report it to anyone. That doesn't feel like nothing to me."

"It was just a prank, ya know, 'cause I'm new," she laughs awkwardly.

"You can tell me what happened, who did it. Nothing leaves this room," I fold my arms over the desk, watching her continue to fidget.

She looks at me then, dead in the eye, "Really, Mr. Marshall-"

"Flynn."

"Really, *Flynn*, it was just a prank. I thought it was funny."

She absolutely did not think it was funny. The same way that my little brother, Raiden, despite snapping the door handle, also, did not find Lynx's removal of the entire door *funny*.

"Okay," I relent, a small smile on my face. "And what about tonight, the reason you wanted to see me, you wanted to talk?"

"Not really," she responds quickly, her cheeks glowing red, she stutters, "I mean, well, what I mean is, that, um, well, I-"

"Whatever it is, Poppy, that's what I'm here for," I interrupt her stuttering, wetting my lips.

I smile again, this calculated warm pull of my mouth that has people spilling some of their most terrifying secrets. I have blackmail on most attendees at this college, staff and students alike.

Chin tucked, her eyes lifting, gaze ensnaring my own, she licks her lips, tucking a strand of hair behind her ear, before quickly recovering it. Another habit I've taken note of, hiding her ears, like she dislikes them, they stick out a little and I want to see them more, makes me want to take scissors to her hair, but I have plans for that too, so I probably shouldn't. Although, she could probably pull off a pixie cut if she wanted to.

"I feel safe when I'm here," she whispers, the rough words drawing me back to the present. Her eyes never leave mine, like a tight cord of tension readying to snap, my spine straightens, my breath held, waiting, "With you."

It's as though something inside of me implodes and then explodes, little, itty bitty, gory pieces of me splattering all across the room. I sit so still I'm not sure I'm even breathing as I hold her gaze, wanting to hold her face in my hands, cover her mouth with my own, use my knife on her inner thighs, slice down her shins, curl my blade around her ankle bone.

Her chest inflates, not going back down, the tight ribbed, black fabric of her floor length dress clinging to her tits. I lick my lips, staring at her. Her cheeks are red, her throat, and I'm sure the color spreads further, down beneath the high neckline of her dress. I want to uncover it, feast on it, sink my teeth into her, take her collarbone between my canines and suck at her skin.

I suck in a breath through my teeth, cold air fills the office like a window is thrown open at my back, a chill of ice racing up my spine.

"Poppy," I say lowly, watching her watch me.

This is the first time she's really said anything about me, and it's already fucking with my head.

Lynx keeps calling her a whore, it's all I hear, the words wreaking havoc inside my skull, rattling around, picking away at each lobe of my brain, day in, day out. Poppy's only a whore in his eyes because he treated her like one, and it makes me want to shove my fist through my best friend's face.

Why couldn't I have found her first? Why did it have to be them? I wouldn't have let Bennett take her away from me. I could have done something else, hidden her from him. From them. She could have been my little secret.

Perhaps she still can.

I'm standing from the chair, rounding my desk, perching on the lip of the wood. Hands sliding down my thighs, resting on my knees. I lean in towards her, her own upper body moving in to meet mine, our chests almost brushing as she looks up at me, wide eyes, parted lips.

There is silence between us, and it's anything but uncomfortable.

"Tell me about your father, Poppy," I say quietly, needing to dig, needing to gather something on the man we're set to ruin her for, she has to give me something.

"I don't want to talk about him," she informs me quietly, but I don't have time for this.

"I do."

She gasps a little at my firm tone, the way I broker no argument, her eyes widening just a fraction as she tilts her chin up towards me.

"We aren't close," she half shrugs, lifting one shoulder, letting it drop heavily.

Our lips are so close I could devour her whole in less than point-two of a second, but I don't, holding her gaze.

"Why not?"

She squirms, dropping her gaze to her lap, her fingernails clawing at the thin skin of her inner wrists.

"Is it because he wanted a son?" I ask her, lots of rich men are only interested in a male heir, daughters are redundant spawn.

"What? No… I don't think so, he- I don't think he cares about stuff like that," she shakes her head, frowning down at her hands.

"He didn't want kids? Your mother was his mistress? You were a mistake?" I'm rapid firing questions here when I know I shouldn't be, desperation gripping my neck like a hand to the throat. "Is it because you went a little mad?"

She sucks in a sharp breath, her eyes finally snapping up to meet mine, shining and red, and not from the drugs she so often loves to take.

"Briarmoor, correct?" *I know it is, don't lie to me, baby girl.*

"How do you know about that?" she whispers, shame filling her eyes as quickly as the tears.

"I know a lot about you, Poppy. Even the stuff you tried to hide." I let that register before I confess, "I can find out most things about a person if I really want to."

Poppy says nothing, the air thick with tension, unease, her eyes flicker quickly between my own.

"But what I can't understand, Angel, is, why you were sent there in the first place, why not just rehab?" she flinches, but I keep talking, low and deep, slow, making sure my words penetrate. "You and I both know you've got more than a small problem with pills, Poppy, so why didn't he send you to rehab? Why didn't he get you help there? Why a high security psychiatric hospital?" Poppy eyes me, tears gathering heavier at her lash line, I lean closer, "What did you do, Angel?" I whisper over her mouth, sharing breath.

She swallows, her gaze never leaving mine, "I attacked a girl at my school," she breathes as though she were unprepared for the secret to spill out of her so easily, her lips brushing mine with every semi-relieved word. "She set me up, got a-" she glances away, pulling in a shuddery breath, her gaze reconnecting with mine, and I feel excitement bolt up my spine. "She got a guy to trick me into thinking he liked me, and after he took my virginity, he laughed in my face, told me it was all for some bet with this girl. So I found her, and hit her and hit her and I didn't stop, until the guy came and pulled me off of her, *protecting her*, and then I hit him too," she whispers the final words, shame swallowing her whole. She looks at me, unblinking, "And I didn't want to stop," she confesses, "I wish I hadn't," she shivers. "That's why he sent me there." She swallows, "I hate them all." Her last words are said with such bitterness that even I tremble. "So, that's why I don't want to talk about my *father*, there's nothing else to say."

I lick my lips as she looks away, turning her head to the side. I reach up, fingers splaying over her cheek, thumb pressing to her bottom lip, I turn her back to face me. Dropping my forehead against hers, breathing her in. Her breaths are heavy, her chest heaving, but she doesn't pull away from me, doesn't shrink back like she has so many times before.

She just confided in me, something real, something with substance.

"Flynn," she says cautiously, divot digging between her brows.

Whatever expression sits on my face is what's giving her this worried look, probably wondering what it is I'm doing, her wide eyes, furrowed brow, parted lips so very close to my own.

"This is a very dangerous game, Angel," I rumble, thick and deep.

Poppy eyes me, blinking those heavy black lashes over her lilac gaze, "What game, Flynn?" she whispers between us, her sweet, creamy scent filling my nostrils, infecting my brain.

My lips curl up in a smirk, eyes tightening at the corners, "Us."

She freezes, just like that, the combination of her and I is something that should never be, but we become an *us* as soon as her mouth collides with mine.

We both move, teeth clacking against each other, a hiss escaping her at the contact. My tongue thrusts between her lips, my hands gripping her biceps, her whimpers vibrate my tongue as it curls around her own. Her hands fist at the collar of my white button up shirt, pulling me closer. I force her back into the chair, pressing my knee to the arm of it, caging her in with my other between her thighs.

Lust licks through me like flames, firing me up to devour her as I groan into her mouth. She kisses me back as violently as I kiss her, biting at my lips, sucking on my tongue. Heat lashes my spine and I lift her up from the seat, my grip punishing on her arms, I flip us around, sweeping everything off of my desk, I slam her down on top. The air bursting from her lungs as I shove her back onto the cold surface.

Gathering the stretchy, ankle length fabric of her

dress in my hands, I wrench it up to her waist, bring myself back down on top of her, cupping her waist, and continue devouring her mouth with my tongue.

She grinds against me, her legs wrapping around my waist, her knees sharp in my sides, digging into my ribs. I groan into her mouth, bite down on her tongue, thrust my hips into her, the hard ridge of my rapidly growing cock placed perfectly between her thighs.

"Flynn," she gasps, the sound of my name on her tongue shooting liquid fire directly into my balls.

Nipping and sucking on my lower lip, bucking against my cock, grinding her hips into my own, she whimpers into our kiss. I rear back, hands smoothing from around her waist, down and over the jut of her hips. Hooking my fingers in the sides of her panties, her chin dipped, she stares at me down the length of her body, holding my gaze, I wrench the clingy lace down her thighs, hooking them off of her combat booted feet and bring them up to my nose. Inhaling deep, her scent drenching the fabric, arousal wetting my nose, I groan into the damp black lace.

"Flynn," she pants, my name like a fucking death knell for the both of us.

Shoving her panties into my pant's pocket, hooking her legs over my inner elbows, I lift her up, her shoulder blades, palms of her hands, crown of her head, the only parts of her still in contact with the desk. Dragging her cunt directly to my mouth, I blow over her glistening pink slit, dragging the tip of my nose over her clit. She whimpers, a soft, breathy, panting cry, and then I dig my teeth into the little swollen bud and she wails.

I huff a laugh into her cunt as I feast on her. Teeth dragging down both sides of her folds, tongue dipping inside her tight little hole, quick little prods, once, twice, before flattening it out and lapping upwards from asshole to clit. I swirl my tongue over her, sucking on every swollen part of her flesh, suckling and nipping. All of her flushed red just like I hope her cheeks are.

Lifting my head, a grin on my face, I keep close enough to her that she can feel every breath on her tender flesh where she's lifted in front of my face. Her eyes are fucking huge, pupils blown, the lilac color more blue than gray and her cheeks are bright scarlet, that crimson hue like creeping fingers dipping down her throat, stretching out beneath the fabric of her dress. The soft slope of her exposed lower stomach is flushed pink too, and I want to see more of it. *Her.*

"Show me those pretty tits, Angel," I rasp, demanding, her hands shakily moving towards the gathered black material pushed just above her navel. "I won't drop you," I reassure her, voice thick with desire, my chin wet with her as her elbows slowly lift from the table.

Her arms tremble as she carefully takes hold of the stretchy fabric, before quickly yanking it up, clamping it beneath her chin. I stare down at her like a virgin sacrifice picked out especially for me, but Poppy, Poppy stares up at me like I'm her fucking god. It's heady, the look in her eye, the *awe* etched in her petite features.

Her small, teardrop shaped breasts jiggle lightly on her chest as she slaps her hands back down to the polished wood of the desk for balance.

I groan, pressing forward once more, my lips vibrating against her cunt, a needy whine corkscrewing its way up her throat in response. I lap at her, my tongue a firm pressure over every exposed part of her, my lips suckling, tongue twisting up into her tight hole, violent little thrusts forcing through her clamping walls. I eat her like I'll never get enough, her sharp, earthy tang my newest addiction.

"Flynn, Flynn, Flynn," she chants as I worship her.

Thumbs spreading her wide, fingers splayed over her thighs, digging in, her legs trembling in the crooks of my elbows, I bite down on her clit. Easing the sting with a long, firm suck on the little bundle of nerves, she groans, long and low. Thighs quivering, she explodes on my tongue, feeding me the evidence of her arousal. Her cunt pulses, trying to suck my tongue back inside. I nibble and suck at her clit, the tip of my thumb pressing just inside her soaking entrance.

Poppy spasms in my arms, her body jerking, palms slapping at the wooden desk, head thrashing side to side as I continue to lick her, sucking up everything she gifts me into my mouth, fucking her with the tip of my thumb as she rides out her orgasm, her hips stuttering with uneven little jerks.

Slowly, I lower her back to the desk, bending over top of her, covering her with my body, she trembles, her chest heaving between us. I grip her face, squeezing her cheeks until her lips part wider, mouth open, I bite her lip, drag it from her teeth, and then I spit in her mouth. Groaning as she stares up at me, the taste of her on her own tongue.

"Swallow, Angel," I rasp, nipping her lips with each word, the top then the bottom.

Hand sliding from her chin to the front of her throat, I watch her eyes, waiting to feel the moment she swallows. My cock thick and pounding with my pulse between us, the taut fabric of my slacks wet with her juices where I lean into her. I watch her wide eyes flick between my own, unsure, anxious, and then her throat works down my saliva, the taste of *us* on her tongue as she swallows.

"Always knew you were gonna be a good girl," I grin, and it. Is. Menacing.

Poppy

CHAPTER THIRTY

F lynn's rough fingers gently tug my dress down, just enough to cover the tops of my thighs as he sits me up on the desk, stepping between my legs. I can't look at him.

Air stabs like daggers in my lungs as I heave for it, trying to catch my breath. Flynn's big hands plant down over my thighs, fingers flexing against my skin, and his extremely pale complexion makes my own very light skin look tanned in comparison. Blue veins ridge over the backs of his hands, disappearing beneath the buttoned cuffs of his white shirt, something else that makes him look even more ghostlike.

Menacing.

My mind races back to this morning momentarily, the video finally made its way into the world, and it was so much worse than just seeing me naked. They, whoever they are that filmed it, recorded the entire thing. The sounds of Lynx fucking me, the loud, choked sounds from me as he did. Then the words, crystal clear in the audio of it. Lynx ripping my heart out. The look on his face as he stormed from the bathroom. The look on my own as I stood there in shock. I think it's worse reliving it than I thought it would be.

Flynn's thick fingers move from one of my legs, hook beneath my chin, sandalwood and vanilla heavy in my nose, his scent so thick I can almost taste it on my tongue. He lifts my chin, angling my head back, arching my neck, so unless I completely close my eyes, I have no choice but to look into his.

His black hair is shaved short on the sides, left long on top. Thick, inky curls springing gently up and down on his forehead when he cocks his head, the ends just brushing over his onyx eyebrows. Sapphire blue orbs, the outer rings so dark they're almost black, are wide on mine.

Assessing.

Measuring.

Calculating.

I'm not sure what to say to my college counsellor now that he's had his face between my thighs, his tongue buried in my cunt.

"You don't belong," he whispers, my body jolting at the words, "do you, Angel?" he says nonchalantly, as though the cutting words are meant to do no such thing. "You've never really belonged anywhere before," he licks his pale pink lips, the tip of his tongue lapping over the bottom one to get another taste of me, my eyes dipping, watching. "Not even with your own family."

It's like a slap to the face. Sharp and stinging, and I suddenly don't want to be here anymore, in what I thought was a safe space, with a safe person.

But then you let him have a taste, fucking whore.

Speaking low and slow, unfeeling, "You came here because your daddy doesn't love you, can't stand you, your mother-"

Chest heaving, my hand slaps hard across his face, shocking us both as his head snaps to the side, "Don't speak about my fucking mother," I spit, anger quivering through my veins.

I shove against his abs, fingers flexing back, he grips them tightly in one of his, locking his fingers around both of my wrists, shackling them together, he holds them down, pinning them to my thigh.

"You're all alone in a big world full of dangerous people, and you don't care," Flynn says calmly, turning back to face me, not at all affected by my violence evidenced in the red handprint blooming bright on his cheek. "You just want to be normal. You want people to *think* you're normal."

I blink up at him, my bottom lip trembling, but he keeps hold of my chin, forcing me to look at him.

"You get no love at home. Shipped from school to school, nanny to nanny, and you don't fit in there either because you're not like them. You're not like anyone else and you hate it. You hate it so much that you stopped trying to fit in and turned to something that will guarantee you do, without any effort at all. You pop pills because, for just one moment, you fit, you're just like everyone else, *normal,* you're afraid of the world and all of the people in it, but the person you're frightened of the most," he licks his lips, pausing, those deep blue eyes flicking between my own before he whispers, "is you."

My eyes close, tears streaking down my face. A sob wracks my chest, shaking my core, my belly jumping with the choked sound as it erupts in my throat. I want to drop my head, but Flynn doesn't let me go. He doesn't release my hands or my chin, instead, smoothing his thumb over my quivering bottom lip, stroking his fingers over my hands where he grips them tight. But he must feel it, when the fight leaves my body, amongst the desperate sobs, because he steps closer, releasing my hands, which I don't move from my thigh, and wraps his arms around my shoulders, cradling me to his chest.

"It doesn't have to be like that, Angel," he whispers into my hair, his warm breath blowing strands of it around my face. "You can make your own family, you can be whoever you want, do whatever you want."

I cry harder, knowing that's not true at all, "I can't," I stutter out, shaking my head against his solid chest, heaving for breath, "I already ruined it all."

"You could go, leave here, start fresh somewhere new," he breathes against the crown of my head.

His lips pressing to my scalp in some semblance of a kiss, drawing me in with his touch as his words push me further and further away.

I think of Rex, of King, how they're currently making my life hell, not quite as much as Lynx, usually just mean, petty shit, calling me names, sabotaging my classes, which has been harder than the other shit, but still, I can't imagine not being near them. My head tells me to go, but my heart, as much as it hurts, tells me something else entirely.

I'm a masochist.

My gut churns, heart burning in my chest. It would be easier just to go. To run away again, but my dad holds the power, he has the paperwork from the judge that gives him rights to me even though I'm a legal adult.

The only way I could leave Briarmoor was with my dad having legal power of attorney over me, my finances, health. It's basically a muzzle and collar. A shackle.

Men with power can get anything they want with the right connections and money to accompany it.

I'll never truly be free.

Not until I'm dead.

Flynn leans back from me, looking down at me with his hands on my shoulders, my arms limp at my sides. I feel empty, hollow. He's right about everything he said, I'll never fit in anywhere. Still, I can't help thinking back to the first couple of weeks here when I thought I *did* finally fit somewhere.

Saying nothing, Flynn steps back from me, and I slip down from the desk, letting my dress fall back down over my legs. He clears his throat, but I don't look up, awkwardness filling the now stifling space.

"Thanks for seeing me," I swallow, bending forward to grab my coat.

I don't look at him as I round the chair, fingers curling over the door handle.

"I can help you get a transfer," Flynn says somewhere at my back in a tone I can't quite decipher. "Just let me know and I'll sort it."

"Right," I nod, solemnly swallowing the lump in my throat, because even after all that, even *he* doesn't want to be near me.

Lynx's words rattle through me as I leave the office.

'Fucking junkie whore.'

I think of the supporting evidence of that statement, how I like to pop pills, forget who I am. He's right. I have an issue with pills. I have done for years, but no one has ever called me a whore before. I think that's why it's been playing on my mind so savagely, keeping me up at night, I didn't expect it to hurt. But perhaps, it's not the words that hurt, so much as who says them.

I seem to drift down the stairs as I descend, moving further and further from Flynn's office.

Lost inside my head.

I think of my mother, hear the *thud, thud, thud,* see the pool of red surrounding her head like a bloody halo. Feel the cold of the darkness as it creeps its way across my vision, wrapping itself around my neck like a noose.

By the time I push out of the glass doors, my hands are shaking, breaths raspy as my feet hit the brick walkway.

As I think of the other night, my head spins. Dreams of King infecting my sleep, but I woke, and he was there, touching me, kissing me, trying to convince me it wasn't real.

Heat floods my cheeks, shame gripping me when I think of Bennett. How he fucked me in the exact same place as his younger brother did. How I then got into a car with him, even though both of us had too much to drink. He stopped by the pharmacy, dropped me off at the front steps of campus and I slid out of his fancy car, slamming the door too hard on my exit, doing all of it without looking at him.

And now, Flynn, my fucking counsellor, who was done with me the second I came, encouraging me to leave.

Fisting my hair, I grip hard, nails clawing my scalp, I groan through gritted teeth at my stupidity. I don't know what I'm doing. Everything is a huge mess, and I've done it to myself.

I never should have slept with men I just met, let myself fall for them, especially all three of them, when I knew, I *knew* they were going to break my heart. I latched on to the first people who showed me any sort of affection like an addict. Like the addict I am.

And the worst part is, Lynx broke it off with me because of the drugs, something I continued to take in hopes it'd make them like me more.

Icy wind lashes my skin as I blow out a hard breath. I probably should leave, it would save my father the embarrassment of having the college Dean call him, I suppose. That would definitely make things worse for me. I could call my dad's housekeeper, Jeanie, she might be able to convince Dad to let me leave, to go somewhere else, before anyone finds out about what's happened here.

The phone is in my hand, the dial tone sounding strange in my ear as I call my family home from a foreign country. I didn't check the time, but it can't be late there.

I consider hanging up when no one answers on the fifth ring, anxiously lifting my gaze from the toes of my boots to the view of the quad, my teeth in my lip, when I see him.

Lynx.

His red-brown eyes sharp on mine where I suddenly stop in my tracks.

We still share a dorm room, now that it has its door back on. Just one of many intrusive things I'm trying hard not to think about. They don't really bother me, but knowing that it was Lynx who did it hurts.

"Yes?" my father's voice booms through the phone, and my mouth instantly dries, heart pounding, I swallow, steeling myself for whatever's to come, he never answers the house phone, that's what we have staff for.

"It's me," I rasp out, my throat thick, tongue floppy.

"What in God's name have you done now?" he bellows and I shrink in on myself on instinct, but feel relief he hasn't heard about the video yet.

"Nothing, Dad, *Sir*, I'm not- I haven't done anything, Sir."

He grunts with distrust, "You called Dr Soren," a statement.

"I did, Sir," I swallow, thinking of the call with my psychiatrist back in England, the nasally judgement I felt through the phone.

Staring at my boots, the heavy grey sky reflecting in their rough polish.

"Good. And your pills," not a question.

"Yes, Sir, I'm taking them," I shift my weight from one foot to the other at my lie, I only use them to sleep, three or four at a time seems to work. "Da- Sir, I was wondering if I could transfer to the other colle-"

"I knew it. What did you do, Poppy? What the fuck did you do?!" His voice cuts down the line, vicious in my ear, and my tummy cramps with my nerves.

I thrust a hand over my hair, gripping atop the strands at the nape of my neck, squeezing the muscles.

"It's nothing, I don't not- I just, the other place has a progr-"

"I am getting sick and tired of listening to your blithering, girl. I warned you. I told you before you left that if you fucked up once more, I would have you sent straight back to Briarmoor, did you not understand me?"

"No, Sir, I did. I do understand you, but I-"

"Enough," he barks, cutting me off. "Now, you listen to me, and you listen well. A very prominent colleague of mine helped secure your place at that college, Poppy, a very *powerful* man, and it wouldn't make me look very good if you fucked this up on purpose now. Would it?"

"No, Sir. I would-"

"Right. So here's what we're going to do. You want to leave, here's the compromise. I'm going to send Jeanie to you on a plane to bring you back," my breath sails out of me, heart thudding loud in my chest with something like strangled relief. "And you can go for a nice long stay in Briarmoor until you learn to be more fucking grateful!" he spits down the phone, my lungs screaming.

"No, no, Da-, Sir. Please, I'll stay here, I'll stay, I can do better, I'll make it work, whatever you want, I'll do it, I wil-"

"Enough! Now that that's settled, you will go to your classes, you will take your pills, you will check in regularly with Dr Soren and you will *not* disrespect my generosity with you again. Do you understand?" I can almost see the snarl in his top lip as his last word curls with each syllable.

"Yes, Sir."

"I could take it away just like that, Poppy. Do not forget that, girl."

"Yes, Sir. Thank you, Sir."

And then he hangs up on me, the line dead, and I can finally take a breath, when a gag is pulled across my mouth, a cloth bag tugged over my head.

A muffled, menacing voice in my ear hissing, "Surprise!"

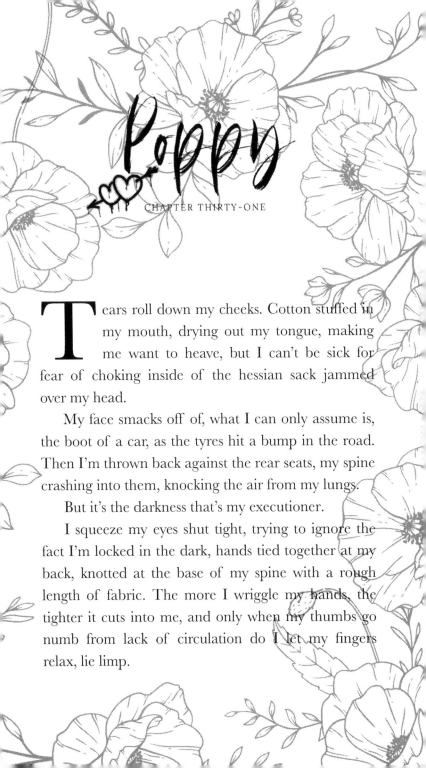

Poppy

Tears roll down my cheeks. Cotton stuffed in my mouth, drying out my tongue, making me want to heave, but I can't be sick for fear of choking inside of the hessian sack jammed over my head.

My face smacks off of, what I can only assume is, the boot of a car, as the tyres hit a bump in the road. Then I'm thrown back against the rear seats, my spine crashing into them, knocking the air from my lungs.

But it's the darkness that's my executioner.

I squeeze my eyes shut tight, trying to ignore the fact I'm locked in the dark, hands tied together at my back, knotted at the base of my spine with a rough length of fabric. The more I wriggle my hands, the tighter it cuts into me, and only when my thumbs go numb from lack of circulation do I let my fingers relax, lie limp.

It goes on and on. I don't know how much time passes as I try to calm my breaths, try to follow the twists and turns of the car inside my head, left, right, another right. Try to count seconds, but it's no good, I can't even get past the count of thirty-three. I'm thrown about like an insect in a glass jar, a small child with boisterous hands shaking it up.

The car engine rumbles, vibrating through my bones, rattling my teeth, and then it's slowing, what sounds like gravel attacking the paintwork as it spits up the sides of the car. And it goes on, the slow, seemingly endless movement of the car, the same road surface, gravel, then something smoother, before more lumps and bumps and potholes.

My brain is rattling and my skull pounds with a headache fogging through the front of my cranium like a heavy, dense cloud as we finally come to a stop.

And I realise, very quickly, that maybe this is worse.

Perhaps being stuffed in the boot of a moving vehicle, gag tied around my face, cutting into my cheeks, bag over my head, that this was okay, fine even, compared to whatever it is that might come next.

Doors open as if in unison, then they close, *one, two, three,* a moment's pause, shuffling, *four.* My breath whistles through my stuffy nose, pulse pounding in my ears as I strain to listen to footsteps, but they all move at the same time, giving me no indication how many there are until the noise of movement stops right beside my head.

Holding my breath, I wait, trying to listen, my ears full of nothing but the shooting of adrenaline flooding my veins. It's all I can hear, the loud buzzing like locusts stripping a farmer's harvest field bare. The boot lid clicks and I am silent as a corpse as it opens, unknown abductors presumably staring in at me.

That's when big hands grab my upper arms, and I scream. I scream even though it's muffled, even though it hurts my own head. I scream like I haven't since I was five years old, locked inside of a kitchen cupboard by my mother to keep me safe. To hide me.

Protect me.

The only person who ever gave a fuck about me.

She should have locked herself in the cupboard and let the intruder rape and murder me instead.

I kick my legs as I'm lifted from the car boot, my heel catching something, a grunt loud as it does. I'm spun in the air and slammed into a rock solid chest, air *oomph*ing from my lungs at the impact. Sandal-wood and vanilla instantly filling my nose.

Flynn?

Chest rising and falling, heart hammering, knocking at my sternum, threatening to crack its way through, I drag in quick, hot breaths through my nostrils. Throat constricting as the gag seems to work its way further back along my tongue, I try to chew it forward, gagging anyway as the person holding onto me plants me down onto my feet, small scattered stones beneath the soles of my boots, hands behind my back making balancing harder.

The air is icy, my long, clingy dress on, it has thick ribbed fabric and long sleeves, calf-length boots beneath it. I wanted to wear the cowboy boots that Lynx gave me, but looking at them this morning made my eyes blurry, so I slammed the wardrobe door closed on them and dug out my combat boots instead.

My jacket was stripped off of me before my hands were bound. Temperatures below five-celcius, wind chapping my cheeks, my ears, it feels like my first day in Groveton all over again. The unexpected cold.

Shivering, my jaw works, teeth trying to clack together in a chatter, but the rag stops me, saliva leaking from the sides of my mouth, down my chin.

Suddenly, I'm shoved forward, curled knuckles in semblance of a punch, hitting me sharply between my shoulder blades. I jerk forward, toe of my boot scuffing in the loose earth and I go down. Hard. The side of my face smacking the solid ground, cheekbone and temple thudding the hardest, making me see stars. Sickness swirls in my belly, and I resist the urge to gag, just barely, by breathing slowly through my nose, but it's taking gargantuan effort to do just that.

Breathe.

"Jesus fuck," someone hisses under their breath, as

large, warm hands hook beneath my armpits, pulling me back to my feet. "Easy, Kitten," he whispers, revealing himself to me, *Rex,* as he grips my upper arms.

Smoothing his thumbs down the backs of my arms as my head spins and my body sways and the sickness I felt before comes rushing up the back of my throat. I swallow down the feeling, abdomen jumping as I do, my empty belly churning, burning in my chest, my throat. His heat at my back, warming my spine, it should feel safe, but it feels anything but.

I think this is worse.

This is so much worse because whatever is happening, whatever is going to happen is going to be so much worse because I know them. These boys, ones who have kissed me and touched me and fucked me. Brought me lunch and gifted me boots, lent me a coat, and genuinely cared for me.

Rex's hands still grip my arms, holding me up as my head drops forward on my shoulders, chest tight.

The sob comes out in full force then. My entire body trembling as it does. I know they were the ones who released the shower video, my naked body plastered across websites and social media, every mobile phone on campus, and now I'm just waiting for that dreaded phone call from my father. Telling me to get on a flight he'll have arranged and not put up a fuss when I get sent back to Briarmoor.

I'm not a person who should ever have been

admitted there. I have depression and anxiety. I use drugs to numb my brain, to make me more social, more fun. Briarmoor houses criminals, people with severe mental health issues who are dangerous. I thought he sent me there as a punishment, now I think he's just trying to get rid of me.

And he can.

With that court ordered piece of paper, essentially making him my owner.

Sobs wrack my chest, choked and muffled with the gag and the sack and the lack of air, as my heaving breaths suck the rough fabric tight to my nostrils. And all it does is make me panic more.

"For fuck's sake," another male voice snaps, someone familiar, but deprived of my sight, and flooded with panic, I don't know who it is.

The bag is torn from my head, Rex still at my back, holding onto my arms.

Blinking to clear the darkness, it does nothing, the night having fallen fully now, plunging us into pitch black, but having my sight back, it's a little like relief.

Until, I blink away my tears, clearing my blurry eyes, and find myself staring into eyes the colour of onyx. Even when it's not dark, unshadowed, his brown eyes are soulless black orbs that want to destroy anything in his path.

Bennett is a demon, and in this moment, he looks absolutely terrifying.

He stares at me, his face angled down, eyes flicked up, cheekbones casting shadows down his jaw, carving him into a ghoul. His dark brown hair is short, pushed back, the sides shorn, but it looks messy, unkempt, like he's been carding his fingers through it again and again.

He tilts his head, and I think of the first time we met, the way his arrogance boiled my blood, at the same time his broad smirk devastated my insides, but I couldn't wait to escape him. Escape the forbidden feelings he elicited inside me. Because there were warning bells ringing in my head within seconds of breathing the same air as him.

My thighs twitch, heat gathering in my lower belly even as panic flares bright in my chest, thinking of the last time I saw him. Fucking him as easily as I did his brother. In the same grimy bathroom. Because I have no class, easily spreading legs, a brain that doesn't ever tell me to stop, stop, *stop*.

I wonder if he told them.

If any of them know.

About Bennett.

Shrinking back against what I hope is the lesser evil, I squeeze my eyes shut tight, feel the last drops of salty pain slip from them. Rex's fingers flex into the muscles of my biceps, almost like reassurance.

Whatever is going to happen here isn't going to be good.

And Rex is no hero either.

Bennett steps into my front, but I don't open my eyes, feeling the heat from his body roll into mine. The backs of his fingers graze my icy cheeks, he hooks them into the rag, pulling on it and shoving it down.

A great gasp leaps into my lungs, making me cough, hunch over, splutter and heave. Sickness sits low down in my belly, but acid burns my oesophagus anyway, like a reminder it's still there, won't take much to spill out. But as I try to remember the last time I ate, coming up with nothing, I let that worry die a death.

Rex rights me when my coughing subsides. Holding onto me once again. I stare at Bennett, trying not to fucking cry. I want to lunge at him, smack that smug, dark look off of his handsome face and demand to know what the fuck his problem is.

Because I don't understand what the fuck I've done to any of these wicked, vile, noxious boys.

"This is your reckoning," Lynx's voice snarls, and it almost breaks the bones of my chest cavity, the viciousness in which he speaks it.

His voice is at my back, and I know that must mean Raiden is here, somewhere out of my line of sight, too. But then I remember that first scent, vanilla-sandalwood, the huge, hard body I was thrust into, *Flynn.* And I don't understand why he would be here, if he is. Are they friends?

Heat flushes over my skin like a sweat laced tsunami and I forget all about it being cold.

God, what if he told them my secrets, the things I have confessed to in the quiet, dark seclusion of his office.

Bennett steps back, giving me space, and my head pounds with the throbbing pain in my face, an ache in the base of my spine from being tossed about in the car boot. I try to look over my shoulder, to see who is here, but I don't need to bother as the three men at my back, bar Rex who still holds onto me, step into view.

All of them in black, four men now stand before me, each of them I'm intimately familiar with. It makes my heart riot in my chest, my eyes pinging between them all.

Bennett and his dark, delving eyes. King's stern expression, his cold glare. Lynx's snarling upper lip, lifted brow. And Flynn, a familiar tilt to his head of black curls, lift to one corner of his mouth, the unexpected one. I think it hurts the worst.

Is this why he was trying to get me to leave?

But I couldn't have gotten away that fast, and he knows that, if he knew about this, what was going to happen to me.

Before I can ask, force my jaw to unlock, teeth to unclench, Flynn steps closer, eating up the few feet of space between us with his long legs. And even in the dark, my eyes track the way his thick thigh muscles twitch and flex beneath his tight joggers, something I have never seen him wear before. Rex leaves my back as Flynn reaches us, the warmth of his big hands leaving an icy shudder in his wake.

Flynn's deep blue eyes look like ink in the dark as they glide across the mess of my face, taking in the tears, spit, a culmination of my fear. I don't know what I look like, but I can feel all of these things drying on my face.

It feels uncomfortable, my vulnerableness now, in front of Flynn. I thought he was something different, but then, I thought that about them all not more than six weeks ago.

The ways they touched me, held me, fucked me. All of it had feeling and it wasn't one sided. No matter what my father tries to convince the world of, I'm not crazy. I know what I felt. The way they treated me.

It was real.

Flynn leans in, head canted to one side, the tip of his nose runs along the curve of my jaw, up past the front of my ear, stopping at my temple as he breathes me in, slow and deep. My entire body trembles, but I don't move, there's nowhere I could go, even if I ran, my hands behind my back, I'm no match for these five.

I stare into his blue eyes, shadowed in the night, his thick, black curls dancing across his pale forehead in the wind. His cheek comes to mine, his lips beside my ear, he scruffs his short stubble against my skin, marking me, despite the tacky mess on my face.

"I guess I should have mentioned before, Raiden's my little brother," Flynn says, answering my unspoken question.

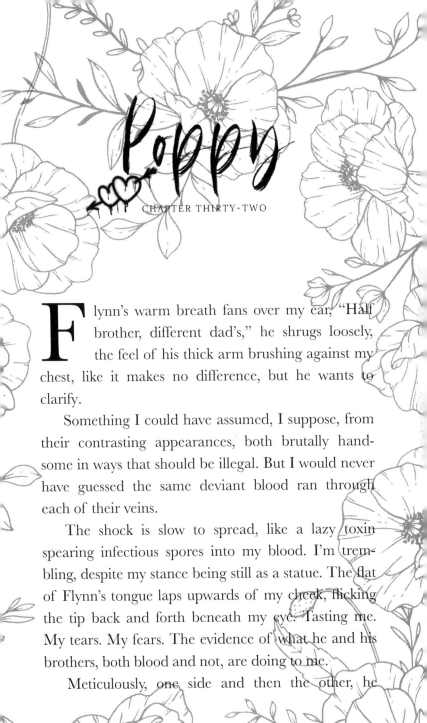

Poppy

CHAPTER THIRTY-TWO

Flynn's warm breath fans over my ear, "Half brother, different dad's," he shrugs loosely, the feel of his thick arm brushing against my chest, like it makes no difference, but he wants to clarify.

Something I could have assumed, I suppose, from their contrasting appearances, both brutally handsome in ways that should be illegal. But I would never have guessed the same deviant blood ran through each of their veins.

The shock is slow to spread, like a lazy toxin spearing infectious spores into my blood. I'm trembling, despite my stance being still as a statue. The flat of Flynn's tongue laps upwards of my cheek, flicking the tip back and forth beneath my eye. Tasting me. My tears. My fears. The evidence of what he and his brothers, both blood and not, are doing to me.

Meticulously, one side and then the other, he

cleans my face with his mouth, using his tongue, his lips, his teeth. Pain bolts through me as he nips at my newly swollen cheek, the impact with the floor making it bruise, I'm sure, and I squeeze my eyes shut tight. Keeping him out.

He doesn't touch me with his hands, and it's almost worse, the ways in which I wish he would. If only for the pretty lie. Comfort in a time of panic. Something that is usual for him, the way in which he soothes me, makes me feel at ease, even though, I know, there's darkness hidden in those pools of blue, I still felt safe.

Now, everything is different.

My heart thuds erratically loud as he steps back, making a slow show of licking his pale pink lips, his cupid's bow overly defined, pretty, almost too delicate for his face.

"You're confused," he whispers over my mouth, breath blowing across my lips. "It's okay to cry."

I swallow thickly, eyelids loosening from their tight squeeze. I sway in the cold breeze, thinking about doing just that, but I don't. Instead, I think about Flynn's hands running all over my naked body, it can't be more than an hour or so ago since he had me splayed out on the desk in his office, his face between my thighs, tongue in my cunt.

Please, don't let me go, Flynn. Don't you hurt me too.

But then I think of all the sessions we've had, the way that sometimes, things just aren't as they seem.

How the things he says are worded to coerce me, to tempt me, to pry information from the darkest recesses of my brain and twist them like a knife in my gut.

I came here trying to forget about everything that happened, but Flynn just wouldn't let me have that. I told him what I did, where they locked me away.

I think of Mum, feeling the guilt, as though it were my fault. Never being reassured it wasn't.

Swallowing hard, throat jumping as I do, I open my eyes, locking them onto Flynn's, "Just do whatever it is you're going to do."

Without another word, Flynn takes my shoulders in his hands, spinning me around, his waft of heat hitting my spine like I'm thrown into the fire. And he's walking me forward in the night.

In my mind, I go back to just this morning.

I reach my long, thin fingers towards a little bump of bright green, grainy powder. Bonnie crushed pills, Venom, *she says, non-addictive, supposedly. And I retract my hand as she says it, unsure if I want to consume substances not designed to kill me. Emma frowns, her beautiful dark skin creasing just between her perfectly sculpted brows as she dips a spit-slicked finger into the luminous green sand, bringing it to her lips.*

Pressing her fingertip to her tongue with a raised brow, then a dipped brow, a wince, and then, "Shit, that's dry."

She coughs, grimacing, before a beautiful smile curls her

plump, deep rose lips, a laugh leaving her like an accident, she couldn't stop it and I wonder how any drug could work that quickly.

Then another thought crashes through my skull, maybe she's just happy.

I wonder if I ever could be.

The space is open, I can feel it, without having to look, but I do, I *am* looking at the huge clearing as we push through the last of the dense forest. Bare trees that Flynn steered me through with ease, his grip on my bound hands, keeping me from falling face first onto the ground again.

I stumble a little, nerves making my legs jelly, five men around me who want to play with me in the dark.

That's the worst part of it all.

The dark.

But the boys all have torches, other than Flynn, and I cling onto the long beams of light like a lifeline, trying not to think of how close the sky feels, hanging low with the forecasted rainstorm.

Flynn knocks me to my knees, pain bolting through my femurs as I hit the uneven ground, thick wooden slats and frozen earth digging into my bones. But I bite my tongue, holding the feelings inside, locking the pain behind my teeth.

Lynx steps around me, grabbing my chin with

brute force, yanking my face up, his cold skin against my own, the harsh vice grip of his hand cupping my chin, his thumb and fingers digging into my skin. He towers over me, those red-brown eyes almost black in the darkness, he scowls down at me, upper lip curled in disgust.

"You're not getting off of this train track until every single one of us has used you exactly how we want," he spits at me, shock penetrating me like a bullet, the pain secondary to the realisation of what he means.

"What?" I blink hard, rain starting to spot against my frigid skin. "Train track?"

Lynx sighs hard, his Adam's apple bobbing in his throat with his swallow, "Yes, train track, so you probably wanna do a good job and get it over with before the train comes."

My entire brain short circuits as I look down at the ground, my knees uneven, thighs parted over a wooden slat of the track. I suck in a sharp breath as Lynx steps back, eyes narrowed in on me as he steps off of the track.

I glance left and right, the track long and straight as far as I can see both ways, and I shiver, my heart hammering. Heat covers my spine as someone sinks to their knees behind me. Smoke and sugary sweetness, a hint of tobacco filling my nose and my panicked sob threatens to choke me.

Rex's lips brush my ear, his warm breath feathering down my neck and I hate how I automatically sink back into him, seeking his comfort even as his big hands ruck up my dress.

My focus on the four men fanned out before me, but it's fuzzy, my vision, as though my eyes are trying to shield me from the men I thought I found my place with. Each of them gifting me something different, something safe, something new.

And now they want to destroy me.

And I don't even know why.

A hiss escapes Rex as he sucks in a sharp breath through his teeth, finding me bare beneath my dress, his thick fingers splaying around the tops of my legs, index fingers digging into the crease of my thighs.

I glance at Flynn, finding the knowing smirk on his face, his hand shifting from his pocket, my knickers balled in his fist. He brings them up to his face, pressing them to his nose and breathes in deep.

I shudder as his eyes roll, his head dropping back, eyes fluttering closed, like he's drawing in the scent of something he craves. And it makes my heart shatter.

Rex places a soft palm to my lower belly, splaying his fingers possessively, holding me to him, his bare, hard cock pressing against my spine, the cold metal through the tip like ice against my skin.

"I've got you, Kitten," he breathes in my ear, making me shudder, my eyes close, a tear rolling down my cheek. "I won't let anything bad happen to you."

It sounds like a false promise, like a pretty lie, and I hate that I wish it were true.

"Just get on with it," I grit out, teeth chattering, I bite the inside of my cheek, swallow the rush of bile up the back of my throat.

"Poppy," it sounds like a plea and I fucking hate it, like there's sadness in his voice, as if he's not the one about to violate me.

"Shut up," I whisper, squeezing my eyes closed, "just shut the fuck up." I sing it inside my head like a chant, a mantra, trying to go somewhere else, anywhere that's not here.

Rex sighs, his huff of breath skating down my neck, blowing hair across my face, little strands catching in my eyelashes, and I do nothing as he takes his cock in hand, lines it up with my entrance, already wet and desperate for him. And I hate myself for it.

I have hated myself since I was five years old, but never once have I hated myself quite as much as I do in this very moment.

Rex's cock is a slow, smooth glide of steel flesh as he enters me. His hand over my belly, holding me to him, other hand clasped over my hip, his grunt of satisfaction in my ear as his teeth snap onto the lobe, biting and sucking as he fucks me, my bound hands crushed between us.

"Angel," Flynn rasps, my eyes fluttering open, lifting to his dark blue ones where he towers over us,

Rex's face buried in the crook of my neck, his lips and teeth mouthing at my scarred shoulder.

Flynn brings his big fingers to my lips, sweeping the tips over the flesh, applying pressure to tug the bottom one down, dragging it away from my teeth. His gaze flicks from his hand to my eyes, his fingers still resting heavily on my lip.

"Suck my fingers like you're gonna suck my cock, Angel," he rasps, low and husky, pressing the tips of his three longest fingers against my teeth, forcing me to widen my lips, open my mouth, let him in.

And like an idiot, I part my lips, suck his fingers inside, let him slide them to the very back of my tongue, down into my throat. I gag, my lips stretched so wide it feels like my cheeks are going to split at the sides to make more room, saliva running out of the corners of my mouth, dripping down my chin as he presses hard on the very back of my tongue, the knuckles of his fingers grazing the roof of my mouth.

"Suck harder, Kitten," Rex breathes, his canine dragging down the curve of my ear as his cock punches against my cervix.

I try to suck on Flynn's fingers, his eyes blazing as he focuses his gaze between my mouth and my eyes, but with a low groan, a deep rumbling in his wide chest, he tears his fingers from my mouth. Air burns my lungs as I heave in a big breath, saliva dripping from the corners of my mouth, my chin. My head dropping forward, my back still flush with Rex's front.

The tip of Flynn's cock is pressing to my lips before I have time to fully catch my breath, the wide head of him a salty musk on my tongue as he fills my mouth in one brutal thrust, my teeth catching the top of his shaft as he taps the back of my throat.

All I can do then is let them use me. The pair of them moving in sync, Rex glides out as Flynn slides in, the walls of my throat and cunt tightening in the same rhythm. Both men groaning as they move inside of me, the two of them clinging onto me as they do. Flynn's hand tangled in the top of my hair, his other tight around my throat. Rex's hands on my body, one on my belly, the other curled around my hip.

They hold me like they're not trying to hurt, but they want to, wish they could, or maybe they don't want to hurt me at all. Maybe that's all just me. What I want. Because if they hurt me more, maybe I'll start to hate them more than I hate myself.

It's as that thought crests that Rex's hand glides down my stomach, over my pubic bone, his middle finger finding my clit. Rough circles dance over the swollen flesh and heat gathers in my lower belly, threading through my limbs, sinking into me like I couldn't stop it if I tried. And that's fatal, because I don't want to. I don't want to stop it and that's the thought that makes me come.

A slow unfurling climax rocks through me, firing through my blood at a lazy pace, but I tighten hard around them all the same. My pussy clenching tight around Rex as he pounds into me one last savage time, before pulling free, his cum painting my lower spine, my dress shoved halfway up my back, and Flynn's salty musk floods my mouth. I swallow it down, spluttering at the volume, his cock still tight in my throat as I swallow around him.

They both pull out of me, Rex's cum dripping down my back, Flynn's thumb catching a small drop of his own that escapes my lips, pushing it back inside, before they both move away from me.

King instantly takes their place, stepping in front of me, his light grey eyes glinting under the warm glow of the torch in his hand, something he silently places beside me as he bends towards me, tipping my chin up to him.

"Raiden," I whisper, my bottom lip quivering as searing heat fills my eyes, but he's my protector. "What did I do wrong?"

King stares down at me, my insides swirling with want and panic. I think about the first night we met. The way he offered me light then too. He was my saviour. And now we're just... this.

His lips part, his expression blank. I can't get a read on him at all. King licks his lips, shoving his hands in his pockets with a loose shrug, clenching his jaw, he looks away from me, down the still empty track.

Cold air whirls around me, whipping my hair across my face, the thick strands slashing at my skin like knives. I, too, stare down the length of the track, peering into the darkness, listening to the near silence surrounding us. We're in the middle of nothing but trees and night and I wonder if I'll ever get off of this track.

Slowly, I rove my gaze back onto King. I peer up at him, hopeless and desperate. Seeking something, anything.

And I suppose he gives it to me.

Silently, he moves around me, taking Rex's place, his hands brushing my sticky skin as I wobble in place, hands still bound at my back. King shoves down his joggers, his cock hard and hot, tapping at my spine. He says nothing as I hear him spit in his hand, feel him grab his cock, working his saliva down his length. He breathes hard, one of his hands curling into mine, holding onto the fabric that binds me, he slams inside of me, a scream piercing the air through my gritted teeth as his hips punch into mine.

Body bowing forward at the rough intrusion, his hold on my hands yanks me back into him as he fucks me hard and fast, my brain rattling around inside my skull.

"I could kill you," he grunts into my ear, and it's like relief.

Hope.

Do it.

My knees dig into the shingle and frozen earth beneath me, thighs straddling a wooden plank, but I don't feel the razor sharp stones breaking skin, the cold seeping into my bones. I don't focus on the man I trusted at my back, fucking me without a care in the world while his friends, his brothers, watch. I don't think about the very real prospect of a train racing down this clearing and splattering me into pieces against its windshield.

Instead, eyes open, vision glazed over, I think of the cupboard. The darkness. The pool of red surrounding my mother, the broken lamp, shattered glass. And I let myself fall into it. Even as I start to feel the way King's free hand begins to stroke down my thigh, his grip careful and possessive. Like he's trying to comfort me, he's murmuring death in my ear as he fucks me harder, faster, harder again, and his hand is planted on my chest, over my dress, directly atop my heart and I know he can feel how it hammers ruthlessly against his palm.

I hear nothing he says to me, whispers in my ear, I block them all out, focusing on the drumming of my pulse as Bennett steps up in front of me, taking out his cock, and shoving it into my mouth, all without looking at me.

Something is snapping and breaking, rotting, inside of me, putrid, decaying, and it feels like it's my sanity.

CHAPTER THIRTY-THREE

King comes in his hand, leaving me cold and trembling as he stands up, rejoining his brothers, thankfully not dragging it out longer than it needed to be. All of this punishment for an unknown crime I don't know I've committed.

Bennett pulls out of my mouth, taking his place at my back, silent and sullen with eyes darker than pitch, and I hardly feel it when he thrusts into me. His fingers tightly curled over my hips, the fabric of my dress clenched between his teeth, his nose to the nape of my neck.

He fucks me coldly, detached, like he's bored, trying to get it over with and I'm glad, because the tears that fill my eyes are barely clinging on and I don't want them to see it. I don't want to show it.

Lynx steps up in front of me, a sneer on his mouth, hate in his eyes. It makes my heart clench, a tightness to my chest that aches and stabs and unfurls like razor sharp talons, hooking deep, and ripping into muscle.

My breathing is rough, pussy sore, but the look on Lynx's face is my undoing.

He doesn't close the couple of feet between us, just unzips his jeans, takes out his cock, but I don't look, even as I see his shoulder rise and fall with a steady rhythm.

I don't tear my gaze from his face.

Those narrowed eyes shining more red than brown in the shadow of night, the devil throwing himself into Lynx, pushing himself to the forefront.

Lynx is just on the other side of the metal rail, my head tilted back, chin up, eyes wide on his. He holds my gaze as his older brother fucks me from behind, my entire being numb to everything but the way he looks at me.

Lynx was the first guy I met, in a time of a panic, he kept me calm, kept me safe. Held me.

I sense the tears fall more than feel them as they roll down my cheeks. Drip from my chin.

Bennett's breath is like lava over my skin, his nose flush with the side of my neck, breathing hard. His short grunts vibrate down the column of my throat, ricocheting down my vocal cords like they're sounds of my own making.

That's when I hear the train.

My head snaps to the right, and I can see it, the

flare of light in the distance, moving closer, getting brighter.

"Your life is in my hands," drawing back my attention, Lynx chuckles darkly, glancing down at his cock. "How does it feel to know that your life hangs on the time it takes for me to come, little slut?"

A sharp breath pierces through my lungs, erupting in my chest cavity, catching in my throat.

I almost loved myself.

When I was with them.

I almost did.

I miss the way he said my name, the way he'd call me Treasure with some semblance of love. Caring and soft, and it was all just for me. The way no one had ever been like that with me before. I think of watching him on the ice, gazing up at me, in front of thousands of people, the way he smiled, beamed at me like he couldn't wait to get me in his arms. The night it all changed.

"Why?" the words rasp from my tongue, like knives in my throat. "What did I do?" I whisper, my voice catching in the wind, Bennett slowing at my back, like he wants to listen, maybe he wants to say something.

Does Lynx know the things I've done with his older brother? Raiden's older brother? Perhaps it was a plan of theirs all along, maybe this was all just some sort of game that I don't understand, not knowing the rules, I could never win.

"Why?" Lynx grits out, still working his cock, clearly not wanting to touch me. *"Why?"* it's a snarl, the second time, the way he repeats it, his upper lip curling, his bleached-blonde hair flapping over his eyes in the wind. "You want to know *why?*"

"Yes," I swallow, throat dry, "I want to know why."

Slowly, he grins at me, this ominous, sadistic smirk that shows too many teeth.

He steps right up to me then, his cock level with my face where I'm still on my knees, his brother fucking into me harder and faster than before, but I don't take my eyes from his.

"Because you ruined my family, you ruined our lives, you forced my brother into a life of crime, you fucking little whore. That's fucking why," he snarls and then his cum is hitting my face.

Eyes snapping shut as he paints me with his release, the hot sticky mess hitting my cheek, my chin, my brow, the tip of my nose, dripping onto my cupid's bow.

The train sounds its horn, getting closer and closer. I can feel the vibration of it thrumming through my bones as Bennett pulls out, finally comes, jets of cum hitting my backside, his big hands rubbing his release into my flesh, mixing it with his brothers', slapping each cheek.

Lynx spits on the ground between my knees. My line of sight following it with morbid fascination.

"Get up, Lollipop," Bennett says in my ear, something cold cutting through the ties binding my hands, before he shoves away from my back.

Forcing me to flop forward, pins and needles fizzing through my fingers as I plant them on the ground to save myself, little stones pricking the soft skin of my palms.

Bennett tucks himself away as I blink open my eyes, I watch the two Adams brothers join the line up of the other three.

The train races down the tracks, all of them staring at me, except for Lynx, his back is already to me, pushing his way back through the trees. I glance between them all, wondering why I ever trusted any of them. Wonder what is so broken inside of me that I allowed myself to latch on like a fucking leech to the first people to pay any sort of warm attention to me.

Except for Bennett.

There's not really affection there, no real tenderness, but I think back to the car journey, the way he took care of me that night after we met in the bar. And I wonder if what happened there meant anything to him at all.

Rex takes a step forward, lines cutting deeply through his features as he stares at me, and I feel nothing. Desensitised, in this moment, to my feelings.

I think of my father, how he hates me. How my mother loved me but was brutally torn away from me, leaving me like this, with him, someone who despises me that is supposed to be my family.

I see the darkness, the edges of my vision shadows. All of me like an old, disintegrating house, creaky doors and shattered glass. So much pain, so much sadness, I wish a passerby would set me on fire.

I see her then, my mum, long golden hair, blue-grey eyes, soft skin, a warm smile, light freckles across the bridge of her nose.

I wonder, if she were here now, if she would take me into her chest, welcome me into the cradle of her arms, squeeze me tight, hug me, and love me, and never let me go again.

I feel numb, pushing to my wobbly legs, cum and spit and tears a mess all over me. The skirt of my dress falls down, covering me, hitting just above my ankles. I see Rex closer, unsure of when he moved towards me further. I step just off of the track, closer to them, and a look of something like relief washes over Rex's face. A crease appearing between my brows in confusion.

I look between the four men, and I'm suddenly not sure why I ever thought I could fit there. Between all of these muscles and ink, smirks and curled upper lips. But the way they each took their time with me, comforted me, together and alone, the way they genuinely *liked* me.

Was all of it only ever a lie?

Lynx's words, his explanation, comes back to me,

telling me how I ruined his family. Forced his brother into a life of crime. I don't understand any of it, I've never done anything to purposely hurt another human being in my entire life. Even when I hurt that girl, it's only because of what she did to me first. It was a reaction, a bad one. A compulsion to stand up for myself for the first time in my life.

Nobody ever really cares about the other side of the story, though. Not when it comes to me.

The train is so close now, I can feel the heat of its roaring engine, like a wall of fire rolling into me.

I glance to my right, dragging my blurry eyes away from four men who have destroyed me. Mind, body and soul. All of it like thick, black tar, seeping its way out of my cracks and fractures, nothing of *me* left now. Whatever that ever was anyway.

Without drugs, without forcing myself to fit, who even am I?

Worthless.

Troublemaker.

Pathetic.

Waste of space.

Should have been you that died instead of your mother.

The train's headlight is like staring into the sun as I take one large step back onto the tracks, my wobbly legs holding me firm, the train horn blares loud enough that I momentarily go deaf and then it hits me.

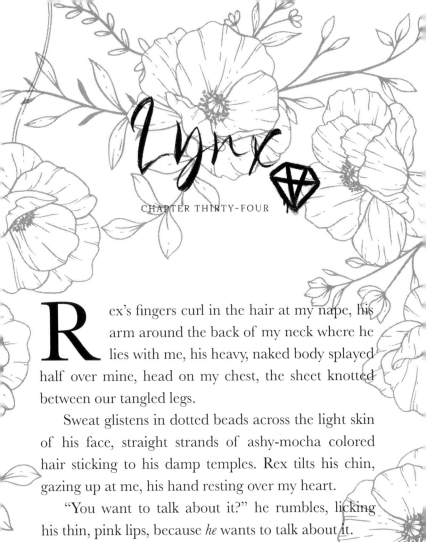

Lynx

Rex's fingers curl in the hair at my nape, his arm around the back of my neck where he lies with me, his heavy, naked body splayed half over mine, head on my chest, the sheet knotted between our tangled legs.

Sweat glistens in dotted beads across the light skin of his face, straight strands of ashy-mocha colored hair sticking to his damp temples. Rex tilts his chin, gazing up at me, his hand resting over my heart.

"You want to talk about it?" he rumbles, licking his thin, pink lips, because *he* wants to talk about it.

I stare down at him, flicking my gaze over his light green eyes, the black metal hoop through his straight nose, the sharp cut of his square jaw.

Licking my own lips, swollen from a night of no sleep and half a day full of fucking, finally, I rasp, "No."

Hendrix is silent, his fingers tracing over my chest,

our breathing soft and even. Eyes drifting shut, I'm almost asleep when he shifts, turning so his chin rests on my sternum, his gaze boring a hole in my head but I don't open my eyes, I don't look at him, knowing the expression he wears. I can see it even through my shut lids, the pleading softness in his very masculine features. I've only seen it once before, before I was leaving for rehab, before it was voluntarily.

"I'm worried about her, Lynx," he says quietly, the bone of his chin digging into my sternum, but it feels like a blade in my heart. "She's not- I don't think she's okay," he sighs.

I think of her beautiful face full of fear, tear-tracked cheeks, and something worse.

Acceptance.

It's why I walked away. Before she stepped in front of a train, Flynn and King launching themselves at her just in time.

I imagine her dead, and bile bites at the back of my tongue.

I wish I could hate her as much as I pretend to.

"I don't give a fuck if she's okay," I snap back, eyes opening, gut twisting like my intestines are tying a noose around my heart. "Her family ruined mine, don't you fucking forget that," I inhale sharply, reminding myself, anger pulsing through my veins. "She put my dad in jail," I bite down on my teeth, pressing my tongue to the inside of them.

Rex doesn't move, his light green eyes on mine, a

little sadness in his frown that I want to smooth out, but I don't, I don't reach for him.

Can't.

"*She* didn't, Lynx," he settles on finally, "she was five."

I suck in a breath, rolling away, forcing him off of me. I turn to the edge of the bed, kick my legs over the side, stoop down to reach for my boxers.

"What we did… You liked her," Rex says lowly, attempting to get his deep rumble to sound soft. "I think you more than liked her, if we're being perfectly honest, Lynx. The way you look at he-"

"*Looked,* the way I *looked* at her. Past fucking tense, Hendrix, leave it the fuck alone."

"I don't like what we're doing," he says next as I stand to pull up my underwear. I glance over my shoulder at him, "In fact, I hate it. You bruised her fucking face, man. Shoved her to the ground with a *punch* to her back. You're like a hundred pounds heavier than her!"

"Yeah," I agree, nodding, gritting my teeth so hard, I think they may snap. "And that was just the start."

I grunt under my breath, thinking back to all those weeks ago, fucking her in the shower, slamming her into the wall. How I couldn't sleep for two days because of it, the guilt. And then last night.

Purple bruises, bloodshot eyes, pleading and crying and-

"We could have killed her last night," Rex replies sharply, an involuntary breath sucking sharply through my nose. "She could have died."

Hands trembling, jaw locked, teeth clenched, my eyes burn.

I hear him shifting up from the bed, my back still to him as I thread my legs through my sweatpants.

"Why are you fucking being like this? This isn't you," he sighs, sounding a messy mixture of exhausted and disgusted.

Two things I am overly familiar with.

"You did it too," I remind him, thinking of how he smiled at her cries, fucking her on the tracks, his lips to her ear.

She cried less when Raiden said he could kill her. Like she was... relieved.

My blood runs cold, and I push thoughts of last night out of my head.

Rex moves around the bed, stopping at the end of it as I turn towards the door. He steps in front of me, blocking my exit. Rex is taller than me by a couple inches, a little older, broader, he's more weighty than I am, he weight trains in the gym with Flynn, but he's not going to keep me inside this room if I want out of it.

"Move."

"No."

"Rex, get out of my way," I sigh, scrubbing a

hand over my bleached blond hair, too tired to find my fight.

My body aches, bruised, tired, I'm bone fucking tired, and I don't want to do this now. I want to shower, to wash thoughts of her off my skin, her scent, her tears.

Rex doesn't move, staring down at me, and I drop my gaze, noticing he, too, now has sweats on. His tattooed feet bare, I stare at the swirls of intricate, colorful ink so I don't have to look at his face.

"Is this because of the drugs I found in your room?" he asks me almost silently, my head snapping up so fast, I almost give myself whiplash.

"What?" I blink, fury flooding through me like my fight or flight instincts have finally kicked in. "You went through my fucking stuff?"

"Yes," he deadpans, unashamedly, holding my gaze. "Because you came home from the bar the other week looking shifty and I wanted to check on you."

I think back, *her*, again. *Her* fucking drugs, *my* fucking sanity. I wanted to help her. Not see her go down the same path as I did. Maybe we could have helped bring her out of the dark. Memories of last night hit the forefront of my mind, and I know that's never going to happen now. We've broken her. She's done.

It's what we -*I*- wanted.

I scoff, "You're fucking unbelievable."

"Because I care about you?"

"Because it's an invasion of fucking privacy!"

"Are you taking drugs, Lynx? Because that Molly I found hidden down the back of your toilet system was definitely not my Venom."

"Ohhh," I drag out, chuckling darkly. "That's what this is about?" I scoff again, shaking my head. "If it's *your* Venom, then it's okay for me to get fucked out of my head? But because that was not *your* Venom, I have a fucking habit? That it?"

"If you have nothing to hide, why are you so angry?"

"Because I'm not taking any fucking drugs!" I scream it, spittle flecking his cheekbone as I get right in his face, knocking my nose into his as our foreheads grind into one another.

"Bro, what the fuck?" Raiden's groggy voice sounds from the room opposite, even over the erratic pounding of my pulse, the drumming in my ears, I can hear him, like a voice of reason. "Why are you fucking screaming? Isn't it bad enough I've had to listen to you two fuck all day? And just when I think you're finally done, you decide to have a fucking fight."

He pushes the door open wider, forcing both me and Rex to part, move further back into the room, only for him to leave it open, blocking the exit with his shoulders brushing frame to frame.

"Why'd you have it then, if you're not taking it, why'd you hide it? Where'd you get it from?" Rex questions, ignoring our exhausted best friend completely.

"Get what from where?" King blinks, trying to wake up, scrubbing a hand down his face, hissing as he catches his eyebrow piercing with the side of his palm, it almost makes me smirk, the kick she landed to his face when we dragged her out of the trunk.

Hands balling into fists at my sides, I grit my teeth, look over his shoulder, out of the doorway, at King's open one opposite. It feels wrong to say it, even though I can't stand her. But to out her like this feels off. Then I think of not being allowed to visit my dad in jail, my mom lying blank faced in bed for months at a time. How I lost both parents, just like that, and I remember why I shouldn't fucking care.

Don't fucking care.

I feel some sort of smug satisfaction as my eyes find theirs, my gaze flicking between the two of them, steely gray and pale green, "You really want to know?" I raise a brow, the corner of my mouth curling up with a smugness I don't truly feel.

"I wouldn't be asking if I didn't," Rex huffs impatiently, King glancing between the two of us in confusion.

"What's going on?" he asks gruffly, tattooed chest inflating with a deep inhale.

"Hendrix went through my room and wants to know where I'm getting my supply from," I stare at

Rex as I speak to King, Rex's eyes narrowing with each word.

"The fuck?" King splutters, face turning ashen, "What the fuck you got drugs for, man?"

Roving my gaze from Rex to King, "I took them off of your little whore," I spit. "Tryna save her from her fucking self," I scoff like I can't believe I cared enough to bother. "She's got a nice little pill habit," I laugh harshly, something sharp spiking in my chest as I do, but I ignore it, keeping the cockiness plastered on my face like a well worn mask.

King looks at me in disbelief, but he doesn't try to argue with me, doesn't deny it. It's clear he didn't know, but his brow creases in thought, as though maybe he saw signs and didn't add them together.

But Rex, Rex drops his gaze down, shifting his feet uncomfortably.

I bark a laugh then, loud, raucous, it's not even forced when tears fill my eyes with emotion I can't place.

Feet thunder down the stairs from the third floor, both Flynn and my brother, Bennett, appearing in the hall now.

"What the fuck is going on down here?" Bennett snaps as though it's not five-p.m., but considering we were up all night, I get why he's pissed at being woken up. Dark eyes glancing over all of us standing in Rex's door frame, he sucks on his teeth, "Well?"

"This is gold," I chuckle, keeping my attention on

Rex. "You knew," I scoff, shaking my head. "Lemme just get this shit straight-"

"Lynx, what the fuck is going on?" my brother demands.

I think of how Bennett fucked her last night when my eyes meet his dark ones, like it wasn't new to him, but equally, like it meant nothing. I don't buy it. She's getting under all of their skin.

I turn to him sharply, a snarl on my mouth, "Shut the fuck up, Bennett." Jabbing my finger into Rex's chest, his light green eyes flicked up on mine, "So you," I spit. "Got a problem with your booty call taking drugs, but forced me off to rehab, so you could do what? Find a new little junkie to take my fucking place?!" I'm bellowing my words now, rage like I have never felt swarming through me.

Jealousy.

"Lynx, dude," Flynn starts, stepping closer to Bennett's back.

I cut him off with my sharp crack of laughter, "*You* spend *hours* watching that little cunt on camera, fucking with her head in your office. Manipulating her so she *trusts* you. She's your newest obsession, so stay the fuck out of this."

"You do?" King asks, turning to look at his older, crazier brother over his shoulder.

"Is that what this is about?" Bennett interrupts, removing the attention from Flynn, "Poppy?" he asks cautiously, a strange look on his face, a wince, as he says her name.

It's like a hammer to my eye socket.

"No, *actually*, it's ab-"

"Drugs," King says slowly, dragging the word out until it's ringing inside my head like a war cry.

Nobody speaks, all eyes on Raiden. He turns slowly, facing his half-brother, Flynn's deep blue eyes already locked on him.

"Has Poppy got a drug *habit?*" not wanting to say addiction, he licks his lips, rolling them together, his jaw popping with the squeaky gritting of his teeth.

A smug thrill rolls through me at the thought of her suddenly not being good enough for him now. That he'll be disgusted he ever let himself get invested. But the way Flynn watches his younger brother, the rest of us silent, makes my belly flop, a weight dropping into it. Because Raiden was never disgusted with me, by me, he was only ever support-ive, worried about me.

Even now, the way he checks in, it's like he...

"You feel guilty," I say quietly, cutting in before Flynn can reply to his brother.

I look up at King as his head slowly turns back towards me, my meaning clear, he knows I'm not talking about Poppy anymore. His dark gray eyes slowly roll back to mine, almost as though he hopes it's not him I'm directing my comment at.

"You think it was your fault," I say coolly, as if the words come from someone else.

It's like a wrecking ball slams into me, knocking me back a step, a new wave of heat overwhelming me.

Embarrassment.

I step even further back into the room. Dropping my gaze to the floor. Raking my hands through my hair. There's a buzzing in my ears that makes everything sound muffled, my heart beating erratically inside of my head.

"It *was* my fault," King swallows, the words raspy, thick, uncomfortable. "I never should have-"

"Your fault because why? You're not a fucking mind reader, of course it isn't your fault! YOU DID NOTHING! It was me! I took the drugs, King, you didn't shove them down my throat! Stop with the fucking guilt! You can't control every fucking thing all the goddamn time. I took drugs because *I* felt better about myself, it had nothing to do with anyone else."

There is silence then, as my chest heaves, thinking of how every person in this house feels like it's their fault. What I did to myself. How they feel like they shoulda seen the signs, they should have said something when they did, not have let it get as far as addiction.

King still sending me out on runs, that's what he feels guilt over. Rex finding me blacked out with a needle still in my arm and not telling anybody those first few times, not until he found me slicing myself open with a razor.

That was the catalyst of it all.

That's their guilt, but it had no impact on my own actions.

That's not how real life works.

We are only ever in control of ourselves, our own actions and reactions. I took drugs because I thought I needed them. They made me feel better. For a moment. I hid it all well, until I couldn't anymore.

I blink.

"This why you're making your new wonder drug?" I interrupt, diverting my attention back to Rex. "Because of me?" Rex lowers his eyes, glancing between Bennett and King. "You think I'm going to fuck up again," a statement.

Hurt tumbles through me with more heat, more flushing of my face, more drowning embarrassment.

"You thought you could give me another option, something that won't ruin all of our lives if I fall off the wagon again. You can let me get away with my merry little addiction and continue living your everyday lives like it doesn't matter. Like it means nothing. Like I'm not broken."

"Lynx, *no,* that's not it, not at all-"

I nod, cutting Bennett off with a sad laugh, "I'm just a fuck up that keeps fucking up."

I rake my fingers through my hair, silence filling the space, but it's suffocating. I can't breathe in the stifling heat any longer. Swiping a shirt from Rex's open top drawer of his dresser, I shove my arms through the tight white fabric, tugging it down.

I push through them all, pausing when I get to the top of the stairs, all of their guilty eyes on me, "Don't wait up for me."

Bennett

"He wasn't supposed to find out," I sigh, dropping into the leather armchair in the basement den. "This was supposed to be an *in case of emergency*."

"Well, he knows," Flynn shrugs, dropping into the corner of the large L-shaped couch opposite me. "He'll get over it."

I lift my gaze to my best friend, his black curls falling over his pale forehead, bright blue eyes focusing on mine. Bare tattooed chest on full display, one hand shoved down his sweatpants, cupping his dick like I'm not right here, the other arm thrown over the back of the couch. His milky skin, a sharp contrast to the chocolate brown leather, icy blue veins stark ridges in his flesh.

"I want to protect him," my vision blurs, thinking of Lynx, out there somewhere, probably doing something fucking stupid.

"He's a grown man, he's beaten addiction, he'll get past this."

I'm nodding absentmindedly, listening but not taking anything in.

Instead, thinking of Poppy in my car. Curled up in the passenger seat as I ran through the snow, into the pharmacy, buying Plan B, and a bar of chocolate. Something I snapped into pieces inside the package before opening it on my way back to her, offering her up the first square of dark chocolate as I dropped a condensation covered bottle of water into her lap, the box in her hands and the chocolate in my fingers. She looked surprised, uncertain, but she parted those plump lips, extending her tongue to me as I held it up to her mouth, leaning over her in the open passenger door of the car.

"We gotta pull the boys off this shit." Flynn cracks his neck, twisting it as the small bones pop, his eyelids fluttering closed as he cranes it back.

Lilac eyes lifted to mine, she smiled, just a little, her pupils still blown, drugs, liquor, a chemical concoction I didn't want to think too much about still heavy in her veins.

"She trusted me," I say slowly, swirling the short glass tumbler of liquid courage around and around. "I wanted to hurt her." I throw the amber liquid into my mouth, fire burning its way down my esophagus, I swallow with a wince. "Couldn't do it." I think about the way I fucked her, rough, without care. "Not really." I lift my gaze to Flynn's then.

"She was already hurting herself enough," he says lowly, holding my eye, his jaw clicking as he grits his teeth. "I fucked her up a little extra, though. *For you.*"

I squeeze my fingers around the glass in my hand, the rim of it suctioning to my palm.

"You told Lynx you fucked her?" My gaze slides to his, a black brow raised in a high arch on his head in question.

"Pretty sure he knows, you all fucking watched me."

"Before last night," he says lowly, "at Graves. You fucked her in the restroom."

"I didn't tell anyone." I wrinkle my nose. "...You saw," I shoulda known, Flynn has eyes everywhere.

"You ashamed?" he swirls his own drink before knocking it back, "Or Disgusted?"

"I'm angry." A frown tugs hard at my lips, my eyes narrowing, "Disappointed," I sigh, "in myself."

Flynn's nodding, like the therapist he is, *should be.* Instead of working for a corrupt businessman like me. He's a little unhinged, but he could be better. *Without me.*

"I wasn't supposed to get involved with her."

"That what you are?" Flynn rasps, rubbing his hand over his short, dark stubble, his thumb smoothing up and down the length of his jaw. "Involved?"

"No," I frown harder, staring at the carpet. "I don't-" I cut myself off, forearm dangling over the arm of the chair, fingers almost brushing the coarse carpet, I let the empty glass slip free, thud softly to the floor.

"You like her," Flynn rumbles, all factually, unquestioning, he always knows.

"I don't want to." A truth, tangled in a lie. "I should hate her."

"You shouldn't, she never did anything to you, to us, your family. She's never done anything but trust us, been as genuine as she's able to be. But this shit, this is high school, bully-boy bullshit." Flynn shifts, leaning forward, forearms resting on his knees. He lifts his chin, expression open, "She's not okay," he swallows, I hear it, my gaze on the floor, unblinking, unseeing. "She might need to get help." He swallows again and guilt clogs my throat. "I think she might really need help now."

I nod.

"We call the boys off."

I nod again. Without argument. I've never been a bully, neither have my brothers. But Lynx, my blood brother, he seems a little too good at it for a boy who's soft.

I did that.

Made him hard.

Made him mean.

He's in love with her.

You fucked your brother's girl.

I look up. At Flynn. An unfamiliar seriousness to his sharp features, wide jaw, crazy fucking eyes.

"You want her too." I grind my teeth, flex my jaw, bite the inside of my cheek, digging my molars into the flesh.

"Her dad is still a problem, Benny."

I think of the phone call, the voice, the shouting. The memory makes my ears ring.

"I know."

Flynn doesn't ask me how, what, why, he just says, "She won't want us." He swallows, still holding my gaze, blue eyes flashing. "We need to talk to Lynx first." I sniff, nodding. "He needs to know we trust him, we love him. That we believe in him."

"I fucked up."

"You didn't, you're his brother, *we're* his brothers and we tried to do something to protect him."

"We should have told him. About the Venom, the why."

"We should have," Flynn agrees with a single nod, still holding my gaze. "We can fix this, *you* can fix this, with him, with her, for them." He finally looks away from me, breaking the taut snap of tension, but his deep blue gaze returns to mine with his final words, "For us."

"It's not her fault," Hendrix grinds his teeth, rolling his shoulders. "We have fucked up," he pronounces clearly, licking over his upper front teeth, his pierced tongue clicking against them. "This is your fault," he spits at me, and I can do nothing but agree.

I am silent, listening, taking everything they throw at me. Lynx still nowhere to be found. King and Rex side by side on the couch Flynn vacated to sit in the armchair at my side. King lifts his gray gaze onto mine, the half full, plastic water bottle between his hands crinkling as he flexes his fingers.

"I didn't wanna fucking hurt her," he swallows the thickness in his throat, self loathing, something heavier. "But I'm loyal," he sniffs hard, his grip tightening on the bottle, the cracking of thin plastic loud in the room. "To you." I hold his gaze, watching his braids fall into his eyes before he sweeps them back, palming the crown of his shaking head. "I should have fucking said no."

Flynn shifts, clearing his throat. Rex watches silently, his eyes darting between his two leaders. One he looks to to lead because it's the role I fell into when we were young. Whereas, the other, the other earned his loyalty through trust, friendship, all things that felt just a little harder for me to find with them. Because I was harsher, I was sterner. I had to be. To help us survive, to thrive.

"What do you think we should do?" it's clear, my question, but silence is what greets me.

I look between all of them, from Rex to Flynn, back to King. His dark brow furrowed, he nods, light gray eyes flicking over the room.

"We need to get Lynx back here," he says naturally, taking the lead without making a big deal out of it, and I let him.

Want him to.

Flynn's hand comes to my knee, his chin dipped, eyes lifted to mine, his fingertips press hard into the muscle of my thigh, and he's nodding at me. Reassurance, because I'm doing the right thing.

I'm letting it go.

Handing over the reins.

I'm gonna take a back seat and let King clean up my mess.

I just hope we still have a chance to fix things. To make it right. For me, my brothers, for her.

I think of the video posted to social media, the printed photos, all of her wet, naked body plastered over every corridor, classroom and student car windscreen. Her having to deal with it all by herself.

"Is she alone?" the question sort of tears out of me in a choked fashion, the words cracking as they escape my lips.

And as I look up, I realize they were all talking,

each of them staring at me from beneath scrunched brows, slightly narrowed eyes.

"She has two friends," King says then, licking his lips, almost nervously. "I texted one of them to go to her."

She stepped in front of a train.

I can't even blink. Seeing it, the train, the way she just… stepped back. The look on her pretty face. Something dark. Something like relief. I froze when I should have moved like the others, Flynn and Raiden getting to her before Rex, all three of them nearly sucked under the train. It was long, long seconds before the train flew past, my heart the only thing I could hear, and the three of them, bodies tangled, were revealed unharmed.

King holding her face in his hands, kissing her lips, smoothing her hair, speaking too low for me to hear his words, but I can imagine. And the way that Flynn was solid at her back, letting her trembling body lean against him. Between the two brothers that might actually be worthy of her. The way Rex barrelled over towards them, sliding through the earth on his shins to get his hands on her. He, too, probably the worthiest of us all.

I'm no good for her.

"Are they…" I swallow, not even really sure of my question.

Are they safe? Can we trust them? Will they hold her when she cries?

"She's fine with them," Raiden says sharply, and I wonder for a moment what they were talking about before I interrupted.

What things I should have been listening to. Paying attention to. All the ways in which Raiden will undoubtedly attempt to fix this shit.

If it's even possible.

I clench my jaw, thinking of fucking her, pulling out of her and coming on her fucking back. Because she's not on any birth control and I don't think it's the worst thing in the world to knock her up with my demon spawn. But also, I'm not a fucking terrorist. I wouldn't put my kid in her just to fuck up her life more. She doesn't need shit from me to aid in that.

"What're you doing?" Poppy whispers from my passenger seat as I pull into the parking lot of the pharmacy.

Slowly, I drag my gaze over to her, putting the car in park, and releasing my restraint, leaving the engine running so the heat stays on for her. Her long legs are pulled up tight to her chest, the seat belt wrapped all the way around her, I'm not sure it'd save her if we were to crash, but she's a smart girl, she probably knows that.

"Getting you Plan B," I look away then, her long, gold-streaked dark hair heavy in her lilac eyes.

"Why?" her voice is like a haunting in the dark space of the car, the scent of leather and liquor and her flooding my senses.

It's intoxicating. Being around her. Someone I'm supposed to want to destroy.

"*Because I protect you,*" I tell her, even knowing it's a lie.

Lynx

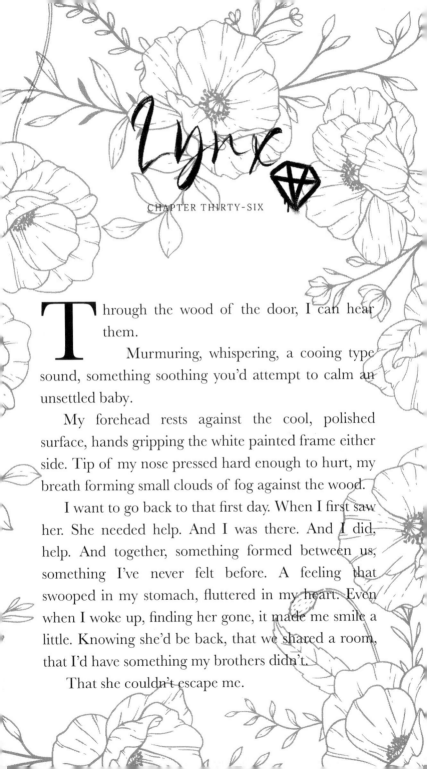

CHAPTER THIRTY-SIX

Through the wood of the door, I can hear them.

Murmuring, whispering, a cooing type sound, something soothing you'd attempt to calm an unsettled baby.

My forehead rests against the cool, polished surface, hands gripping the white painted frame either side. Tip of my nose pressed hard enough to hurt, my breath forming small clouds of fog against the wood.

I want to go back to that first day. When I first saw her. She needed help. And I was there. And I did, help. And together, something formed between us, something I've never felt before. A feeling that swooped in my stomach, fluttered in my heart. Even when I woke up, finding her gone, it made me smile a little. Knowing she'd be back, that we shared a room, that I'd have something my brothers didn't.

That she couldn't escape me.

It's why I didn't tell them right away. A little self-ishly, I wanted to keep her to myself. Make her want me, know then, that even after meeting *them*, Rex, King, she'd never look at anyone but me. *See* anyone but me.

I've had so much torn away from me in my life, it felt as though the world was finally gifting me something.

Only then to laugh in my face, stab me in the heart and rip it all away.

I think of her wide, wet eyes, the bruises to her cheekbone, the way she was so fucking high, she laughed as she sobbed in that shower. And I let the world see it. I exposed it to the world, the pain that *I* caused her.

It wasn't only my cum and her tears that were washed down the drain in that shower.

I feel doors banging shut up and down the length of this hall, hear whispers as people pass at my back, but I don't care what they say about the junkie hockey player. I don't really give a fuck what anyone says about me. Thinks about me.

Except for her.

Sucking in a sharp breath, opening my eyes, I rap my knuckles against the door. Silence now beyond it. My head spins, and I think of pills, of powders, of needles, razors and blood. And I wonder if she'll do it all with me.

Lose herself with me.

Me with her.

The two of us together.

Oblivion could be a beautiful thing if we weren't lost in it alone.

There's movement beyond the wooden blockade separating us, like shuffling knees on the rough carpet. I could use my key, the door probably not even locked anyway, but I don't, slowly, finger by blanched finger, I release my hold on the frame, take a step back from the door. My eyes never leaving the wood, I trace the grains, the darker lines, deeper colors. Studying it as I listen to my pulse pound in my ears, my breathing too hard and too quick, chest heaving with every breath.

Anticipation.

To see her.

To do something.

All of it confusing inside my head, but after last night, what we did, what I orchestrated. Knowing full well that Hendrix and Raiden alike were not happy about it. But they are loyal, to a fault. I wish they weren't so catering to me since I've been back. I wish my brother had never seen her, that Flynn never looked into her. I wish that I'd hidden her better, kept her safe, kept her just for me.

"Oh, fuck no," the blond from the dorm opposite ours half screeches as she opens the door. "Sleep somewhere else, *buddy*," she clucks her tongue, throwing the door in my face, but I place my foot over the threshold, the flimsy door ricocheting back in towards her. "Lynx!" she whines, stomping a foot. "Get the fuck out, you're not welcome here." Her arms are flung wide, blocking the opening.

The room is dark beyond, the lights around the window aglow, but I can't see anything with the way she holds the door, shielding her friend.

It makes my heart happier, knowing Poppy's not alone, but it thuds harder with pain all the same.

"Let him in," it's another female voice, not the one I"m aching to hear, but it's familiar all the same.

"Emma," I say her name with a thread of relief.

She's a smart girl, when she isn't high, we shared a couple classes last year, a few too many lines, too, but she's sensible, mostly.

"What?!" the blond before me half-snarls as she whips around, still barring the door to glare at her friend.

But Emma isn't looking at her, her dark eyes are lifted over the blond's head of thick, curly hair, locked on mine.

"You need to deal with this," she warns, volume low, coming closer, standing tall, shoulders back, unafraid. "You have royally fucked up," she hisses, real anger in her tone that makes my gut pinch. "What is *wrong* with you?"

The blond turns back to me, a smug grin on her plush mouth, realizing her friend is taking her side after all. I don't say anything for long moments, staring into her rich brown eyes, narrowed on me with her temper. It feels good, someone not babying me just because I'm fresh out of rehab.

I think of her question.

'What is wrong with you?'

And I do and don't have an answer.

Everything feels appropriate. But I'm not talking to Flynn. I'm not in fucking therapy, AA, I'm in the open doorway of my dorm, *my* girl on the other side of it and I don't gotta answer to these two.

"Move," I snarl at blondie, shoving her into the door, sending it wide.

She squeals with a grunt at my back as the door thuds against the wall with her weight falling against it. I step inside, blinking in the dim light, eyes scanning the room to find her. And when I do, nothing inside of me seems to work right.

Emma stands right before me, unmoving like a brick wall. I make to step around her, but she follows my movement, halting my steps, dark eyes on mine. I sigh, yielding, shoving a hand through my hair. Waiting.

"If you hurt her again," she whispers, dark and threatening, "I'l-"

"I won't."

Not unless she wants us to hurt together.

Emma's dark eyes narrow the tiniest amount, squinting at the inner corners, the skin tightening and then she smooths out her expression, nods, glancing back over her shoulder at Poppy, the girl I can't stand to look at yet.

"I'm gonna come back later, sweetie," Emma says softly, waiting.

Chin over her shoulder, her gaze on Poppy. My own focusing on the top of the wall over her head of thick braids. When she waits a few more long seconds, eyes still on Poppy, and still gets no response, inhaling deeply, she sighs, turning back to me.

"I'm right across the hall," she glares at me as she says it, low and slow beneath her breath, a warning I grit my teeth at, but I'm nodding all the same, wanting to get fucking rid of her.

I don't move, barely breathing as the two girls from the dorm opposite leave. I wait for the door to click closed at my back, the tapping of their soft footsteps across the corridor, whispering as their own door opens and closes.

There's silence, the drumming of my heart loud in my ears, but I can still hear her breathing, the soft, low sound of it. Slow, even inhales and exhales of air and my eyes drag to her without permission.

Poppy sits atop her bed, her body upright, leaning against the wall in the corner of the room. Her mass of thick hair curtained around her face, forward over her shoulders, knees drawn up to her chest, but she doesn't cling to them. Her arms lie limp, one in her lap, the other at her side, palm up on the bed. She stares off towards the other side of the room, side onto me where I still hover just inside the center of the room, door at my back.

"Poppy?" I whisper unintentionally, my voice cracking, I lick my lips, moving closer, my eyes only on her.

My insides swirl, sickness like a razored lead weight in my gut, as I get a clearer look at her, the bruising on her beautiful face, the red marks around her wrists. I edge closer, holding my breath, watching, waiting for her to react, to see me. To tell me to get away. To scream. To do something. Anything.

I reach out, fingertips just brushing her inner elbow and she flinches so hard her shoulder thuds into the wall.

I retract my hand, letting it hang at my side, her eyes on me now, arms crossing tight in her lap, to her chest.

I don't know what to do, how to stand, what to feel. Let alone know what to say. I hover, it feels like, between time and space. Indecision warring inside of me as she continues to stare, unblinking, unseeing. The tips of my fingers burning like I was singed by her skin when I touched her.

I take a step back, licking my lips, holding her gaze, but it's as though she looks right through me. As though I'm not even here.

Sweat forming beneath my arms, I feel uneasy, hot, cold, goosebumps rippling my flesh. I could walk away, say nothing, leave her the fuck alone. It's probably what I *should* do, but, instead, I shuffle towards the end of her bed, leaving her at the top end, me sitting at the foot of it. I clasp my hands, lacing my fingers together, elbows to my spread knees. I stare at the carpet between us, a glow from the little twinkling lights around the window cast my shadow long, my eyes tracing the silhouette of myself, her shadow not beside mine, her body too curled up in the corner to reveal her.

I think about telling her I'm sorry, it's what I should start with. An apology. But it just feels wrong. Not authentic, pointless. I don't have any way of showing her how sorry I am. I just want to explain to her. Not so she *understands,* just so she knows. I just want her to know what happened, why I did what I did.

That it wasn't her.

You did nothing wrong, beautiful girl. It was all me, me, me. I'm the one that's broken.

I'm fucked up.

I ruin things.

People.

I wanted to keep you.

"When I was fourteen, I drank beer for the first time." I think back to that, Raiden's dad held a family barbecue, all the neighbors came. "We snuck some cans from the ice buckets, drank them down the side of the house in some bushes." I glance up, looking at her still looking through me. "I hated it," I shrug, "but that didn't stop me from always joining in. It was Hendrix who smoked first, King was never into it, he just cared about sports. And I just wanted to make sure I always fit in. So I did both. Whatever either one of them did, I made sure I did it too."

So they couldn't leave me behind.

I shake my head at myself, thinking of all the stupid shit I've done because I wanted to fit. I spent all my life attempting to fit in with people who never needed me to. I fit with them because they liked me for me. Loved me.

"Senior year of high school was when I really started partying, hard liquor, hard drugs. I thought it was like social smoking. Thought I'd just get high on the weekends, Fridays, Saturdays. I was more fun, people wanted to hang around me. I was popular, it was... heady, I guess, which is dumb, cause I never really gave a fuck about popularity. Then I got here and it was the same, but free-er. Drugs were now Wednesdays after eleven because I didn't have class on a Thursday, only hockey practice at seven and I could get high all night, sleep it off for a few hours, drag my ass to practice."

My brow furrows a little, staring into the shadowed room, my bed, I've slept in twice, pushed flush against the opposite wall, my crinkled sheets still in a ball, untouched from the last time I slept here. It makes me think of last year, how I was never in my own bed then, either.

"When I started bursting into my classes at the wrong times on the wrong days, sleeping in random houses, cars, abandoned buildings." I swallow. Hard. "I wanted to die," I whisper the words into the room, "I tried to," I swallow, "I switched pills for needles and hoped an accidental overdose would take me out. And when that didn't work, I cut myself open, trying to end it all, but Rex found me." Focussing on my shadow, climbing the opposite wall with the soft orange glow at my back from her lights around the window, a sliver of light slicing in from the streetlamp beyond it. "What does..." I trail off, thinking about my question. Words hushed, "What does it feel like for you, getting high?"

Chin dipped, I glance right, looking at her from beneath my lashes. She still stares at me. Silent. I'm not sure she's blinked the entire time. The air feels heavy. With my question, it feels heavier. I watch her chest rise and fall, slow but fast, heavy but light. My own doing something similar.

"I think," I lick my lips, dropping my gaze with a gentle shake of my head, "I think I miss it some days." I lift my head then, looking at her, my arm shifting, fingers unlinking.

I let my fingers crawl over her light colored bedding, towards her bare foot, chipped dark polish on her little round toes. Her eyes finally move, rolling to the bottom of their sockets, tracking the slow creep of my thick fingers, she doesn't try to stop me. And this time, when my warm skin meets her cold, she doesn't flinch, her eyes flutter closed, nostrils flaring, she draws in a shuddery breath.

"I can be whoever you want me to be." I swallow, the whisper cracking as it slips free. "I can be whatever you want." My fingers smooth over the tiny bones in the top of her foot, little solid ridges beneath her light skin. "We can get high together, right now, Treasure." I think of pills, of needles, of blood. "I can be whatever you need, we can fly off of the edge together."

I watch her face, bruised, her lip split, swollen on one side, shiny, with something slick, like a balm to soothe it. Her light eyes lift to mine, dead and dull, and it has nothing to do with the darkness of the room.

"Go home, Lynx," she whispers shakily, like she's frightened, can't quite catch her breath.

Brow creasing, fingers digging harder into her foot, my lips part, ready to protest, when her eyes snap shut, squeeze closed. Her foot slipping out from beneath my fingers, quickly tucking up beneath her, shielding it from me.

"Please," she whispers again, chin quivering. "Please."

Bottom lip rolling into my mouth, I push to stand, turning away from her, towards the door.

"Not that it means anything," I say, staring hard at the wood of the door. "But I wish I could take it all back." I swallow, hating myself. "I don't think sorry really means anything, it's just a word people teach their children to make it look like they're well behaved, polite. And I didn't even explain myself. I guess, maybe, I didn't want to make an excuse for my behavior. I just want to be sorry without saying the shitty word. I-" I almost choke on my runaway words, but I lick my lips, make sure to say them clearly anyway. "I loved myself. That first week. I loved myself. And it was because of you." I feel my lip tremble, voice cracking. "You deserve the world, Treasure." I sniff, palming the doorknob, and without looking back, I pull the door open, leaving my heart behind.

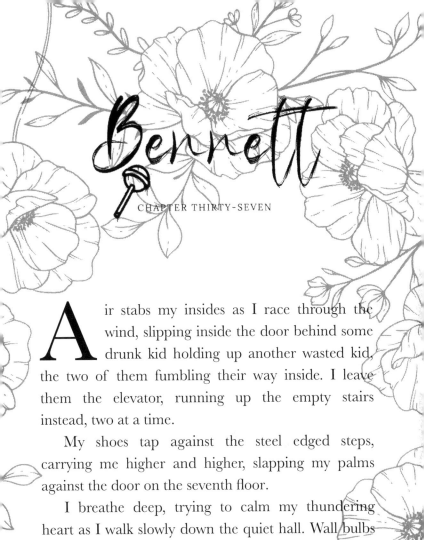

Bennett

Air stabs my insides as I race through the wind, slipping inside the door behind some drunk kid holding up another wasted kid, the two of them fumbling their way inside. I leave them the elevator, running up the empty stairs instead, two at a time.

My shoes tap against the steel edged steps, carrying me higher and higher, slapping my palms against the door on the seventh floor.

I breathe deep, trying to calm my thundering heart as I walk slowly down the quiet hall. Wall bulbs click on as I pass their sensors, automatically lighting the path ahead of me.

Curled fist to the wood, I knock, rapping my knuckles against Poppy's door, eyes fixed to the floor, the scuffed toes of my shoes.

There's no movement, no sounds, nothing beyond the thin blockade separating me from her. I test the handle, both pleasantly and unpleasantly surprised to find it unlocked, and I'm inside the dimly lit space, closing the door at my back.

I don't wait for her to speak, I don't wait for objection. I stride towards her, huddled in the corner of the room, her eyes wide on me, lips parted, I bend over her, grip her waist and heft her up. Spinning us and sitting myself down in her pillows, I pull her into me, straddle her over my lap, band my arms around her and hold tight.

"What are you doing?" she whispers, my chest heaving, hers slow and steady, but I can feel her heart through her back, thudding harder and harder against my palm.

She's stiff in my hold, uncomfortable, but I've done far worse things to her that made her uncomfortable, this, this is nothing.

I cock my head, licking my lips, stare up into her eyes where she's hovering just above me, her knees trembling where she's pushed herself up onto her shins, trying to avoid being flush with my cock.

"We need to talk-"

"I don't have anything to say to yo-"

"Don't give a fuck, Lollipop, I'm gonna speak, you're gonna listen. That's how it's gonna go-"

"What is wrong with you? Why are you always like this, you talk over me, and I talk over you and you smirk as you do it, and yo-"

"Are gonna keep doing just that until you hear me

out," I finish for her.

She huffs, her thighs trembling with the way her legs are angled, weight on her shins. My arms clamped around her back, she plants her hands on my chest, pushing against me, her back into my hands. She squirms on top of me, huffing and puffing and my dick is getting harder and harder and she keeps moving, keeps struggling, but I only grip her tighter. And then she just… stops.

Slumping into my hold, hands slipping from my chest, like lifeless dying tree branches hanging in our laps. She stares off over my shoulder, at the wall, her eyes going dead in her head like someone took a gun to her, splattered her brains against the ceiling.

"Poppy," I say, my body feeling tense now, like I just broke her, and she's not responsive to me as I chant her name over and over.

She's in a loose, oversized shirt, nothing but tiny sleep shorts hanging low on her hips, spread wide, the leg holes on them gaping where she's pulled over my lap. My fingertips press harshly into her spine, digging into her flesh and she does nothing, she doesn't look at me.

"Lollipop," I say, licking my lips, breathing her in, fall, pumpkin, vanilla, warm and comforting, soft. "Lollipop, I need you to fucking hear me when I say this, please, fuck, pay me attention. I'm not going to give up and leave just because you ignore me, you little brat."

That gets her fucking attention.

"I'm not a brat, you're a fucking arsehole," the way she pronounces it, rolling the R in the slur, all prim and proper and British, makes my lips twitch with a laugh and she hits me, her splayed hand, the heel of her palm colliding with my collarbone in a harsh smack. "Stop laughing."

She scowls at me, her split lip pouting, slick with something shiny. That's when I notice the bruises, really taking them in.

Poppy staggers forward, long, black dress clinging to every bone and curve, bag tight over her head, a gag, I tied, beneath it, in her mouth, tied at the back of her head, stopping her from objecting.

And Lynx is shoving her between the shoulder blades. Too hard. *I think, blinking as I watch it happen, as though slow motion, her body slamming face first into the earth. I'm curling my fists and I'm staring down at her as Rex is gentle, lifting her beneath the arms, righting her, holding onto her like she's a jewel, precious,* his. *Scowl on his face for my brother who keeps walking.*

But she's breathing hard, too hard, she's panicking and I feel my own chest tighten with panic. Panic for her. I don't want you to die. *I'm tearing the bag over her head, yanking the gag down her cheeks, rubbed red from it.* Too tight. *I tied it too fucking tight.*

· · ·

432

"Nothing you've ever done to me is funny, Bennett."

It sobers me like a slap to the face. I swallow. Dryly, licking my tongue over my teeth, gritting them.

"I should take you to Urgent Care," it's raspy, the words, the way they come out, concern lacing them even though she wouldn't know it. "You should get this looked at," I breathe, my breath over her mouth where she's glancing down at me, still in my lap, her hands coming up to rest on my shoulders. "I don't think anything I've done to you is funny, Poppy."

She drops her gaze, staring down between our bodies, where she finally, finally, is resting on me now, my cock limp beneath her, unthreatening. She swallows at the same time I do, and I smooth my hands up her back. Cupping the back of her neck, guiding her to look at me, my other splaying over the center of her spine. Holding her to me, her tits brushing my pecs.

"Baby girl, I'm sorry." I might choke, waiting for her to say something. When she doesn't, her lilac eyes on mine, shadows and bruising on her delicate face, I continue. "Those boys," she flinches, but she doesn't look away, this is how she was in the passenger seat of my car, soft, placid, all of her attention on me. "They hurt you because I told them to. After I met you, I got Flynn to look into you."

She says nothing, still staring and then, "Because you wanted to check out who Lynx was going to be living with."

"Exactly, I didn't want him living with a-"

"An addict," she says quietly, still holding my gaze and somehow it feels better and worse all wrapped in one.

I nod slowly, her fingers curling tighter into my shoulders. "And then," I glance away, just trying to form the words in my head, the way everything seemed to spiral. "Then I found out who your father is."

Her brow scrunches, confusion etched deep, because she doesn't fucking understand, she knows nothing.

"What does he have to do with us?" she whispers, worry in her throat.

The way she says *us* has my dick twitching, that means she thinks of us as something singular, in the present, not the past. I smooth my hands over her spine, squeezing her nape just a little tighter, my thumb pressing into the side of her throat.

"A long time ago, mine and Lynx's dad was sent to jail. Money fraud, tax evasion. A whole host of other shit, but my dad is as straight laced as they come, never missed a receipt, always double checked everything he had to declare. He was a good guy, bit of a math nerd to be honest. Turns out it was his construction company's offshore accountant that set it up. Moving money, pushing through fake contracts. Our dad ends up getting twenty years."

Poppy gasps, fingers flexing in my shoulders, tightening, "Oh, that's…" her forehead wrinkles, brows drawing in, beautiful, this girl, she's fucking perfect. "I don't understand…"

"What that has to do with your father," I finish for her, nodding. "My dad's accountant's name was Michael Edward Carrington, an office in Kensington, a home address in Surrey, England." I watch her as I tell her, my tone softening with each word as she takes it in, processing, and I'm staring into her eyes as they seem to glaze over, still on mine.

"You're sure?" is all she says, a little blankly.

Disconnected.

Where do you go inside that pretty, dark head of yours, beautiful girl?

"Yes. I'm very sure."

"I'm sorry," she tries to duck her head.

Her hair swishing around us, curtaining us with it, but my grip on her neck doesn't allow her to move too far from me as I feel her try to lift up. Her fingers clench harder in my button down and I'm clutching her tighter to me. Our chests flush.

"Look at me," I demand it, and her eyes snap to mine, glossy with tears. "You *never* apologize to me, Poppy," I tell her seriously, meaning it with my whole fucking soul. "Never. You understand?"

She trembles, her entire body vibrating and I think back to her in my car again. That night screws with my fucking head. Fucking her in the bar.

"That's why Lynx finished with me," she says

solemnly, and my heart pangs, the look on her face, distraught. "You," she breathes in, shuddering, "you wanted to make me suffer. Because of *him*."

"Poppy, I-"

"No, I," she shakes her head, dropping her gaze, just briefly, before bringing it back to mine. "I get it," she twitches her nose, her eyes squinting a little as she bites on her bottom lip, wincing as she does, the swelling making her thick lips even bigger.

"I don't want a fucking acceptance, Poppy," I frown, lines etching deep in my face. "That's not, *Jesus*, I just wanted to explain so you understood, so you knew it was never about you. And I directed my anger wrong, and I ruined what y- I fucked up. I fucked the *fuck* up and I set those boys against you and they are loyal to me. And they shouldn't be. I led them wrong and you suffered, and it's all my fault. I'm not asking you to forgive any of us. Especially not me, but I want you to know." I swallow, the lump in my throat suffocating.

She has no idea how good she is. What she does to me. How she makes me feel. All of us. God, she's so beautiful and sad, and fucked up, but so good.

"You are so perfect," it's a raspy whisper, the confession pulled deep from my blackened heart. "You are brilliant, and beautiful, and lost." She looks at me then, tears dripping down her swollen cheeks. "Lost is okay," I reassure her, dropping my head against hers, a small smile curling my mouth. "You deserve people who love you, will put you first, who will keep you safe." She trembles in my arms, my shirt gripped so tight in her hands. "A family who will love you no matter what, will help you and hold you and love you." I take a deep breath, ducking my head so I'm inside the waterfall of her dark hair, our lips almost touching as I lift my head from where it rests against hers. "We can do that for you," I tell her, meaning it. "Even though we don't deserve you. We could do that. Can. Will."

Poppy squeezes her eyes shut tight, her breath held in her chest as she tries to control her cries. And with a shuddery exhale, her chest deflating finally. She licks her lips, looking at me, the vision of her a little fuzzy at the close proximity, but I hold her gaze.

"I can't," she breathes, my insides heavy, weighted, useless. "I can't," she shakes her head softly. "Knowing, *that*. I… I can't."

My eyes are burning, and I cling onto her harder, tighter, wanting to claw my way inside of her. I'm moving, closing the distance between our mouths and claiming hers in a kiss meant to say goodbye. She's frozen, lips unmoving as I lap my tongue over her mouth, tasting antiseptic and iron and pain. I knot my fist in her hair, gentle as I tug her head back, my mouth kissing her face, lapping at her tears, mouthing along her cheekbones, down her jaw, and she's kissing me back and I'm drowning in her.

She's kissing me back, her lips parting, my tongue

pushing between her teeth, and she groans into my mouth, my hand slips down her spine, gripping her ass and she moves with me. Grinding down over my lap, little breaths fanning over my lips as she breaks our kiss, untangling her fingers from my shirt to close them around the back of my neck.

"Bennett," she gasps, moving her hips with me as I use my grip on her ass to work her over my cock, hard and pulsing beneath my tight slacks.

"That's it, Lollipop," I hush, grinding her into me, hissing as her panties slip to the side, exposing just a little bit of her heat. "Fuck," I'm panting, kissing her again, directing her lips back to mine with my hold on her neck. "Good girl," I say between kisses, "good fucking girl, come for me, don't stop, Lollipop."

She nips my jaw, dropping her head to my shoulder, both of us watching her move. The heat of her cunt like lava enveloping me, a shiver tears up my spine as her nails dig into my skin.

"I don't forgive you," she suddenly gasps, her eyes flicking to mine, "this doesn't mean I forgive you."

"I know, I know, just, keep going, Poppy, don't stop, beautiful."

She moves faster, pushing herself down harder, grinding along my length, the crown of my cock catching on the inside of my zipper every time she hits me just right.

"You don't forgive me, I don't want you to." She groans with me, her hips stuttering, she's close and

I'm fucking close and I grit my teeth, hissing, "Don't fucking stop."

"Bennett," she cries, my grip on her neck punishing, my fingers digging into her ass as her pace slows, faltering as she starts to come, and I'm climbing higher, my heart hammering inside my chest, trying to break free, and I'm coming too.

Her breathy voice in my ear, "Bennett, Bennett, Bennett."

A chant, my name, as she comes and I'm finishing inside of my pants and I don't care as she slows, but she doesn't stop, whimpering against my cheek, her lips parted and wet. Her breath humid down the side of my neck as she slows to a stop, her chest heaving in an uneven rhythm with my own. Slumped in my arms, my head thudding back against the wall. I cradle her to my chest.

"Let me stay with you, Poppy. Hate me tonight, Lollipop, and then hate me again in the morning, but let me stay."

"I don't forgive you," she whispers, but she's still in my fucking arms.

It feels like a losing victory.

"Good."

Raiden

"What do we say?" Rex asks as we stalk down the hall towards Poppy's final class of the day.

I peer at him from the corner of my eye, keeping up with the original pace I set that feels a little like running.

"I don't know," I confess, Rex's steps faltering for a moment, leaving him behind me, but I don't stop, students parting as I make my way through the halls.

"Wait, *what?* I thought you had a plan," he jogs back up beside me, falling into step, his eyes on me, burning into the side of my face, but I don't waste time looking at him. "You always have a plan."

"She spent the night with Bennett," I say it through gritted teeth, every single part of me fucking hating it, but also, not, I don't want her to ever be alone ever again.

"What?"

"He forced his way in, then he never left," I swallow and it feels like razor blades on the back of my tongue.

"That fucker."

My thoughts exactly.

"You think this is because he wanted her for himself?" Rex is almost breathless at my side as we take the stairs up to the Math department.

"You smoke too much," I inform him, but he ignores me, keeps talking.

"I know he explained how they met, but, shit, man, we had her first. If it wasn't for him, we wouldn't even know about the connection. That would have been better wouldn't it? We wouldn't even have to be sorry right now because she would have just been ours! Safe and loved and we could have helped her. All of us together, we could have helped her and we wouldn't have had to share her. Don't you think, King?"

All of Rex's questions swirl inside my head, anger nipping at my heels like a dog in chase, and I'm just about ready to explode. Anger at Bennett, at Flynn, at Lynx, myself.

How did I not see it?

Her using.

Why didn't her words click in my thick fucking skull when we talked, our whispered confessions in the night. She was telling me then, wasn't she? A plea that I couldn't figure out. Silent desperation for help.

"'Yeah, I get like, anxiety and stuff now," she frowns hard like she's somewhere else. "It took me a long time to try and move past it," she rasps, her voice low and cracked. "Don't think I ever will.'"

I didn't understand, baby girl.

Just like I didn't with Lynx.

"Hendrix," I bite his name off as it tears up my throat like a growl, my feet stilling. "Please, stop talking, I can't- I can't focus and your voice is like a screwdriver being pushed in through my ear."

"Wow," he says with a scoff, a laugh, half-hearted as he tries to shrug it off.

I'm walking again, seeing the door to Poppy's class up ahead, breathing a sigh of relief that it's not let out yet. And then I'm planting myself in front of it, glaring through the small circular window, up into the lecture hall, my eyes scanning over the sea of faces, only searching for one.

I didn't think she would attend today, but Flynn said something about credits, and her dad, and then I tuned out, grabbing my keys and getting in my truck. Driving straight here. Finding Rex already in the parking lot as I haphazardly pulled in.

I spot her, far in the back, her head dipped, shoulders drawn in, slumped down as low as she can with her tall frame in her seat, nobody sitting around her, three or more seats between her and the nearest student. Nobody looks at her, their gazes all fixed on the professor, or their phones hidden in their laps like they think they're being really sneaky about it.

I keep staring and I think I like the way she looks when she's lost inside her own head, alone, no distractions around her interrupting her thoughts. And then her eyes lift, those pretty silver-lilacs, and they're on mine, like she knew I was here. A short crease digging between her brows, staring back at me, and, momentarily, I don't breathe. Can't quite catch my breath at the sight of the blues and reds and purples, the plume of them down the side of her face.

We did that to her.

Rex is talking at my back, talking and talking and I'm staring at someone I wanted to protect, wearing bruises crafted by my brothers, by me, and my heart thuds so hard inside my chest, I think I might go into cardiac arrest. And then I'm spinning around, my clenched fist aimed at Rex's jaw.

But he's ready.

Rex leans back, ducking, his hands coming up to block himself from me, my fist colliding with his forearms as he staggers back out of my way.

Arms dropping to my sides, my chest is heaving. I'm breathing so hard and Rex is now too, his chest rising and falling fast. All I can hear inside my head is the roar of my own blood, the thud of my heart. Anger is a dense, red cloud that I can't clear. Rex's hands up in front of him, palms face out, towards me, his brow low. He could beat me in a fight on skill. But

I think, maybe, because of my anger, I could win on rage alone.

I don't wanna fight with my brothers.

We promised we'd never let anyone come between us.

Not something we really had to worry about, *we* are the ones who came between us.

We ruined everything ourselves.

"It's okay," he says smoothly, automatically. "You didn't do it, you didn't hurt her," he coos like he can see inside my fucking head. "It's okay."

"None of this is okay," my voice breaks as I say it, fisting my hands, Rex dropping his, slowly to his sides.

How could I not know?

I think of Rex, of Lynx, their fight, the way Lynx laughed maniacally because Rex knew about Poppy and the pills, and didn't say anything. He never said how he found out about it either.

"How did you know?" the words slip off of my tongue as easy as breathing and I don't need to add anything else to my question.

The way his pale green eyes narrow, seeming to darken as his pupils flare, a hand shoving through his ashy brown hair, he drops his gaze, shifting his feet, sneakers squeaking loudly in the empty hall, before he lifts his gaze back to mine.

"I saw her in the library," he sighs, tapping his fingers over his mouth as he tries not to mumble. "Her eyes gave her away, she was sluggish, but she was sad and I got angry." He shakes his head, still holding my gaze, confessing. "I didn't handle it how I should have," he says these words lower, quietly, despite the abandoned hall, only he and I, and the class beyond the very solid door. "I was scared." Shame highlights his cheeks in a bloom of pink, his fingers drumming over his lips harder. "I scared her, I think, being so... and she'd been with Flynn before. I fucked up and then I said nothing about it because it was after. Ya know, everything. I thought it didn't matter because we weren't supposed to care." He shrugs his shoulders, arms limp, fingers still fidgeting over his mouth.

When did we stop communicating?

Why have I missed all of these things?

She brought me back my light, and I let hers die.

"It's okay." My turn to reassure him now, it's what we do, whenever one of us fucks up, acceptance, quickly followed by forgiveness.

Why couldn't we do that for her?

"I don't wanna lose her, Raiden," Rex breathes deep, breath rushing out of his nose as he sighs.

"What about Lynx?" I swallow, thinking of Lynx's silence.

A punishment for himself.

We need to stop that, and soon.

"He slept in my room last night," Rex glances at the door at my back, a stampede of feet quickly approaching. "I think he'll be all right, whatever happens," he says reluctantly, like it's only half a lie if he tells it to himself. "He's in love with her," he smiles, dropping his gaze as his lips twist with a grimace.

"And?" I coax, stepping closer, hearing the door click open at my back, but I don't look even as Rex takes a couple steps back, watching for Poppy, before he switches his gaze back to me.

"And *I'm* in love with *him*, but I don't want that to interfere," he swallows, gripping the nape of his neck. "I don't want that to interfere with his feelings for her. And I'm happy for him, if that's what he wants."

"You want her too?" I ask it, knowing he does, but Rex has this nervous habit of catering too much to everyone else's feelings and shoving his own to the bottom of the pile.

Something else we all need to pay closer attention to, too.

"Not if it-"

"Hendrix," I hush, stepping into him, his back almost flush with the adjacent wall to the lecture hall. "Do you want her too?" My eyes flicker between his, his fingers dropping from his mouth, curling into his palms, I can tell by the way his shoulders flex.

"Yes," he nods, just once, his hair brushing my face as he does.

"Good," I say, "then you should tell Lynx how you feel," I tell him, drawing in a breath, glancing over my shoulder, his green eyes running over everyone passing at my back. "Let's go get our girl."

❦ 447 ❦

Poppy

Eye socket knocking with every too deep breath I take, pain strikes through my brain cavity, skull aching from the bruising in my face, to my head.

It is constant, the pound of physical pain, memories haunting me night and, now, day.

Train.

Heat.

Cupboard.

Thud. Thud. Thud.

Heart erratic in my chest. Heat rolling down my cheek, painful pinching in my gums, even my teeth feel bruised. Everything hurting and aching and sore. But I ignore it all for thoughts of the man I know to be in the hall.

Raiden's grey gaze funnels into my mind's eye without even having to try summoning visions of him. His light brown skin, glistening with beads of sweat, the roll of his hips, the feel of his braids against my face where he hovers over top of me. I see it all, feeling it all, my belly rolling with a dangerous mixture of want and anxiety.

He's actually in the corridor. Here. Outside of *my* class. Something none of the other boys take, but maybe he has another friend in this class he's waiting on. Perhaps, he's not here for me at all.

My eye blurs and I blink to clear it, a couple more blinks until I can see and then it's okay.

'Let me take you to Urgent Care.'

'Let me stay with you, Poppy.'

'You don't forgive me, I don't want you to.'

'Hate me tonight, Lollipop, and then hate me again in the morning, but let me stay.'

Today it all feels like I let myself down. All of Bennett's words really translating as *let me love you even though I hardly know you and I tried to ruin your life.* And I just said *okay.*

We cuddled.

And I didn't hate him.

Not even a little bit.

I hated myself, though.

All I could think about was Lynx. How he and Bennett are such stark contrasts of each other in so many ways, but so much the same in others.

Yet, it was Bennett, the mastermind, that I took into my bed.

I shake my head, bundling books up into my

arms, closing my computer, the snap of it making me flinch, dragging me out of my head and back into the room. I blink again, blurred vision, a swirl of sickness in my gut, but I grip my laptop between my fingers, slide it onto the very top of my book pile and straighten to fully stand, clutching it all to my chest.

I think I'm the only person in this class to have physical books and not an e-reader. Seems like a dumb idea of mine now, wanting *real* books, when they're such a ballache to carry without throwing them all over the floor as I juggle.

Turning towards the stairs of the auditorium, I shuffle past the now empty seats, peer down the length of my nose, through the blurred vision of my eye, over my stack, the cold metal of my computer pressing to my chin as I find the steps. Cautiously taking them one at a time as everyone else files out as quickly as they can. I'm halfway down when I feel him.

I don't look up, but my feet still, pausing me in the centre of the steps.

"Princess," King rasps, his voice gravelly and rough, not broken, but it feels like it's damaged.

My eyes squeeze closed, bottom lip trembling.

"Kitten," Rex drawls, lazily, but sad, so sad, and I can't get my legs to work, my knees shaking at the realisation that he's here too.

They came for me.

I stumble back, collapsing against the nearest

desk. My books and computer clattering to the floor but I don't care, bringing my hands up, burying my face into my palms. A deep, wracking sob stifled in the cup of my hands. Cold and clammy against my aching face.

Hands smooth over my shoulders, down my spine, a chest pressing to the top of my head where I bow forward, the other body wrapping himself around me. King at my front, Rex draping over my back, both of them holding me and saying nothing, and I breathe them in, through the humid breath in my hands, oranges, black pepper, and smoke and sugar. A mixture of scents that feel like home.

Strong muscles, and firm hands.

Warm and safe and mine.

"Sit down here with us," King rasps, clearing his throat quietly.

Thick fingers circle my wrists, gently drawing my hands down and away from my face, he drops down into a crouch before me. His chin lifted, eyes flicking between my own as I blink them open, steely grey orbs tracking over my face, and I want to hide. I want to drag my hair further forward as Rex is dragging it back, holding it at the nape of my neck, his knuckles a welcome pressure against the top of my spine. Unveiling me like some sort of broken object for review.

My shoulders curl forward, arching inwards, trying to hide myself in some way as the man before me continues to shackle my wrists. His thumb and finger a cuff around each of my hands, his other fingers splaying wide, like they're trying to touch as much as possible, keep hold of all of me.

Rex's arms slide beneath my own, hefting me up as King rises to his feet, and then they're settling me on the steps between them, Rex at my side, King at our backs. His knees spread wide, feet parted for me to fit perfectly between his trainers.

Kings hands crawl over my shoulders, pads of his thumbs to my collarbones, holding me against him, Rex clasping one of my hands inside of both of his, King's leg between us, but it doesn't stop him claiming my full attention. I glance up at Rex, my hair a welcome hiding place to peer at him through the strands, but with his free hand he's hooking hair behind my ear, one and then the other, his fingers brushing over the spiked backs of my earrings.

He smooths his big hand over the top of my head, rough palm snagging stray strands, combing through its lengths until his long fingers are knotting in the ends, taking grip with his fist, giving him control over the movement of my head.

"Kitten," he swallows.

My chin lifts, gaze on his light green one. Lids lined with thick, dark lashes, hollows tinged blue beneath his eyes, his skin paler than normal. It makes me frown. His carefree smile absent from his thin, pink lips, a pursing to them replacing it that makes my skin itch.

"I will never be able to be sorry enough," he says quickly, biting on his bottom lip, chewing the skin, picking and picking and picking at it with his front teeth.

"Please don't do that," I whisper, his hands on me, still but twitching, "you'll make yourself bleed." I reach up with my free hand, tugging gently with my thumb on his bottom lip, popping it free.

Rex yanks his head away, surprising me, clenching his jaw, before he swallows, his throat bobbing up then down, "I should bleed after what we did to you."

"I feel like everyone's been hurt enough." I shrug, King's hands rising and falling with the subtle lift of my shoulders, his fingers digging deeper. "I don't want that, for any of us." Slowly, I bring my hand back up between us, my thumb smoothing across Rex's bottom lip, fingers curling around the wide, square bone of his jaw. "I just want it all to stop now."

"It has," King growls, low and deep, his voice vibrating down the length of my spine where I rest in the cradle of his thick thighs.

"For everyone," I say, licking my lips, glancing from Rex up to King.

His head angled down, a few loose braids dropping forward from their band at the crown of his head, hanging in his eyes. His mouth is so near my own, I can taste his breath, minty and fresh, cold against my lips. I shiver, fluttering my lashes, knowing this is our goodbye.

It's why I let Bennett stay last night, it's why I listened to Lynx. And it's why, now, I'm sitting so closely between these big men, letting them hold me. Selfishly, because I'll miss this, their smell, their eyes, chiselled muscles and big hands. The names they use, ones that are just for me.

I think of King's confession to me, how he was hurt too, a different way to I, but pain doesn't discriminate. It only emanates. Infecting, poisoning, polluting.

If you let it.

I won't let it be that way for these noxious boys anymore.

"I don't want any of you to hurt ever again." It feels like a confession, the way I whisper the words, staring up into dark silver eyes.

"Even Lynx?" Rex asks quietly, drawing my attention back to him, his fingers squeezing mine tight, deep crevice between his dark brows.

Especially Lynx. I think to myself, he just wants to fit too, have someone love him. I feel like I relate more to him now, after last night, than ever before. It was no wonder I thought our connection was the deepest the fastest.

None of this is forgiveness, but I can't change the past. I can only control the future.

"Even Lynx," I swallow the razors in my throat as I nod, just once, and Rex smiles, dipping his head, pressing a kiss to my knuckles, our hands still linked, relief easing the tension a little in his shoulders.

"Poppy," King's voice rattles my insides in the best and most terrifying of ways.

I look up, arching my neck, Rex releasing the ends of my hair to plant his hand on my thigh, his other still laced with mine. The top of my head brushes King's abs where he sits on the step one up from us, the rock hard planes of muscle rolling beneath his t-shirt at the contact. He lets go of one of my shoulders, his fingers smoothing up the column of my throat instead. Cupping my chin, my jaw, cradling it.

"I will spend the rest of my life making it up to you. And even that will never be enough. I am broken without you, and you should stay far, far away from us," it hurts, his words, like a knife twisting in my gut. "But I'm too selfish, Princess, I *need* you. *We* need you and I know we don't deserve you, not even a fraction of you. You are more than too good for us. But I will follow you to the ends of the earth, even if you don't want me, we'll pave the way, make sure you get there safely. Wherever it is you wanna go, whatever it is you wanna do. With or without us. We're gonna protect you, every step of the way, even if it means protecting you from us."

I look to Rex, tears filling my eyes, the backs of them burning, and I watch, numbly, as, with sad eyes, he nods his agreement.

And I cry.

I sob so hard, I can't breathe. There's no time, there's no meaning, there's only a slow, piercing, shattering inside of me. My rib bones feel like they're curling inwards, their dull, blunt ends sinking into my heart with poison tipped ends.

King's hand tightens over the curve of my shoulder, his other smoothing up and down my throat, so careful with me it makes me hurt worse.

Rex clutches me close, wrapping himself around me like warm, safe walls.

The rest of the world doesn't matter.

Doesn't exist.

Nothing but their words, because they mean them, they mean them even though it hurts them. There's something like love tangled here, something I can only suspect because I've never really felt it before.

There is a cold absence bleeding in my chest and I think of the ways I have tried so hard to fill it. Nothing even close to stitching me back together, no matter what I do to heal the darkness.

Until these noxious boys picked me. Fucked me, adored me, ruined me. It was inevitable. I thought they would grow bored, that they would find out just how uninteresting I am. That I would do more drugs and pop more pills and they'd think I was *fun*. They wouldn't see the fear, the dread, the anxiety. The ownership of my father. All of these things that make up my entirety. How much effort I assumed it would take to keep their attention, only on me, would take everything I had to give and more and I would give it.

It would kill me in the end but I would give it.

And then I'd be free.

They hold me as I cry, together, brothers not made of blood, but of love and respect and loyalty. Something that twisted them to hurt me, but they'll get over it, me. In a few weeks time this will all have meant nothing.

I'll go to class and earn my grades, keep my head down, my nose clean, so to speak. I won't try to be fun anymore. I don't think, even with all the pills, I ever really was anyway. Barely close to normal. I'm not sure anything could help me achieve that either.

Normality.

Rex brings my head up, kissing my salty lips, swallowing the evidence of my sadness, and he doesn't even know what it's for. I think of the way he kissed me, just like this, after King and Flynn saved me from the train.

How I cried because I wished they hadn't.

King's face is buried in the crook of my neck, his lips suckling along the side of my throat.

It feels like begging. The way they both cling onto me and I hate it.

I'm no good for them.

Everything is so gentle, both of them so careful, handling the stupid, broken girl.

It makes me want to laugh, but I don't, holding my breath as my sobs subside, my crying slower.

I'll wait until I'm alone tonight. Underneath my covers, the sheets pulled over my head, the glow of my string lights peeking through the cotton, I'll cry then. And I'll let the final pieces of my heart dissolve.

I draw in a deep breath, bringing my free hand up to my aching face, swiping away the tears beneath my eyes which makes me wince, contact with the bruises, but I hold my tongue, not wanting to show just how much I really fucking hurt.

I should want them to feel guilty, I should want to make them feel worse, disgusted with themselves, guiltier.

Worse than me.

But I'm not sure I'd ever want another person to feel like I do.

Suffer as much as me.

So I say, "Thank you," soft and quiet and submissive, if only to draw their attention away from me. And then, "I don't need that from you, but thank you. I just need to be left alone now."

I dip my chin, a breath shuddering its way in through my teeth as I try to keep my composure, get myself together. I have another class later today, and then a study group with a tutor, because I'm going to fail, and I need to pass everything, or I'm going to be sent back to Briarmoor.

My father can do anything he wants with me.

I want to scream it, the reminder of it sharp like a rusty nail through my temple, but, instead, I roll my lips into my mouth, between my teeth, locking the words back inside.

"Kitten, I want-"

"That's okay," King interrupts, stopping his brother with a hand to his shoulder, but he's tilting my head back with his other, my neck arching to peer up at him. "Whatever you want, you're in charge."

It's like looking up at a demonic sort of god, his beautiful face, his smooth skin, silver eyes. It's like he shouldn't be real. His fingers loose around my throat, I swallow, I know I need to shove him off but I want him to never let me go.

"I have a study thing," is what I say, shifting so they'll release me, which they do, and I hate it.

The ease of it.

"You have Art Studies," Rex replies as I push to my feet, nodding my head, dipping down to collect my scattered books, my computer that's already in Rex's hands, as he too comes to stand.

We're eye to eye, our noses almost brushing and he doesn't ask before his lips mould to mine.

Devastating me with his mouth, the way his tongue punches through my teeth, curling around my own. Owning me and ruining me and I kiss him back, with everything that I have. I kiss him back and I die a little more inside as I do, but I let him take his fill.

He pecks at my lips, breathing hard, kissing me

lightly as he draws back to look at me. Scanning me with his beautiful green eyes, tight at the corners, a small smile curling his pink lips.

Pain.

I know it so well, I feel like I can see it in others so easily now, like I have some sort of detector. It's why I don't want a confrontation. They're hurting too.

"Princess," King rasps, his breath a slice of warm air down the back of my neck.

I turn from Rex, offering him a cracked smile, my nose blocked, my eyes hot, I feel uncomfortable, and I want to get out of here. Away from them.

Facing Raiden is like having my soul torn open, all of my nerve endings raw and exposed. Because he sees me. He reads me so well, even I'm unsure of what it is I'm feeling when he sees it. Untangles all of it and smooths it out with his mouth.

Thick, dusky rose pink lips connect with mine, soft, coaxing, such a contrast to my own cracked, dry, split skin. King kisses me like he did that night in his bed, like he's trying to meld us together, not consume, just merge. Drag me into him as much as he pushes himself into me.

It's a kiss that speaks of finality, but his version of it is different to mine. As he tangles his hands into my hair, breaks free of my lips and slides his tongue softly over my bruised skin. I shudder in his arms, my eyes sliding open, I peer over his head, Rex's heat at my back, too close, too far. Like they both know they have only precious seconds left with me like this.

I don't want to come between brothers.

Not these ones anyway.

"I have to go," I whisper the words with a shudder, King drawing back, my hands very still at my sides.

Rex stops breathing at my back, I think King does too, it makes my head spin. I think the way I spoke the words came out differently to the way they sounded inside my head.

They know this is a goodbye.

But none of us address it as they release me, help me to take the stairs the rest of the way down without having to worry about tripping over my own feet, arms too full, eye too blurry, because they hold my stuff. My purple pen tucked behind Rex's ear, books and computer stacked between them, secure in their large hands.

They pile me back up when we reach the art building, the pair of them walking either side of me the entire way. We don't speak, the wind blows, the cold lashes my cheeks and it feels good against my bruises.

"Thank you," I tell them both quietly, the wind whipping my words away, swallowing them in its own howl.

"Anytime," King rasps, meaning something else entirely.

I can't bring myself to look at Rex, silent at my back now, angled towards me, but my eyes can't rove in his direction because I'll see something in his eyes that devastates me, and this is for him.

I'm doing it for both of them as I tear my gaze from Raiden, make my way up the brick steps of the building, shoulder my way inside, clutching my books so hard each of my fingertips crack.

I hear a noise at my back before the door is closing all the way shut, Hendrix, some sort of choked wail escaping his lips.

But I'm doing this for him.

For them.

The five brothers who stole what was left of my heart.

Flynn

CHAPTER FORTY

Spring Break seems to tumble its way into my lap.

March hits me like a freight train and I laugh. The irony of that statement.

I can't get the imagery out of my head, hers splattered all over the tracks.

Spinning side to side in my leather office chair, head thrown back. Curved, butterfly knife in my hands flicking open and closed as I stare up and up and up. It feels like time slows more and more, everyday at four. As I wait, and she doesn't come, but at five, I mark her as attended all the same.

I follow her around campus with digital eyes, I wiped those fucking videos and pictures of her off of the internet again, just like I did before, but it felt redundant the second time. Everyone had already seen them. But I thought of her dad as I did it.

Briarmoor.

Somewhere I've looked further into and decided I don't fucking like it. And if Poppy ever gets sent back there, I will go and get her the fuck back.

Whether she wants this separation from us or not, *from me,* I don't. I don't want it. I want her, and everyone is telling me to give her space, and I've been trying. I have been *fucking* trying, but my brain just doesn't work that way. Every time King tells me it's the right thing to do, I think about breaking my little brother's nose.

I am unable to just *let* someone go.

Thoughts of her infect me, dreams of fucking into her, something I never got a chance to do. Marking her up with my knife, carving my name into her chest while I suck the blood from the wounds. I picture her tongue running up the flat of my blade, my cock buried so deep inside of her cunt she can feel me in the back of her fucking throat. I picture her taking the blade between her fingers and carving her name into me.

I groan hard, the heel of my hand grinding into my cock, hard and pulsing, weeping at the tip beneath the tight restriction of my pants. All of my thoughts are of her, her, her.

It feels like I'm suffocating.

I push to my feet, staring at the time, four-eleven, I shove my hands through my black curls, frizzing the ends, but I do it again, and again and I don't stop. Checking the time, over and over.

It feels like when I was little, before Raiden was born, when Mom lived alone with me in our trailer and my biological father had left her when I was just a few days old. I'd never met him, but when I was four, he told Mom he wanted to meet me, take me to see a game.

I felt excited, lots of kids in my park didn't have a dad to take them anywhere, but I was going to.

I paced the front room of our little trailer, always clean, always tidy, neat and smelling like my mom's homemade lavender oils that she would spritz the drapes with, on pick up day. I waited hours for him to never arrive. I think I trod a hole through the carpet.

I finally met him, a lot later on in life.

I had Raiden's dad then, he treats me like we're blood and I treat him the same way. He's my real dad, DNA or not.

My sperm donor was a piece of shit and I've never thought about him again.

Not until now.

Four-thirty-six.

I flick my blade closed, gripping it hard in the curling of my hand, feeling the warmed metal dig into my skin. I take in a deep breath, smooth out my shirt, grab my jacket from over the back of my chair and slip my arms through the sleeves. I lock up my office behind me as I make my way towards the quad, I know she likes to sit out there, regardless of the weather. Snow, rain, fucking lightning.

Stupid, reckless, addicting girl.

My dress shoes tap each step as I make my way down the stairs, hands in my pockets, knife clutched in my left. And I'm thinking of how I sort of want to strangle the life out of this girl, the way she's doing exactly that to me with phantom fucking hands from what feels like a billion miles away.

Choking the life out of me with her fucking absence from it.

I'm on the second floor and I'm running now, gritting my fucking jaw so hard it makes my ears pop, jaw crack and I'm slamming into another body as I round the square cornered railings.

My hands fly out of my pockets on instinct, knife still clutched in the curl of my fingers, but I'm gripping warm upper arms, pinning the body into the wall, all before I realize who it is.

There's a snarl on my upper lip, ready to fucking destroy whatever sorry-ass kid just got in my way when I'm stopped all at once by the color of her eyes.

I blink. Making sure I'm not dreaming. Not hallucinating due to the immense stress of having to stay the fuck away from her.

"Flynn?" she questions on a whisper, like she, too, is questioning reality right now.

Ironic.

'Stay away from her, Flynn, don't freak her out with your stalker bullshit.'

Raiden's words flash through my brain like blistering fry oil and I smile through the feeling of my brain combusting.

"Angel," I purr, "you fell from the sky for me," my lips curl sinisterly.

Lilac eyes are the only thing I see, flaring gray then blue, a bright violet hue like a fork of lightning striking my heart, her pupils large and dark and calling me to madness.

My hands are squeezing her biceps as I lift her, throwing her over my shoulder, bracing for the impact of her fists to pound against my spine as I continue down the stairs, not giving a single fuck who sees us.

But there's nothing.

No struggle, no fight, no words of protest.

It's almost like her body loses all of its tension as she hangs over my shoulder, muscles going lax.

And then her arms lift, curling around my waist, her fingers locking together, she holds onto me, tight.

"I missed you," I tell her, my brain short circuiting with her body wrapped around mine. Willingly. "I've been praying to the devil to deliver me my fallen angel, guess he was listening after all."

"I missed you too," she says, upside down, hanging down the length of my spine, her face nestled in the back of my thigh.

"Yeah?" I rasp, her words infecting my melting brain like an antidote.

"Yes," she says quietly.

"What were you doing on the stairs?" I ask her,

calmer, breathing slowing because she's not fighting me and this isn't technically a kidnapping.

I push out of the stairwell, the halls empty. My hand firm on her ass, the other around her thighs.

"I was on my way to see you," she whispers and for just one second I am still.

My steps pause and I blink, staring down the long, wide hall, think of how far the parking lot is, the spaces in the very fucking back where my car is.

I can feel her breathing, the rise and fall of her chest, the thud of her heart against my lower back. She smells like fucking cream-butter pumpkins, the scent from her shampoo, *her*, everything about her is intoxicating. And I...

"Why?" I ask, perfectly still, unseeing of the white and green hallway, the closed doors running down either side of it, floor to ceiling glass windows at the very end.

She squirms in my hold, blood probably rushing to her head, her face likely a little red. I think of her blush, the way it works its way down her throat, over her pretty tits, and her heart hammers now, with my silence, my question.

"I- We have a session today."

"Yeah, but you've missed the last seventeen," I think of all those minutes spent in my office watching her traipse around the halls, her head always down, as though she knew where every camera was stationed and avoided them all.

She says nothing in answer, but I feel her breath heave and it prompts me to move. Closed knife digging into my palm, cock grinding into the zipper of my pants. I'm looking at the doors in the hall as I pass them, unsure what I'm looking for, but I need to see her face when she answers me.

I push into the girls bathroom, shouldering my way in, checking the stalls are empty with a foot to each door, before I bend, placing Poppy's feet on the white speckled lino. Smoothing my way up her body as she comes to stand, a little wobbly on her feet but I hold her up. My hands secure on her waist, contracting with deep breaths.

My back to the door, I smooth my thumbs over her front, feeling the bumps of her ribs as I grip a little too hard.

I look at her face, taking her in, the bruising gone as though it were never there to mark her pretty face. Yellows finally dissolved from her skin. There are bags beneath her eyes, hollow and icy blue in her light skin.

"Why were you in the stairwell, Poppy?" I ask again.

She drops her head, her feet shifting, she flicks those pretty lifeless eyes up onto mine, holding my gaze and I never want her to look away.

My knife is like an itch, thumb still locking it in the palm of my hand. Sweat beading at the top of my spine, blood roaring in my ears.

I stare at her mouth, her thick lips are cracked, the

bottom one dry and bitten, and I want to sink my teeth into it.

I step into her, hands tightening on her waist, her feet tracking her backwards until she's stumbling back into the end stall. Flicking the lock, I spin us around, slamming her back into the door, the lock bolt rattling as the door shakes.

I dip my head, catching her eye, my nose brushing over the tip of hers, my hands slipping from her waist, splaying on either side of her head instead, caging her in.

"I missed you," I breathe, lips slanted over her mouth. "They kept me away." I swallow, catching the split in her bottom lip with the tip of my tongue as I lick my own, tasting iron. "I never would have left you alone again."

"It's for the best, Flynn," she whispers.

My fist with the knife slams into the door beside her head, making the entire row of stalls shake at her back, but she doesn't flinch.

"It's not for the fucking best!" the words seem to rip their way up my throat, tasting like battery acid on my tongue. She flinches then, my empty hand smoothing over her head, "It's not what's best," I say quietly, breathing deep. "Us, Angel, that's what's best. Me and you." I drag my nose along her temple, breathing her in. "I can make you happy," I kiss her cheek, mouthing along the arch of bone, down towards her cupid's bow. "I can keep you safe." My mouth glides over hers, my bottom lip grazing the skin. "Let me keep you, Angel, let me have you, Poppy."

Her breaths are loud in the echoey room, her chest touching mine with every inhale. I kiss her cheek, open mouthed down her face, one side and then the other, my eyes never straying from hers. She watches me too, never closing those dying eyes. Her hands are flat to the door at her back, body pressed into it. Her loose shirt gaping at the torn neckline, exposing the delicate, pale flesh of the curve of her shoulder.

My tongue glides down the side of her neck, circling the hollow of her throat, my teeth nipping along the length of her collarbone, sucking on her shoulder. I stare at her as my teeth dig in, tongue licking around the inside of them. I bite free of her shoulder, scraping my teeth closed over the fresh bruise to her skin.

"Tell me to stop," I breathe, her chest heaving, I hold her gaze, her eyes flicking frantically between my own, searching. "I'm not going to ever let you go." It's a promise, I cannot warn her away from me. "You'll never be able to cut me free, Angel, I'm your own personal disease." I peck at her lips, "I'm bone deep," I breathe, licking over her mouth. "There's no fucking cure for me."

She groans like the sound's been bubbling in her

throat, desperate to break free, and I swear to fuck, I almost die.

Our lips collide, desperate and needy as our teeth clash. Her moans echo their way down my throat, my tongue in her mouth, her hands digging into my shoulders. I'm pawing at her skirt, stretchy, tight, knitted fabric. Fingers clawing at the loop of her baggy shirt tucked into the high elastic waistband. I bend my knees, our mouths still connected as she pushes her fingers up into my curls, nails dragging over my scalp as she holds me to her, not letting me go.

I'm panting, shoving her skirt up as I straighten my knees. I flick my blade free with a *snick*, her lips fused with mine, she stills, her eyes opening, slowly, so slowly, rove to the knife in my hand beside her head. The glaring strip bulbs above us glint off of the blue tinted steel. She draws back, her lips leaving mine, crown of her head flush with the door, but she doesn't let go of my head, her nails curving into my scalp.

"Tell me why you were on the stairs," I pant over her mouth, drawing back just enough to see her face clearly.

"To see you," she whispers, holding my eye, and my heart flip flops in my chest, but she drops her gaze again, that thick bottom lip being abused by her top teeth.

"What for?" I cock my head, ducking down just a little to see her beneath her hair.

"To hurt," she whispers, eyes on the sliver of space between us.

"Poppy," my exhale is shaky, adrenaline like a livewire in my veins. "Look at me," I tilt her face up to meet mine, blade beside her cheek, she doesn't flinch.

"Why d'you wanna hurt, Angel?"

Her lilac eyes dart between mine, her tongue catching my mouth as she licks her lips, her fingers tightening impossibly hard on my head, it feels good to have her hold me.

"To feel," she hushes, shame thick in the choked words.

"Why me?" I think of Bennett, of Raiden, Rex, even Lynx, all of them could do this for her.

"Because I trust you the most," it's a broken confession, something that seems to pierce my heart. "Because I feel safe with you."

I shudder as she claws her nails across my scalp, my eyes fluttering closed, open. My hand cupping her jaw, the knife dangerously close to her eye, but she doesn't care, she doesn't even look at it. She's only looking at me.

"You want me to look after you, Angel?" she nods, slowly, once, twice.

My fingers slip down the door with an uncomfortable squeak, but it's like neither one of us hears it, the clamminess of my palm against the plastic coated door. Hand coming to her hip, skirt and shirt shoved up high between us. Flat of the blade to the jut of her bone, I flick my eyes between hers.

"Yes," she breathes. "Make me feel, Flynn."

I drag the blade down lower, the knife's edge against her skin.

"I can do whatever I want to you," I say softly, glancing down, eyeing the lilac lace sitting low on her hips, before I'm focusing back on eyes of the same color. "I can mark you up, make you bleed. Bite you, bruise you, cut you, fuck you." I press the knife to her flesh, a little red line forming, the skin unbroken. "I can scar you."

"Yes, Flynn. *Yes.*"

"I can do all of that. But, Poppy, I'm not going to hurt you to make you feel small. To put you in a place you think you need to be. To punish you for something you think you need to be punished for."

I can see it in her eyes, the way she wonders if I can read her fucking mind. I can't but I fucking wish I could. I run my mouth over hers, taking my time.

"But I can ruin you, and keep you, and make you mine."

She says nothing, frowning slightly, the tip of the curved blade slipping beneath the edge of her panties, her tits brushing my chest with her heavy breaths, only funneling in through her nose. Lips pressing tightly together.

"I can't do this with you and let you go, Poppy," I drop my forehead to hers, our eyes still on one another but the view is blurred, we're too close, but we don't stop looking into each other's eyes. "You give yourself to me now, I will keep you forever, Angel."

Her breath shudders in through her mouth as she parts her lips, the bottom one trembling, I feel it against my own, my tongue darting out to taste her, lap at the chewed skin, slip my tongue into her mouth.

"Give in to me," I dig the knife in harder against her pelvis, so close to drawing blood with the controlled pressure, I can imagine the red indentation in her pale skin. "Give in to me. Stay with me. Let me make you feel and feel and feel. I. See. *You*." I swallow, "Be mine."

She is trembling, the door rattling at her back, the lock tinkling, her breath is heavy over my mouth, and I want to fucking eat her. It takes everything to keep off of her, to wait, to be patient. Something I'm not usually good at.

"Do you want me to beg you, Angel?" I huff a laugh over her mouth, her lips parting wider. "I can beg," I whisper, nuzzling the tip of my nose over hers. Working my mouth to her cheek, lips beside her ear, our cheeks flush, "Please, beautiful Angel, please, let me devour you." I nip her ear as I whisper the words.

Her hands fist tighter in the roots of my hair, my curls a frizz around her fingers, she yanks my head back, hard, my neck twisting, lips parting with a smirk. I'm wondering what it is she's going to say, but she says nothing, a glint in her eye, a crease between her brows. She is panting, pushing me down to my knees, my hand slipping from the door, curling around her outer thigh as my shins hit the ground. The knife still held to her other hip.

I'm staring up at her, her down at me, and she's hesitating, I can see it, she wants this without the connection. Something I have always wanted, until now, until her. I won't do this unless she gives in to me.

"You want my mouth on you?" I ask her from her feet, my fingers tight in her skin, indenting her flesh. "You want me to beg you by shoving my tongue in your needy little cunt because you're such a dirty little angel?"

"*Yes*," she finally breathes, making my scalp bleed as she beds her nails into it, it makes my cock impossibly hard.

"You're going to be mine after this, Angel," I don't ask it, I tell her.

And she's pushing my mouth closer to her cunt and I'm holding still, only my breath blowing over the wet fabric between her thighs.

"You are, or we stop, I would never beg anyone else, Poppy. Only *my* girl." She blinks heavily, her frown deepening, her nails like knives against my fucking skull. "Are you going to be my girl, Angel?" I swipe my tongue up the length of her, through the lace of her panties, tasting her on my tongue with a groan. "I want to fucking ravish you," I tell her. "I want you to be mine, Poppy. I will be yours. Only yours." I suck on her lips, the lace rough in my mouth. "Give in *to me.*"

"Okay," she whispers, my neck arched so far back I can hardly breathe. "Okay, Flynn," she nods, her lips parted, shining and swollen with our kisses.

"Spit in my mouth," I command her. "I'm gonna eat you so fucking good that you sob as you come on my tongue," I tell her earnestly. Pink blooms in her cheeks, bright and high, and she worries her lip between her teeth, "Spit in my mouth, my filthy fucking angel."

My lips part wider, waiting, and without further hesitation her saliva hits my tongue. My groan reverberates throughout the echo of the room and she's moaning, peeling the skin off of my scalp with her nails in my skull and my blade is slicing through the flimsy fabric separating us. My mouth is suctioning over her clit, lips parting wider, consuming as much of her as I can. My tongue finding her entrance, teeth scraping over her lips, nibbling and sucking, feeling her drip down my chin.

My thumbs part her folds, stretching her wide, exposing all of her to me, to my mouth. My lips suck her wet flesh, earth and tart sweetness heavy on my tastebuds. My tongue laps up the length of her, swirling around her clit, sucking hard, teeth biting into her flesh.

I glide the blade over her mound, scratching but

not cutting, and then I'm dragging it down towards her clit, my fingers and thumb spreading her wide so I can see every part of her.

I tap the flat of the blade over her clit, her teeth gritting, she groans, panting, but oh so still.

"You want to bleed for me, Angel?" I whisper, words blowing over her swollen, red clit. "Right here?" I ask her, pressing the point of the blade against it. "You want me to suck your blood from this pretty little clit and then fuck it into you with my tongue?"

"Flynn," she breathes, her pulse thrumming in her inner thigh beneath the harsh grip of my splayed fingers. "Yes," she cries. *"Please."*

"Oh, Angel, I thought I was the one doing the begging," I prick her skin as I laugh the words, barely a hiss escaping her teeth as she moans.

A bead of blood blooming on her swollen clit, I suck on it, drawing her blood onto my tongue, groaning at the taste of her. Feeling heady with her eyes on me, flicked down so she can watch me feast.

Holding her gaze, her thighs trembling, I suck the handle of the knife into my mouth, slathering it in her flavor. She stills, her teeth chattering, but she doesn't stop me as I circle the wet handle around her tight little entrance, her cunt squeezing on nothing but air.

I push the knife handle into her, twisting it slowly as I grip the blade in the curl of my fingers, the blade just breaking skin, but I don't focus on the slight sting as I watch the handle slowly disappear inside of her.

"Oh my god, Flynn," she whispers it fast and hard, my name like a summoning and a curse from her swollen mouth.

I watch her cunt squeeze around it as I start to fuck it into her, slow, hard thrusts in and out, the sounds of her sloppy and so wet like an injection of adrenaline directly into my heart.

My mouth is on her clit, her fingers a permanent attachment to my head now where she grips me so fucking tight. I groan against her wet flesh, biting down onto her clit and then she stills, her entire body turning to stone as I continue to lick her and the bath-room door opens, two sets of footsteps entering the restroom.

My free hand reaches up, slapping over her mouth, fingers digging into her cheeks, lips detaching from her cunt, my chin glistening with her, I look up, holding her panicked gaze, and keep fucking her with the knife.

The two girls are at the sinks, talking about shit I don't fucking care about. Blood from my palm holding the blade drips beneath the cuff of my shirt, soaking into the white cotton. Poppy's pussy grips around the handle so hard it's a struggle to hold onto it with my hand as wet with blood as it is, but I keep twisting it up inside of her. Latch my teeth onto her clit, feel her thighs tremble.

Listening to faucets switch on and off, the door opening and closing as I suck her harder.

My hand slips from her face, groping her tits, pinching her nipples, and she's crying out my name, *"Flynn, Flynn, Flynn."*

Her orgasm tearing through her, her entire body trembling, eyes squeezing shut before they're snapping back open. Lilac-blues hooked on mine as I lap slowly over her clit, slow the thrusts of my knife as she comes down from her high.

She looks like the fucking devil as she stares down at me, and it drives me fucking insane.

Poppy's skull bangs against the door as she throws it back, still gripping my head, pulling on my hair. She's dragging me up her body, my knife popping free of her, clattering to the floor between my feet.

Bloodied hand slapping against the door beside her head, she finally releases her hold on my head. Dragging her nails deeply down the skin of my face, leaving stinging marks in her wake, but as she claws down my throat, our mouths reconnecting, the taste of her all over my fucking face.

We're both fumbling with my belt, the clang of it dropping free like a shot signaling the start of a race. She palms my cock as she tears me free, grip hard and sloppy and spiteful. The drag of her nails along the underside of my cock, catching my crown, squeezing me tight in her slim fingers.

I'm hissing into her mouth as her teeth sink into

my tongue, silencing me with her groan as it ripples its way through my own vocal cords. And I'm lifting her leg into the crook of my elbow, my bloodied hand swiping over her cunt.

Both of us look down, breaking our kiss, foreheads together. We stare at the mixture of our blood, her wetness, my saliva, all of it messing up her pretty, perfect skin.

Her hand on my cock, she pumps me hard, not gentle, *hurting me*, and it feels so good. I'm groaning, watching her work me, bringing me closer to her clenching cunt, lining my dick up with her entrance.

She brings my bleeding palm to her face, and holding my gaze, she buries her face in my hand. Lapping her tongue over the cuts in my fingers, sucking the slice in my palm, getting my blood all over her. She moans as she tastes me, blood slicking up her cheeks, the tip of her nose. Unable to hold off any longer, I'm slamming inside of her.

Her cunt clenching around my cock, sucking me deeper. I'm wrenching her leg higher, forcing her thigh wider. We're both groaning and her teeth are savage as she tears at the broken flesh of my hand, like she's trying to peel back the skin, expose all of my nerves for her to pluck at.

Our hips crack as I fuck her. My hold on her thigh bruising as she keeps sucking on my hand, but I want her to taste both of us. I yank my hand away from her hold, shoving her head back against the door with my palm to her throat. I run my bleeding hand down her body, over her clothes, her pale skin, and press my fingers beside my cock where it thrusts in and out of her. Knowing it's too much too soon, but I'm doing it anyway, her hands gripping my shoulders as I work two fingers in beside my cock.

A ragged breathy moan tears out of her as I fuck her hard, my balls drawing up, heat rushing down my spine, settling in the base. Fire unfurling in my lower belly as I pull my fingers out of her, blood and *her* shining on them like a blessed offering.

"Open your mouth," I demand breathlessly, her lips parting, face slack as she does as I say.

I push my fingers between her teeth, her mouth closing around them as I caress the back of her tongue. Reaching into her throat, feeling it tighten around me as she gags, salvia pooling on her tongue, dripping down her chin.

"Come again," it's a bark, the order, her moan vibrating through my fingers, her teeth driving into them as I push further into her throat, my knuckles trying to get inside. "Come with me, Angel, fucking come with me. Come now."

I pull out as I come, grinding my length into her belly, cum painting her, running down and over her pussy, covering her in my release. Her cunt pulsing around air, I arch back, spit on her clit, drop her leg, reaching for her clit, mashing harsh circles on it with my thumb. And she's coming too, spit running down my hand, her release pushing free, slipping down her as I hold her open with my fingers. The heel of my hand a hard pressure against her clit, watching her release ooze free.

She bites down on my fingers, breaking skin, her tongue working around them as we both moan. My eyes find hers, blood and saliva all over her face.

"God, *fuck*, Poppy," I rush out, breathless, my chest heaving, I pull my fingers free, push them into my own mouth, sucking the taste of us off of my own fingers, ignoring the way my split skin stings.

Poppy stares up at me as I remove my hand from her cunt, her hands on my shoulders, one moving to my hair, her fingers carding through my curls.

"You're mine now," I tell her, and I can see in her eyes, my blood all over her face that she didn't mean it, any of it. "You're not going to walk away from me," I say, even though I know she's going to. "You're mine, Angel."

"I'm yours," she whispers, and we both know it's a lie.

Poppy

Four days speed and slow as they simultaneously drag and race by all at once. It's been that long since I let myself completely go with Flynn. I feel like I still have his blood all over my face, his knife handle inside my cunt. I flush with heat, digging down deeper beneath my sheets.

It's the first Tuesday of Spring Break and I didn't go home. I didn't turn up for my flight, I've ignored all of my dad's calls, the voicemails. And I switched off my phone after getting a text from Lynx.

LYNX

I'm sorry.

Lynx's bed beside me, empty, cold, made. I miss his scent, his skin, his eyes. I groan, pushing thoughts of him out of my head too. Tearing the sheets in closer to my face where I'm curled up beneath them. I wonder if I could suffocate just like this. Would I be able to smother myself?

I'm not sure how long I doze for but the thump on my door, the opening of it, the crash of it against the wall startles me awake so sharply I clench my thighs to hold in my pee as I struggle to fight my way out of my blankets.

"Jesus," Bonnie chides. "It's like a crypt in here," grabbing them and tearing them off of me.

Emma trails in behind her, closing the door at her back, a teasing smile on her face. I groan, trying to snatch back my sheets, but Bonnie bundles them up in her hands, throws them atop Lynx's empty bed. Hands on her hips, she looks me up and down.

"Fuck me, we have got our work cut out for us today, Em," she clucks her tongue, and my mouth is gaping, looking at Emma as Bonnie turns her back on me, pulling open my dresser and rifling through it.

"What are you doing?" I finally ask, Emma flopping down atop the other bed, her cheeks lifting high with mirth as she lets Bonnie reply.

"Getting you out of this room," she glances over her shoulder, her thick blonde curls bobbing with the movement of her head, her blue eyes bright, lined with thick mascara coated lashes. "We're going out," she says matter of factly, turning her attention back to the dresser.

"Bon-"

"It's no use arguing with her," Emma shrugs coolly, crossing the room and opening up the blinds at my back, my dry eyes blinking hard with the sudden brightness. "We're in this shit together." she smiles at me, leaning over me, her hand lifting to my cheek. "You look tired, sweetie."

"I'm fine," I lie, my voice cracking.

Emma likes getting fucked up too, but not like I do. She does it for fun, I do it to forget.

"Your cell is off," she cups my cheek, sweeping her thumb beneath my eye with cool fingers.

"Yeah," I swallow, her dark eyes seeing too much, "it died."

I shuffle so she has to step back, push to my feet, diverting my attention to the bubbly blonde maniac tearing through my drawers of clothes.

"Bon-Bon," I laugh as she slaps a pair of ripped jeans over her shoulder.

"Don't you have any little dresses?" she huffs, stuffing all of my now balled up clothing back into one drawer.

"No, I don't, I'm not wearing a *little* dress."

"You are," the pair of them sing in unison, making me laugh.

"Why am I wearing a dress, what are you doing with me?" I press the heel of my hand to my tired eye, rub my sleep clumped lashes.

"We're going to a frat party!" Bonnie squeals and Emma laughs as I groan, dropping my head back on my shoulders, slumping back down onto the end of my mattress.

"I don't wannnaaaaa," I whine, knowing I'm going regardless.

The boys don't do frats, they won't be there, which washes me with relief, but at the same time, I think of how they won't be there... and my insides knot.

"We won't leave your side all night," Emma frowns, like she can read my mind.

"I will," Bonnie calls from over her shoulder as she pulls open my door, not giving a fuck who's out in the hall when I'm in nothing more than knickers and a t-shirt. "I wanna get laid!" she shouts from across the hall, someone wolf-whistling her comment from further down the corridor.

"Oh my god," me and Emma echo, hers with a laugh, mine with a groan.

"All the girls are going, it'll be fun, I'll be your buddy," Emma touches her shoulder to mine, winking at me.

Her dark twists and braids are pulled up in a high ponytail on the top of her head, the ends whipping over her bare shoulder as she crosses to my dresser, refolding the clothes Bonnie tore out.

"Fine, I just-"

"Don't wanna see them," she finishes casually with a shrug, her back still to me.

Belly twisting, I drop my gaze, studying the tops of my feet, knotting my fingers, the bones popping. The familiar rush of dread and anxiety swirls in my gut, and I squeeze my eyes closed. I just need something to take the edge off.

"Right?" she asks, her shuffling hands on my clothing stopping.

I don't look up, hearing Bonnie's steps in the hall, stopping just outside the open door.

"I miss them," the confession drags out with a trembling lip and I think of the pills on my desk.

The little clear bag of them tucked just inside a notebook. How badly I want to swallow them, drift into semi-consciousness with a smile. To make me more fun. Sociable. *Normal.*

Neither of them say anything and I don't look up, but my mouth doesn't stop either.

"I think I'm broken," it squeezes out of me, my lungs choking me. "They felt like my family."

A tear drips down my cheek with my huffed laughter, and I rush to wipe it free, keeping my head down, eyes squeezed shut.

"They hurt you," Emma says plainly, no judgment in her tone, just a statement.

"They did," I nod, and then, "I think I probably deserved it," I say the words with a shudder, mixed feelings about everything I know now, someone has to take responsibility for what my father did to theirs.

"You definitely did not deserve it," Emma says coldly, bluntly, and I feel my heart squeeze.

"I fucked Bennett," I shove the heels of my hands into my eyes, shaking my head, sucking in my sob. "I betrayed them with that."

"They were already messing with you by then, sweetie, that's got nothing to do with why, at all. You know that," Emma says, and I hear Bonnie step closer, one step, into the room, the door still open, and I can't stop my mouth.

"I had sex with Flynn on Friday," I shove my hands into my hair, tugging on the roots, it's easier to confess without looking at them, seeing their reactions. "I fucked him and then I left him in a fucking bathroom stall." I laugh at myself caustically, spinning around so my back's to them.

Opening my eyes, shaky fingers rushing through the pages of my notebook, I pop open the bag of pills with blurry eyes, throw two into my mouth, drop my head back and dry swallow them down, staring up at the ceiling.

"Pops, you're allowed to fuck whoever you want," Emma says quietly as I exhale heavily.

"They'll never want me back now," I sob, my shoulders shaking violently. It's what I've been thinking about for the last four days. "They'll never fucking want me now." My knees tremble, and they hit the floor before I can stop myself falling, my face buried in my hands as I have my breakdown.

"Is that what you want?" Bonnie asks, "You want them back, babe, all of them?"

It's all I want.

"It doesn't matter," I breathe out, sucking in air, wiping my nose with the back of my hand. "It doesn't matter."

It's like a chant to myself, as I relax into the fact the Ecstasy will start to work soon, too fast probably, and I'll have to take more to get through the night, but we're going to be drinking and mixing it with alcohol will make my high feel like it lasts longer. Either that or it'll knock me out for the night and I'll finally sleep properly. I've not taken anything since I saw Flynn, my nerves frayed and I've been fucking miserable. But I'll start to feel better now.

"It doesn't matter, I'm better now," I smile even though no one can see me, showing my teeth, resting back on my heels, I breathe deep, wiping my eyes. "I'm better now."

The door slams at my back and I whip around, glancing between the two girls.

Bonnie's mouth works soundlessly for a moment and then she smiles, shrugging one shoulder, her other hand going to her hip, "Wind."

This party is fucking wild.

I suck on some fruity vape shit that some kid in pressed beige chinos told me tastes like mangos. I said no, because I hate smoking, I cough more than I smoke, but then he told me it was flavoured cannabis oil and I snatched it right up.

I dunno if I wanna take more pills than the three I already swallowed today and the one I crushed to snort in the bathroom when we first got here and I saw how many people were crammed inside this huge mansion. I didn't think it was possible for this many people to be wall to wall when the square footage of the place is at least in the five figure range.

The acrid taste is still present in the back of my throat like a reminder not to take anymore. But my skin feels tight and my muscles feel loose, and I'm just waiting for the right moment to go back upstairs, to the bathroom we used when we first arrived, and take more.

Wind whips the thick cloud of fruit scented smoke away where I sit out on the back deck. Too many faces of girls I don't really know surrounding me, but they all seem cool. No one tries to talk to me, but there's no creepy guy like the last house party I went to, so I don't mind.

Resting back in the corner of an L-shaped sofa, glass coffee table set before it, topped with crushed cans, plastic cups, cigarette packets and spilled drinks.

I ignore it all, the mess, fingers twitching to clean it up so I can focus on something other than my crippling anxiety threatening to make a sharp return. I stare out over the back garden. Past the dancers, into the woods at the back, the dense trees are both inviting and terrifying. Quiet, away from the people I don't know at this party. There's no light in there, though, which means it's definitely not for me.

I inhale the fruity concoction from the vape in my hand, my lungs filling with artificial sweetness and I look up at the moon as I blow it back out.

Hands grab my shoulders from behind and I flinch, jerking in the tight hold, relaxing just as quickly at the sound of the familiar raucous giggle.

"There's a hot guy in there I wanna fuck, come dance with me!" Bonnie laughs.

Her nails pinching my bare skin, my shoulders, chest and upper back exposed in the dress Emma leant me. Too much of my legs on show to really feel at ease. Something short, strapless and tight, thankfully black.

"Pleaseeeeeee," she jumps up and down, pressure on my shoulders.

I laugh then, feeling light as I stand, tossing the vape to the table, nodding my head, stepping between the angled feet of the girls along the couch beside me.

I let Bonnie take my hand, lead me back into the overcrowded house and I don't mind it. Can hardly feel the people around me, their sweat slicked skin, their eyes.

I let my own fall shut as Bonnie's hands grip my waist, mine looping limply over her shoulders, our hips flush with her in skyscraper heels and me in flat boots, drawing her closer to my six-feet.

Music pounds through the speakers, flooding through my veins as we grind together, our breaths mingling as we work our hips to the grungey playlist thumping through the surround sound speakers.

She giggles, her lips against my neck as I tip my head back, a smile on my mouth that feels real in the moment.

"He's looking," she whispers, running her bottom lip over my pulse, my ears buzzing with the volume in the room, the voices, the music, the rushing of my blood. "He's coming over here," she breathes, and I can feel her smile against my skin, and I don't hate it, liking touch when I feel like this, when I'm floating.

I feel movement at my back, masculine words spoken over my shoulder, one of Bonnie's hands leaving my hip, her arm brushing my waist, reaching past me to the mystery guy at my back. I smile, still dancing as her fingers flex over my hip bone. Pressing me between them, the three of us dancing from song to song.

I'm flying now, my body weightless, stress a dying

thing shrivelling at my feet. I don't think about my father, the consequences for switching off my phone.

I'm hot, bladder tight a while later, as I spin my way free of them, letting Bonnie and her boy grind without me as their buffer.

She grabs at my hand, twirling me back, "Thank you!" Smacking a kiss to my cheek, her lips beside my ear, "You good?"

I nod, laughing as I back away, watching them dance, Bonnie's smile a beam of light in the dense cloud of smoke that swirls across the ceiling.

Turning, pushing my way through the crowd, needing to pee. I make my way through the dancers, a laugh bubbling in my chest as I find the stairs, following the route we took earlier as a group to a quieter bathroom.

The empty bathroom is through a bedroom, and I flick the light on as I hurry though it, the large room clean and spacious, no personal effects, a plain navy bedspread.

I take care of business, washing my hands in the sink. Bracing my hands on either side of the basin, I stare at myself in the mirror, the marble counter cold beneath my palms. I feel a little off balance, like I could fall if I sway too hard, but I smile all the same, the risk welcome when I don't want to feel anything else.

My makeup is sleek, courtesy of Emma, smokey eyes and a dark lip. I can hardly notice my bloodshot eyes, or find the bags beneath them as I search my face for any telling signs of being less than okay.

My fringe hangs low, parted a little in the centre, and using my fingers, I sweep them over my brows, flicking the ends of hair free of my lashes and take a deep breath, staring at my pinprick pupils. Lips pulling into a smile, even though sadness burns in my chest, I focus on smoothing down my hair, the top half of it up in a little bunch at the crown of my head, the rest of it in loose waves down my back.

I look good, I should feel good.

But I catch sight of the almost healed scar in my shoulder, turning side on to the mirror so I can see it better.

Lynx's teeth.

I wish I hated that it's there.

Permanent.

But I don't.

I sigh, dropping my gaze.

I want to leave, as much as I want to stay.

If I leave, I'll be going back to my empty dorm, and I don't really wanna be alone. I don't want to think of how Lynx should be there but isn't. And even though I'm kind of by myself here too... At least there's people. I can play pretend.

Opening the door, flicking the bathroom light off, I sigh, click the door shut at my back and I'm suddenly plunged into darkness.

I blink. Certain I put the light on when I came in. I never leave lights off.

Heart pounding, I march towards the door, slapping my shaky fingers over the light switch. It clicks uselessly, nothing happening when I flip it up then down, over and over. Gripping the door handle with a sweaty palm, twisting it hard, it does nothing, the round knob rattling uselessly as I tug on it. My other hand curling atop it, pulling with all my might.

In a panic, I spin around, thinking about the phone I switched off and left in the dorm. Eyes focussing through the darkness on the bathroom door I just exited, I start to walk back towards it and that's when I see it.

The shadowed silhouette of someone.

I stop still, broad shoulders blocking the bathroom door, my chest heaving for air I just can't seem to get.

"What are you doing?" my voice is loud, eyes straining hard in the dark, my brain short circuiting as I silently pray for light.

The laugh that leaves the man is terrifying, my feet are backing me up towards the locked bedroom door before I have to put any conscious thought into it at all. He doesn't move, but I hear him breathe deep, a long, satisfied sort of sigh.

He stalks forward, slow, predatory, and despite my high, everything inside of me is screaming danger. But I've got nowhere to go as he closes the space between us, stopping just a few feet away.

"Don't you remember me, Poppy?" he chuckles, and it isn't funny, the sound, it's haunting.

I shake my head, my tongue not willing to work as I grip the door handle hard at my back, trying everything to get it open. The man doesn't move closer, doesn't try to stop me which fills me with dread, because there's no way he can't hear me yanking the door. But with confidence, he stands still, unmoving, unflinching, and that's worse. It means he knows I'm not gunna get out of here.

"Oh, shucks," he tuts, and I imagine a faux pout on his lips. "I'm hurt I made such little impact on you that you don't remember me at all."

His words slur a little and my head pounds with my pulse. I've barely spoken to anybody at this college at all, let alone guys, and I'm blinking harder in the dark, eyes slow to adjust, blurring the harder I strain them to see. But I see light skin, dark hair, and I think back to the night I first met Raiden and make an educated guess.

"Chris?"

"Ding, ding, ding, we have a winner!" he yells loudly, laughing as he does. "God, I'll have to try harder in future, make sure I'm not so *easily forgotten!*" he bellows the last words so loudly I flinch back, my spine connecting with the door with a thud.

"I'm sorry," I rush out, still twisting the door knob at my back, my breaths a rush of hot air in and out of my lungs. "I didn't forget you, I just, I can't see you well in the dark."

"You think I'm that fucking stupid?" he growls, drawing another flinch from me. "God, my dad said you were a fucking bimbo, but I didn't think you'd be this dense."

"Your dad?" my face screws up, confusion rolling through me.

"Yes!" he snaps. "They go way back. Your dad works with mine, he told us all about *you*."

My brain tumbles through everything since Christmas. Things my father's said, done. I think of him shouting at me down the phone when I mentioned a transfer.

A very prominent colleague of mine helped secure your place at that college, Poppy, a very powerful man.

"Chris," I say, a breath shuddering as it leaves me, I lick my lips. "Why don't we put the light on, and we can *talk*, you can-"

"You know the only reason you're not back in the psych ward right now is because *I* told my father you were spending Spring Break with me," he says sharply.

I stutter, trying to process what it is he's saying, "What?"

"You think you were sent here *coincidentally?*" he barks a sharp laugh, my head shaking, mouth gaping.

"You were promised to *me*, Poppy. All part of another successful business transaction." *What?* "But then you had to fall into bed with *them*, didn't you, like a no good fucking whore," Chris snarls and the tension in my body tightens as he takes another step closer. "I was told I was getting a meek little virgin, not some junkie slut!"

"Chris, I-"

He lunges forward, a shriek leaving my mouth, as his spittle hits my cheek, "Shut it!" his stale beer breath wet against my ear. "Shut the fuck up," his hand slams over my mouth, my body squirming against the door, his weight crushing me to the textured wood. "I'm gonna make this real nice for you if you just behave."

Panic surges like a red hot poker up my spine, my hands going to his face, nails gouging his skin. He roars in my ear as I drag them down his face, his forearm batting at my hands, he grabs hold of one, slamming it down at my side, my other scratching into his eyes. The thudding of my head against the door at my back is drowned out by the thundering music downstairs as he slams me harder into it.

"Fuck!" he screams at me. "Shut the fuck up!" he fists my hair, slamming my head back into the door making me dizzy, ignoring my struggling hands slapping against his face, my feet kicking limply at his shins where his body pins mine. "Fine!" he grits his teeth, his hand over my mouth, fingers digging into my cheeks, crushing against my teeth, muffling my screams. "You want it the hard way, fucking fine."

Chris releases my mouth, wrenching his head back away from my hands and tosses me onto the bed. My body bounces on the mattress, wind knocked out of me, not prepared to be thrown.

Before I can catch my breath, trying to roll onto my side, he's there, pinning my arms at my sides, launching himself on top of me. Straddling me, his knees squeezing either side of my ribs, my arms between his legs and my sides, pain spiking through me, forcing a cry to wrench its way up my throat.

"Hold fucking still or you'll have a needle snapped in your neck," he hisses in my face, ducked over me, his lips against my own. "I couldn't give a fuck if you wanna die that way or not, but I'm still gonna fuck you."

I don't stop struggling, despite what he says, but then his open palm connects with the side of my face, my temple, and I go limp. Momentarily stunned. Seeing the glint of a syringe held up in front of my eyes, I blink, a whimper catching in my throat, sickness swirling in my gut.

"Please," I whisper, my voice cracking. "Please, I'll do what you say, just-"

"Ohhhh," he sniggers, "now you come with the begging," he laughs then, sinister and raw, cutting me off, bending down so his nose touches mine. "Tough shit, I've heard enough of your fucking noise. My dad warned me about you Foster women and your disobedience. Like mother like daughter." And then he stabs me with the needle, a short, sharp prod in the side of my throat that has my mouth opening on a silent cry.

All at once, I can't think, goosebumps are flying up over my skin, breaths panting through my nose, a wash of cold flares through me, just below the surface of my skin and I'm on fire and cold all swirling into one.

My head goes limp, Chris tosses the needle to the floor, lifting himself up and off of me, the mattress dipping by my feet. My chest feels heavy, my lips parted and although my mouth feels so, so dry, I can feel saliva leaking down the side of my face, pooling atop the bed covers.

I can't lift my arms, flex my toes, and every touch feels cold as Chris' hands grip my calves, thrusting my legs apart. I feel like I'm dead, unable to turn my head, to see, my eyes roll in the dark room, trying to see him, what he's doing from the corner of my eye. And all I want is some light.

Monsters are always more terrifying under the cover of darkness.

The sob is locked inside my chest, but the tears stream free as his hands ruck up my short dress, his fingers tearing my underwear down my legs, exposing me to him. It's hard to blink, my gaze locked on the light carpet, the needle right there, like a taunt. I want to shut my eyes, lift my arms, turn my head, but nothing works, nothing will move and I realise with a sudden shock like a bullet to the heart that I don't want to be fun anymore.

I don't want to be fun.

I don't want to be anything anymore.

I just want this to end.

Everything.

I long for an uninterrupted silence, somewhere I can just be.

Alone. Happy. Quiet.

At peace.

The sound of Chris' zipper is louder than the slow thudding of my heart even as my pulse seems to scream in my ears. His hands grip my waist as he climbs over me, his knees between mine, my limp legs splayed wide. Heat floods my cheeks, knowing he can see me, even in the darkness, with the ways my own eyes have adjusted to the absence of light, I'm sure he can see just fine.

He groans as he positions himself between my legs, and I can feel him, nudging at my dry entrance. My cheeks are wet, my lips trembling, even as nothing else is able to function. I stare at the needle, his thumbs coming to my sex, pulling apart my lips like he wants to see everything.

"So fucking dry, *jesus,*" he complains, shifting away from me, but it all seems so far away now, numbness a slow crawl through my veins.

Eyes unfocused, I feel him shove me higher up the bed, trying to position me and himself better. My head hangs off of the side of the mattress and I think this might be better. Unable to see.

It's a dullness where he touches me now, only mental awareness causing me harm. I feel him nudging between my legs again, fingers on my inner thigh, trying to force his way inside of me. Harder, angrier. His grip on my hip is a weighted pressure, the shifting of his hips, the way the mattress moves beneath him as he shuffles his knees, all of it making me want to throw up.

Then I feel nothing.

There's panic.

It shows itself like red spiderwebs in the whites of her pretty blue eyes.

She speaks to me, but I hear nothing as my nails claw into the back of her hand splayed over my little chest. She pushes me back, with a finger to her red lips, the top one shaped like a little heart. She forces me to the back of the kitchen cupboard, pressure on my shoulder making me sit. My bottom hits the wood beneath me, knees drawn up to my chest, but I don't release her hand and she yanks it away, leaving me with bloody fingers on my chubby hands.

The door is closed on me, and I breathe harder, my eyes wide, trying to see in the dark.

I stay quiet as I hear Mummy speak, but she's too far away from me to hear what she's saying.

There's thudding, and I don't move. It's a constant sound, and my mummy cries.

Thud, thud, thud.

Over and over and over, and then there's screaming.

In a panic, I push on the cupboard door. The kitchen is dark too as it opens, and when Mummy first pushed me inside this cupboard it was light outside, the sun warm as its rays fell through the arched glass roof.

I crawl to my feet, my hands cold on the tiles as I push to stand, brushing my hands down my dress. I peek around the corner of the counter, staring down the hall, fingers gripping the edge of the cupboard.

"Mummy?" I whisper, my voice echoing back to me in the dark house.

I stand taller, straightening my spine, being brave, even though I'm frightened.

"Mummy?" I call it now, braver, knowing she would be brave and come and find me. "Mummy!" I smile, even though it's dark because I spot her, lying on the floor… "Mummy!" I giggle, "what are you doing lying down in the hall?" I place my hands on my hips as I approach, my head cocked to one side, smiling. "Mummy, why are yo-" my bare feet land in something sticky and cold.

Frowning, I lift one foot, trying to see what it is, I touch it with my hand and when I bring it closer to my face, I see what it is. Blood. Like when I cut my knee, but there's a lot of it on my feet and I haven't cut my toes. I stumble back a step, peering at the wooden floor, so much of it, all thick and dark and cold, painted around Mummy's head.

"*Mummy?*" *my bottom lip wobbles, and I'm trying to be brave but tears wet my cheeks and I try to swipe them away but I can't lift my arms.*

There's thudding, and I don't move. It's a constant sound, and I hear my mummy cry even though her eyes are wide open and staring up and there's no tears on her cheeks.

Thud, thud, thud. I hear it, unsure where the banging is coming from and I clamp my hands over my ears. But it doesn't stop, the thudding.

Thud, thud, thud.

Over and over and over, and then there's just screaming.

The screaming is me.

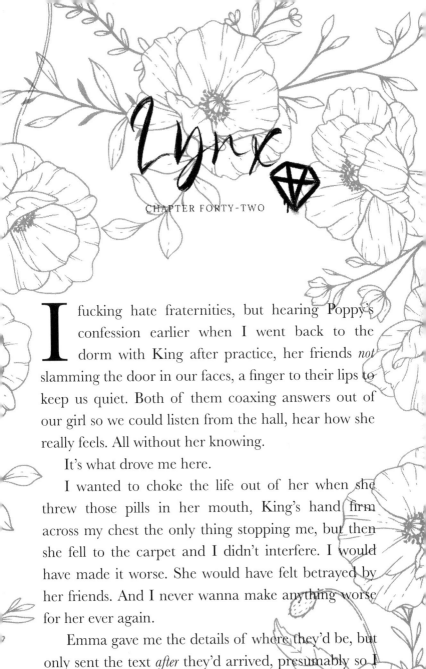

Lynx

I fucking hate fraternities, but hearing Poppy's confession earlier when I went back to the dorm with King after practice, her friends *not* slamming the door in our faces, a finger to their lips to keep us quiet. Both of them coaxing answers out of our girl so we could listen from the hall, hear how she really feels. All without her knowing.

It's what drove me here.

I wanted to choke the life out of her when she threw those pills in her mouth, King's hand firm across my chest the only thing stopping me, but then she fell to the carpet and I didn't interfere. I would have made it worse. She would have felt betrayed by her friends. And I never wanna make anything worse for her ever again.

Emma gave me the details of where they'd be, but only sent the text *after* they'd arrived, presumably so I wouldn't try to stop Poppy going out completely.

Which I wouldn't have tried to do, but Emma's just protecting her friend and I'm good with that. It means she's got someone decent in her corner. Besides, I could have found the party in ten seconds flat. I'd only have had to ask around, take a twelve second stroll down Greek row, but as it stands, I waited, like I promised I would, on tenterhooks until the text came through.

Now, a full, warm beer in my hand that I'm not going to drink, I scan over the sea of faces until I find her. Short black dress, arms around her blond friend's neck, a guy at her back. I want to slit his throat, my fingers squeezing my cup until the plastic cracks, the liquid draining right out of the bottom. I drop the cup, grab my cell and open the group chat.

KING
Where the fuck are you, Lynx?

REX
I wanted to go too!

KING
You don't even know where he is

REX
Okay… Fair, but I wanted to go, regardless

FLYNN
I wanted to go too :(

BENNETT

Jesus Christ. What's going on?

Lynx?

KING

You better not be at that party, Lynx.
What did I fucking say?

BENNETT

Party?

REX

I wanna go! Nobody lets me do
anything fun

KING

We literally just got back from
paintballing

FLYNN

Why did no one invite me
paintballing?!

KING

Because last time you pulled a knife
and almost stabbed a kid

That's why

FLYNN

He had it coming

KING

You literally attacked him because he
shot you.

Like he's supposed to

FLYNN

I stand by what I said

REX

He was twelve

Plus, you're shit at it

BENNETT

Someone tell me what the fuck the problem is, right now.

LYNX

I'm getting our girl.

Shoving my cell back inside my jeans' pocket even as it vibrates, again and again, I glide my line of sight back to where Poppy is dancing. Blondie's there with the guy I want to kill, but Poppy's gone.

Frowning, I stretch up onto tiptoes, searching the dark, smoke filled space for her. I circle the room, making my way into the kitchen, onto the back porch where she was sitting when I first arrived, search through the bathroom queue.

What the fuck?

It takes me ten minutes to get back to my original position beside the wall, and then I shove through the dancers, tapping her blond friend on the shoulder. She spins around, still dancing, a frown etching her forehead.

She rolls her big blue eyes, "I've already helped you once today, what could you possibly want now?"

"Where did Poppy go?" I shout over the music,

someone bumping into my back making me grit my teeth.

Blondie rolls her eyes again, smirking at me, her lips sealed.

I raise a brow, dipping my face into hers, "I need to know, I just wanna make sure she's okay." I hate that I'm telling her this like I should have to give some sort of reason, but I'll do whatever it takes. "She's not good in crowds, I just wanna keep an eye on her. That's all."

She sighs, another eye roll and I'm wondering how it'd feel if I plucked them out of her fucking skull, "She had to pee."

I frown harder, "She wasn't in that line."

"No, upstairs, I showed her where when we first arrived, last door on the right."

I'm moving before she's even really finished, and I hear her yelling something that sounds like *be nice* at my back, making *me* roll *my* eyes now.

I take the stairs two at a time, the halls are long, splitting off into wings when I reach the top and I don't fucking know which way to go to make it to the right door.

"For fuck's sakes," I groan, turning right and heading all the way to the end of the corridor.

I hammer my fist on the last door as I push it open, a shriek that is *not* Poppy's greets my ears and I walk through anyway. Ignoring the threesome happening on the bed, I head straight for the bathroom. Empty. I huff in frustration, slamming the door shut behind me. I don't stop, crossing the hall, entering another bedroom, this one much fuller…

"Poppy?" I call out.

Gritting my teeth, glancing over all of the naked bodies to pick her out, praying like fuck she's not fucking in here. I stride through, stepping over tangled arms and legs and holding my breath to avoid the smell of stale sex as I open up the bathroom door, lots of shower sex but no Poppy.

Exiting the room, I smack right into Rex, lazy smile on his face.

"Two guys fucking in the shower invited me to join them in there," he announces proudly, gesturing towards the room I just exited. "I told them thank you, but no thank you, someone already owns my dick."

I raise a brow, rolling my eyes, "You're an idiot," I toss over my shoulder as I turn, King falling into step beside me.

"They're waiting outside in the truck," Raiden says at my side, referring to our older brothers, gray eyes sweeping across the hall as we make our way to the other end of it. "Saw Bonnie downstairs, she told us you were up here."

"I meant you!" Rex says at my back, hurrying to catch up.

"Shut up, Hendrix," King mutters, but Rex's words do funny things to my insides.

We've never talked about *us*. What we're doing. What we are. We just always sort of fell into bed together and neither one of us ever ordered the other one out of it.

"What?" I say, stopping even as King keeps walking.

I turn to face Rex, blinking at him, his ashy hair flopped in his light green eyes, a lick of yellow paint on the edge of his wide jaw.

"What?" he echoes, blinking at me in the same way, his lazy smirk slowly being replaced with a frown. "You think you don't own me?" he murmurs, a crease denting between his brows, he steps closer. "Baby boy, you've owned my heart since I was fourteen years old and you punched Jake Jones in the face for calling me a loser. I knew right then, I'd pick you over fucking anyone."

"You-"

"I love you," he says casually, a simple shrug of one shoulder. "Always have, always will."

"I-"

"This door's locked," King grunts, both of us snapping our attention to him. "Poppy?" King's twisting the door handle and my heart is pounding in my chest.

"She wouldn't lock the door," Rex murmurs beside me as we close the distance between us and King.

The air seems to change, thick, tinged with panic,

and something feels off now, it didn't before, I just wanted to see her. To get her back. Make her ours. Now everything just feels wrong.

"Poppy!" King pounds his fist on the door, shouting her name.

My chest is rising and falling, heart pounding in my chest, and a heavy sense of dread drops into my gut.

"Break the door," I say sharply.

"What?" Rex snaps his head over his shoulder to look at me.

"Break the fucking door down!"

Without hesitation, hearing the panic in my voice, both of them step back, and then barrel into the door, splintering the wood, the hinges groaning as they break through. King steps onto the door, his heavy footsteps crushing it more, getting inside the dark room, quickly followed by Rex, his big body like a battering ram.

And all I can think as my feet track me forward, over the broken door, into the shadows, across the carpet, is, she wouldn't be in the dark.

She wouldn't be in the fucking dark.

Adrenaline deafens me to the sounds of the room. King is overtop of someone sprawled out on the floor, his fists pummeling into them again and again. It's a dull thudding overridden by my hammering heart, my pulse storming in my ears.

Rex is on the bed, murmuring, and I can't make

out his words, but I can see him, straddling someone. A long arm, fine-line floral ink, a bloom of darkness against her pale skin, hanging limply off of the edge of the bed. I don't want to see, but I need to.

This is my fault.

My feet don't stop, drawing me closer like everything's in slow motion. Like a punishment, to drag the moment out, make me see everything. Poppy's limp on the bed, her eyes fixed open, unseeing, and for just a single moment, I think she's dead.

My body rushes cold, then hot, stars spark across my vision, little dots of white then black, and I'm hardly able to stay standing.

"I've got her! But stop King before he kills him, Lynx!" Rex barks at me.

His shout muffled but I'm moving towards Raiden on instinct.

Protect your brother.

Protect your girl.

Get out of here without anyone seeing.

My arms go around Raiden's neck and I'm hauling him towards me, his elbows connecting with my sides as I fight him back, the body on the floor unmoving. King knocks me to my ass, my spine connecting with the floor, my legs wrapping around his, wrestling him down.

"Raiden, Raiden, Raiden," I chant.

His heaving back to my chest, my arms tight around him, pinning his arms at his sides. He throws his head back, connecting with my collarbone as I wrench my chin out of the way just in time. A sharp pain jolting up my neck, but I don't let him go, holding him to me.

I say his name over and over and my hearing is coming back, and Rex's deep voice meets my ears and I hear him say my brother's name. *Bennett.* And I've never been so relieved. I've always needed my big brother, but right now, in this moment, I feel like I could cry. Grateful to have him.

"Raiden, man, please," I grunt, tightening my thighs around him, squeezing his legs, his torso, every hard inch of him rebelling against my hold, twitching and fighting. "You gotta get it together, she needs us, you gotta stop. She needs *you.*" My lips are to his ear, the taste of him on my tongue, and finally, finally, he stills, but I don't release him. "You gotta stay with me, man. We need to do this shit together. If I let go of you, you gotta work with me, not against me, as a unit." I'm panting, his weight crushing my lungs, but I'm not letting go, not until he agrees. "Yeah?"

He heaves for breath, panting and then, "Yeah, okay." I wait, still holding onto him, he sighs, his body deflating, and then I release him.

Effortlessly, he rolls to his feet, offering me a bloody hand, he pulls me to my feet just as Bennett stalks into the room.

He looks between all of us, the bed last, I can't look, so I keep my eyes on my brother, watch every tiny twitch of his face, witness the mask of pure rage transform his hard features into something murderous.

"Rex, take your hoodie off, put it on Poppy," his eyes come to us, onto King, "Raiden, the door." Bennett turns fully towards me, his eyes going to the body at my back. "And that is?"

I turn then, at his question, peer down. Bloodied face, dark hair, bruised, split skin.

Not enough.

"Chris Matthews," I swallow, clenching my fists, staring at his broken nose, torn brow, tracking down, over his rapidly rising chest, over his abs to find what I already knew, his dick flopped out, legs bare.

"Break his arms," Bennett instructs and I glance back, watching my brother's face, expressionless as he stares down at this piece of shit.

"I want to break his neck," I seethe, the words slithering their way out through my teeth. "I want to break his *fucking* neck." my hands clench harder, short nails cutting into my palms.

"We will." Bennett nods his agreement, clenching his jaw. "But for now, his arms. Do it now."

He flicks those dark brown eyes up onto mine, a dangerous curl to his upper lip, something I mirror on my own and then I'm stomping my foot onto Chris' chest to hold him down. Snatching up his left arm and yanking it from its socket. He cries out, something gurgled and semi-conscious, but it's like I don't hear anything at all. All I can hear is Bennett's hushed voice, King's deep boom, Rex's gentle murmurs and then there's one tiny whimper at my back.

And it makes my brain pulse, anger threading hot through me like I'm never going to be able to purge it.

Everything merging and mixing, movement at my back, my brothers taking care of our girl that this fucking cunt *touched*, and I'm snapping his forearm. Reveling in his agonized scream. I lift my foot, kick him in the face, and then stomp back down on his chest. Taking his other arm, his fingers bent backwards in my palm, I twist and twist and *twist*, his arm at an obscene angle, one that almost makes me vomit, and then there's a long, drawn out, *crunch, click, snap*.

Hands are tight on my upper arms, King's voice in my ear, "We're a unit, she needs you."

My breathing comes out in a rush, my hearing coming back as he echoes my own words, the low, dull thud from the music downstairs filtering back in.

I spin around, eyes flying over my two lovers, Poppy slung up in Rex's big arms, Bennett already leading them to the door. I hurry up beside them, King at our backs, and as a unit we make our way out of the room, down the stairs, through the crowd.

No one pays us any attention, the way each of us is practiced in slinking through crowds. The hood is pulled up and over Poppy's head, hiding her from view, her legs limp over Rex's arm, but she's not on display. No one can see. I try not to think about what was happening to her while I was downstairs, texting with my brothers, aimlessly circling the first floor, while she was upstairs, being-

"Raiden, pocket your hands," Bennett utters at my front, loud enough for King to hear at my back.

Drawing my attention, his head down as we weave our way out the front door, he slips his busted knuckles inside his pockets, and we make our way down the huge mouth of brick front steps.

Bennett leads us straight to the truck, speeding up the closer he gets to Flynn in the driver's seat, who he promptly turfs out, directing him into the back. And it's the look on Flynn's face as we approach, the anger, the rage, the murder that pulls my mind from the pit of darkness. My fingers circled around one of Poppy's calves, I release her, step into Flynn's chest as he makes to lunge forward, Bennett already buckling his seat belt in the driver's seat.

"We'll give her to you, but you've gotta get in the car, bro," I tell him, shoving him back with all my strength.

My open hands to his shoulders, my body against his, I can't hold him back, he's bigger than us all, only Rex would stand a chance but not with Flynn this angry, it's like he has super strength. I grab his face in my hands, squeeze his cheeks, his nostrils flaring, blue eyes flicked over my shoulder on Rex closing in on us.

"Get in the truck, Flynn," I shove him again, squeezing his face, jerking his head towards me.

"Look at me," I order sharply, his eyes finally coming to mine, "get in the truck," I instruct softly, releasing his face.

His eyes glide behind me once more, but with a swallow, Flynn slides back into the truck, across the leather seat. I'm stepping back, Rex moving in front of me, ducking inside the back door of the truck, Poppy in his arms.

"We've got you, Kitten," he hushes, a cracked sound catching in his throat, he passes her like broken glass into the cradle of Flynn's body, a muted whimper as she passes hands.

"It's okay," Flynn whispers. "You're okay, Angel."

Rex sits down beside them, King slamming the front passenger door as he climbs in, and Rex is pulling me onto his lap. My hand on the door, tugging it closed, Bennett already driving us down the bricked driveway.

I shift myself, Rex's hands helping me out of my sweatshirt to drape over her legs. I catch sight of her thighs, deep purple fingerprints covering the insides. I grit my teeth as I lay the fabric over the curl of her in Flynn's arms.

"You're safe," Flynn says, feral, threatening and soft.

There are so many promises in those words, but I cling onto the most violent translation.

We're going to kill for you.

Bennett

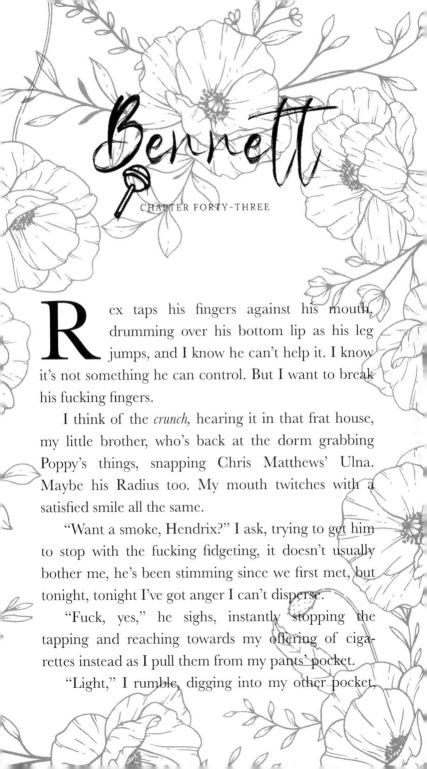

CHAPTER FORTY-THREE

Rex taps his fingers against his mouth, drumming over his bottom lip as his leg jumps, and I know he can't help it. I know it's not something he can control. But I want to break his fucking fingers.

I think of the *crunch*, hearing it in that frat house, my little brother, who's back at the dorm grabbing Poppy's things, snapping Chris Matthews' Ulna. Maybe his Radius too. My mouth twitches with a satisfied smile all the same.

"Want a smoke, Hendrix?" I ask, trying to get him to stop with the fucking fidgeting, it doesn't usually bother me, he's been stimming since we first met, but tonight, tonight I've got anger I can't disperse.

"Fuck, yes," he sighs, instantly stopping the tapping and reaching towards my offering of cigarettes instead as I pull them from my pants' pocket.

"Light," I rumble, digging into my other pocket,

he leans into me, his fingers still twitching, but as soon as he inhales, leaning back in the chair, he stills. "Flynn?" I ask my brother as I light my own, he shakes his head, flicking his curved pocket knife open and closed.

I drop my head back, stare up at the ceiling as I exhale.

The three of us sit inside Flynn's suite on the top floor of the house, the door open, the one opposite, my room, is closed. Poppy inside with a doctor, with King.

I grit my teeth. I want to be the one in there with her. But I'm too angry, I wouldn't be thinking straight. Raiden's got anger that bleeds out of him, but he needed his hands looking at and only one of us could be in there with her.

"Did you see what he did?" Flynn asks, elbows on his knees, the flipping of his blade paused, chin dipped, his blue eyes flash up, onto Rex, waiting.

Rex shifts, exhaling through his nose, thick white smoke slowly drifting up to the ceiling. "I don't think he could get it in." He cringes as he says the words, "But he was right… *there.*"

I feel relief at that, having already heard the same thing from him when I first arrived inside that house, pocketing a syringe and leaving behind a battered body.

Flynn nods, resuming his knife play, dropping his gaze to his bare feet. Dark sweats the only thing he has on. His silky black curls in disarray, a frizzed mess atop his head. Other than that, he is so very serene it is unnerving. I know Flynn better than I know myself. This is when he's most dangerous.

"Flynn," I clear my throat, pinching out the cherry of my cigarette between my finger and thumb, flicking my gaze onto Rex, gesturing for him to go find an ashtray, he climbs to his feet. "Look at me," I say, diverting my attention back to Flynn. Very slowly, his sapphire blue eyes lift to mine, "I will find you an outlet, you will get your blood," I am very clear with my words in that respect, making sure he knows as I hold his gaze that I'm being serious. "But not without proper planning. There will be no vigilante-"

He scoffs, cutting me off, a sinister smirk curling his mouth, dark brow dropped low, "Vigilante would imply I'm some sort of fucking hero."

I raise a brow, slow to climb my forehead as I look at him, and I have a million and one things I could fucking say, but I go with, "Poppy needs a hero right now, and if you fuck off to god knows where and she wants it to be you, what the fuck do I do then, huh?"

He grits his teeth, Rex returning, placing a crystal ashtray down on the glass table between us. Three short couches perpendicular to one another.

"She's got y'all," he shrugs, dropping my gaze again. "She doesn't need me."

"Flynn, brother," he glances my way, closing his knife, "she needs you."

I need you.

After too long, bright blues flicking over my face, finally, he sighs, "Okay," sweeping pale, clammy fingers through his wild hair.

"Got any weed?" Rex asks Flynn, but he's already moving, opening drawers, closing them, tapping his fingers over his goddamn mouth. "If I were a knife-wielding, sociopathic psychiatrist, where would I stash my weed?" Flynn tosses the open knife at Rex, his broad back to us, and he drops down, just as the blade spins through the air, hitting the dresser. Turning his head of messy ash-brown hair over his shoulder, he licks his lips, cocks his head, looking Flynn in the eye, "Missed me, pretty boy."

"I missed on purpose," Flynn grunts, sighing heavily, he leans back against the couch.

"Like the last time we went paintballing, you mean?" Rex stands, turning back to face us, little baggie of weed between his fingers. "You miss on purpose then, too?"

"You're a little shit, Hendrix," Flynn mutters, not rising to it, exhaustion heavy on all of us, but Rex's energy never wavers.

"Sit the fuck down and shut the fuck up, Rex. It's rude not to share a spliff, so hurry up and roll one," I say as he crosses the room, grabbing his sweats pocket and yanking him back down onto the couch.

"Jesus," he chuckles, "okay, okay," he says, leaning towards the table, already rolling a joint.

I hear the front door open, close, my brother's

light gait trudging up the first set of stairs, then the next.

"Got her stuff," Lynx announces, duffle swung over his shoulder, bright blue colored cell phone in his hand.

He comes over, dropping the bag beside the open door.

"It's off," Lynx says, swallowing, holding the cell, screen up, "probably dead, we should probably charge it." Flynn holds out his hand, Lynx places it into his waiting palm, dropping down on the cushion beside me, closest to the door. "They're still not done," he states, a crease digging between his brows, scrubbing a hand through his bleached blond hair.

"I'm sure it won't be long," I say, counting down the seconds myself.

"When did you first fuck her?" Lynx whispers from beside me, my entire body coiling with tension, I turn my head, glancing at him, his head dropped back on the back of the couch but his red-brown eyes are on mine. "It wasn't at the track."

I swallow, but I don't say anything, no one knows anything except for Flynn and he wouldn't rat me out, but do I want to keep it a secret? Do I-

"I love her," Lynx says calmly, killing my thoughts, still watching me, and I don't drop his gaze, even though I want to, I've never heard my brother say he loves anyone except our mom. "I want to keep her." I nod, understanding, Poppy was his first, he doesn't want to share a woman with his older brother, and I will respect that even if it hurts. "I will do whatever the fuck she wants, but I'm not leaving her again, I'm not," he blows out a breath. "I'm not pushing her away, and I'm not giving her up for you, unless that's what *she* wants."

I think of the bar, the car, the parking lot, the ride home.

"I'm not giving her up either," Rex rasps, eyeing his lover, "I'm not exchanging one of you for the other," he tells Lynx. "I love you," he says confidently, making the tops of my little brother's ears flush red. "And I love her. She makes my head quiet." I blink at that. "And King won't give her up, either."

All of this feels like it's coming outta left field, and it shouldn't really, should it. I've seen the way they rally around her. They orbit her like the fucking sun. Like I do. Like I think, maybe, Flynn does too.

"She already gave herself to me," Flynn says, looking between the three of us. "I'm already hers."

I work my jaw, gripping my thighs so tight, my knuckles feel like they're on fire, but I don't say anything. I don't have anything to fucking say. I can't add to that. I don't love her. I'm not sure I even have the capacity. I love my brothers and I feel as though I'm maxed out with that. I don't have a big heart or a tender bone in my whole body. I'm not a man built for the love of a soft woman. I could never reciprocate.

"Fine," I swallow, my throat dry, voice raspy, drawing the attention of the room. "I'll back off," I say, nodding, owning it, we're not good for each other, I'll break her heart and she's already dealt with enough shit from me. "If you're what she wants, and y'all are gonna share without fighting," I swallow again, still nodding my head but I can't stop. "You can't fight," my words and my thoughts are all getting blurred as I think about her with my four brothers. "She's got enough shit in her life, you cannot be fighting." I think of her dad, his words, threats. "You need to protect her."

And I know they can, Flynn was made for protection, so was Raiden. And Rex is easygoing, carefree, he could drag a smile out of a corpse. She needs that. Happiness. Lynx is soft, usually. He's the buffer. The four of them fit her. I just... I just don't. I'm hard and angry, unfeeling, I run a corrupt business, and create non-addictive substances like I think I'm some sort of hero.

I could never be that for her. I'm the reason tonight's even happened. Why she pulled away from them. Everything is my fault. I wonder, not for the first time, if they'll all be better off without me. Especially her.

"Bennett," Lynx says.

But I'm already pushing to my feet. Shoving my hands into my pockets as I jog down the stairs. I grab my keys from the kitchen counter and climb into my car, start the engine. I sit inside the car, the engine rumbling as it warms up. I could peel out of here, drive and keep driving, hit highway after highway.

Instead, I'm tapping a number into my phone, the cell connected to the car speakers. It only rings three times.

"Benny," she sighs, "I missed you," she says, soft, happy.

Tears spring to my eyes, and I choke them down as I answer, "Hey, Mom."

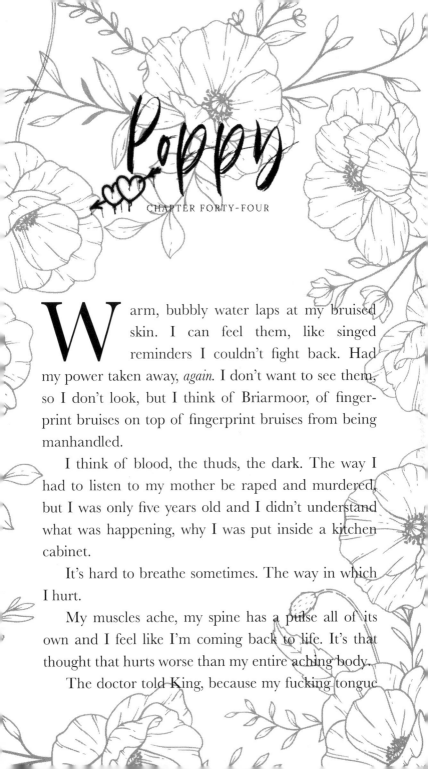

Poppy

Warm, bubbly water laps at my bruised skin. I can feel them, like singed reminders I couldn't fight back. Had my power taken away, *again.* I don't want to see them, so I don't look, but I think of Briarmoor, of finger-print bruises on top of fingerprint bruises from being manhandled.

I think of blood, the thuds, the dark. The way I had to listen to my mother be raped and murdered, but I was only five years old and I didn't understand what was happening, why I was put inside a kitchen cabinet.

It's hard to breathe sometimes. The way in which I hurt.

My muscles ache, my spine has a pulse all of its own and I feel like I'm coming back to life. It's that thought that hurts worse than my entire aching body.

The doctor told King, because my fucking tongue

wouldn't work, that there was no signs of rape. It confirms what I thought I knew, *he couldn't get it in.*

I close my eyes, inhale through my nose.

The doctor also said that I'm lucky the shit Chris shot me up with didn't kill me with the amount of other drugs already in my system.

I wish it had.

I don't want to face them.

Anyone.

After seeing that.

Saving me.

I wish I'd never gone out tonight. I wish I'd never taken those pills. I wish the men I'm addicted to weren't inside this house.

I want to peel off my skin, inch by inch, I want to boil my blood, drink bleach, step into fire, anything to get the feel of *him* off of my skin.

Tears burn the backs of my eyes as I think of Raiden, holding my hand, kissing my knuckles, his own split, *for me.*

Lifting a shaky hand to my face, I touch my cheek, still hot from where Chris smacked me, but I'm fucked up too, because I like the feeling, what it reminds me of.

My worth.

I drop my head back, hair down my spine, the ends in the water, think of Raiden running this bath for me, in Bennett's bathroom. All slate grey tiles and silver accents. Fluffy black towels and an unnecessary amount of mirrors on the walls, only a small window set high up in the wall to my back. It smells like him in here, bergamot and tobacco. A scent I've tried to block from my memory.

Candles flicker, the overhead lights off and it's like my own personal cave. Warm light, hot water, steam wafting off the top as I lie chin deep in the tub.

I think of the men, just on the other side of this door, how I wish they were mine, but they can't ever be.

I slept with Flynn.

I slept with Bennett first.

I'm in their house, but I can't get reattached. I'm supposed to be keeping my distance. I'm supposed to be letting them live their lives. Be free of burdens. I'm always going to be a burden. I wonder how long until Dad gets completely bored of dealing with me and locks me up in Briarmoor for the rest of my life. He could do that, if he wanted to, what with his Deputyship. A court ruled piece of paper that makes him my owner.

I will never have control over my own life.

I hear Chris' words inside my head, *'You were promised to me, Poppy.'*

My skin crawls, and I want to tear it off.

My father's just moving my ownership from him to another. Like a blind adoption from the pound. I'd rather be euthanised.

I bury my face in my wet hands. Breathe deep,

catch Bennett's scent again, and hate that it calms me so easily. Soothes me. Like he did in the passenger seat of his car. I don't think he really wanted me inside his car, I don't think he even really wanted to fuck me. I don't know what the fuck that was. But I remember the feeling of self loathing that followed me afterwards.

I think of red chestnut eyes, bleached blonde hair and golden tanned, tattooed skin. Full peach lips, a straight nose, tiny dimple in the centre of his chin. A freckle beneath his right eye, another along the curve of his cheekbone, just beneath the other.

Lynx and I, we reached somewhere high up in the galaxy together on that first night that the rest of the boys couldn't have imagined.

I wanted Lynx to be mine.

Right then.

When he held me and we were strangers, but we tangled and it was so right, I wasn't even scared.

The feelings that flooded through me, something like love, a welcome dagger in my chest.

That's why, I think, he hurt me the most.

Because even when he thought he wanted to, he didn't really want to hurt me at all.

King was the one I fell for next.

Solid and surly, his presence like a wash of ice, a flash of heat, goosebumps, heart pitter-patters and rushing blood through my veins. He was my foundation. Sure and stable, smart and confident. Gentle with me in a way I'm not sure he's ever been before. His heart felt like it was for me. Violently torn from his chest and placed gently in hands, delicate and fragile. I would keep it safe.

Rex, I think, I sort of tripped and fell into. A little head over heels, sort of like I was drunk. Champagne bubbles bursting in my veins with his attention, fun and carefree, loving. His heart on his sleeve, a teasing smirk on his mouth. Confident in himself enough not to hide his affections for me, or for Lynx, even if Lynx doesn't see it. A tether that only seemed to tighten us closer together.

I'm not sure when I fell for Flynn. Terror strangled with a strange curiosity, a noose of daisies around my neck, something that made me fall into him instead of away. Letting that fear bind me to him, in blood, in lust, in love. Possessive protection. Something I have craved my entire life and found in a man with brutal hands.

I finally think of Bennett.

Just on the other side of the door, I can see his shadow beneath it, the gap darkened by his presence, so close to the door, and my own throat chokes me, stopping me from calling out to him.

He is easy to just exist with, in silence or laughter. Even with his overbearing nature, the way he needs control, to protect the people he cares about most. He is darkness and goodness and home.

That's what each of these men ground me with. A

feeling, I'm not sure I've felt, even before my mother was killed, of home. Warmth and comfort and love.

So much love it makes my chest cavity squeeze. Too tight. Too much. Suffocating. I've never known love because I'm not designed for it. It's undeserved, and I don't know how to convince myself otherwise. I'm not even sure I could, I just, I haven't earned it.

I almost came between these men, they were fine before me, they'll be fine after me. It's only me who won't be.

The razorblade glints under the flicker of candle-light as I pick it up from the edge of the tub, swaying orange waves of warmth splashed across the bath-room walls. I stare at it between my fingers, having found it easily in Bennett's cabinet below the sink, the mirrored surface catching the reflection of the water. Of me.

I stare at my eyes in the blade, red licks over the whites, the colour of my irises bland and dull, I look lifeless. I wonder what it would take. How long.

Warm hands cover my own, lifted out of the tub, above the water, taking the razor from my numb fingers. I don't know how long I was spaced out for, but I blink, my teeth suddenly chattering, my body alerting me to the cold temperature of the water.

And the room is full, as I look up, five faces all staring down at me in the now bubbleless, clear water. Nothing shielding me from them, but not one of them looks at me like that, all of their eyes only on my own.

"Sorry," I say, voice cracking, dry, underused, I blink, looking down, holding their gazes just too much.

I catch sight of it then, the colour of me, a sharp inhale sucking in through my teeth at the mess of purples, blues and greens.

"You're perfect," King says automatically, drawing my gaze, not looking at my body, and I see him looking at me like he did that night we were together, alone in his room, confessions in the night. "You're perfect, Princess."

A sob chokes up my throat, and I'm so tired of crying, but I can't seem to stop.

"Come on, Angel," Flynn rumbles, his blue eyes tight, inky curls a frizzy mess, torso bare, jogging bottoms sitting low on his hips.

Rex steps up closer beside him, a big black towel open in his hands, "Let's get you out, Kitten," he smiles gently, before pulling his bottom lip between his teeth.

It's Bennett that reaches for me, his strong hands, long fingers, warm tanned skin, slips beneath my arms and I grit my teeth at the pain, my entire body hanging limp as he lifts me, everything feeling so heavy. King lifting my feet over the lip of the porcelain with a gentleness you wouldn't think him capable of.

Lynx reaching down into the water, pulling the plug as Rex helps get the towels around me. Raiden squeezing the ends of my hair in another, all whilst Bennett and Flynn have hold of me. Two such different men, strong and hard and soft, all in different ways. But they treat me like a glass doll as they take care of me and I can't stop the tears as they carry me into Bennett's bedroom.

A freestanding corner light, a table lamp on the other side of the large bed switched on. Dark grey walls and silver sheets, heavy curtains drawn across what I suspect is a large window behind them.

Flynn settles me in his lap, cradling me to his chest, I bury my face in the hollow of his throat, breathe him in, vanilla and sandalwood. His big hand covers the entirety of my head, thick fingers gentle as he smooths my damp hair.

"We wanna talk to you, just for a minute, if you're up to it," Lynx is the first Adams brother to speak, finally, my back to him as Flynn settles me closer in his lap.

"You okay to listen, Angel?" Flynn rumbles and I know it's not me he's looking down at as he says it, despite my eyes being closed very tightly, my nose pressing to the top of his bare tattooed chest, I nod my head against him. "Good girl," he whispers and he presses a kiss to the top of my head, scalp tingling as he rests his chin there.

Smoothing my hair back, exposing my ears and I push into him further at the uncomfortable feeling.

And like he knows, he drags my hair back down, recovering them and I relax again.

Blinking, I open my eyes, lift my chin, turning my head just enough to see Lynx dropped into a crouch between Flynn's feet. Pain in his eyes that makes my own heat, my bottom lip trembling as I stare at him and think of all the ways he hurt me, and I don't care about any of it.

"I'm so sorry, Treasure," his voice cracks on his whisper, the back of his thick fingers coming to press lightly against my hot cheek. "I'm so sorry, for everything. I don't have an excuse, I'm just sorry."

"I'm sorry, too," I whisper, my throat sore, tight, "I'm sorry," my chin quivers, my chest vibrating.

Lynx frowns, his fingers a welcome coldness against my burning cheek, "You never did anything to me to apologize for." I lift my gaze slowly, raising my eyes over his head, overtop of his bleached blonde hair, my eyes locking on Bennett's dark brown ones. "Oh," Lynx says quietly, following my gaze and still looking at Bennett, my heart thudding harder and harder, Lynx directs my chin down, the other side of my face still pressed to Flynn's chest. "I don't care about that," he murmurs, just for me, "I want you to be happy," he swallows, wincing as he looks back up at me, those gorgeous warm eyes flicking between mine.

It makes my mouth dry, the way he is just so beautiful.

"We all do. But if it's Bennett you want, I'll back off." He swallows again. "*We'll* back off," Flynn's arms tighten around me in silent protest, enough to make me gasp, but I lift a heavy hand, place it over his heart, and he instantly loosens his grip.

"What?" I ask, frowning, I glance up at Bennett, but he's not looking at me now, staring down at his feet.

"We'll be okay with whoever it is you choose to be with, if you want that," Lynx says, him frowning too now as my gaze returns to his. "We just, we all agree we just want you to be happy, and safe, and if that's with Bennett, that's okay, Treasure."

"No," I stumble over the word, my tongue thick in my mouth. Bennett's eyes come to mine, his jaw clenched, "I mean, yes," I shake my head, pressing the heel of my hand to my temple. "I mean, what?"

My brain feels like it has pins and needles, nothing fucking firing right. I blink hard, fluttering my lashes, trying to get my thoughts together, but I can still feel the drug cocktail in my veins. A brightness that hasn't finished dying yet. And everything is confusing.

"What I mean is, I'm not choosing anyone." All of them stare at me with hard eyes as I stumble through my words, panic lodging itself in my throat. "I'm not coming between you. I won't. And I can't do that anyway, even if it didn't, it's not up to me, I'm just- That's not what it is."

"What does that mean?" Raiden asks, stepping

closer, his light brown skin glowing warmer beneath the orange light as his abs roll with his deep breath.

"What?" I mumble, licking my dry lips.

"What does '*it's not up to me*' mean?" Rex asks, looking between me and King.

My lungs squeeze, not meaning to have said that, I drop my gaze, Flynn's big hand squeezes my waist gently, I look up at him, sapphire blue eyes dark on mine.

I shake my head unable to find the words, but I can't help glancing back up at Bennett.

He's the furthest away, in a pressed, white button up shirt, the sleeves folded up to his elbows. Tattooed, tanned arms exposed, corded with muscle, green veins thick ridges beneath his skin, over the backs of his hands, down his fingers.

"Tell us what that means," he finally says and it's like my chest caves in, hearing his voice, a relief.

But he's still got that hard look on his face, and I'm wondering if he thinks *differently* of me now, after tonight. He steps forward, tall, imposing, hard edges, strong, commanding. He's still moving closer, looming over his brother still crouched down on the floor.

"Lollipop," he rasps, and I see his nostrils flare. "What does that mean?"

I blink, trying to think of what to say, not knowing if I really have anything *to* say. I wonder if I'm even getting this right, it's a swirl inside my head, and there's sickness now, low in my belly, and I press a hand there as I bite down on my teeth, squeeze my eyes shut.

Fingers grip my chin, turning my head, a hand clasping my ankle, and I know who each of those touches belong to. Flynn's breath is heavy down the back of my neck and I like it, the reminder of him so close. As Bennett turns my face towards him. Lynx squeezing the circle of his fingers around my ankle. Comforting. Coaxing. All of them together.

"I could never choose just one of you," I say it all without opening my eyes, it feels easier, the pain, to blurt it out without seeing their faces. "But Chris," Flynn growls at the name, his breath harder against my skin. "He said I was part of a deal between his father and mine and that's why I'm here." My chest heaves and no one speaks, but I can't open my eyes.

"We won't let that happen, Kitten," Rex says. "We won't let anyone have you if you don't want them, even if you don't want one of us, we won't let anyone else force you into something you don't want."

I lick my lips, slowly opening my eyes, looking between them all, my gaze gliding across each of them, taking them in, brown, grey, red, blue, green, all focused on me.

"It's not that simple," I whisper, and a lump lodges itself in my throat, I turn my head, Bennett releasing my chin, turning my head, I blink up at Flynn.

"Is this about Briarmoor?" he rumbles, a line between his black brows.

"Kind of," my voice trembles, "my father, he has a um," I suck in a breath. "It's called a Deputyship." The room is silent and I keep my eyes on Flynn's, his dark blue gaze a pool of safety. "It's called something else here I think-"

"A Conservatorship," Flynn says, grinding his teeth, "keep going," he encourages, nodding his head.

"It's granted to someone, a guardian, or another responsible person, to act on behalf of someone else. Take control of their whole life. Money, health, living arrangements." I'm speaking to the room, but I don't look away from Flynn. "He owns me, and there's nothing I can do about it."

Flynn looks away then, grabbing the side of my face, he presses me into his chest, and even though it hurts my bruised cheek, I let him, because I need it too. The way he holds me like he'll never let me go.

My breath gets caught in my throat, "That's another reason why I tried to stay away. I knew it would end in heartbreak one way or another. So when you broke it off with me, it was somewhat of a relief." Tears run down my cheeks, my body trembling in Flynn's lap. "I knew it couldn't last." I suck in a sharp breath, trying to find my composure. "So, please, please stop fighting with each other over me, I'm not worth ruining your lives over. I'll go back to England if I refuse to cooperate with my father's plan, which I will. And you will move on with your lives and forget all about the disruption I caused you. I never wanted any of you to fight because of me. And I-" I bite my lip, stopping myself from confessing more, from making even more of a fool of myself.

"And you what, Lollipop?" Bennett rasps, something breaking in his voice.

I roll my eyes onto him, connecting with his, I lick my lips, "Even if I had the option of making my own decisions, I could never choose one of you because I'm in love with all of you."

Flynn turns to stone beneath me, his grip tightening impossibly around me, making my bones ache. Lynx sucks in a sharp breath, and I see in my periphery as King and Rex move in closer. Bennett's eyes are hard to read though, he blinks, his jaw clenching, something I've never seen before settling in his expression. But then as the other three each place a hand on me, Lynx's fingers circling back around my ankle, Rex's going over the top of them as he crouches beside Lynx, tangling their fingers together atop my foot. King leans over Rex, dipping his face to mine, kissing my temple fiercely, all so I can still see Bennett.

Breath held, I hold his dark gaze, even though I want to shrink under it, I watch him lick his lips, his cupid's bow a smooth curve.

"You would choose all of us," he states, like he's just spitting facts, and then as I open my mouth, he speaks again, "if you had a choice, you'd choose us all."

I swallow, "I would," I reply nervously.

He drops his gaze, and I feel sick, I guess he wanted me to choose him.

"Then you'll have us all, Poppy," he announces simply, his shoulders rolling back, his fingers coming back to my chin, he looks like Bennett now, strong, certain.

Lynx and Rex at my feet, Raiden at my side, Flynn at my back, my body curled in his lap, Bennett grips my chin between his thumb and forefinger.

"Whatever it is you want now, Lollipop, you'll have, because between us, we can give you the fucking world." He presses his lips to mine in a fierce kiss, my eyes closing as tears fill them once again when he says, "And we will."

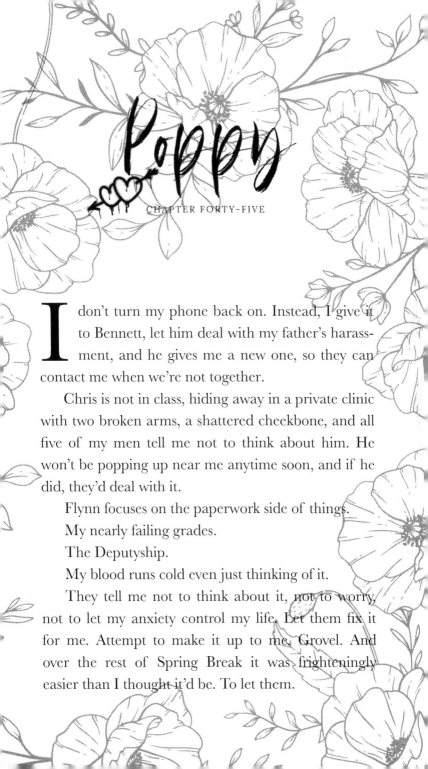

Poppy

CHAPTER FORTY-FIVE

I don't turn my phone back on. Instead, I give it to Bennett, let him deal with my father's harassment, and he gives me a new one, so they can contact me when we're not together.

Chris is not in class, hiding away in a private clinic with two broken arms, a shattered cheekbone, and all five of my men tell me not to think about him. He won't be popping up near me anytime soon, and if he did, they'd deal with it.

Flynn focuses on the paperwork side of things.

My nearly failing grades.

The Deputyship.

My blood runs cold even just thinking of it.

They tell me not to think about it, not to worry, not to let my anxiety control my life. Let them fix it for me. Attempt to make it up to me. Grovel. And over the rest of Spring Break it was frighteningly easier than I thought it'd be. To let them.

To fall back into the arms of men who were my lovers turned tormentors, now, I think, maybe, they could be my saviours.

I walk to my last class of the day, take a seat high in the back and bury myself in my books. Taking notes like a maniac because I'm running on no sleep and caffeine has been my only vice. And I don't think I've felt this uncomfortable or irritable in my own skin before, never in my whole life.

I miss the drugs.

And that alone is terrifying.

I don't know when it got so bad. When I became so frighteningly dependent.

My hands shake, my guts churn and I want to vomit constantly, but there's nothing to expel, food tastes like chalk.

The nib of my pencil snaps against my page and I blink out of my haze, staring down at the lined sheet, frowning at the nonsense I've scrawled across the paper. I'm not even sure what made me press down so hard, the little tip of lead rolling to the edge of the desk, plinking softly as it hits the ground.

"Poppy Foster!" the professor snaps, my knee hitting the underside of the desk with my flinch.

"Yes, Professor?" I answer, my voice tight, embarrassment bright in my cheeks as sixty pairs of eyes all turn to stare back at me.

"The dean wants to see you in his office," I blink,

panicking, I want to say I haven't done anything, but whispers start, and my professor frowns, "right away."

"Right," I nod my head, looking back down at my unintelligible notes.

I heft it all up into my arms, shove it into my canvas bag, papers fluttering everywhere as I try not to make a scene. My cheeks flame, my ears burn hot and itchy, and I hurry to get down the stairs as quickly as possible.

My heart hammers in my chest as I start making my way to the office. My head pounding at the temples, sickness washes over me again, and I have to pause, knuckles to my mouth as I close my eyes, breathe deeply through my nose. God, this is the fucking worst.

I pluck my phone out of my pocket, finding Rex's name and shooting him a text letting him know where I am. Classes are almost over and he's supposed to be meeting me. Bennett made me promise not to go anywhere alone, but I can't exactly ignore my professor. *The dean.*

Christ. What if this is about my grades, oh my god, what if it's about the video, the pictures. I'm going to need Flynn. He's going to need to help me. I don't ever know what to say to authority figures. And if this *is* about my grades... He said he was going to fix it.

I dial Flynn and wait and wait, and it's still ringing and then *'This person's mailbox is full.'*

Rex hasn't texted me back and I'm climbing the stairs, on the other side of the campus now.

Phone to my ear, I bite my lip, waiting, it only rings once.

"Lollipop, what's wrong?"

I'm panting, sweating, cold, a chill creeping down my spine, it makes my head spin. This fucking *withdrawal*.

"I don't feel well," I suddenly say, not meaning to tell him that at all.

Slumping against the wall, resting my shoulder against it, my temple, breathing hard through my mouth, I close my eyes.

"I'll come and get you, just wait for me to-"

"No, I can't, that's not why I called. I think I need Flynn, and I- oh shit! I've forgotten my computer," I huff a breath, my head spinning.

"Lollipop, take a breath," and I do, at his instruction, making my brain still, just enough to do as he asks. "Now, where's your laptop?"

"In my class," I say, still focussing on my breathing.

"And you are…?"

"Not in my class."

"And that's because you are where exactly?" he asks, I can hear a door closing, the snap of his fingers, his voice saying *King*.

"I got called to see the dean and I'm worried I'm in trouble, why else would they call me there? What if it's about my grades, what if it's the," I swallow, "video?" I whisper, biting my lip, even though Flynn assures me it's gone, is it ever really? "What do I do?" my body starts to tremble and sweat beads along my brow, my insides feel like they're curdling. "And I really don't feel good, Bennett."

"I'm on my way," his voice sounds further away and the purr of his engine comes through. "I'm going to fix everything, Lollipop, just wait for me."

"How long will you be?" I whisper, palming the front of my throat with my hand, fingers flexing on the sides of my neck as bile sits on the back of my tongue.

"We're at my office downtown," his engine purrs louder and I know he's speeding because that's exactly how he drove in the snow.

I liked it.

The fear.

But I know that means he's at least half an hour away and even with the insane way he drives, he's going to be at least fifteen.

"But they want me in there now," I whisper, biting my lip, real fear and something worse making my mouth dry. "And my computer," I knock my head against the wall, gentle but it thuds all the same in the empty stairwell.

"Get Flynn on the fucking phone!" Bennett snaps, presumably at Raiden, sensing my panic. "Baby," his tone is so different with me, like the other side of a coin, "we've got you, they can't do anything to you. Please don't worry. And Rex can get your computer."

"Told him to grab it already," King says to Bennett, and then, "Princess, everything's gonna be fine."

"What if I'm getting kicked out? I haven't met any of my conditions to stay," my chest is heaving, breaths coming too short and fast.

My ears are buzzing and Bennett's voice is drowned out by the erratic thudding of my own heart.

"What if this is about *him?*" I shudder as I think it, *Chris,* what he did to me, what these boys did to him.

"It isn't," Bennett says with certainty.

I drop my bag to the wooden steps, follow it down, settling into a crouch. I hold the phone between my ear and shoulder, fiddling with my stuff. I reach into the bottom of it, retrieving a small zipped pouch, finding a little white pill in the bottom of it.

I stare at it for too long, turning it over and over in my clammy palm. And just when I grit my teeth, deciding against taking it, another cold sweat washes over me, nearly making me fall to my knees. I toss it back, swallowing it down dry, and I breathe out long and slow.

"Poppy?" Bennett's voice is low, like he knows, and I bite my lip so hard I taste blood, squeezing my eyes tighter.

"I'm sorry," I breathe, a sob jumping in my chest.

I hear Raiden swear, and Bennett sigh, his engine

revving harder, and I hate myself all over again. I swallow, the back of my tongue bitter, my throat burning, but it feels like all of my other symptoms dissolve, just like that, with the knowledge that that little white pill is going to fix me soon.

"Poppy, wait for me, we're- *fuck*, we won't be long. Can you go to Flynn's office instead? Go there first and just go in and get him."

"I'm so far away from there now," I whisper, cursing myself for not being smarter, but I felt so shitty, I didn't think about anything except my overwhelming panic.

I drag my papers and books back towards me, stuffing them inside my canvas bag, my pens, snapped pencil.

"Poppy, what did you just take?" that's King's voice and I stall in my shuffling of items, my fingers trembling. "I'm not upset, I just want to know, okay?"

Their silence in the car, the engine loud, my own ears rushing with my pulse as it picks up.

"Ecstasy," I say it blankly, factually.

I don't want to feel emotional right now and I'm already feeling lighter, not because the pill's started working, just because I know it will soon.

And it feels like relief.

Shouldering my bag, I stand, continue up the stairs, push through the door. Walk down the corridor towards the office.

"I'm here now," I tell them, swallowing.

"It'll be fine," Bennett says, "if they bring that little fucker up, you know nothing, and you wait for me. You fucking wait, okay?"

"Yes," I whisper, staring at the wide wooden door, gulping down air, my mouth so dry, my voice cracks. "Okay, bye."

I pocket the phone, draw in a deep breath and enter the office.

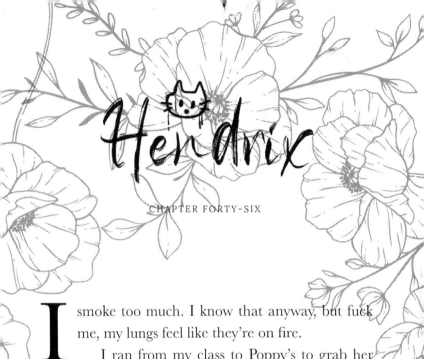

Hendrix

I smoke too much. I know that anyway, but fuck me, my lungs feel like they're on fire.

I ran from my class to Poppy's to grab her laptop, then I raced all the way to Flynn's fucking office, where he wasn't. Then sprinted here, to the administrative building, and I can already hear the dean shouting before I'm even halfway up the stairs.

I'm wheezing as I get to the final step, bracing my hand on the railing and bowing my head, breathing in deep through my nose, I shove my hand through my hair, trying hard not to cough up a lung.

Fuck, I need a cigarette.

"If you don't release your fingers from her arm, right now," Flynn seethes, his voice deadly as I rush through the door, "I will cut your *fucking* hand off."

The dean's secretary is standing behind her desk, ear to the phone, fingers to her mouth, Flynn's huge back to the open door of Dean Groveton's office. I grab the phone off of her as I pass, wrap the cord around my fingers and wrench it from the wall.

"Sorry," I whisper as she gapes at me in horror, planting my hands on her desk, I lean over it towards her. "Sit down, and shut the fuck up if you know what's good for you." She falls back into her chair, a whimper escaping her throat. "I'll deescalate the situation, okay? No one needs to call for security." She nods frantically, and it's almost comical, the way it bounces on her shoulders.

I stalk towards Flynn, clearing my throat as I slink in beside him. And in true Flynn fashion, he doesn't look at me, keeping his hand wrapped around the handle of his blade.

"Put the knife away or you are fired, Mr. Marshall!" Dean Groveton is bellowing, spittle flying from his mouth.

He's leaning over his mahogany desk, suit straining over his carved chest, his chestnut hair combed back, deep green eyes glaring at Flynn.

Poppy's standing on the wrong side of the desk in the far corner, and there are too many other people in this room. Three men, all white clothes, scrubs, I realize, stationed around the walls. One of them is gripping Poppy's bicep, his fingers digging in where he holds her too tightly. She's shaking in his hold, her lilac eyes locked on Flynn.

"You okay, Kitten?" I ask her directly, taking

another step into the overcrowded office, drawing her attention.

She licks her lips, trembling so hard I think even her teeth might be chattering.

"Oh, and what number is this?" a mocking voice says from the chair in front of the desk, British accent thick, his back to us.

He doesn't turn around, clearly doesn't give a fuck that Flynn is armed with a knife no more than a foot behind him.

Poppy doesn't look up, dropping her gaze to her feet, a wince on her face. I side eye Flynn, his jaw locked, teeth gritted, but he isn't looking at me, his dark blue eyes only on her.

"Mr. Marshall!" the dean bellows, "I will not tell you again!"

"I don't give a fuck," Flynn says lowly, roving his gaze onto the dean, "I quit." He shrugs, a sinister smile curving his mouth, he dips his chin, flicks his eyes up, "Now, hand over the girl."

The man seated in the chair before the desk laughs, sighing as he pushes to stand. He's not Poppy's dad, Bennett showed us pictures of him, and this man is older, his lips curled in a mocking snarl.

"Mr. Marshall, is it?" he lifts a dark brow, holding his smirk. "I believe we've spoken on the phone. He reaches out his hand, as though inviting a shake. Flynn doesn't react and I am so still, I forget all about my poor lung capacity as I stare at him. "I'm Dr. Soren," he smiles then, retracting his hand. "Head psychiatrist at Briarmoor." I know about this place, it's a prison for people with mental health illness, and Poppy's dad has threatened to send her back there too many times to count. "Unfortunately, Miss. Foster has had another psychotic break and we are here to take her back into our care. You cannot stop us. There is a police escort outside, I am more than happy to call them in here if you plan on making it difficult for me to leave with her."

"You're not taking her anywhere," Flynn rumbles, low and deep, knife still held out between them, mere inches from this so-called doctor's gut.

"Oh," he huffs a laugh, "but I am, Mr. Marshall."

"Flynn," Poppy's voice cracks as she says it, a whispering plea. "It's okay," she says then, her sad lilac eyes coming to mine, pupils blown, I feel my heart clench. "Rex, please," is all she says, and I know what she's saying, don't make it worse.

We will come for you.

My entire body is trembling as I think it, chanting it over and over inside my head, praying she hears it.

We will never leave you again.

The room feels heavy, oppressive, it's a ticking time bomb of pressure. We are not going to win here. I feel sick, my insides like lead, I need to be the sensible one now, not something I usually am, I try to channel Bennett, King. I breathe hard, gritting my teeth even as my heart feels like it's breaking.

"Flynn," I say without taking my eyes from hers, "let them go, man."

"What?" he whips to face me now, lifting the blade higher, and I try to ignore the smile lifting on Soren's face.

I swallow, my eyes leaving hers as she drops her gaze to her feet. I stare at Flynn, he's a little bigger than me, and a lot angrier, but I need him not to get arrested.

"Let them go."

I turn, flexing my fingers, curling my fist. My heart pounding in my chest so hard it feels like it'll tear free, flop to the floor, bleed out right here on the hardwood.

"You're out of your fucking-"

My fist collides with Flynn's cheek, the smack reverberating around the office. Flynn tries to shake it off, his inky black curls falling onto his forehead, I cringe, biting down on my back molars. I swing again, hitting him in the same place, and he folds, crumpling to the floor with a thud, knife clattering from his fingers.

"Get the fuck out," I order, not looking away from my brother, his dark lashes fluttering. "Get her and get the fuck out."

Soren laughs, but wisely, he says nothing. I look up, my eyes finding hers as they march her past us, I turn into her, halting their exit.

I lean in, kiss her cheek, breathe her in, filling my

lungs with her, my lips to her ear, I whisper, "We will always find you."

And then she's yanked away, and I don't watch her go, listening as they march down the stairs, their footsteps fading. Flynn stirs on the floor at my feet, and I drop into a crouch, smoothing his hair back and pocketing his knife.

"Mr. Connors!" Dean Groveton barks, and I roll my eyes, breathing deep.

"Yeah, yeah, I know, he's fired."

Flynn

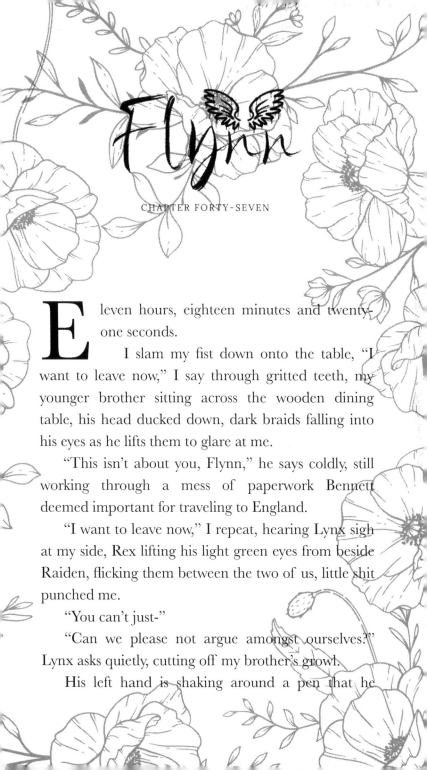

CHAPTER FORTY-SEVEN

Eleven hours, eighteen minutes and twenty-one seconds.

I slam my fist down onto the table, "I want to leave now," I say through gritted teeth, my younger brother sitting across the wooden dining table, his head ducked down, dark braids falling into his eyes as he lifts them to glare at me.

"This isn't about you, Flynn," he says coldly, still working through a mess of paperwork Bennett deemed important for traveling to England.

"I want to leave now," I repeat, hearing Lynx sigh at my side, Rex lifting his light green eyes from beside Raiden, flicking them between the two of us, little shit punched me.

"You can't just-"

"Can we please not argue amongst ourselves?" Lynx asks quietly, cutting off my brother's growl.

His left hand is shaking around a pen that he

drops to the table, shoving both hands through his bleached blond hair.

"I want to leave now," I repeat again, ignoring him, like a dead chant, something that requires blood to summon such a thing, I suppose.

But I could bleed, if it's for her.

"Good, I'm ready, let's go," Bennett's voice is all business as he strolls into the room.

White button up, the top button open, ink revealed by the rolled sleeves. His black slacks pressed, a silver buckled belt on his hips. His dark brown hair slicked back, gold watch on his wrist.

He looks like a fucking mafioso.

"About fucking time," I rumble, shoving back from the table, the wooden legs of my chair screeching across the hardwoods as I come to stand.

I'm wearing the same thing, minus the white, my shirt is black and my long sleeves button at the cuffs, but we're dressed for business, which is funny, because all I have on my mind is violence.

"We'll meet you at the airport," Bennett says then as I twist open the front door. "Make sure you get on that plane with or without us. I have told the pilot to go with or without me. We'll catch up if we have to."

King says something I don't hear in response as I take the three front steps down and climb into the passenger seat of Bennett's car. Tapping my fingers against the top of my knee as I try to wait for him without losing my fucking mind.

I see blood and bones and sinew. Hear screams, painful moans and desperate pleas.

I keep the soundtrack of the near future on repeat inside my head as we drive to Ackerman Medical Clinic. Ignoring Bennett and his incessant rambling about behaving until he says otherwise. I roll my eyes, staring out of the window as we pull up to the clinic, the place in darkness.

Bennett switches off the engine, and we wait in silence, staring at the backdoor of the building where one of our guys is already inside. The door opens, and together we step out of the car, closing the doors quietly. We make our way across the near empty lot, and enter quietly. Bennett talks with our guy, but I'm already slinking my way down the hall to the room at the very end.

Applying pressure to the handle, it goes down silently, and I slip inside.

The guy in the bed is asleep, low lighting is on around the clinical room, all white floors and walls, white sheets. There's a TV playing silently, subtitles dancing along the bottom in white lettering rimmed in black, and the picture flickers over the patient. Two arms propped up in blue casts.

Chris Matthews.

Bennett wants to question him after Poppy told us all the weird shit he said about their dads working together and Bennett then spent the last nine hours on the phone with *colleagues*, trying to piece together more than what Chris divulged as he attempted to rape my Angel.

Bennett says he knows everything now, but I didn't ask him what that meant. I don't really give a fuck about the facts. Not while my mind was wholly consumed with Chris Matthews' murder.

"We aren't murdering him, Flynn," Bennett says as he tucks his hands into his pant's pockets, having silently entered the room from my right.

I hum, clicking my jaw.

I'll do what I want.

"Let me lead, get the answers I want out of him, and I'll let you break his leg," Bennett says, cocking his head, both of us staring at the slimy little rapist in the hospital bed.

"I want to break his fucking neck."

Bennett hums as though in thought, "Lynx said something similar," he pauses, sniffing with disgust, "I suppose you could fuck up the other side of his face to match what your brother did."

My eyes tighten, *it's not enough.*

"We aren't killing someone in a hospital, Flynn, use your brain," he rumbles lowly, tutting at me like I'm an irritation.

I sigh, staring up at the ceiling, praying for fucking patience, knife burning a hole in my pocket, I blow out a breath, "Whatever, start talking."

I stalk toward the bed, stare at his peaceful fucking

face, bruised, fractured cheekbone, purples and blues and yellows a wild bloom over his skin.

Licking my lips, I glance up at Bennett, a smile curving my mouth that has him shaking his head, and then I slap my palm across Chris' face, pinching his nose closed.

He jolts, groaning as I squeeze his fucked up face. His fingers twitching but his arms are on some sort of fucking stilt contraption, holding his arms up and away from his body.

"Hello, Chris," I hiss, bending down, leaning into him so we're eye to eye, still crushing his face with my palm, the side of my hand pressing on the bridge of his broken nose. "If you'd like to live to see another miserable fucking day, you're going to be real silent while you listen, then you're going to answer all of my brother's questions." I turn away from him, smiling ferally at Bennett. Locking my eyes back on Chris's, I lick my lips, catching the back of my hand with the tip of my tongue. "In fact," I breathe, cocking my head, "I think you're going to sing like a fucking canary." I flick my eyes between his wide, watery ones. "Aren't you?" Using my grip on his face, I forcefully nod his head, yanking it back and forth. "Yeah?" I urge, my nose pressing against my knuckles over his face.

He nods on his own then, kicking his legs because I know he's running out of oxygen, and I love it, the way I can practically taste it on the air.

"I'm going to release your face now, and you," I

say lowly, "you are going to be very fucking silent. Understood?"

He nods again, a desperate plea in the motion of his head. I pinch his nose harder, just for good measure, his eyes squeezing shut in pain, a tear rolling down his cheek, and then I release him, and he does exactly as I expect.

He screams.

And I, I punch him so hard in the side of the head that I hear something crack.

"Flynn," Bennett snaps, stepping closer, and I narrow my eyes on him.

"Chill," I whisper, and he frowns harder, grabbing my wrist and yanking me away, taking my place at the bedside, leaving me to pace at the end of it.

He slaps the side of Chris' face, the little fuck groaning as he comes to, and I want to rip his tongue out of his head. Bennett wipes his hand down the thigh of his pants like he'd really rather not have to touch this fuckwit ever again.

But that's okay, because I'm itching to.

"Your father, Chris," Bennett says, hands coming to the thick plastic railing on the side of the bed, fingers curling over it, he squeezes it tight, veins rippling beneath his olive tanned skin. "He works with a man called Carrington. Michael Carrington."

Chris really wants to die, because the idiot rolls his eyes like the self-entitled little rich prick that he is, but

Bennett doesn't give a fuck, he keeps talking, obviously already knowing everything…

"Your father used Carrington to move money between business accounts, funneling money back to your dad while making sure it all left an overly obvious paper trail that would point right to Jason Adams Construction company instead. Correct?"

"How do you know tha-" Chris starts, paling as Bennett steamrolls over him, ignoring him completely.

My gaze flickers over Bennett, his posture straight but relaxed, as though he didn't actually know this, he just knew this boy would be dumb enough to confirm his suspicions after spending all day and most of the night making calls, connecting dots.

It's what he does, that's why Bennett is the leader.

It's why we follow him.

That, and we love him.

I frown, my heart thudding harder and harder as Bennett keeps talking and talking and lead sinks into the pit of my stomach as I take it all in. What he's saying, what it means.

It's only when I knock Chris out, twist his ankle at a one-eighty degree angle and spit on him for good measure. That I look to my brother, our leader, as he races us towards the airport, and know that he'd do anything for Poppy, just like he would for us.

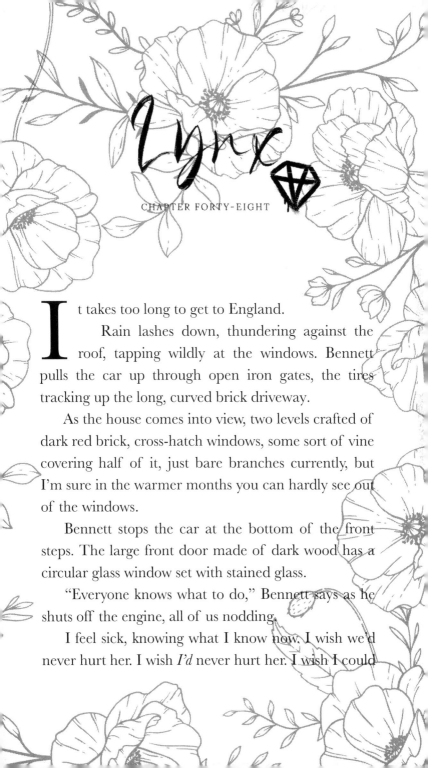

Lynx

CHAPTER FORTY-EIGHT

I t takes too long to get to England.

Rain lashes down, thundering against the roof, tapping wildly at the windows. Bennett pulls the car up through open iron gates, the tires tracking up the long, curved brick driveway.

As the house comes into view, two levels crafted of dark red brick, cross-hatch windows, some sort of vine covering half of it, just bare branches currently, but I'm sure in the warmer months you can hardly see out of the windows.

Bennett stops the car at the bottom of the front steps. The large front door made of dark wood has a circular glass window set with stained glass.

"Everyone knows what to do," Bennett says as he shuts off the engine, all of us nodding.

I feel sick, knowing what I know now. I wish we'd never hurt her. I wish *I'd* never hurt her. I wish I could take it all back, but if I did, maybe we would have lost her. Maybe we wouldn't be able to save her.

Like she's saved us.

Flynn works on the door, gets it unlocked and open in no time at all as we all stand around him. Cold rain soaking us right through, but no one objects, all minds focussed on the task at hand.

Flynn and King go in first, Bennett, Rex, me at the back. I click the door closed. Hearing the commotion beyond this hall. I glance down at the hardwoods, think of puddles of red, a woman, too much like Poppy, lying dead in the middle of it.

I blink, passing a large oval mirror, a slim dresser pressed up against one wall, stairs on my right.

They already have Poppy's father in a chair when I enter a large open room, a living and dining space combined with the kitchen. Glass walls make up the back of the house, all of the furniture wood and expensive fabrics with swirling patterns.

Michael Carrington is a tall, broad, man, thick, brown hair pushed back, white skin, his face extra pale, and I like to think that's due to our presence. His dark concrete colored eyes narrowed in on my brother, thin lips pursed.

"Like I said," Bennett says calmly, sitting down opposite him at the table, his fingers lacing together, King holds Poppy's father in place with his hands on his shoulders. "We're here about your business with Christopher Matthews."

He scoffs, "I don't know what you're talking about."

"Fifteen years ago, you moved money between business accounts, funneling money that wasn't his, back to your business associate Christopher Matthews. All while making sure it left an overly obvious, *false*, fraudulent paper trail pointing fingers right at Jason Adams Construction company. Making sure you and Matthews got rich quick, and poor, innocent Adams got sent to jail for *twenty* years, for embezzlement among a long list of other crimes he was innocent of. Correct?" Bennett is eerily calm, the way he spouts off the information like some sort of emotionless computer program.

Michael's mouth moves, but no words come out and Flynn's fist connects with his cheek, his head snapping to the side. He spits, sniffing hard, before lifting his head back up.

"But you didn't agree to work together right away, did you Michael? No," Bennett laughs caustically, resting one palm down on the table. "There's a period of time, you supposedly stopped working with the Matthews because you wanted to keep all the money for yourself. And then what happened? Because you did, in the end, start working with him again. That's what I can't figure out, what did he give you, to convince you? How much money did it take for you to *ruin my family?*" Bennett snarls in Michael's face, slamming both hands down onto the table as he leans forward.

Snot drips from Michael's nose, blood dripping from his eyebrow, breath heavy through his mouth.

He brings his eyes up onto Bennett's, holding his gaze, "Get. Fucked."

My brother stares at him, and then slowly, his hands slipping back across the wood as he straightens to stand, his dark eyes roll to Flynn. And with a single nod of his head, Flynn smiles.

Flynn strikes Michael across the face, his knuckles a dull thud as his fist connects with bone, King holding him in the chair, hands pinned behind his back.

Flynn beats Poppy's dad's face, blood dripping from his mouth, brow, nose, but Flynn keeps going, waiting for Bennett to speak again.

I tune the noise of violence out, peering around the Carrington family home, no pictures, no personal effects. Nothing to indicate a family does or has ever lived here.

"Anything you'd like to divulge yet?" Bennett asks the bloody man, drawing my attention, staring down at his phone as he reads a message on the screen, "I already know everything, Michael, I'd just like to hear it from your mouth."

"He murdered my wife," Michael bites out, gnashing his red stained teeth, and I can tell my brother is momentarily stunned, even though he mutes his reaction like a pro. But Michael isn't done yet, "I had him murder my wife for an extra cut of money," he shrugs, like it means nothing. "Her parents left her millions and I fucking wanted it. She was always gifting it to charities and bullshit, wasting it, she was standing in the way of my business. So I offered him a partnership and a little slice of her money."

Bennett stands, his jaw clenched, stare hard.

And it's me that asks, thinking of Poppy, the way she trembles when anyone mentions her dad, "Why'd you send Poppy to him? Why give her to Chris? What was in it for you?"

Michael stares at me with a snarling, split upper lip, but he rolls his fucking eyes as he says, "She is nothing more than a burden, soft like her mother. I have no use for her, and the Matthews boy wanted to play with her, he'd get her inheritance when they married, after that," he shrugs. "He could kill her, sell her, do whatever the fuck he wanted." He shrugs again, spitting blood onto the floor as he props himself up in the chair. "I got fifty-five percent of the inheritance money in advance, that's how desperate he was for her, taking out loans worth more than his life. So why not let him have her."

It's as though the room spins, so easily discarding his own flesh and blood, all for the sake of more money he doesn't need.

I can't help but laugh, "That's the most ridiculous thing I've ever heard."

"I don't care what you thugs think," he snaps back. "I'd have given the bitch away for free. Would have saved me a whole lotta hassle, but that boy doesn't know how to haggle to save his life. Pathetic little shit."

"You know your five year old was gonna be in the house at the time?" Flynn asks calmly, his blue gaze sharp as knives from his place on the other side of the kitchen island now, his bloodied forearms resting atop it, hands laced together, crimson on his knuckles.

I can't help thinking of a tiny Poppy closed inside one of those cabinets at his back. The front hall can be seen from here, where we're all crowded in the dining space. She must have been able to hear every single thing that happened to her mom.

He grunts, but it feels exasperated, like he doesn't care enough to attempt an explanation, it just is what it is.

This man is pure evil. The way he corrupted so many, organizing the killing of his own wife. Selling his only daughter. All in the name of money.

But we're not the police.

Our dad's only got a few years left to serve.

Our mom's happier.

I'm better.

Bennett saved us.

We only came here for our girl.

So we can save her too.

"I want you to sign this document," Rex says from the head of the table, sliding over a small stack of crisp white papers, his thick, black framed glasses on his nose, little green stickers poking out of the pages. "Sign at each marker."

"What is it?" Michael asks, already taking the pen.

"It's a conservatorship, among other things. Each document is already signed by a judge, multiple doctors." Flynn smiles as Rex explains. "This over-rides and dissolves your deputyship. Placing Poppy into Bennett's care. She will be his ward, he takes full legal, medical responsibility for her."

The only thing he doesn't have any say in is her monetary assets that she inherits from her mother at twenty-one. He doesn't want to take power over any part of her, but if we want her out of that fucking *hospital*, we needed something drastic.

"And you think I'm just going to sign this?" Michael scoffs, his dark hair a mess.

"I know you're going to, Michael," my brother chuckles, "because if you don't, I'm going to ruin your entire fucking life just like you did mine."

"Yeah? What about Mathews?" he laughs, like a challenge.

Bennett, leans back in his chair, rocking on the back legs of it, the creak of wood loud in the room.

"Firstly, Matthews is your fucking problem, not mine. I'm sure you'll find some cut-throat way of dealing with him. And secondly, I've got video evidence of all your little rendezvous with some very powerful people, Michael. I know many don't think The Cartel has any presence here in good old England, but you and I," Bennett lifts a dark brow, "we know differently, don't we, Michael?"

Michael swallows, staring at my brother in challenge, sweat beads along his temples, and then he lifts the first page, signing at the first green marker.

I hold my breath the entire time, watching with sweat rolling down my spine as Rex taps at each line and Michael signs beside his finger.

I feel dizzy when it's over. Heart hammering in my chest when Bennett slides his cell across the wood of the table. Rex retrieves the documents, passing them over his shoulder to Flynn to look over once more, pushing his glasses up into his ashy-brown hair. We can't afford any little slip ups.

Michael stares at the phone, the dial screen pulled up, a frown pulling at his lips.

"What's this for?" he sneers, King's hands tightening painfully hard over his shoulders.

"You're going to call Briarmoor and tell that *Dr.* Soren that he's about to lose his favorite patient."

Poppy

Fingers pinch my upper arms even though I'm not struggling. Fingerprint bruises are already forming over my light skin in just the small number of hours I've been here. My bare toes catch the grout between the tiles as they haul me down the corridor. Rain lashing the roof so hard I can feel the vibration of it in my bones.

Mouth dry, I try to swallow, the powdery dryness at the back of my tongue, caught like thick sand in my throat, almost chokes me. It's the first thing they did to me, Dr Soren. Feed me a fistful of pills that'll have me hallucinating or vomiting, perhaps both, in next to no time at all.

Jelly legged, I hang limply between the two porters, they're big hands clammy and cold. It sends a shiver up my bare spine, a paper-thin medical gown tied in the back, exposing me to the elements of a place I never wanted to come back to again.

Dr Soren is smug, I can tell, even from only being able to see the back of his head as we follow him down the endless bright white corridors. He's whistling, the echo of it like thunder down the long, wide space. Paired with the rain above, it feels like an unending darkness is finally settling in. Something I'm not going to be able to shift.

What if I never get out of here?

A sob is locked behind my teeth, and everything inside of me feels so dried out already, I don't think I could cry if I wanted to. Which I don't. I'm not giving these people my tears. Not anymore. I have cried too much over things that *actually* matter. People who, despite everything, love me.

I know they do.

I know I love them.

I think of Rex's face back in the dean's office, his promise.

'We will always find you.'

And I shiver for an entirely different reason now.

Dr Soren stops before a familiar steel door, only four rooms on this entire top floor.

Solitary.

'It helps clear your head, Poppy.'

That's what he told me when I was first brought here all those months ago. And each time I've been back since, he's said something similar.

Now he just pushes open the door, the porters

dragging me inside the space, empty except for a single bed.

Without fight, I let them shove me down on the cot, no sheets, no pillows, nothing I could attempt to damage myself with. Leather cuffs are quickly fastened around my wrists and ankles. Bands buckled over my thighs, belly and chest. I am limp, so still it feels like I am dying. I can hardly taste my own breath, my chest such a slow rise and fall, you could likely mistake me for a corpse.

I am dying and I just found life.

They broke me.

They're rebuilding me.

We're fixing things.

They're still showing me how sorry they are.

This can't be how it ends for us.

Not after everything.

"Welcome home, Poppy," Dr Soren calls from the doorway, a taunting, evil smile revealed in his voice. "It's so wonderful to have you back. Sleep well, we've got a lot to catch up on in our sessions."

Flicking out the light, he plunges me into my own personal hell.

That's when I start to scream.

"Poppy."

Stuck somewhere between conscious and not, I feel like I'm floating, like I'm falling. As though I am both very heavy and very light, a boulder and a feather.

"Miss Foster."

Frowning, my eyes glued together with sleep, I try to peel my lids open, squeezing my eyes shut tighter, fluttering my lashes. I reach up, scrubbing my knuckles over my eyes. A pinch of pain in my wrists as I press them to my face has me gasping. Eyes flying open as I remember where I am.

But my hands are free of their cuffs, there's feeling back in my toes. I shiver with the cold, finally dragging my eyes open just enough to squint. There's too much light in the room, the bulb overhead flooding the oversized, clinical white space with a bright, almost blue, hue, forcing my eyes to squeeze closed again.

I can't understand why my cuffs are free. Why I'm not being dragged up from the cot, why nobody's hands are pinching and pulling at my skin, yanking at my sockets.

Working my eyes open with fluttery blinks, I frown harder, shivering again in the icy chill. It's like being locked up in a deep freezer, barely clothed, no sheets. My spine aches as I push up to sit, swinging my stiff legs over the side of the bed.

"Miss Foster, your guardian is here, and he is very

eager to get back on the road, so if you would please get up quickly."

Scanning my eyes in the direction of the door, a tall, curvy woman I have never in my life seen before, stands just a few feet inside of it, the door open at her back.

"Guardian?" I ask, mouth dry, tongue too heavy.

My dad's never been here before.

He never does the dirty work himself.

What new game is Soren playing?

"Yes, your guardian, Mr Adams, very insistent young man."

I look up sharply then, cracking my neck.

Guardian.

"Adams?" the word cracks as I repeat it, blinking past the violent light.

The woman shifts her weight from one leg to the other, her ashy blonde hair falling across her shoulder as she looks over it, out of the open door, at something I can't see in the hall.

"Yes," she says slowly, looking back at me, dipping her chin, "please hurry."

Placing my hands down on either side of the painful spring mattress, I attempt to push to my feet, but my elbows just can't take my weight, sending me straight back down to the cot.

"Porter!" the woman calls, snapping her fingers, "get a wheelchair, quickly, quickly."

My breath is heavy, too fast, lungs burning with the sharp, fast inhales of air as I'm moved *gently* into a wheelchair, my feet lifted and placed on the footrests with care.

Everything seems to blur as I'm wheeled into a lift, the woman in a pale pencil skirt and navy blouse pressing the buttons, scanning her ID card to get us moving.

"Where's Dr Soren?" I rasp, my throat sore from screaming myself to sleep. "Isn't he supposed to discharge me?"

The woman glances over her shoulder, peering down at me, a strange, pinched look in the pull of her mouth, "He's with another patient now." And then she turns back to face the opening doors.

I think it's the first real breath I take. Knowing he's occupied elsewhere. Not with me.

He can't fight to keep me here.

Then I hear *him*.

His deep rumbling floods the room, the glass front to the building is dark beyond the windows.

How long have I been here?

Bennett crowds the reception desk, leaning far over the curve of wood in a threatening pose, the person behind it pushed back from the desk, attempting to avoid his wrath. He lifts a hand, pointing a finger at them and murmuring beneath his breath.

Relief washes through me like my insides just melted into a puddle.

"Mr Adams!" snaps the lady leading me down the hall, a porter pushing the handles of my wheelchair just a few feet behind.

I feel dizzy, watching as slowly, so menacingly slowly, Bennett flicks his gaze onto the woman with a look that I truly believe could kill just as efficiently as a bullet or a knife.

But that's when he sees me.

As the woman keeps talking, and I'm being pushed closer and closer, and the doors at Bennett's back are opening. Ice cold air rushing in. My teeth chatter and my eyes water and then those obsidian orbs are pulled from me, back to the woman before him as she passes him a clipboard.

My wheelchair is stopped, and Lynx is racing towards me. Bleached blonde hair a crazy mess on his head, red-brown eyes wild, he skids the rest of the way across the floor, his shins bashing into the tiles as he drops to his knees before me.

Tears slip from my eyes as his big hands dwarf my cheeks, cupping my face. He's pushing up onto his knees, pressing his lips to my forehead, over and over.

"I'm so sorry," he whispers. "I am so fucking sorry. We've got you now. We'll always have you. I'm sorry, I'm sorry, I'm sorry."

Lynx gathers me in his arms, cedar and red berries engulfing me, his heat seeps into my skin as he holds me up, my toes just barely grazing the floor as I sob into the crook of his neck, my arms limp at my sides.

"We will never let anything happen to you, Treasure. Never again."

"You okay, Princess?" Raiden's comforting rumble reaches my ears at the same time his warm hand finds my bare back, and my eyes lift, finding his steely grey ones.

I nod, even as I sob harder, King's lips coming to the top of my head, his hand cupping my crown.

Flynn appears on Lynx's other side, his hands grabbing me, mouth coming to mine, a fierce press of his lips to my own, "We've got you now, Angel. Forever."

Rex is walking up behind him as our mouths separate, Flynn's forehead resting against my temple, King's hand still cradling my skull.

I turn my attention to Hendrix, his light green eyes warm, a soft smile on his face, he lifts one shoulder in a slow shrug, "Told you we'd always find you, Kitten."

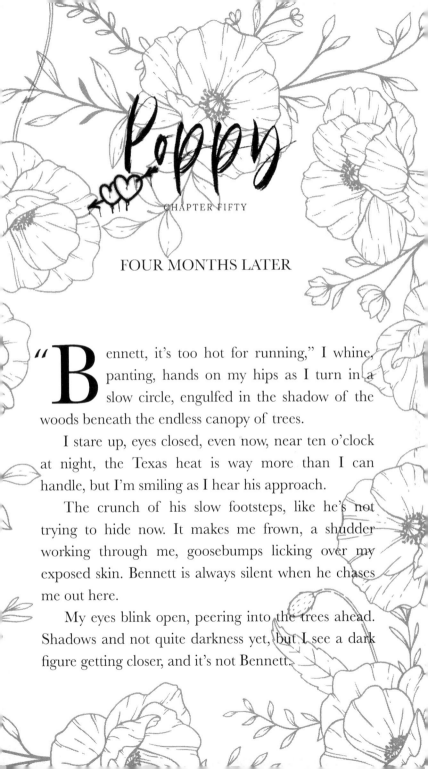

Poppy

CHAPTER FIFTY

FOUR MONTHS LATER

"**B**ennett, it's too hot for running," I whine, panting, hands on my hips as I turn in a slow circle, engulfed in the shadow of the woods beneath the endless canopy of trees.

I stare up, eyes closed, even now, near ten o'clock at night, the Texas heat is way more than I can handle, but I'm smiling as I hear his approach.

The crunch of his slow footsteps, like he's not trying to hide now. It makes me frown, a shudder working through me, goosebumps licking over my exposed skin. Bennett is always silent when he chases me out here.

My eyes blink open, peering into the trees ahead. Shadows and not quite darkness yet, but I see a dark figure getting closer, and it's not Bennett.

Even still, I call out to him, hoping it is, and my eyes are playing tricks on me, "Bennett?" I almost choke, fear a lump in my throat.

I tremble, hot and cold with goosebumps all the same. I lick my lips, my heart pounding, my arms fall to my sides, and I take a step back. I smell him at the last second, bergamot and tobacco, but I'm already stepping back into him, my back connecting with his hot, sweat-slicked chest.

"This was no fun, Lollipop," his breath feathering down the side of my throat, I can hear his pout, his lips skimming the slick skin behind my ear, my long hair sticking to my nape. "You didn't even try to run from me," he whispers. "Are you that desperate for my cock?" his breath is unnaturally cool for this heat, and my goosebumps prick harder, erupting over my flesh, my nipples tightening into diamond points. "Let's play again," his knuckles skim my outer biceps as he brings his hands up, planting them over my shoulders. Making me tremble, my knees feel weak, my heart knocking against my sternum, "I'll count to ten and if you can escape us all. You can have anything you want."

I shake in his hold, his thumbs massaging my shoulders, all of our bare skin touching. Only loose basketball shorts and trainers on Bennett. Short-shorts and a strappy vest top on me, trainers on my own feet.

"All?" I whisper the question, we've never done this with the others before.

Trembling harder, my eyes scanning the shadows, night not yet fully fallen.

I'm getting better, being in the dark. Now that I'm going to therapy, getting real help.

"Hmm," Bennett hums, huffing a laugh, his nose against my neck, *"all."* I lick my lips, lean back into him, feel the long, thick length of his hard cock like steel pressing against my lower back. "I let them join us tonight," he says lowly. His lips grazing along the length of my neck, towards my shoulder. His teeth bite gently at it, his lips sucking, tongue licking. "Because they, like I, are positively *feral* to get a taste of you, Lollipop."

I shudder, my teeth chattering, my body not knowing whether it should be hot, cold, frightened or turned on. I see them approaching now, a second darkened silhouette joining the first.

"You want me to run," I say, staring straight ahead as Bennett mouths at my skin, his brothers slowly coming into view.

"You know I do," he chuckles darkly, sending my trembling into overdrive. "What else do you think we want from you, Lollipop," he breathes and I stiffen, his thumbs stroking soothing circles into the soft skin of my upper arms.

"You want me to fight," I whisper, my eyes darting between Flynn and Raiden, the only two I can see clearly, but I know Lynx and Rex will be out there somewhere too, beyond this small clearing.

Bennett groans, the sound vibrating down my spine, "I do." He mouths along my jaw, his left hand coming to the other side of my face, tilting my head over my shoulder, his cock jumping against me. "You okay with that, Lollipop?" he asks seriously, and my legs tremble, he knows, regardless of what happened to me, that I love it when he pretends to force me.

I nod my head, his mouth slanting over my own, those dark brown eyes coming to mine, our breath mingling, and then he says it out loud, the reassurance, "It doesn't make you wrong, beautiful. You can like what you like," he breathes, the words dancing across my own tongue as he breathes them into my mouth. "I like it too, we all like giving you what you need."

Our lips connect in an innocent kiss and I reach back for him, my hands finding his sides as he arches my neck. Twisting my chin further over my shoulder, the hard ripple of muscle rolling beneath his skin at the contact with my fingers.

"Okay," I whisper, blinking hard as his mouth continues to tease mine, his lips brushing my own, but he goes no further.

He smiles then, a wide toothy grin that sets my heart aflame and my insides coiling tight like a striking viper.

"Run, little Lollipop, run like your life depends on it, and don't make it easy for us to catch you," he places an open mouthed kiss against my cheek as he releases his hold on my face, lapping his tongue along the length of my jaw.

And then he releases me and I bolt as he shouts ten, too quickly followed by nine.

I jump branches, and race through bushes in the opposite direction to where Raiden and Flynn were. Hearing noises all around me, my heart pounds harder and harder, sweat dripping down my back, my chest, rolling down the valley between my breasts.

I breathe in, my feet pounding the hard, dry earth, the leaves rustle around me in the light evening breeze and a scream rips from my throat as fingers twine through the ends of my hair.

But it isn't over until they really catch me, and I don't stop, strands of my hair snapping free of my scalp. I don't stop and I hear a grunt at my back that sounds like Rex. He's the slowest, he smokes too much, even though he says he's trying to quit like I've quit pills, but he still smells of smoke and marijuana and I think I just like it.

I see a figure fly across the path ahead of me, and I don't doubt it's Lynx when I hear his laughter, the collision of bodies as he runs straight into Rex at my back, the latter grunting, immediately following the sound up with a groan as their big bodies collide with the hard packed earth.

I laugh then, wanting to turn around and find

them, fall into their centre, but I keep going. Arms pushing me forward, I fly through the woods, around trees, ducking beneath low hanging branches that scratch and snarl my skin. I'm breathing hard, my heart thudding in my throat, there's rushing in my ears and I can't pick out any sounds above my heaving breaths.

That's why I don't hear him.

"Hello, Angel," Flynn rasps against the shell of my ear, his big hand wrapping around the front of my throat, long, thick fingers squeezing tight.

Sandalwood and vanilla flood my nose and I want to melt into him, those big blue sapphires glued on mine, that small little freckle high on his right cheek-bone. His pale pink lips curve, like he knows what I'm thinking and he loosens his hold, tucking a strand of gold-streaked dark hair behind my pierced ear, his finger tracing the shape of it, pinching and tugging on my lobe.

His bare chest glistens, sweat rolling down his shoulders, over his chest, down the valley of his abs. I trace the little droplets with my eyes, his own still on my face and that's when I stomp on the instep of his foot, spit on his cheek and twist out of his hold.

I don't look back as he laughs raucously. The cackle of a villain in the night.

My villain.

I run, and he isn't chasing me, but I feel when

Raiden drops into step beside me, six-feet separating us. He doesn't try to close it, his grey eyes on the path ahead, a clearing coming up, he watches me as I run, a smirk on his face, he has fucking insane stamina. He's hardly even out of breath and my lungs are working overtime just to try and keep me alive.

"Keep going, Princess, I know he wants to catch you," he whispers loud enough for me to hear.

A brow lifting on his head as his muscles pop beneath his light brown skin, making sure they make themselves known. He falls back, and I twist my head over my shoulder, watch as he tackles his older brother to the floor.

I'm laughing as I turn back to face the path ahead, the trees opening up. I come to a slow in the large circular clearing, hands folding behind my head, trying to catch my breath. I stand in the centre, breathing hard, eyes scanning over the surrounding trees.

I feel him before I see or hear him, and I drop my arms, running straight ahead. I make it into the trees, the fresh scent of pines and oaks filling my lungs as the warm breeze blows through the leaves.

"Gotcha," Bennett whispers in my ear and I scream. His hard body connects with mine, and I keep screaming, squirming beneath him, until my ears ring. "That's it, Lollipop, fight me, it only gets my dick harder."

He chuckles in my ear, his hands on my waist, he flips me over beneath him, the back of my head connecting with the hard earth, he drops his weight onto me. Grinning at me as I let out another blood curdling scream. He slaps a hand to my mouth. Adjusting his hips against mine, shutting me up. A groan escapes my throat, the vibration a tremor up his forearm, and he stops grinning, licking his lips.

Staring down at me, the hard length of his cock against my lower belly, he drops his nose to the back of his hand, my hands clawing over his arms. I watch as deep red lines raise across his hot flesh. Gouging at his skin, I curl my nails in, making him groan, grind himself against me.

"You want me inside of you?" I shake my head frantically, still playing our game and he laughs, licking the sweat from my forehead with the flat of his tongue. "You taste like a liar, Lollipop," he chuckles, shoving his other hand down between us, yanking my shorts and underwear down my legs. "You going to keep denying me?" he asks.

His weight pressing against my face where he still smothers my mouth and nose. My breath a wet vapor inside the cup of his palm. I groan as his forearm brushes over my pussy, my thighs shut tight together. He shoves down his own shorts, no boxers beneath. He lifts up, kicking them free, and then he's tearing my thighs apart with his free hand, settling between them.

I kick him, draw my knees back, up to my chest, plant the soles of my trainer covered feet on the front of his thighs and push with all my strength. Throwing my head from side to side as he tightens his hold on my face, cutting off my breath as he tightens his fingers together.

All I can smell is tobacco and bergamot, and I want to fucking lick it from his skin, but I keep kicking, planting a foot on his chest, my knee at my chin, almost resting against the back of his hand, I shove at him with all of my might and then he's rolling us over. His back to the dirt, my back to his chest, and Flynn is towering over me, Bennett's legs pinning my own open from beneath me. My hands curled over his scratched forearm.

Flynn stares down at me, dropping his shorts, his cock bobbing free, the moonlight above us now highlighting all of the slivers of his pale white skin between his dark ink. He grips his cock in hand, my head craning up from Bennett's heaving chest.

"We're going to destroy you, Lollipop," Bennett bites my ear. "I'm going to release your mouth, and if you try to scream we'll find someone to fucking fill it," he grits out the words just as King saunters up beside us, a smirk flitting across his devilish thick lips.

"I got you covered," he licks over his teeth, taking his time to admire the length of my body, then he, too, drops his shorts.

My heart is thudding in my chest, breathing raspy,

I lick my lips, Bennett's arms banded around my torso, my chest, his legs still curled through mine, pinning them wide open, my thigh muscles pulled taut, straining and trembling.

Flynn spits onto my pussy, my eyes blinking up at him as he drops to his knees.

"Angel," he rasps, rubbing his spit into my flesh. "Such a pretty little cunt," he praises, his bright blue eyes on his thumb as he circles me, spits again. "We're gonna need to get you real nice and wet for Benny, huh?"

I pant as I crane my head up to see him, Bennett not loosening his grip on me. King dropping to his knees on our right, but I don't take my eyes off of Flynn as he spits on me again, and I can feel myself getting wetter as he pushes his thumb into me. My legs trembling as he fucks into me shallowly.

"How else will we get him in here, Angel?" he whispers, dragging his thumb from my entrance to my back hole, circling the tight ring of muscle, he spits again and my pussy clenches on air making him chuckle. "Desperate little holes on a filthy fucking angel."

I suck in a sharp breath, Bennett stroking his hands over my skin, goosebumps prickling their way across my flesh as Raiden pinches my chin. Dragging my attention to him as he shifts upwards on his knees.

"Suck me, Princess," and then he's forcing my mouth open, shoving his cock into the back of my throat making me gag, at the same time Flynn's thumb breaches my arse.

Raiden's stroking my face, Flynn's mouth is on my clit, thumb inside of me, and I shout as Bennett's hands tweak at my nipples.

"Knew they'd start without us," Rex says and I can hear the pout in the tone of his voice.

My eyes are a blurry, watery mess as I blink them open, look over Raiden's shoulder as I hollow my cheeks, making Raiden hiss.

"Should have made me come quicker with that filthy mouth of yours like I told you to, you little brat," Lynx replies, a lazy smile on his perfect face. "Hey, Treasure," he greets with a teasing grin, his tongue lapping across his bottom lip, he thumbs it as he bites into it, stifling a groan.

Rex is beside Flynn who suddenly pulls his thumb out of me as Rex says, "Let me eat her cunt, you can have her ass," and at that they settle their huge shoulders beside each other and two mouths begin to feast on me.

I pop off of Raiden's cock, the wet head of him slapping against my chin as I cry out.

"Oh, good, my turn," Lynx laughs and his cock is thrust into my mouth, stroking shallowly over the flat of my tongue before I close my lips around him.

"You're such a good fucking girl," Lynx bites out as I reach out a hand to squeeze Raiden, run my hand up and down his wet length.

Bennett bites and sucks at my throat, his hands driving me crazy as he runs his thumbs over my nipples, plucking them into even sharper points. I groan, my entire body trembling as Rex pushes two long fingers into my cunt, his tongue bar cold against my clit. My pussy clasping them tight as Flynn fucks his tongue into my arse.

Groaning around Lynx's length, my teeth grazing him.

Bennett bites into my shoulder, and it feels like the exact same place his younger brother scarred me with his own bite and an orgasm rips through me. My shout loud as I throw my head back, my skull connecting with Bennett's collarbone.

"Fuck, fuck, fuck, fuckkk," I pant, crying out as Flynn and Rex both lick over me, the two of them drawing back to look me in the eye as I blink them open, and they both spit on me. "Oh," the word is a breathy whisper as my body shakes between the five men who love me.

"That's right, Lollipop, *oh*," Bennett chuckles darkly, and then he's craning his own head up, looking down the length of my body at his brothers between our feet. "Put me in her ass, Flynn," he orders and I almost die.

Flynn just grins, Bennett still pinning me down, my trembling body pulled open. Flynn's arm brushes my pussy as he grabs Bennett's cock, lining him up, he holds my eye as he leans forward, opening his mouth and letting saliva drip from his mouth directly onto me and Bennett.

Both of us groan and as Bennett shifts, crowning me, I push down, trying to take him in faster, making him hiss and Flynn laugh.

"Greedy little pussy," Rex laughs, slapping the flat of his hand over my clit.

I bite my lip, unidentifiable noises falling from my throat, as Rex takes position between my legs, Flynn shuffling up beside Raiden.

Bennett keeps pushing inside of me, my arse burning but the good kind of burn, Rex spits directly on Bennett's length, and I groan at the sight as he strokes his own cock, piercing glinting in the tip. He pushes into my cunt, filling me up as Bennett finishes getting inside of me. Both of them making me feel so fucking full.

"That's it, Princess," Raiden says at my side, Flynn stroking my hair back from my face, him and his younger brother both tangling their fingers in my hair. "Suck his cock, Angel."

"Lynx," I call out first, panicking as he steps back from us, he comes back to me quickly, dropping down into a crouch on my free side, leaning over me.

"Kiss me, Treasure," he rasps, smiling that playboy smirk at me, dimple carving his cheek.

Our mouths connect in a slow, heated kiss, two of my other men's hands in my hair, pushing me harder into Lynx's kiss. His groan vibrates down my own throat, the rumble of it stirring in my chest. His tongue laps over my own, long, luscious licks into my mouth. Lips plucking, tongues curling, he slowly draws back, my eyes blinking open.

"I'm going to fuck our little brat," he smiles, thumbing my bottom lip, "I wanna make sure he's getting inside you deep enough," he chuckles over my lips, his words caressing my tongue.

I laugh then too as I hear Rex's huffed protest, his hips clapping against mine as if to prove a point. Both Bennett and I shouting as he drives himself deeper.

"I love you, Treasure," he says over my mouth, his eyes hard on mine.

"I love you so much," I tell him honestly, everything we've been through bringing us here.

He smiles, chucking my chin as he stands, moving behind Rex.

I look up at Raiden, reaching out for Flynn's cock at the same time my mouth suctions around Raiden's. I suck him deep, drawing him into the back of my throat as Lynx gets inside of Rex, the combined thrust of the two of them together making my eyes roll.

"That's it, Lollipop, suck my brothers deep," Bennett rasps and I'm coming again, everything inside of me tightening as I lift a hand to Raiden's length, thumbing his tip, as I angle my head and take Flynn into my mouth.

"So fuckin' pretty," Raiden rasps, making all of me clench, and everyone else groan.

Alternating between the two brothers, my orgasm rolls through from one into the next, everything almost numb as I come again. And Raiden's coming in my mouth, his cum hitting the back of my tongue. I swallow around him, lapping at his head as he spills into me. Pumping his cock into the very back of my throat, cutting off my breath as he finishes. He pulls out, dipping down and plunging his tongue into my mouth, curling it with mine as he kisses the breath out of me, the taste of him between us.

"I love you, Princess," he presses the words against my mouth, my lips parted, his tongue lazily rolling just inside of them, across the top of my teeth.

"I love you, Raiden," I reply, meaning it with my whole heart.

"I know you do," he smiles, real and pure, "but my brother looks like he's in pain," he chuckles, making me grin and Flynn groan as I twist back to face him and swallow him down.

He fists my hair so hard my eyes stream as he comes, but I know he so likes it when I cry. *For him.*

"Fuck, I love you, Angel," he beams, pulling out of my mouth, thumbing my chin, catching the dribble of him that escaped.

He pushes his thumb into my mouth, and I suck the digit hard, swallowing the taste of him and smiling around him.

"I love you," I grin, before my head is hauled back against Bennett's chest.

Palm of his hand across my forehead, he holds me tight as he fucks brutally into my arse, "Come again. Fucking come again, Lollipop," Bennett demands, my pussy tightening around him as the groan in his chest vibrates down my spine.

Heat coils in my belly, everything tightening, and then Lynx is grunting, his arms banded around Rex's chest.

"I'm coming, I'm coming," Rex chants, mashing his thumb over my swollen clit as he fucks me harder and harder.

I cry out as Lynx bites into Rex's shoulder, breaking skin in the same place he bit me, holding my gaze as he does.

"I love you, Kitten, fuck, you feel amazing. Fuck, Lynx, I love you, fuck, fuck, *fuuuck*," Rex chants, pounding into me, his head back, eyes squeezed close, his cock punching my cervix, and everyone is finishing, cum filling me.

Lynx in Rex, Rex in me, Bennett in my arse.

"I love you, Hendrix," I whisper, letting my eyes close.

Bennett's lips to my ear, he rasps, "I love you, Lollipop," dropping his head back down to the earth, his cock stilling as he finishes filling me with little jerky movements of his hips.

"I love you," I breathe, Bennett's arms around me squeezing me tight.

And when we're all dressed, walking hand in hand

back to our house, Bennett nuzzles his nose against my throat, breathing me in.

"You happy, Lollipop?" and I can hear his smile before I feel it against my skin.

I lift my gaze to the full moon above and smile.

"Very."

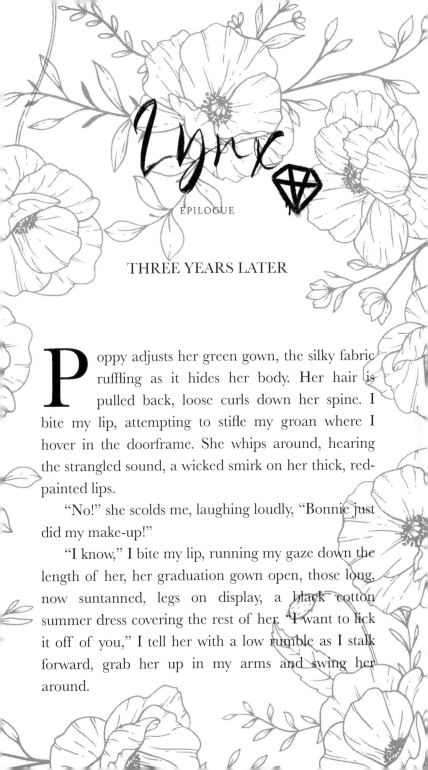

Lynx

THREE YEARS LATER

Poppy adjusts her green gown, the silky fabric ruffling as it hides her body. Her hair is pulled back, loose curls down her spine. I bite my lip, attempting to stifle my groan where I hover in the doorframe. She whips around, hearing the strangled sound, a wicked smirk on her thick, red-painted lips.

"No!" she scolds me, laughing loudly, "Bonnie just did my make-up!"

"I know," I bite my lip, running my gaze down the length of her, her graduation gown open, those long, now suntanned, legs on display, a black cotton summer dress covering the rest of her. "I want to lick it off of you," I tell her with a low rumble as I stalk forward, grab her up in my arms and swing her around.

"Lynx!" she squeals, swatting at my shoulders. "Put me down!" she laughs, burying her face into my neck, wrapping her legs around my waist.

I perch her on the edge of the basin, flick my gaze over her beautiful face, feel my heart thud that much harder.

"We're graduating," I beam at the smile that takes over her very pretty mouth.

"We are," she breathes, her hands adjusting my shirt collar. "And your dad's here," she smiles shyly, looking up at me from beneath her thick fan of lashes.

I swallow around the lump in my throat, tears gathering in my eyes.

Dad was released two years early after anonymous evidence found its way to the authorities, proving his innocence and Christopher Matthews *Senior's* guilt. Chris' dad killed himself before he was ever locked up, and Chris and his family *moved out of state*, but not before he was charged with sexual assault and attempted rape. At least, that's the story Bennett told Poppy.

Dad was released just days before Raiden and Rex graduated, so he got to come to their ceremony, and now, he gets to see ours.

I bite down on my teeth, Poppy's arms linking around my neck, her nails scratching over my scalp.

"Are you happy, Treasure?" I ask her in a whisper thinking of how happy she makes all of us.

Our family loves her like their own, and I think

she feels a little like she has her mama back in the form of both of ours. Raiden and Flynn's mom is obsessed with her just as much as mine and Bennett's.

She hasn't had contact with her dad since he was sent to jail not too long after Matthews' conviction. She doesn't ever want to talk about him, she says she hashed it out in therapy, that she still attends regularly, and doesn't want to waste her new life with thoughts of him. It's the only reason he's still breathing, in case she ever needs closure.

Poppy smiles up at me, those red lips finding mine, "Always with you."

And later, once our green, tasseled caps are launched into the heavens and we're all eating together in my dad's favorite restaurant, passing plates of good food down the long bench table filled with all of the people we love.

I smile, and I know as long as she does the same, we won't ever stop.

Afterword
xo

Thank you so very much for reading!

I truly hope you loved this story. I know it was tough to get through in parts and then even tougher in others, but hopefully you enjoy emotional whiplash as much as me. And if you didn't, perhaps, now, I've converted you?

Anyway, lots of my ARC readers wanted to know why our bloodthirsty Noxious Boys didn't *'finish off'* good old Dr Soren.

Totally valid question.

Well, as all of my books are written in the same 'world'… we will, unfortunately, be seeing him again when we revisit Briarmoor Sanatorium in *Delirium*, coming early 2025.

Acknowledgements

Firstly, thank *you*, the reader, for being here and reading my work, whether this is your first book by me or your tenth! Because, holy hell, this is book number ten being published and I couldn't have done any of them without you. So thank you for reading, it means the world to me.

Mark, as always, for everything, thank you. You have my heart.

Mum, you didn't have anything to do with rescuing the plot of this book, *this time…* but I know you'll read it anyway. Thank you for looking after me still, even though I'm in my thirties.

Inga, for everything. This one really *is* for you. You are one of the most amazing people I know, and I am so lucky to have you in my life. Thank *you* for rescuing the plot of this book, I'm sure Mum's very grateful!

Raeleen, you're a queen and you better know it. Thank you for organising my life and reassuring me I'm not a complete wreck, at least, well, not everyday, right? Dunno what I'd do without you.

Kins, you fucking rockstar. Thanks for teaching me all about hockey, I cherish our joint spreadsheet and all the knowledge you bestowed unto me. *Check hard, play hard, fuck hard!*

Kayla, for keeping me going and going and going. You are amazing, and you deserve all the success I know is coming your way.

Els, I am so very lucky to have you as my friend. Thank you for being wonderful always.

Agnieszka, for loving all of my characters as much as only I do, your posts and messages never fail to make my day, thank you for always putting a smile on my face.

Monica, for being supportive of everything I do, thank you endlessly.

Thank you so much for reading, I hope you enjoyed this book. If you have time, I would be so grateful if you could leave me a rating or review <3

Also by E. L. Taylor-Lane

.

SWALLOWS AND PSYCHOS

<u>KYLA-ROSE SWALLOW</u>

A Dark Mafia Why Choose Romance

PURGATORY

PENANCE

PERSECUTION

SWALLOWS AND SAVAGES

<u>CHARLIE SWALLOW</u>

A Dark Mafia MMF Romance

RUIN

TBC

TBC

THE BLACKWELL BROTHERS

HUNTER BLACKWELL

A Dark Gothic Horror Stepsibling MF Romance

HERON MILL

HERON MILL TENEBRIS

THORNE BLACKWELL

A Dark Gothic Mafia MF Romance

ROOK POINT

WOLF BLACKWELL

A Dark Gothic MF Romance

CARDINAL HOUSE

THE ASHES BOYS

A Dark Bully Gang Why Choose Romance

TORMENT ME

BURY ME

TBC

RAVEN RIDGE HALLOW

BILLY BLACKWELL

A Dark Gothic Horror-Gore Cult MF Romance

HAUNT

LOVESICK

BRAM BLACKWELL

A Dark Gothic Horror-Gore Cult MF Romance

DEATHWISH

TOLLY BLACKWELL

A Dark Gothic Horror-Gore Cult Romance

HEARTLESS

GORE BLACKWELL

A Dark Gothic Horror-Gore Cult MF Romance

CRUCIFY

STANDALONES

NOXIOUS BOYS

A Dark College Bully Why Choose Romance

DELIRIUM

A Dark Gothic Romance

Coming 2025

Find K. L. Taylor-Lane

BOOKBUB - @KLTaylorLane

AMAZON - K. L. TAYLOR-LANE

INSTAGRAM - @kltaylorlane_author

TIKTOK - @kltaylorlane.author

PINTEREST - @KLTaylorLane

FACEBOOK - K. L. Taylor-Lane Author

GOODREADS - kltaylor-lane

FACEBOOK READER GROUP -

K's Southbrook Psychos - Reader Group for K.L. Taylor-Lane

Content Listing

⚠️

Age Gap (11 yrs) | Dub-Con | Non-Con | Physical Assault | MMFMMM | Strong Drug Use | Blood Play | PTSD | Sexual Assault | Graphic Violence | Attempted Rape | Addiction | Somnophilia | Mental Health Topics | Drugging | Suicidal thoughts/ideations | Abduction | Physical Harm to FMC | Stimming | ADHD Representation | Voyeurism | Primal | Hockey Players | Needles | Student/Counsellor | Bullying within the harem | Begging | Knife Play | Good Girl, Good Boy | CNC (Consensual Non-Consent) | Primal Play

This list is not exhaustive - although I have done my best to include all potential triggers, there may still be other content contained in these pages that could be found triggering by some

Made in United States
Orlando, FL
13 November 2024

53858719R00352